C0-AAU-730

JAN TISSOT, J.D., is a child of the old days in America. Born in 1940 – before the nation's corporate coup and its attendant shopping malls, suburbs, TV sets, plastic substitutes, super highways, and paid-for politicians – he survived the transformation as a rebel, fighting a state/corporate synergy that he believes is bent on casting us as background extras in its virtual democracy.

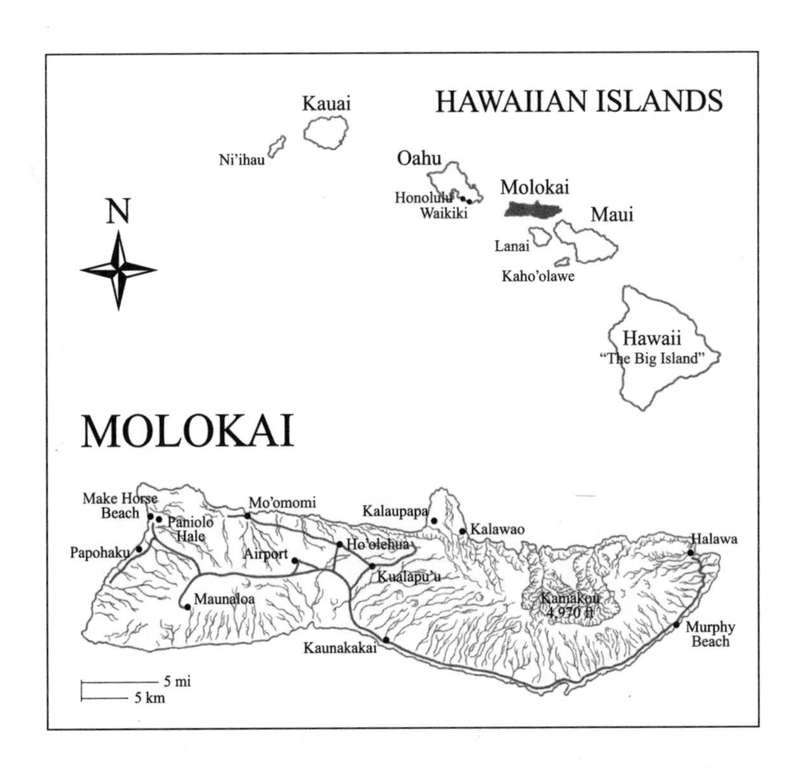

GLOSSARY

words not defined in context

ho'oipo – to make love
ipo – lover
kane – man
okole – buttocks
ono – good
paniolo – cowboy
pau – finished
puka – hole
pupu – snack
tita – sister
tutu – grandparent

VOWEL PRONUNCIATIONS

a like *a* in ma
e like *ay* in day
i like *y* in city
o like *o* in so
u like *oo* in too

NAME PRONUNCIATIONS

Keiki – kay kee
Make Horse – ma kay horse
Pale – pa lay
Kale – ka lay

ALSO BY JAN TISSOT

Kali Yuga, 1994

Crow Speaks, 1992

Sudden Rain, 1975

The Hidden Seed, 1963

KEIKI

JAN TISSOT

ISBN 0-9717825-0-4
Printed in Canada

P.O. Box 2115, Kapaa, HI 96746
808-821-0046
www.sundogarts.com

Look where you will among those associated by blood or marriage with the Tissot name and you will find creative people . . . artists, filmmakers, writers, and musicians.

And it is we – the Tissots, the Ibrahims, the Storeys, the Martins, the Houstons, and the Sherwoods – who present to you Jan Tissot's first novel, Keiki.

This book is dedicated to our newest member, Isabel Sofia Ibrahim

ACKNOWLEDGEMENTS

Undying thanks to Kelly Tissot,
my wife and editor.
This book is not mine, but ours.

Thanks also to NYSU professor,
Julia Boken, and movie pro, Paul Sylbert,
who read and critiqued
the developing manuscript.

KEIKI

A story of the child in us all . . .
of children who pose as adults,
of adults with redeemingly
childlike traits.

PROLOGUE

"Morgan's almost three years now in maximum security. It's time to step her down, maybe put her into general population, but she refuses to confide."

"What's to confide? Good behavior's not enough?"

"Considering her offense, I'd need more to justify the referral."

"Like what?"

"A little background to show that she's redeemable. Some way to grasp her state of mind."

"Why come all the way to Molokai? We could have done this on the phone."

"I noticed your name on our register. The frequency of your visits. Mind if I ask why?"

"Is this about Morgan or me?"

"After what she's done to you, why would you continue the relationship?"

"Some enemies make better friends."

"Would you be friends if she were free?"

"The fact that she's locked up is part of the equation. I feel, in part, responsible. She has an innocence that makes me hurt for the hell she's in."

"How would you define her problem?"

"I'm not an expert. I can only tell you what I know."

"Has she talked to you about her childhood?"

"Her classmates taunted her in school, particularly the boys. They called her 'White Bread' and 'Dough Baby.' She described herself to me as having been a fat, off-white child."

"Molokai's definitely browner than the other islands. I noticed it as soon as I got off the plane. It's like entering the third world."

"Her father made her Hawaiian side a source of shame. He scolded her mother for speaking Hawaiian in the home, despised pidgin, and wouldn't allow association with the locals."

"Sounds like she was branded from both sides. Her father's background?"

"Latvian. A physicist. Left his country in '48 during their post-war exodus. Got a job on Oahu working for the feds."

"Her mother was Hawaiian, then?"

"A quarter. A real beauty. Poor Morgan takes after her dad. She's wracked with body shame. She responded very young by turning inward. That's what you're dealing with now."

"But she opens up to you."

"I'm her ki'i pepe, her baby doll. She can talk to me."

"You two were more than friends?"

"No, not like that. We were never intimate. As a child she came to prefer the company of dolls. Her father nurtured the involvement, bringing dolls home on the weekends from Oahu. A way to reduce contamination from the local kids. When she wasn't studying, she'd play with her dolls – her society of dolls."

"Good, good, go on. This is the stuff I need to know."

"She became excessively concerned, even as late as the fifth and sixth grades, with her dolls' imagined bodily functions, physically punishing them for pooping and peeing their pants, that sort of thing. It evolved into a kind of sexual outlet."

"A doll fetish."

"To make herself feel better after being teased by her classmates, she would hide in her bedroom and nurse water through her wetting dolls."

"Through?"

"You need me to be more graphic?"

"No. I got the picture. 'Through her wetting dolls.' I'll put it down like that."

"After passing the bar she actually buried the dolls she'd kept from childhood."

"Guess she didn't bury them deep enough."

"It's a shame she buried them at all. During my summer as her legal intern, she fixed on me as her living doll, but kept the longing crammed down in her gullet with her other self-detesting ideations. The problem is not the dolls. They're a symptom of her emptiness – a benign affect. The trouble begins when she ignores them and attempts to translate the connection to the real world. At present, separated from me by bars, she's safe to play with the idea. I'm only as real as she wants me to be. She's taken to calling me Dolly. Her way of admitting the fiction."

"You're buying into her pathology."

"Did you know she was honored for community service?"

"It's in her sentencing report."

"They gave her a plaque for defending indigent clients – the same people who tormented her when they were young. Do you think she was fond of these people?"

"I don't."

"And yet she refused to turn them away. Why would a person with her . . . pathology, as you call it, choose to represent these individuals?"

"Her society of dolls. Only as real as she wanted them to be. Power over her detractors."

"She could have been a prosecutor. That's control."

"Defending them is more intimate. A chance to toy with their distress."

"That's unfair. She was honored for exemplary service. There's no evidence of betrayal."

"Okay, enough theory. Any other graphic stuff about the dolls?"

“You like that, huh?”

“Everyone likes dolls. Some more than others. I’ve got it under control.”

“She wasn’t practicing voodoo, if that’s the sort of thing you’re after.”

“No, no, just some way to get inside her head.”

“Everything I know, you know. I picked it up in our visits. There was an incident during her arrest, but I didn’t hear it first hand. I’m sure it’s in the police report.”

“Anything to get her talking?”

“If you want to get on her good side, buy her a doll. But don’t overrate your fetish theme. There’s much more to the story. Morgan’s problem isn’t dolls, it’s people.”

PART I

". . . one tough little cookie."

CHAPTER ONE

The town was still asleep. Her consolation in these hours alone was isolation self-imposed. The envelope lay beside her on the desk where her secretary had placed it after sending off the notice of employment. Her summer intern would fly in today. Morgan opened and perused the resumé. When it first arrived, she had merely scanned it and made her decision. Milissa Dogherty had been the only female applicant. Third year law student. Middle of her class. Private investigator, licensed in Seattle. Martial arts. Calcutta for a month. Europe. Excitement buzzed remotely in Morgan's chest. So much experience for such a young woman.

The cover letter was brief and eager. Morgan was reading it a second time when the phone rang. "Zarins Law Firm. . . . This is Morgan. . . . Miss Dogherty. You must be in the air. . . . You needn't have called. I plan to pick you up myself. . . . Arrival time? Let me check."

Pale Gutierrez marched drunk and unexpected through the door, a hunting rifle propped against her shoulder. Lowering it and aiming it around the room, she began to mimic the sound of gunfire.

"You leave Honolulu at nine, arriving here at nine thirty," Morgan told Milissa, not wavering from the muzac cadence of her delivery. "I have a guest. Please hold."

Laying the receiver aside, she walked around the corner of her desk and came abreast of Pale as if intending to pass, but placed both hands on the rifle instead and twisted it free, then leaned it against her desk, grabbed the frail woman by the base of her pony tail and the seat of her pants, tiptoed her out through the waiting area and onto the front porch, and sat her carefully on the second step. "You wait here," she said, straightening her pony tail and patting her on the head.

She picked up with Milissa as though nothing had intervened. "I'll bring you to the office this morning for orientation, a small task or two, and we'll sort things out from there. . . . Your resumé? I have it in front of me. . . . Yes, I see. Seattle Sleuths. . . . I doubt there will be much need for investigation. Only six thousand people on the island. Not much goes unnoticed. . . . Very good. See you in four hours then."

Morgan stood at the gate watching as the last passenger stepped out of the tiny shuttle onto the tarmac. Seeing only a girl in her early teens and an assortment of older couples, she wondered if Milissa had missed the flight from Honolulu.

After being assured by the desk attendant that Milissa was on board, she returned to the baggage collection area near the gate and examined the luggage tags. There it was, *Dogherty*, attached to an enormous backpack/duffle bag.

"That's mine." The girl smiled broadly and hoisted the bag onto her back. "And you must be Morgan."

"Miss Dogherty?" Morgan asked, stunned by Milissa's childlike appearance.

"The same," Milissa said, capturing Morgan with a handshake.

"Ladies," Morgan warbled from the middle of the room, "please welcome Milissa Dogherty, our intern from Seattle U. Five feet, one hundred and five pounds of . . . esprit? Is that the correct word? It sounds so appropriate."

Linda and Leilani, perplexed by Morgan's unaccustomed bliss, eyed each other comically and shrugged.

Milissa stepped into the void. "Some say ninety pounds BS. Is there a required minimum?"

Linda laughed. "After lunch we gonna weigh you in."

"Morgan," Leilani asked, embarrassed for her boss, "you like me to show Milissa around?"

"Yes, thank you, Lani. And when you're through, what time are we expecting Ewa?"

"We have her down for eleven. Dey t'reatening to cut her food stamps off again."

"Linda, Milissa will be working mornings only. To finish up today, she'll be sitting in with you and Ewa. For now, Lani, show her the form bank and let her look through Ewa's file."

Leilani, a small, round spinster of Filipino/Hawaiian ethnicity, attempted immediately to bring Milissa under her apron. "You can call me Nana. All da keiki call me Nana or Aunty."

"The form bank and the file," Milissa replied, uneasy with the parenting urge she inspired in most adults.

Leilani gave Milissa two forms. "Tedious stuff, but gotta have it down for work wit' Morgan. Everyt'ing by da books." She ran her fingers along the slots in the bank. "Da rest you can help yourself. You need Nana, I be right here. Linda's got da file."

Linda spoke quietly to Milissa in passing. "Forget da file for now. Ten minutes we got break. We can take a walk. I'll show you around."

"Big challenge here on Molokai is dealing wit' dat sneaky, sucking apprehension when your mind begins to empty. Boredom. It happens every time. Someone's here for five, six weeks, getting plenty moody by da day. Den by-n-by you see 'em jabbering in pidgin, or handing out flyers for Hawaiian sovereignty, or some other kinda knee-jerk t'ing. Some haoles, dat's da white folks, dey just hang, getting nuts from nothing left to do. Walking 'round unshaven, hair all matted down in dredlocks, forgetting to clean deir clothes. Just like da keiki kine. No words for pictures in deir heads. Den maybe one day when dey looking off da cliff or listening to da surf too long dey snap."

"They snap? Sounds like satori."

Linda slowed her pace and stopped in front of Pono's Bakery. Her face took on a scampish gleam. "Most of 'em end up in here, scarfing jelly rolls and coffee wit' da locals. A buncha little buddhas eating pastry, ya? Da real sticky kine. You like?"

Milissa looked through the window. Inside were rows of maple bars, pershing rolls, bear claws, and yep! jelly-filled donuts glistening beneath a print-smudged, glass display case, peppered here and there with houseflies activated by the morning sun. "Yuck!" she said, flashing back to the coffee cart on the corner by the courthouse in Seattle and the cloud of breath that reassured her after every warming sip. "No lattés? No date nut scones?"

"Hoh, girl," Linda laughed. "Lotta ways you in da fifties here. Local people like Wonder Bread and Nescafé. Can get island grown coffee up da plantation and espresso at da Maunaloa Deli, but none of doze scrumptious, heavy scones."

"Sounds like you've been to the mainland."

"Plenty times da Bay Area. Got some Irish cousins dere."

Milissa jumped away and fanned her skirt, angling her heel against the pavement and lifting her toe in the air. "Irish is it?" she brogued, twirling a jig and coming back alongside.

"My family claims O'Higgins," Linda answered, returning the curtsy in stride.

"You knew I was Irish," Milissa kidded.

"Hoh, Keiki, you one leprechaun, one imp if I ever saw one."

"And you one fiery wahine. But I can see the Irish too."

"Where?" Linda asked, glancing down her sturdy, well-shaped, five-foot-seven frame.

"The eyes. It's always in the eyes."

Linda nudged Milissa playfully, "You fulla da kine."

"What kind?"

"Da blarney kine, dat's what."

"Everybody's got a touch of the Irish. It's contagious. If it isn't in the blood, you catch it."

"He was my great great uncle," Linda announced, pointing at the Mitchell Pauole Center sign in front of the county office complex. "Mitchell Pauole. One famous Molokai cowboy. Honorary mayor of Kaunakakai in da old days. No Irish in him as far as I know. Hawaiian and probably a little bit Portugee. Way back, most da cowboys had some Portugee."

As Linda took Milissa back in time by way of other landmarks in the town, she began to lament the victimization of her people by the white man. To lift herself above the guilt, Milissa tried on parallels in England's subjugation of the Emerald Isle, but she couldn't match Linda's palpable engagement with the issue. "Dat's why we first went call 'em haole," Linda explained. "Ha means breath, God's breath. Ole, without."

"Is that how people here see me?"

"No shame on you, tita, or any haoles 'round here now. 'Cept maybe da big landlords. Dey stone haole from da old days. Haole doesn't mean da same today. Most haoles use it on demselves."

"I envy you knowing where you came from. You have something to return to. My family is proud of being Irish, but we've lost touch in all but name."

"You got no reason to look back. Your kine's already overcome. You had John F. Kennedy and all doze senators. Irish is American. Your past is in da present now."

Milissa looked at her watch. "My God, we're ten minutes late."

Linda picked a plumeria blossom and handed it to Milissa. "Chill out, girl. You still on haole stress time. Trying to catch up wit' da future, ya? We can be late. Molokai time everybody's a little bit late. Only one punching da clock is Morgan. She da kine."

Ewa was sitting in the "next" chair just inside the front door when Milissa and Linda got back. Leilani had already done the intake. Linda scanned the form as she led Ewa to her cubicle. Welfare had put a hold on her food stamps, claiming she was peddling them for marijuana.

Ewa began to whine as soon as she was seated. "Kepa went narc on me. Say I make him do it. Little fucker went steal my stamps and sell 'em for pakalolo. He da one who got arrested. Shit!"

"Shush, girl," Linda chided. "Lemme get steady here." She pulled up a chair for Milissa and settled herself across the desk from Ewa.

Ewa looked at Linda and cocked her head suspiciously in Milissa's direction. "Who dis?"

"Dis Keiki. Morgan's new intern."

Milissa concealed her surprise at this second "Keiki" reference. She had initially assumed the curious word was merely a term of endearment.

"Keiki, dis Ewa Wia," Linda continued, leaning sideways to check Milissa's spelling of Ewa's name as she entered it on the interview form. "She say it wit' da 'v' sound," Linda corrected, "but she like spell it E...w...a... W...i...a, Hawaiian style."

Ewa snuck a peek at the mistake. "She claiming 'Keiki' and cannot spell Hawaiian style?"

Linda wrote *keiki = child* in bold letters on her notepad and handed it to Milissa. "Ewa like know if you claim Keiki for one nickname."

Milissa gave Linda a questioning look. She'd been given a choice, but Linda was looking back, head listing, gauging her response to a well-intentioned gift.

"Blessed are the children?" Milissa asked.

Linda nodded, allowing the interpretation.

"Keiki then," Milissa conceded. "Call me Keiki."

Ewa pouted dubiously. "Keiki's okay," she said, as if her consent was required.

"Good," Linda replied. "Den you no get all stink-face if she sit in wit' us. Now, whatzup?"

Ewa's son Kepa had been caught smoking marijuana with some friends at school and then admitted to having taken it from Ewa's drawer. When the principal confronted her with Kepa's confession, Ewa suggested that Kepa had bought the marijuana with her missing food stamps. After a search of Kepa's friends produced a book of food stamps and new admissions, Kepa changed his story, alleging that Ewa had sent him out that day to make a buy. The school turned the stamps over to the police.

A phone call from Linda to Ewa's case worker, assuring him that Ewa had legal counsel, would secure the release of her stamps. Her regular allotments would follow until a hearing could be held, months down the line, to re-establish her claim. Kepa's charge, since he was on probation, would move ahead with more dispatch, but also in Molokai time. In either case there would be no real consequence. Molokai mothers weren't taken from their kids for using marijuana, and island boys like Kepa were simply kept on probation, despite numerous minor infractions, throughout their teenage years.

Morgan turned off the main highway and headed west on Kaluakoi Road. "I hope the bed's comfortable. It came with the condo. It's never been used."

"I appreciate you letting me stay until I can find another place. The way the ad described the Ono, I had no idea it was such a dive." Milissa read aloud from the classifieds. "'AC, daily and weekly rates, ocean front' . . . which turned out to be a mud flat. I mailed them the deposit weeks ago. They refused to give it back."

Morgan smiled softly. "Quite a few of our nonpaying clients live there. It has the cheapest rents on island, except for Maunaloa Town, which the owners are tearing down. We should have discussed your living arrangements. I had simply anticipated you staying with me as part of your compensation."

She lived at Paniolo Hale in a charming, vault-ceilinged condominium with a screened-in, wrap-around lanai. "That's Make Horse," she said, pointing to a stretch of beach across the golf course. I have a brief to finish, but first I'll fix us a bite to eat. You must be exhausted. Would you like a Caesar salad and some cantaloupe?"

"Perfect," Milissa sighed, surveying the shoreline less than fifty yards away.

In the time it took to return with the food, Milissa had fallen asleep. Morgan eyed her innocent sprawl, then turned away self-consciously, anxious to lose herself in the law.

CHAPTER TWO

In the weeks that followed, Milissa spent most of her afternoons chumming with the characters she met along the surface of the little humdrum town. Sea, the resident transient, standing inconspicuously, in no particular location, at any time day or night, was the first to catch her eye. Brown skinned, but not of local ethnicity, he never spoke unless spoken to and rarely even then.

Intrigued by his reticence, Milissa located Sea each afternoon and asked him pointedly, "How are you today, my silent friend?" When she was able to get him to look at her, usually in response to a pat on the back or a touch on the arm, there was always a question in his eyes.

"Very fine today, my friend," he finally answered one day, forming the words at the front of his mouth in the crisp, distinctive fashion of East Indian English.

From that day on, when approaching Sea, Milissa used the Hindi greeting she'd recalled from her stay in Calcutta – the word for hello. "Namaste," she would say.

"Namaste," he would reply, only when she was close enough to hear him at a whisper, eventually adding "shukria" in thanks for her concern.

Milissa first noticed Cory Adler sitting in the airy little coffee bar at Molokai Community College. She was smoking a cigarette, looking very Left Bank in her loose, colorfully printed gypsy blouse, ankle-length skirt, and head bandana – smoke trailing up through her auburn hair.

Cory was an original hippie who had hired on fifteen years before as the branch's first administrator. Full of acumen and local scuttlebutt, self-trained expert in the island's patois, she had coached many a Molokaian through the throes of late childhood.

"You have this charming way of asking inappropriate questions," she said, after responding to Milissa's initial barrage. "I thought I was good at being up front. All you need is a license. You'd make an excellent PI."

Milissa produced her Seattle license. "And you, a reader of minds."

"That's my job, recognizing aptitude." Cory took the card. "Flashy. Almost like a badge."

The ID's star potential had been simmering half-seriously in Milissa's mind since she arrived on Molokai. The guys at Seattle Sleuths had kidded her before she left, calling her their "Polynesian connection," urging her to show it around. Though the notion took on weight with Cory's insight, in the end it was ennui – Molokai's test of haole character – that tipped the scales. Four hours a day at the office and interminable afternoons in hot, dry Kaunakakai had given Milissa island fever. Her lunch dates with Linda were fun, the highlight of her day, but when she was alone, tedium, more than tedium, a disturbing sense of obscurity – not like she'd imagined it would be.

The waters along Kaunakakai were dreadfully muddy. The best beaches were on the ends of the island at Halawa to the east, and Papohaku to the west, each about fifteen miles from town by way of the "Kam," King Kamehameha Highway. By the time she arrived home with Morgan in the evenings it was too dark to enjoy the out-of-doors. She had already hitchhiked once to Halawa and a few times to the west, heading out early to walk the two mile Papohaku stretch. But this seemed to only deepen her isolation. One might walk the entire way and back without encountering a soul.

During her last few treks along the beach she'd taken to chasing sand crabs. They'd pop out of their holes halfway, eyes erect, as if to say, Ah ha! Your apathy has come to this! And then they'd creep, inching cautiously forward, but yoyoing back at the turn of her head – in out, in out, ten or twelve at a time, able to see her from a remarkable distance. The trick, she'd learned, was to cut them off from their retreats. Once she'd broken their tethers, they'd lose themselves in the surf.

Their abandon made her think of Linda's dredlocked haoles, losing touch from hanging out too far. Not for me, she mused, not on your fly-tracked jellyroll. What she needed was an entrée, a talisman, a way to open doors – and her PI license, though it also smacked of Linda's warning, seemed just the play. "Do it for a lark," Cory had urged, nudging Milissa with a catalystic laugh, never imagining the outcome of her jest, the final task for which the license would be used. "This island needs an upstart."

"Is this allowed?" Milissa asked, holding up the can of beer just handed to her by Moke, spokesman for the small clutch of county park denizens known as the "six pack, half-rack gang."

"Allowed!?" Moke replied. "My grampa drank his stubbies underneath dis tree. Dis one right in perpetuity. Dey put up wit' us," he added, nodding toward the county sheriff's office in the Pauole Center across the street, "we put up wit' dem."

Moke's answer brought to mind the squatters Milissa had seen on her trip to Halawa. Inevitably, their tiny makeshift hovels – constructed of tires, tarp, driftwood, car trunks and hoods, plywood and the like – had conspicuous "No Trespass" signs posted near their entrances. Claims of right like Moke's? She wondered. Evidence of a once more-expansive freedom? Or merely tocsin for the wolves? Adverse possession of public land had been coming under fire of late. The decades-old colony at Makua Beach on the Waianae coast of Oahu – two hundred strong, including families with school age children according to the news – was being threatened with eviction. "Rights can be rescinded," she observed, lifting a toast. "Let's enjoy it while we can."

Cory had given Milissa a cautionary description of the half-rackers before pointing her in their direction. "The politically radical underbelly of Molokai. Always going on, and rightly so, about how Hawaii was stolen by the white man. But they drink too much."

"You guys are all members of Sovereign Hawaii, then?" Milissa asked, as if questioning their credentials.

"Hoh!" Moke spouted, "you one mighty mite, ya? Can call us members, ya. Who you?"

"Morgan Zarins' legal intern," she answered, joining them at the picnic table.

"You one poor man's lawyer."

"Well, not yet. Actually, I'm a poor man's private eye." She pulled her license out of her back pocket, set it in front of Moke, then leaned back to frame his reaction.

He held the ID at a distance with both hands. "Check dis, brah!" he said as the others stretched to get a look. "Less see, you Milissa Dog...her...ty..."

"It's pronounced 'Dor'," Milissa chafed, "not 'Dog'."

"Hoh, you one keiki!" Moke pointed at Milissa's date of birth. "How you get dis already?"

"Keiki," Milissa agreed, snatching back the card, "that's what they call me."

"How you get dat?" Moke repeated, more civilly this time.

"Passed a test and put my money down. And how about you?"

"What?"

"Name, birthdate, and occupation."

"Dey call me da Moke, forty five year old Vietnam vet, well seasoned, a little bit inclined to tip a few too many," he replied, guzzling his beer to the snickers of his sidekicks.

"Hokay, Keiki!" he continued, bringing his beer down with a

thud. “You one private eye. Eye dis. Up on Maunaloa dey gonna subdivide.” He pointed toward the mountain on the west end of the island. “Stockmans Inc., dey own da town, gonna t’row up plenty ticky tacky for one haole bedroom community. Already tore down half da old plantation houses.

“Problem is, dey t’rowing out ohana, families dat been dere two, t’ree generations now, but can’t afford to buy da new kine ticky tack. What’s gonna happen to doze displacees, eh Keiki? You one poor man’s private eye. You like investigate dat for Moke?”

Milissa was a little intimidated, not by Moke’s bombast, but by the problem presented. She looked at the faces around the table and felt her heart beat faster, a slightly uncomfortable pulsing, like after the first few warm-up stretches when the heart’s reacting but the body’s not in sync.

“My people’d like to know what Stockmans got in mind.”

“Your people?”

“Maunaloa Crisis Committee.”

The table’s response to Moke’s claim of allegiance was unanimous. A few strained to keep the beer from blowing out of their noses. Others frowned and exchanged sideways glances. The old man at the end of the table turned and looked into the outfield. “Shit, Moke,” he cackled, flagging his bony hand, “you no MCC. You only one half-racker always puffing like you one beeg radical.”

“Keoni Mikala’s my partner!” Moke protested.

“You see him coming wit’ one six pack, he you partner.”

“What’s the Maunaloa . . . the MCC?” Milissa asked.

Looking around at his friends as if they hadn’t a clue, Moke proceeded to repair his credibility by detailing the hottest political issue in Hawaii. The MCC, he explained, had been organized by independently wealthy Fidel Monzón to champion the plight of Maunaloa’s residents. MCC had fought tirelessly in the press, in government councils, through administrative channels, and on the picket line to stop or stall Stockmans’ demolition of the tiny tradition-laden town.

By and large these efforts had gone unnoticed by the island’s laid-back majority – the rest of Hawaii was more tuned in than the locals – but MCC's pressure had produced results. A work stoppage was presently in place. Xavier Spitz, Stockmans' CEO, was buying time to consider his options. Thus far, no evictions had been issued. Most of the town had heeded the company's intent and moved – forced, the committee claimed, into worse conditions. But those who'd lived there longest intended to be carried out last, if that was the price of resistance.

Moke's already thorough knowledge of the conflict told Milissa he had more in mind for her than mere investigation. His hecklers, silenced by his sudden change of tone, stopped snickering.

"Where do we start?" she asked as the group closed in around him. "I'll need your help."

He looked down his shoulders right and left. "What? You buggers just went blow me off and now we tight again? Come," he told Milissa, lifting himself from the table, "I take you fishing."

Though Moke's acumen gave him some distinction as a minor spokesman for the cause, he had more in common with his friends in the park than not. He was, like most of them, a dedicated hedonist, trained in survival and wary of encroachment. One of his more sensible moves in life was bailing out of Molokai's pineapple bust at age twenty for a three year Navy hitch in Vietnam. Returning home with benefits, he settled in Maunaloa and carved a niche conducting hunting expeditions on her seaward slopes and fishing tours along the western reef. His tourist take sufficed to pay the bills, but to free up income he depended on the island's natural resources.

Milissa scanned the placid western shore and up the mountainside to tiny Maunaloa, barely visible against the skyline. "Where will you go?" she asked.

Moke handed her his spear gun. "I'm staying," he grunted, throwing his catch of parrot fish on board and heaving himself into the boat. "Gonna fight it all da way. Most of da short timers – da ones who took da vacancies when Dole pulled out – dey already moved. Lot of 'em staying at da Ono. Plenty more went Honolulu for da housing projects."

They were anchored off of Kaiaka Rock. The water was clear to the bottom. Milissa peered into the ten foot depths, watching the fish graze on the multicolored coral. Some looked cautiously, even curiously back.

"We let 'em put dat subdivision in, first t'ing to go'll be deer hunting," Moke complained, laying his hand against the mountainside. "Den dey junk da reef. Too many people."

"Where do I fit in?" Milissa asked, not looking up.

"Was thinking you could be one go-between. One goodwill emissary, ya? Everyone's so stuck in deir position now. You, coming from da outside, can maybe shake things up."

As they skimmed and slammed across the surface out beyond the reef, returning to the wharf, Moke cried out above the engine whine, "One tiger shark!" pointing ahead and to his right, and letting up on the throttle. Milissa stood and watched as sixteen feet of darkness, magnified and undulated by the sea, approached. Seeing it cross close beneath the bow, she felt the dizzy pull that causes one to shrink back from heights. Moke revved forward a few feet. Milissa stiffened, but remained standing, not acknowledging his attempt at humor, eyeing the beast out of sight.

CHAPTER THREE

Xavier Kimo Spitz was raised by a wealthy, loving family. "But sometimes you can do too much," Grandma Mary would add, as an admonition to her daughter Rhonda.

James and Mary Spitz' first Christmas following Armistice Day, 1918, was spent in a two room cottage equipped with a hand-pumped well, a wood-burning stove, and an outhouse. They had migrated to the island of Kauai to teach school and, more importantly, to capitalize on post-war animus. Within months of their arrival they had purchased, at drastic discounts, the homes of several German plantation owners, forced out of Lihue by anti-German sentiment.

During the prosperous twenties, they sold this property to Kauai County and later bought several thousand acres at Depression rates on the island of Molokai. After developing their Molokai holdings into a profitable pineapple plantation, they leased the business to Del Monte, but continued to operate it with the help of their three children.

By the early fifties, the family had achieved lasting prosperity in diversified financial markets, and when Del Monte stopped production in response to union wage pressure, most of the Spitz' land was sold to Farley Chisolm of Chisolm Villa Inc. The thousand plus acres retained were eventually planted in coffee as part of Rhonda Spitz' post-graduate, remedial program for Xavier, the youngest by ten years of her four children.

During his formative stay in the remote town of Pullman, Washington, where he had been enrolled in the state university specifically to remove him from the youth culture temptations of the day, Xavier had fallen off track several times. What was intended to have taken six years took ten, and culminated after graduation in three months of drug rehabilitation – the result of a plea-bargained cocaine conviction.

After completing the drug program, Xavier returned dutifully home, MBA in hand and – buttressed by his mother's determination – built the coffee plantation into regional prominence in a mere seven years, finally selling it at a profit. These additional years under the wing had qualified him for executive employment in any of a number of multi-national firms his mother had been courting – the most promising of which was the old Chisolm Villa Inc., by then reorganized and renamed Molokai Ranch Ltd.

Xavier and Chisolm were working out the terms of his employment as the Ranch's incoming CEO when a background check brought up his drug conviction. Given this news, the ranch's controlling interest, Brierley Investments of New Zealand, balked. Their response to X was subsequently repeated by every firm on his mother's list: A few more years in the trenches, and we'll look at you again.

Not to be outdone, mother Spitz, in partnership with Australian stud farm magnates Julius and Harry Stockman, purchased Chisolm's island-wide holdings, including his share in Molokai Ranch, and negotiated a split from Brierley's, which yielded the town of Maunaloa and twenty thousand acres of surrounding pasture land. The resulting Stockmans Inc. of America hired Xavier as its first director.

Xavier had always been capable of hard work and intelligent application. From a young age, he had been made to work the harvests alongside the field hands. But he always resented these stints as personal impositions, and inevitably purged their benefits with episodes akin to his cocaine binge after graduation. Out of the seeds of these early experiences, he developed a lifelong pattern of industry, broken by bouts of melancholy, insulated with intoxicants and indiscriminate sex.

These episodes, which interrupted progressively longer periods of productivity as Xavier grew older, were tolerated because of the work that preceded them and, in particular, because of his admired ability to "knock out the devil," as his mother liked to put it. As a boy, these breaks would manifest in short periods of isolation; as a teenager, all night disappearances; during college, undisclosed stop-overs in large cities on return trips to Pullman; and later, impromptu, extended "business" trips or retreats away from home – all debilitating, all occasioned by simple lulls in the action.

X, still in his robe, leaned out through the door of his den. "Private detective?" He glanced across the room into the foyer but missed Milissa standing behind Renee. "Whatever, he'll have to compete with the game. Send him in. Jesus, I wonder what this is about."

As he turned away, Milissa walked briskly toward him, offering her hand. "I'm Milissa Dogherty. I stopped by to discuss the environment."

Renee held up the ID. X looked at its picture and then at the schoolgirl pumping his arm. "Environment? What environment?"

The sportscaster's voice inside the den caught Milissa's ear. "Who's playing?" she asked, attempting to peek in.

"Mariners and Angels." X pointed at the license. "This is you?"

Renee took another look and handed it to Milissa. "It's her, Xavier."

He stepped aside to make way. "Can I get you a beer?"

"Sure," Milissa heard herself say, "I love the taste of beer in the morning."

X watched Renee's eyebrows levitate as he felt Milissa slip by and enter the den.

"Honey," he said, backing through the door, "I hate to miss the game. Could you . . .?"

"Bring Detective Dogherty a beer?" Renee quipped.

"And another for me," he added as she headed for the bar.

Milissa sat on the opposite end of the sofa from X. A portrait of a beautiful, bare-breasted woman hung on the wall beyond him.

"Is this about our horses?" X asked. "We're constantly mending fence."

"What a lovely woman. Who is she?"

He looked to the end of the room and back. Seeing Milissa's pleasure, he got up and read from the picture's inscription. "'Haumea, sacred mother of Pele and a multitude of Hawaiians.' It's by Kilakane. Grandma Spitz bought several Kilas for us when we furnished the house."

"And that fisherman in the vestibule?"

"The great warrior Wakea. I think the spear he's holding is meant for more than fishing. I don't know much about this stuff. It all comes from Grandma. She's a follower of Ho'oponopono, ancient Hawaiian religion. I have to concentrate to even say it."

"What's . . . Hopono? What do they believe?"

"Ho'oponopono. Not sure. Something about mental cleansing and reincarnation. Sometimes I think these people – the ones promoting it – patch this stuff together out of contemporary religious conjecture and attribute it to their ancestors. I mean all of a sudden the ancient Hawaiians believed in reincarnation? Since when? The sixties? I thought that was the Hindus."

Milissa stroked a carved monk seal sitting on the end table. "It's nice to see that Grandma's trying to preserve the island tradition."

"I got that from Renee last Christmas. It's all original stuff." X reached out with both hands to include the arts and crafts displayed about the house. "Our way of paying respect to the past."

"Does your little town deserve the same respect?" Milissa asked, stretching out to ease the awkward segue.

Disarmed more by her uninhibited release than by her sudden shift to Maunaloa, X sat down as if to focus on the game. "We're mindful of the concern."

He stared blankly for a moment at the screen, then leaned back and took her beauty in, trying not to examine her too obviously as she reclined against the soft arm of the sofa, her body emanating strength and dignity uncommon in a person so young. The boyish quality in her deep-set eyes and full eyebrows seemed almost fierce in its willingness to engage.

She was not an innocent. She could tell by his sudden lack of bearing, the over-long pause and flushing of complexion, that he was enamored. But she could never have discerned so soon how much her unintended charm had compromised his will.

He felt his cock begin to swell. He reached over and turned off the set. "We're putting a small museum in the north section." He retrieved a blueprint of the planned development from his desk. "We're renovating one Portuguese and one Filipino plantation house as part of the exhibit. They'll be right . . ." He opened the plans out on the coffee table, scooted close, and reached across Milissa who was now leaning attentively in. "Right here."

"No glasses," Renee broke in, setting Milissa's bottle on the end table and handing the other to X, who had slid away, abandoning Milissa to the enigmatic plans. "The way Xavier likes it."

Embarrassed by X's move, Milissa kept her eyes fixed on the drawing. Finally, "This?" she asked, pointing at what appeared to be houses in a section apart from the museum. "These are the new houses?"

"Our new rentals," X replied, moving even further from Milissa, but adjusting to face her. "Sixty units. They're ready to go up. But the whole thing's dead in the water right now."

"Well," Renee announced quietly, looking in at them through an invisible partition with an edge in her voice that only X could detect, "if I can be excused, I've been trying to get into the pool all morning."

"Oh!" Milissa looked back at the beer as if her fascination with the plans had been interrupted. "Thank you. Looks nice and cold."

"I'll join you after the game," X said.

Renee gave the empty TV screen a questioning look and left the room.

Reset by the jolt of Renee's intervention, X postured himself against the back of the sofa, crossed his legs, ankle to knee, and took a drink. "What's your interest in Maunaloa? I thought you had some questions about the environment."

"Cultural environment . . . as reflected in preservation of affordable housing."

"Cultural environment as reflected . . ." X repeated, taunting the phrase. "You're working for whom?"

"To tell you the truth," Milissa replied, "I'm on my own."

"You're not with Fidel's group?"

"The MCC? No. I'm a third year law student, a summer intern for Morgan Zarins."

"Did she send you?"

"Not likely. Do you know Morgan?"

"Everybody knows Morgan."

"What do you think of her?"

"No one's more respected."

"Why's that?"

"Hawaiian girl makes good. She does a lot of free work."

"She's Hawaiian? She's so white."

"Off-white, wouldn't you say? Hapa haole they call it. Just a touch on her mother's side."

"She never said."

"Some hapas would rather pass for white. As kids, they take a lot of abuse for their skin. I thought I was asking the questions. So you're not a private eye?"

"I am a private eye."

"A private eye on a personal mission."

"Something like that. I'm always on a mission."

"So what's the mission? Don't forget your beer."

She wasn't sure. *Do it for a lark*, she recalled Cory saying. *This island needs an upstart*. "Basically, it's about displacement."

"'Displacement.' The latest catchword in the local vocabulary. Runner-up to 'da kine'."

"People wanna know what's gonna happen to the families."

"And you wanna save them," X observed, appearing patient and wise.

"I'd like to help," Milissa granted, looking shyly down and fondling the lobe of her ear.

"What can we do?" X asked, his animus confounded by her simple, sensuous distraction, certain only that he needed to keep the small talk alive while he figured a way to work her into his life.

"You're supposed to be the big Satan in all this. I know how that goes – an easy target for a world of woes – but I'd like to hear your version before I decide."

"That's fair. But aren't you taking a lot on here? You already have a job and you have what? A couple months before you're back in . . .?"

"Seattle," Milissa answered. "That's the way I am." She shrugged as if there were no remedy. "I get involved. I make up my mind as to where I can be the most help, and I push toward the ultimate good."

"Ultimate good!" X laughed. "You got a fix on the ultimate good?"

"In the case of Maunaloa? I'm not altogether sure. I need more information. In the final account, ultimate good is when everybody's needs are met."

"But some people's needs are not good."

"Aside from the rare, gratuitously evil exception, all people strive for humanly acceptable results."

"Where'd you get that?"

"I'm quoting myself."

"From some term paper, no doubt."

"Actually, a law review article on the nature and character of the reasonable man."

"Well, it's horseshit. Ivory tower stuff. Reasonable man my ass. The concept is up for grabs. That's what's wrong with the law. No immutable standards. Given the right circumstances, all people are capable of evil deeds."

"Can I tell you a story? I think it'll make my point."

"How 'bout I tell you a story. It may not have a point, but it's what you came to hear."

"Oh." Milissa grinned, trying to get X to lighten up. "It's about the environment."

"Just an account of experience. Which you obviously have little of. And then I have a proposition. You in?"

"I'm in."

X downed his beer and motioned for her to stay put. "I'll grab a couple more."

"Drink this one," she offered. "I didn't really want it. Just being polite."

"Probably flat by now." He tasted it and studied its inscription as if to inspire his muse. "Before I took over, Maunaloa was a sore. When there was pineapple, the companies kept it up. Since then it's become a slum. We got Stockmans to come in with us because I sold them on the idea of a subdivision – a bedroom community for neighbor island professionals – and pasture land for their stud enterprise. You probably noticed the horses as you came up the Kam. That's Stockmans. We're Stockmans. They have controlling interest.

"The master plan" – X waved his palms in broad strokes across the surface of a grand futility – "included riding stables, my mother's contribution. But everyone agreed, first order of business, old Maunaloa had to go.

"Of course!" X complained, flinching from phantom accusations, "we knew we couldn't just throw everyone out! But the situation over there was out of hand. Almost all the tenants were on welfare, some for three generations. You know, children having children, learning by example.

"First thing, we tore down the vacancies that followed our notice of intent. Some were so full of termites they couldn't have been saved. That took out almost all the south side. What you had over there were a lotta bachelor quarters that hadn't been occupied consistently since Dole pulled out. It was the poorer side of town. We also got rid of a big chunk of the north section the same way. Once again the least desirable housing.

"Then Cory Adler came with her idea. First she asked me for a couple of the empty cottages to house a Maunaloa extension of her school. You know Cory?"

"We've talked."

"I thought it was a good idea. Wasn't sure where to put them, but I told her I'd work it in. Every time I gave her a little nod, she'd take it to her board and get approval, and then come back and pile on new ideas. Before I knew it, we were talking about preserving the north side as a historic district. Houses converted to shops and quaint cafés. Craft shows. A little ethnic ambiance for the south side upper crust. She actually got bids for the renovation. Her scheme was meant to address the problem of affordable housing. No one over there could afford to buy, so renovate their houses and let them make the added rent by selling bric-a-brac. My problem back then was that I was trying to please everyone. Especially her. She was around a lot." X lifted his eyebrow suggestively. "And very persuasive.

"Between the time that I took the idea upstairs and got back to her, she'd mobilized the tenants. Actually used my copier to run off notices. They were already hanging out their trinkets. The Aussies didn't go for it. Abbot – he's the hard ass – laughed at me over the phone. 'Oh, mate,' he said, 'sounds like the little tootsy has you going.' I laughed too. He was right.

"Cory was pissed. No more coo chi coo. And that's when Fidel stepped in." When he touched on the more contentious parts of his account, exasperation, a juvenile torment, tantamount to feeling the pain anew, appeared in X's face. "His timing was perfect. He succeeded in getting the tenants to believe that we'd welched on 'em, and they've been entrenched ever since.

"Ultimately, we opted for the cheap south side rentals you saw in the layout, and focused our dream for an upscale community on the north side. We'll sell some houses near the rentals too, but not at the price we'd get if they weren't there. Swear to God, I'll build a wall around that north section once I get everyone out.

"It's all Fidel. He's latifundista. Argentine. Old, old money. We'd known of him through Renee's family. He grew up in the west coast Catholic prep schools. That's where he learned his perfect American. He has nothing to do with his time, so he trips around the world in his half-beard championing causes. Outside of South America he was just another spic until he picked up on the ethnic chic – the educated Latin American politico thing – and made it his identity. He built his reputation fighting Washington's nuclear industry, and then got national attention in the spotted owl thing. He leeches onto issues one after another and takes control."

"How were you lucky enough to attract his attention?"

"He was already here, trying to buy land for his utopian community. He overplayed it in the press and suddenly no one would sell. So, when he heard about our misstep, he latched on. His pitch was preservation of the plantation culture he claims has grown up in Maunaloa over the last hundred years. I saw it as a cover story for him to become a hero at my expense, and for his clique to set themselves up for life, smoking pakalolo and catering to the cultural fantasies of the locals.

"Now, don't get me wrong. My family's admiration for Hawaiian culture is well known. But this plantation culture compost is a fabrication. I mean sixty years of immigrant laborers mixed in with what remained of the old stock is not tradition. Truth is, plantation culture was replaced years ago by welfare culture. The people left in Maunaloa are looked down on by their own kind."

X took Milissa through the hurdles that MCC had set up, including two costly work stoppages. The banks had frozen funding for ten days in March while the county council debated Stockmans' proposed affordable rents. "We got our way on that, but they're still too high for the welfare set. They're used to paying seventy five a week."

"Week to week?"

"I cut 'em all back to weeklies years ago. They could never come through with the monthly rents. They'd get their checks and piss 'em away, then come in asking to pay a week or two. The weekly system keeps the pressure on and shortens the eviction."

"So what's gonna happen to the people who can't afford the higher rents?"

"The displacees? That's what I'm hiring you to figure out."

For the preceding hour, X's unwitting hints of cynicism and snobbery had caused Milissa to see him as a big part of the problem. But there was an internalizing – a painful, adolescent self-doubt in his reaction to stress – that softened her resistance.

"I have a job."

"As long as you're on Molokai, you'll be giving your quality time to this issue. It's where your passion is. I'm offering you a chance to play a meaningful role. You'll have the resources and prestige of Stockmans Inc."

"Resources, I'm sure. Prestige? Maybe in the boardrooms."

"Maybe you can do something to rehabilitate our local image."

"I'm not concerned about your image."

"I think you are, inversely."

"My only concern would be the tenants."

"But you're not bent on destroying Stockmans."

Milissa had to think. How far would she go?

"We're not blind to the plight of the tenants. I'd foot their relocation. You'd have a budget."

"It'd be like in-house opposition."

"If I let you get away, you'll team up with Fidel. That could cost me more than hiring you."

"I'm not into teaming up with opportunists, if that's what they are."

"I see you as somewhere in between. Like an ombudsman."

"Only more proactive."

"I'm comfortable with that."

"Can you give me a day or two? I'd like to write a job description and talk with Morgan about conflicts."

"Here's where I'm coming from." X twined his fingers together in the fashion of a child at prayer. "I've had to put everything on hold. These people aren't going without a fight. I can't afford to let them disrupt things again once I get it rolling. I'm meeting with a couple of board members in a week. I need something in place by then."

"It'd have to be part time."

"No problem. Come around to the office on Monday and we'll look at your ideas. Meantime, unless you decide otherwise, consider yourself on board."

"What was Nancy Drew up to?" She was standing behind him, wrapped in a towel, a gin and tonic in her hand.

He hadn't heard her come in. Always watching, he thought. "You noticed that too," he said without turning around. "I gave her a job."

Renee climbed over the back of the sofa and straddled him from behind. She pushed his shoulders forward, scratching the nape of his neck and checking behind his ears, triggering a shallow, preconditioned drowse. "That's a shocker," she said, squeezing down over-hard on a blackhead. "She came here looking for a job?"

X leaned into Renee's pinch. "No...o...o," he moaned stoically. "My idea. She's perfect. A legal intern. Only here for a couple months. Has a genuine concern. I'm gonna let her mediate, run interference with the tenants."

"Seems a little presumptuous, getting her foot in the door with that ID," Renee remarked, disengaging to retrieve her drink from the end table, lifting herself from the cushion just far enough to give X a glimpse of her bare bottom. "You let her know who's boss?"

"You?"

"You think I'm joking."

"I think you underestimate me."

"I think you're eternally naive. Sometimes you don't know your own mind, especially when you're off task. You get lost. An adolescent bimbo comes into the house and you hire her to run your business."

"Given enough downtime," X laughed, "I could be living in a hut like Fidel."

"He's slumming out there. You in that situation? You'd never pull out of it."

"You're right. I could've gone down like that. A shack on the beach, tokin' the bud and touchin' the sky."

"Um hum, and you're wrong about him sitting out there getting high."

"You don't know that."

Renee's brow crimped with irritation. "I grew up around patricians like Fidel. They're taught to think they're better than the rest. They stay straight to keep their noses up. His people think that he's a renegade. They're wrong. He's got their taste for conquest, but he's part mestiza."

"Indian?"

"His mother's side. He has something to prove. When he cashes in it'll be for recognition."

She lit a cigarette and reflected before going on. "Miss Dogherty? What're you paying her?"

"We're doing a contract on Monday."

"Did she give any references? Or did you hire her because of her 'genuine concern'?"

"She works for Morgan Zarins."

"Did she make you feel guilty? Was that the emotion?"

"In that category my dear, you're still the fairest of them all."

Renee stood abruptly, searching for a kinder sentiment, anything to mask her jealousy. Dead ash splashed against her thigh. "My only regret so far," she said, slapping it away and dropping the butt in X's all-but-empty beer, "is for Cory Adler. After starting out in a Quonset hut and bringing that school to where it is . . . Hessie saw her at Friendly Market after you retracted your offer on those houses. She was devastated."

"She's the one who backed away. The houses were still on the table. I didn't even bring it up with Abbot. But now she can't turn back. And neither can I, God damn it. If she'd cooperated – helped set the pace for the new community – there might have been other concessions. But that wasn't her style. Paying cheap rent and smoking pot with brother Stan, hanging onto her funky little environment, that's what she's into."

"Now you've got Cory smoking dope. Isn't there a term for that?"

"Well for damn sure Stan is. Anyway, that's not my point."

"I think it is."

"No, no, no. We're professionals. People like her and I run this island. We have a common trust. She's betrayed it. Putting in with that bunch of radicals. That's what pisses me."

"The only thing we have in common with Cory and Stan is what they got away with and we didn't," Renee confided, a trust-in-me look in her eyes. "And you resent it – now especially, since they're trying to bring you down."

X deflated. "Me? I remember you stretched out in the sun, stripped to the waist with a pipe in your hand. You can't say you don't miss it."

Renee lowered her head and smiled. "Sky River."

Renee was attracted to X in college because he "wasn't tame yet" like the preppy types she'd dated while attending Dryden's Seminary, an exclusive girls school in LA. She and X had been seeing each other for about a year before they went to the Sky River Rock Festival And Lighter Than Air Fair, a one-of-a-kind event in western Washington that featured not only rock bands, but hot air balloon rides and The Great Piano Drop – a piano dropped from a helicopter at five hundred feet into the middle of a cow pasture. At Sky River, Renee and X shared their first hit of gentle Owsley's, the famous bathtub acid of the day, their first full immersion in hip counter-culture.

As a kind of re-entry from the Owsley experience, they went through a brief infatuation with the "movement," attending anti-war rallies and a few radical gatherings. But X's militancy was limited to combat boots, camouflage trousers, and non-specific outbursts of anger; and Renee favored the Beatles over the Stones, approving especially of *You Say You Want a Revolution*.

By the time the Panthers were being systematically purged from society, X and Renee had become righteous hippies – long hair, psychedelics, peeper glasses, and nudity. But when Kent State happened and the Weathermen started bombing, their bourgeois instincts kicked in, causing them to slowly withdraw from their erstwhile "brothers" and "sisters," spending more time alone, doing their homework, eventually coming to resemble the people they were brought up to be.

But X never completely repaired. The conflict between whom he had played at being and the person he'd become produced distortions. His sophomoric militancy resurfaced in graduate school as invective against Black groups like the Symbionese Liberation Army, and evolved into privately-kept, racist convictions against all dark skinned people as Black gangsterism spread across the land.

In the present he masked his racial hatred with open contempt for the slouchy, low-crotched Hawaiian kids and their emulation of gangster mystique, decrying them and their elders as "savages" or "uncivilized," depending on the politeness of his audience. His racism was, in essence, a projection – a reaction to the stress that spurred his bouts of dissipation.

"We were children then," Renee said, pulling securely away from that day in the sun at Sky River. "Sure, it was good. So were Barbie Dolls."

"Bliss is kids' stuff, huh?"

"We're not talking Bagwan here. We're talking induced bliss and its downside – hangovers, hepatitis, AIDs, addiction."

"The pressure of this job, I didn't need that."

"Your choice."

"Not really. Our choice. You and Mom. I wanted to be an executive farmer, to retire young and independently wealthy so that I could explore life, to find myself. That was my clean dream. Now it's either slumlord or son of a bitch."

"Be the sweet son of a bitch you always turn out to be and stop agonizing."

"No qualms?"

Renee slipped to the floor, suddenly passive. She draped an arm across X's lap and looked up at him suggestively. "The only qualm I ever had was you."

"Nice talk."

"You know daddy wanted me to marry someone with a golden rod up his ass." She traced an inward spiral on his thigh.

He opened his legs. "Most of those super-flushes needed something up their ass."

Renee peeked in. "You were in here all that time without any underwear?"

X placed his hand on the back of her head and pressed her gently forward. "I've been ready all morning."

With only slight hesitation, she nuzzled into the opening, growling playfully and nibbling with her lips. He straightened his legs and spread his arms across the back of the sofa, relaxing to enjoy the show. "Christ, I'm horny!"

"I bet you are, after ogling little Miss Dogherty." She took his distended cock into her mouth.

"Get it good and hard. I'll do you from behind." He untied his robe and watched Renee's lips riding his shaft. "Let the head touch against the back of your throat."

Renee emitted a deep groan.

"Slowly," he whispered. His stomach muscles tightened as he buckled forward to examine it emerging almost completely from her mouth and then sinking back in, giving the impression of interminable length.

He reached down past her belly, prodding, gently unfolding the lips of her vagina. She guided his fingers succinctly into the clitoral area, not removing her mouth from his cock. He massaged her clit delicately as she had trained him to do, almost skirting it as it erected in search of his touch. Properly prepared, she could bring herself to a climax almost as quickly as he.

X pushed his head firmly into the back of her throat, gagging her momentarily, then pulling it slowly out and crawling over her as she remained in position, lifting her ass receptively, eager and exposed.

In studied fashion, he wet his head with saliva and inserted it with progressively deeper thrusts to the hilt. With each increase, she let out a girlish cry until she felt him working it against her sweet spot. To get the full effect, she would alternately tuck and cock her ass in a slow bucking motion. If she felt his rhythm regulating toward a climax, she would arch her back, hold still, and encourage him to come.

Normally X would have contained a couple of mini-climaxes before letting her get on top. After coming she would have given it up to him, allowing him to enjoy his own private, unabated pleasure. But while looking down, he began to imagine Milissa in Renee's place. Within seconds, his fantasy spun out of control and he finished her off, howling "Oh, Jesus! Oh, Jesus!" his agony of pleasure.

"Sorry, honey," he sighed, lying receptively on his back. "Couldn't hold it."

Renee mounted him and locked her ankles below his calves. Purchasing him powerfully with her legs and hiding her face in his neck, she began her belly to belly gyration to the heights. "No problem," she murmured. "Sometimes not so hard makes for better traction."

"Traction!" X laughed, enjoying the sensation of her vagina massaging his still sensitive cock.

As she rotated, taking large gasps and holding them in, he coaxed her on, cupping her ass in his hands, reaching in and fondling her labia, until she finally eased into a high-pitched release, coming three times and then collapsing, lifting her head to pant for air, and then lying still.

They fell asleep in their embrace, not waking till the sun began to set. After they took a dip and lolled in the hot tub, Renee suggested that they go out for dinner. "Harry can fly us to Lahaina. We'll eat at the Ali'i and stay at Mom's."

"And have to deal with the kids? That's Hessie's job tonight. They'll be back home soon enough."

"Someplace else then . . . I love you honey."

"Me?" X replied, playing at surprise.

Loka's large, thickly-shocked head came with a pair of dark, heavy, wrap-around sunglasses, giving him the appearance of an accomplished Hawaiian god graffito. He drove the Molokai Tour and Travel Service van, mainly transporting tourists to and from the airport. He was on his way from Kaluakoi Villas to Kaunakakai when he picked Milissa up hitchhiking along the Kam away from X's house.

He presented himself as an expert on traditional Hawaiian religion. With the slightest prompting from Milissa, he launched into a homily, touting Molokai as the last remaining bastion of authentic Hawaiian belief. He explained that the followers of "da old ways" believe in reincarnation, and that people come to Molokai, whether they know it or not, to learn and progress spiritually.

"Nobody come to Molokai by mistake. You here for a reason – not material, spiritual. If you come to Molokai for sense gratification, beautiful Hawaii, like dat, you'll be disappointed. Take a look." He leaned over the wheel to survey the miles and miles of dry, rocky, mesquite-pocked landscape stretching to the lower ridges of Mount Kamakou in the east. "Dis no physical paradise. Paradise in da heart." He tapped his chest. "Dat what Molokai's about."

As he went on, it occurred to Milissa that what she was hearing wasn't extemporaneous. Not because it was sing-song or uninspiring, but because it was so well-integrated, a concise opening statement, a body explaining the opening by way of personalized example and metaphor, all seeming to lead to a conclusion that challenged reply. There was really nothing she could say without seeming argumentative. For lack of a more critical response, she remained deliberately silent until he pulled off the main street of Kaunakakai and drove, to her surprise, directly to the front door of Morgan's office. She hadn't told him anything about herself.

"Let me see those eyes," she demanded pertly, releasing the force of her stored up energy with inquisitive good humor.

She wasn't disappointed. His eyes were strong, not large and enveloping, but unwavering and kind. The worry of getting caught up in an immature stare-down crept into her mind. He blinked to ease her concern. "Keiki," he said, putting his glasses back on, "t'anks for listening."

As she stood alone watching the van pull away, she reflected on Loka's effort to impress her with his knowledge of her nickname and place of employment. Part holy man, part hack, she mused. Is everyone an event on this island? she asked herself, not realizing that she was fast becoming the main attraction.

CHAPTER FOUR

Perry Dogherty was an investigator for Amnesty International. He had started his career in 1966 with Seattle's first public defenders and moved into international law by way of Greenpeace. Maude O'Neil-Dogherty was an artist and syndicated art critic. Though Maude had taken Perry's name, they'd never married. While growing up, Milissa had lived with one and sometimes both as they travelled about the world scene satisfying their interests and the demands of their professions.

The Doghertys' coterie referred to infant Milissa as "Papoose" because of Maude and Perry's practice of keeping her with them on the job. Her personal development was paralleled by a gradual move from the back bench of the courtroom in childhood, to counsel's table where she worked as Perry's trial assistant in her early teens. But closeness was not to be mistaken for coddling.

From early on, she was kept busy with home-schooling and urged to cultivate her own interests and community of support. "Be there but not in my hair," was Perry's curt advice. But where? With whom? she had always wondered. With Perry's constant tutelage and their frequent change of address, she had never known a place where it was safe to learn from childish mistakes.

By age sixteen she was enrolled at Seattle U and living on her own. Prior to leaving home her only lasting ties had been with adults, initiated by adults and irrevocably conditioned by the difference in age. Since that time – emulating her parents' select circle of intimates, but lacking their more evenly acquired discernment – she had become unabashed in her outreach for peers.

Morgan listened to her emotion-packed account of the visit with X, sorting out legal substance and choking down the rest, exuding an impervious buffer of calm. "Using your out-of-state license without the sheriff's leave is *de minimus*, but unwise. The Stockmans job has clear potential for conflict here. We may find ourselves representing their tenants in evictions. Where possible, we'll keep you off the case. Ultimately, you may have to make a choice between employments."

Milissa was irritated and amused at Morgan's flat response. She had absorbed the details of X's come-on and the breakfast beer without a blink. Over the preceding weeks, Milissa had made innumerable attempts at coaxing Morgan into a fuller, more sociable companionship, with no success. She had never seen her more high than on the day they met, and even then she seemed almost two-dimensional. She had hoped for a confidant, not a legal guide dog. She presents like a priest, thought Milissa. A lifetime by proxy? She wondered. There's gotta be more.

"I have a champion idea," Milissa rose dramatically and placed her palms on the edge of Morgan's desk. "You and I go snorkeling."

Morgan, who had already returned to her brief, replied without looking up. "I don't know when I'd have time."

"You should make time," Milissa scolded.

Morgan didn't respond.

Milissa leaned in on stiff arms. "Are you even listening?"

Morgan traced her finger down a column of headnotes. "I believe

Linda likes to snorkel," she answered, writing out a case name as she spoke.

Milissa moved off to do some filing to justify her presence in the room. "This isn't about Linda," she sang, intoning her intention to play out Morgan's evasive end-game. "You, I believe, need some exercise, not to mention a break from this monotony."

Morgan heard, but wasn't listening. Milissa's voice had blended with the twilight of the unlit office.

"I wonder," Milissa said, posing in fifth position, bringing her right foot to point, feigning distraction by holding up a page and examining its watermark. "I wonder if you're just afraid to show your body." She dropped the paper in a drawer and rolled it closed to punctuate her discontent.

The voice came back small and sticky. "I can hardly swim."

Milissa sputtered out a nervous laugh, startled, not by what had been said, but by its disembodied timbre. She squinched her eyes at Morgan through the lowering dusk. "What was that?"

Morgan switched on her lamp. "Call it a maybe," she hedged, sounding like herself again.

"How late will you be?" Milissa asked, unappeased, but wary of proceeding. "I'm hungry."

Morgan looked at her watch. "Another hour."

"Be right back. You, uh . . .?" She didn't finish. Why disturb her? she told herself. She's off in law law land.

She stumbled over him in the dark as she rounded the corner of the truck yard at the back of the post office. He was sitting in the narrow strip of dirt and weeds between the fence and the street. "What in the hell are you doing sitting out here in the dark?" she shouted in a whisper, quelling her fright with anger and then concern. "They oughtta put some lights up in this town!"

"Please forgive," Sea said meekly.

Milissa stood over him, quizzing him like a friendly beat cop. "Where do you stay?"

He got up and pointed to the ground.

"No. Where do you sleep?"

Sea hung his head, embarrassed and afraid to admit that he was homeless.

Milissa tipped her head and prayed her hands to the side of her face. "Where do you sleep?" she repeated, guessing that, despite his crisp pronunciation, he might have a limited grasp of English. "You no eat for long time?" she added. "You like eat?"

Sea covered his mouth. "You are speaking the pidgin to Sea. I must laugh now."

Milissa smiled at herself. "You like hear more?"

"No!" Sea clasped his fingers together over his diaphragm and bent forward, pressing his elbows in to contain the laughter. "Sea will be eating if you insist, but no more pidgin."

"You wait here . . . Sea, is it?"

Sea nodded.

"You wait right here."

The Molokai Drive-In was only a block away, but when she got back, Sea was gone. She called his name and walked on. He coughed to make his presence known as he caught up in the dark.

She handed him his bag. "What kind of name is Sea?"

"The name having been given to me by Sahib Loka. He is calling it my nickname."

"Loka?"

"Yes, Memsahib. The guru of Molokai I am believing."

"The Hawaiian spiritualist. With dark glasses and a van."

"Yes, he is the one."

A couple of sideways glances from Sea told Milissa he was anxious to get off by himself.

"Go and eat now," she said, reigning in her curiosity.

Sea brought his occupied hands together at chin level and bowed slightly. Catching the scent of meat, he turned away to hide his nausea. "If you please, Memsahib . . ." He took a deep breath to clear his nose. "How shall I be calling you?"

"Keiki."

"If you please, Memsahib Keiki . . ."

"No," Milissa broke in, "just Keiki. You can drop the Memsahib, if you please."

"Keiki. The contents of my package . . ."

She took his food and switched the burger for her fries. "Next time communicate."

Sea called out softly as Milissa crossed the street. "Namaste, Memsahib Keiki. Namaste."

Her zone of inviolability, thought Milissa, reaching in gingerly and placing the bag on the desk, feeling an infantile desire to sit on the lap of the lonely figure trapped in the cage of light. Retreating into the darkness, Milissa sat and observed a big, brooding, country girl concentrating on her food like a seaman at mess, looking blindly out into the penumbra, her expression rough and casual, as if she were alone and unconcerned about appearances.

"Everything alright?" Milissa asked.

"Turn on the overhead," Morgan growled, gulping a yeoman's bite, examining the last fry and popping it into her mouth. "Cannot see you.

"So you'd like to take a dip with Morgan?" she continued, her change in affect bloated by exposure to the added light, elbows on the desk, sucking her teeth and wiping the spread from her mouth with the side of her hand.

"Well, if you'd like," Milissa replied cautiously.

Morgan oozed self disgust as she slouched back and looked down at her body. "You're in for a treat."

Milissa was perplexed. She considered taking the offensive, but wasn't sure who she was dealing with. She rested her chin in her hands and eyed Morgan pensively.

Suddenly self-conscious, Morgan straightened up and held her head erect. Her voice softened and rose slightly in pitch. "We'll go snorkeling tomorrow. Linda's going with us. She recommends the twenty mile marker, east end." She paused as if in thought, delicately brushing her crumbs into her napkin. "You probably look very sweet in a bathing suit. I assure you, I do not."

"I'm sorry," Milissa responded, embracing the more familiar

Morgan with a gracious smile. "I didn't mean to imply anything. It'll only be us girls anyway."

Morgan took down a casebook. "One more item," she said serenely, not certain of the reason for Milissa's apology, yet feeling that she'd lost a chunk of time. After locating her citation, her sense of loss was eased and then submerged beneath the reading of the case law. Closing the book, she put it in its place among the others on the shelf.

CHAPTER FIVE

Milissa was prepared to suggest a hike instead, but Morgan's note was unequivocal. Linda would be coming by. They were to pick Morgan up at the office at eleven. Without thinking, she tapped herself on the shoulder, a gesture the O'Neils used for calling down their angels.

"How long have you worked for her?" she asked Linda as they headed for Kaunakakai.

"Two years. She found me at da community college, taking da paralegal course."

"Does she ever act peculiar?"

"Morgan's one peculiar wahine. Gotta know dat going in."

"Peculiar how?"

"Never can tell what she t'inking. She covers it up. Can be nasty wit' a smile on her face."

"I had a teacher like that."

"Just da kine. Cannot believe she going snorkeling. She's usually so prissy."

"I'm afraid I pushed her into it. How did she sound on the phone last night?"

"Like a voice behind a wall."

The grocery sack contained a pair of purple sweat pants, a package of red tights, and two flowery sun dresses purchased at the Salvation Army on the way to the office that morning. She closed the window louvers and began to fuss, instantly breaking a sweat. She hadn't consciously examined her body for at least a decade. She always slept in a full length nightgown, bathed unceremoniously, and covered herself immediately upon stepping out of the shower, routinely omitting everything but her face in the mirror above the bathroom sink. She put her undergarments on while still wrapped in her robe, and always had her clothes laid out so she could dress without delay. In her everyday practice she wore neutral-colored, calf-length muumuus. In court it was olive or gray, military-cut suits and short heels, absent any item that might suggest she was trying to draw attention.

Despite her studied efforts, she wasn't altogether plain. Her face was large and regular, with gravely intelligent blue-grey eyes. Her shoulders were broad and held back effortlessly. Her chest and belly were disproportionate by comparison to her small butt and narrow hips – giving the impression that she was intentionally sticking her stomach out and tucking her backside in – but one was not necessarily put off by her portliness. To the contrary, she might have been seen by some as having a majestic, matronly appeal.

The sun dresses tucked just below her breasts and hung loose to the knee. She had in mind cutting them off at the hip to create a sort of Raggedy Ann effect, hoping that the drape would make her belly less conspicuous. She cut the first one too short and at an angle downward, front to back, emphasizing what she had hoped to hide. She had succeeded, however, and to her chagrin, in producing the look of a two hundred pound rag doll. She pulled the botched dress over her head, ripping it in her frustration.

Morgan had come out once before, more gradually and more

innocently. But Milissa's tireless efforts at engagement – the goading, the enticing naughty-girl comments – were compellingly familiar. She sat in her chair to cool down, but continued to strain for a way to coordinate the pieces of her ludicrous ensemble. Caving in to her predicament, she began to sob, then slumped into a fantasy. Her hand slipped beneath the waistband of her tights. "Oh, Keiki, Keiki, my ki'i pepe," she moaned. But when the dampness reached her fingertips, the hand jerked back.

Grasping the arms of her chair, she held herself in restraint. Her eyes strayed to the thick line of pubic hair leading from her vulva to her navel. I have hair like a man, she said to herself. *A torrent of phantom insults crackled through the room.* Had I been a boy, she thought – flashing back to her days at Molokai Elementary, to the slaps on the butt, to the racial slurs – I would have fought back.

She imagined herself in the outer office, shielding an abused wife from her husband. He was one of her childhood tormenters. He got in her face, calling her a dyke bitch and grabbing her arm to pull her away from his woman. She seized him by the throat and slammed him to the floor. She was on top of him, crushing his Adam's apple. He gurgled and went limp. She had snapped his neck, but was unable to release her grip.

When she came to herself, her hands were still clasping the arms of the chair. Her body remained stiff while her mind decompressed, letting down from the excitement of the kill. She looked at her watch – a quarter to eleven. She was dripping with sweat. She quickly scissored off her sweats above the knees and slipped them on over her tights. The second dress was given an uneven, zigzag hem to avoid the problem of symmetry. After washing her face, she sprouted her hair into two little tails high on the back of her head. She cranked open her window louvers. They were waiting in the car. One last item, the sunglasses in her desk drawer, and she was out the door. Halfway across the gravelly lot, she noticed that her feet were bare.

As Linda started the car, Milissa made a move toward the back seat. Neither dared speak for fear of revealing their astonishment.

"I'll sit in back," Morgan said grimly.

Milissa stopped abruptly and rejoined Linda in front.

After Morgan got situated, they turned to look. She was grinning now, large and foolish. "Well," she said, rubbing her hands in readiness, "let's go bummin'."

Linda cracked up, but Milissa contained herself, wary from the night before.

Linda reached back and grabbed Morgan by the knee. "Morgan, honey, dat you?"

"Not tellin'."

"You should say somet'ing. I could've brought one of Aunty's bathing suits. She 'bout your size."

"It isn't the size," Morgan replied as the car headed east. "It's the shape." Maintaining her vapid grin, Morgan began to prod with both hands around her navel.

After several miles of odd silence, Milissa recalled aloud that Morgan was a weak swimmer.

"Murphy Beach, da water's shallow – t'ree, four feet da most, way out," Linda assured, catching Morgan in the rearview mirror, head bowed, still examining her paunch.

Morgan remained in physical contact with both women as the three glided forward, breathing slow and deep. Eventually, the experience of weightless ease combined with hundreds of bright colored fish to draw her out of her bodily shame. As she floated, maneuvered about like a freighter between tugs, her companions directed her attention – the golden angelfish, her child released; the red, spotted eel, protruding from her rocky heart, gnawing at the indulgent sea; the coral growths, bizarre imaginings. A sense of womb-like security, nurtured by the loving tow of her attendants, allowed her to absorb unchecked the fantasial thrill. Her breathing shallowed as this fusion of embrace and liberation lulled her into autonomic reverie.

Hobbled by the slope of fist-sized boulders – made slippery by the constant southwest China monsoon season flux – she rambled, slapping her hands on her naked thighs, crying "Mazie! Oh Mazie!" but unable to muster the courage to plunge in and attempt a rescue.

Sweet, petite, spunky, and very homely Mazie Magonigal was the only other English speaking Caucasian within three hundred miles of Fuli Town. She was in the final week of her six month contract at the village school where Morgan had also come to teach. They had bicycled down to the river Li before, but this day was special – requiring some act of initiation, thought Mazie, some way of signifying that they were in it together now that she had decided to stay an additional six months.

Taking her own dare, Mazie stripped down to her bra and panties and waded in. Morgan followed, red-faced and dutiful, but only ankle deep. Mazie went under and came up a couple of times before gaining control of her body. Grappling against the current, she located a root jutting just above the surface and hung on, her body lashing around in the direction of the flow. She was about fifteen feet from shore. Already exhausted from panic, she couldn't gain her feet. Morgan retrieved their discarded smocks and pajama pants and knotted them together. Scooting away from shore along the bottom, she flipped the tangled lead again and again in Mazie's direction. By the time the water had reached Morgan's armpits, hysterics had blended with hilarity.

"Let it wash you down," Morgan pleaded. "I'll send a cab to Yangshuo."

"No fuckin' way!" Mazie shouted, getting her footing for an instant, lunging fiercely forward and grabbing the lifeline. "I'll end up paying the fare."

Mazie pulled herself as far as Morgan and languished. "This'll do," she sighed, half joking. "You do the rest."

Morgan let go of the clothing and gave Mazie a mighty push on the rump, shoving her close enough in for her to crawl onto the strand. After bottoming her way to safety, Morgan collapsed into a momentary daze, then flopped onto her stomach and put her hand on Mazie's back. "Are you okay?"

Mazie turned over. Her bra was around her waist. "Was I a goner?"

Morgan gazed, helpless and exposed.

Mazie smiled in reply. "Oh that's all right, mate. We all have feelings. They're just my little bippies. You can look." She reached up and tousled the back of Morgan's hair. "Sweet Morgan. Did you save my life?"

Morgan gave a bashful shrug and looked into the current. Her eyes drifted to a mangle of fabric flagging off the end of Mazie's fateful root. Mazie saw it too. They walked to the edge to be sure. Plopping down where they stood, they laid back and laughed at themselves until nightfall, then peddled home, swift and inconspicuous, grateful for the narrow, unlit lanes of Fuli Town.

The gentle rocking brought her around. Linda had gone ahead to shore. Milissa had hung on, waiting for her to emerge. "Where were you?"

Morgan stood up. "With you, I think." She leaned through the hip-high surface and sank back up to her neck, surprised by the lack of support. "You'd know better than I."

There was a message on Morgan's answering machine. "Milissa. X here. For Monday. You mentioned a job description. Point of emphasis. Think about how you would handle the most belligerent cases. Is one o'clock okay? If not, give a call. Otherwise, see you then. At the office then. Maunaloa. Right on the main drag at the south end of the warehouse."

Milissa's statement, composed that night, outlined her duties and the policy behind them. She would deal with each household separately. There would be no playing into the hands of the MCC by acknowledging its representative role. "A self-appointed committee like this," she had written, "is rendered ineffective by its raison d'être that all concessions be meted out equally among its following. The opposing party inevitably asserts its inability to satisfy everyone, and the demands are not met, or at best, in the process of leveling down, the most needy receive less than they deserve. The committee looks heroic for its lack of compromise, and the landlord is vilified for his greed."

To rectify this inequity, she would be allowed, if hired, to respond differently to the needs of different households. She would have broad discretion and a dual purpose. On the one hand, she would be an agent for the corporation. On the other, she would be an advocate for the tenants. And finally, though she had been given no real reason to expect hostility, but addressing X's "point of emphasis" nonetheless, violence or threats would be responded to with police presence as a matter of course.

Milissa's mind paced through the upcoming meeting with X again and again, alternately considering Morgan's strange but endearing behavior that afternoon. At last, conceding that nothing could be resolved outside of real time, she fell asleep to dream intense but unremembered dreams.

Morgan lay subdued in the dark, inklings of bliss weeping through the rends in her heart chakra. That afternoon. The tender attention. Had she opened too soon? Something in her was terrified of escape. She fell asleep *walking arm in arm with Mazie. They minced along the rugged shoulder of the Li, propping each other up. Mazie slipped and fell away*. Morgan struggled for conscious control but couldn't bring her Mazie back. *Down the shore, the hungry, bony-faced China boys were throwing pebbles. One came over and plucked Morgan's belly and pointed at her crotch. She was unable to move because of the slimly stones. The little devil knew it. He taunted her hidden sex, trying to look in from in front and behind, calling the other boys over.*

Milissa appeared above them on the slope, looking like one of the immense broadside heroines posted about during Mao's Cultural Revolution. Wide stance. Chest out. Head high. Hands fisted to the hips. Waving her arms, palms exposed, in the stylized gestures of an over-zealous traffic cop, one hand then the other flourishing out and snapping back. The boys whimpered, scattered, threw themselves into the river. Morgan watched them float away. They waved goodbye – round, shaven heads with cherubic, grinning faces bobbing on the surface – cleansed by Milissa's intervention. Milissa waved back, cap in hand.

CHAPTER SIX

Linda's extra large, melonous Aunty Isabella, known by all as Easy, beckoned over her shoulder with a single finger as she walked into her size thirteen slippers and disappeared into the kitchen. "Linda's at church wit' little Maria," she called out. "She say you coming by. You like me take you 'round some neighbors, ya?"

Milissa had assumed that Linda would be her escort. "Can get a look at Maunaloa before you meet wit' X," she'd suggested the day before. "You come by tomorrow. I'll get you started."

"Got just da kine," Easy announced, pointing in the air as she re-entered the room, reacting to the fizz from her coke with a "taahh" and handing Milissa the half-empty bottle, hiding a smidgen of mischief in the corners of her generous grin. "Come," she said, moving in the direction of the front door as Milissa, who had expected chitchat, was lowering herself into an overstuffed chair. "I'll introduce you my nephew."

Taken aback by the pace, Milissa gawked and grumbled, "Just da kine?" – an antic wasted on Easy, who was already trouping down the unpaved road toward the house next door.

The front porch creaked under her weight. "Anybody home?"

A bare chest appeared from the darkness behind the screen door.

"Got one lady here for see you. She from Stockmans Inc."

The man hesitated. A large, short-haired mongrel, apparently happy to see Easy, groaned softly at his side.

"Put Ché in da back. We like come in."

"Ché, come!" he called, yielding to Easy's rank.

Easy stepped inside and did a complete rotation as she inspected the condition of the small, low-ceilinged room lit only by the flash and flicker of a silent TV set at the far end of the couch, situated there so that John could view it while lying down. John had been watching baseball. He came out of the kitchen, tucking in a white, short-sleeved shirt.

Easy took a place on the floor by the shaded window. "Keoni, dis Keiki."

John acknowledged Milissa with a nod as the two sat on the couch, but for a time nobody spoke. Seeing no polite alternative, Milissa turned her attention to the game. "The Big Unit," she finally remarked, recognizing the National League fastball king. How many games in this series?"

"T'ree."

"And they're at?"

"One game each. Whatchu like to talk about?"

Milissa squinted at the semi-dark and returned her gaze to the screen. "I *did* want to discuss Stockmans' plans."

John reached over Milissa and fiddled with the volume control until the sound jumped out. "Switch has a defect. Got a mind of its own."

Milissa pressed her palms into the cushion and turned away from the set. "We were hoping we could help you resettle," she said, watching Easy expand and contract in the hazy coruscation. John leaned forward to formulate a reply. Whap! One of the shades next to Easy furled up.

"Hoh, dat's one sassy window shade!" Easy said, affecting surprise as she leaned away and shielded her eyes from the light. "Mo' bettah I go home now anyway. Keiki, you come see me when you t'rough, ya?" She tapped John's shoulder as she left. "And you, be nice to each other."

"You're jumping ahead of yourself," John told Milissa. "Lemme say goodbye to Aunty, den we talk."

Definitely saying more than their goodbyes, thought Milissa as she watched John and Easy through the screen door, shoulder to shoulder at the edge of the porch, facing into the yard.

Across the room, the caption above the erstwhile leader sitting on his wicker throne read: *Huey Newton, Chairman, Black Panther Party for Self-Defense.* On another wall hung the familiar beretted head of Ché Guevarra. SOVEREIGN HAWAII was permanently emblazoned in a rainbow above the entrance to the kitchen. A small framed picture sat alone on an end table in the far corner. It was Gandhi sitting alone by a young couple near a river bank with people gathered 'round. His autobiography was lying on the floor. As Milissa opened the book, the screen door creaked.

"How far ahead was I?" she asked, leafing purposefully through the book.

"Dey gonna have to put me out," John answered without apparent concern as he pulled up the other shade.

"Put," Milissa remarked, locating the page on which the description, *Gandhi Witnessing an Intercast Marriage*, had been left behind. "Sounds less than passive."

"Let 'em know dey gonna hafta send da sheriff in for . . . to remove me."

Milissa set the book down and joined John on the couch. "My job is to help people resettle, not to arrange political settlements."

"You have da information," John shot back, pinched by her impertinence.

"You'd like to minimize the personal danger of your protest by announcing it in advance. That way everyone will know and they'll have to do it by the book. Easy's idea?" Milissa had stated plainly what John was loath to admit.

"If dey decide to shoot one son-a-bitch, dey gonna find a way," John replied, his pidgin thickening, distressed from having to explain, but smiling wryly at Milissa's insight. "I leave dis t'ing for chance, dey maybe send one swell head local boy to make da bust. Dey send one brah to blow me up, no look so racial on da news, ya?"

The two stared at each other for a moment.

"Of course, I'll make sure they have it under control. If you'd like, I'll be on hand. In which case, you'll go willingly?"

"Dey gonna have to arrest me, but otherwise . . ."

"Cuffs and that?"

John nodded. "Da whole production."

"You got a deal, then." Milissa started sorting through the books lying beside John's end of the couch. "You keep your reading on the floor."

"I keep it at hand," John said, picking up his current read. "Dis whole state's a good ol' boy club. Been like dat since Kamehameha went in cahoots wit' da haoles. Check it out."

Milissa took the book, a local sovereignty press bestseller on the history of the islands.

"Brown folks work deir way into da cabal, dey harder on da locals dan da rest."

"Is that in here?" she asked, furling the pages.

"A little bit, ya. But most of it's still locked up wit' internal investigation files in Honolulu." He reached down behind the couch and pulled out two cans of beer hanging from a plasti-pack retainer. "Can call it insider information." He snapped one open and sipped enough to wet his lips.

"Dewan Jackson," he began, as if he were referencing a noted authority, "San Francisco County Jail. Used to call dis one black guard Ol' Crimson Neck 'cause he was so hard on da brahs. 'Here come Ol' Crimson Neck,' Dewan used to say, 'da blackest peckerwood on C deck.'

"And den he had dis song, dis poem he was composing. Was kinda like a rap, but never had no rap back den. Da first two lines stuck in my head. 'Ring around da resources. Race follows da buck.' He'd go around rapping doze two lines and den add t'ings on like maybe, 'You in bed wit' Crimson Neck, you black ass outta luck,' or somet'ing like dat."

"What was he in there for?"

"Bank robbery."

"And you?" Milissa asked, smiling at the irony. "What were you following?"

"All political stuff. Demonstrations. Resisting arrest. Assault while resisting arrest. San Francisco in da seventies. Stockmans probably has a file."

"So you're doing what they expect you to do?"

"Everybody expects Keoni to fight eviction. Dat's my book on Molokai."

"Are you comfortable being perceived as a radical?"

John laughed. "Sounds like you're reading from a script."

"Just trying to be a tough guy like you. Actually, I envy you the opportunity to stand for something."

John glanced past Milissa at the score on the screen. The sound had gone out without them noticing. "My Angels're going down da tubes."

"You've got more in common with Stockmans than you think."

"How's dat?"

"When I was over at X's a couple days ago, he was watching the first game of this series."

"Doesn't count." John adjusted the knob and whacked the set, with no result. "Even La Cosa Nostra follows baseball."

"Maybe you all have something in common."

"Ah yes, da big betting pool in da sky."

"There must be something that unites us all. Don't you believe?"

"Beer and baseball."

"No, I'm serious."

"Let's see," John mused, taking a chug. "Race divides most of us. Religion inspires bloodshed. We're all glued to da tube. Dat's it. Da Circus Maximus syndrome. Everybody's fetished wit' consuming entertainment, products, ideas."

"How about love?"

"Love? Love helps, but human bonding comes down to control of limited resources. Lotta times love doesn't count."

"That's a pretty cold outlook."

"Most people're out in da cold. Where you come from poverty's transcended, so you t'ink everybody can be friends."

"You think I was brought up in utopia," Milissa chided. "You can't be that naive."

"Mo' bettah put, your people got no reason to be unfriendly wit' each other. Dey under no pressure to hang in. Independent men and women travelling da globe in search of deeper meaning, like dat. Den dere's you. You over da top. You t'ink *everyone* can get along, and you gonna make it so, ya?"

It was Milissa's turn to react. "My membership in the human race isn't limited because I've had material advantages. How would you know anyway? What're you basing your assumptions on? The color of my skin?"

"You da kine," John answered, mirth in his eyes. "Besides, your fame precedes you."

"Who've you been talking to?"

"Who you been talking to?"

Milissa paused as if to bring John into focus. "Wait a minute," she said, pointing in fun. "Keoni Mikala! The big MCC radical. One of Moke's people, the way he tells it."

"Milissa 'Keiki' Dogherty," John replied, pointing back and releasing a little gut laugh after taking another drink, "law school, private eye, two shoes."

"Gimme one!" Milissa demanded.

John dangled the remaining beer playfully beyond her reach.

"Come on, share the resources."

After feigning deep consideration, he handed her the can.

Milissa held her prize in the air. "At present then, as you see it, our relationship is contained herein. Limited to the contents of this can. Do I dare open it?"

"Got to admit," John ribbed, half serious, "was plenty nice, me going fifty fifty wit' you like dat, wit' you just up here slumming. Gave you a feeling of acceptance, ya?"

"Whatta you think friendship is anyway, a materials contract? Loosen up!"

"Friendship's a matter of degree like everyt'ing else," John replied, returning to his premise, "but in hard times, friendship, call it community, gives way to self-interest."

"Two men on a plank."

"Sounds like one circus act."

"Grim entertainment. It's a seminal case in law, a clash of morality and necessity brought on by hard times. Two sailors, lifelong friends, are shipwrecked in the Atlantic. They find a small piece of the ship floating in the water, a plank large enough to hold only one at a time. For three days and nights they cooperate, spelling each other until it's apparent that neither will survive if they continue to share – one too exhausted to continue swimming, the other too exhausted to give up the plank. The one in possession paddles away in the dark. Two hours later, at sunrise, he's pulled from the sea. His friend is never found."

"He did what he had to do. Maybe not what I'd do, but can't blame a man for saving his life."

"That's what he claimed – his defense was necessity. On appeal, the court noted that the law had never recognized an unqualified right to save one's own life. They gave the example of a soldier at war. The sailor's conviction for murder was upheld and he was sentenced to hang."

"Too strict, da verdict, ya?"

"Queen Victoria thought so. She commuted his sentence to six months, credit for time served."

"Hoh! dat Vicky's one ono lady."

"She was a good one," Milissa agreed. "But the court was right. You can't lay down a law that necessity is the rule. I mean, who's to be the judge when things are happening?"

"Da guy who profits from da act."

"Exactly. That's the problem."

"Like when Stockmans tore down half of Maunaloa."

"That's quite a reach."

"Not really. Two vying claims to property. Like da guys on da plank. One has possession, but both got a stake."

"The cases are easily distinguished."

"You're saying dat 'cause you t'ink your boss deserves clemency."

"Oh, no. Don't pin X on me!" She paused to decompress. "Look at the facts of each case."

"Let's say plank man kicked da other moke in da chops when he wasn't looking, whacked him good so he couldn't catch up. You t'ink Vicky's gonna give him a break? No way. Just da kine when Stockmans tore out half da town."

"I understand they gave notice."

"Folks aren't of one mind. Dey can't react as quickly as a corporation. Stockmans, deir mind was made up. We could consult wit 'em to plan da new community. Everyt'ing had da appearance of fairness. But doze bulldozers all da time were coming our way. To us it was just like a smack in da chops. But we caught up. Dey got dis far, and now we're digging in."

"Daddy, Chase went pinch me!" Maria cried, barging through the door in frightened glee.

Out on the porch, scowling, stood Maria's playmate, afraid to venture in but holding his ground, considering revenge. Maria glanced back and giggled, leaning safely on her father's knee.

"What's up, Chase?" John asked. "Come here, boy."

Plump, round-faced Chase stood in the doorway, ready to flee, pointing to a red smudge on his khaki pants. "Deze are my church pants. Mama going whack me for get 'em dirty."

"You do dat?" John asked, looking gently at Maria who had already delivered her eyes to the floor. "Den you gotta clean 'em. Now, time out on da back porch till Chase brings 'em back."

Maria peeled off stiff-legged into the kitchen.

"My baby," John explained.

"You're married?"

"Her mama died. Back in San Francisco. Maria was only t'ree months old."

"You miss her?"

"Angel? She's over six years gone. We never was too close. She took an overdose. Mo' bettah dis way for Maria."

Maria bounded back into the room, plopped down cross-legged on the floor, and stared curiously at Milissa.

"Maria, dis Keiki. Now, what'd I say about time out?"

"She no keiki," Maria protested, pointing proudly at her chest. "I da keiki."

"Hoh, you bad today," John said, sweeping her into his arms. "T'ought you went to church dis morning." John looked sheepishly at Milissa. “Aunty makes her go to church. She insists.”

Chase came in holding the pants at arm’s length. Maria rounded her shoulders and brought her hands to her chest. John put her down, clapped a hand on each child’s head and pivoted them toward the kitchen. “Now, both of you go to work.”

“Uncle!” Chase whined, “why me? Maria went . . .”

“You in dis too,” John cut in. “Maria didn’t just walk up after church and t’row dirt on you. Besides, work’s good for you. Make you strong.”

“If it’s so good, why don’t you help? I’m already strong.”

“I’m going to my workshop.”

“Aunty Keiki going to?” Maria asked, peeking at Milissa from behind her father’s leg.

“You never mind.” John fanned Maria’s backside as she and Chase scampered away.

“Where were we?” John asked Milissa.

“I should be leaving. You have things to do.”

“Not really. Come, I’ll show you my creations.”

Milissa followed John through the tiny tacked-on utility room. As they passed the children, who were already lost in a mountain of suds, John turned off the water and cautioned them not to leave a mess.

Milissa crouched down on the back porch and tugged at the base of Ché’s ears. “He didn’t even open his eyes.”

Ché’s moan was deep and acquiescent.

“Daddy say Ché can see wit’ his nose,” Maria offered, taking the opportunity to decorate Ché with a pile of foam.

“Eh!” John scolded, directing Maria back inside.

Ché pressed jealously between John and Milissa as they headed across the yard to John’s weather-worn retreat.

“What kind of work do you do?”

“Silversmith,” John answered, removing the padlock. “Dis is my treasure house.”

An immense valley dropped away from the grate-covered window at the back of John’s shop. Flanked by descending promontories, it rolled for miles down into the foothills blocking the southern shore.

To the east, Milissa recognized X's estate perched on an isolated plateau.

John popped open an airtight container and set it on the bench. Inside were earrings – precise pairs of cowry, auger, scallop, and puka shells with gold and silver findings, and delicate, silver-laced baubles of beach glass. He also laid out a number of gold and silver ankle bracelets exquisitely inlaid with petroglyphs and Tahuna crosses made of semi-precious stone.

One of the bracelets caught Milissa's eye. It was made of small, hinged silver plates, each inlaid with the same intriguing turquoise design. John suppressed a smile of delight as she admired it. He took a seat at the side of his workbench and motioned for her ankle. She slipped out of her sandal and propped her foot on the edge of his chair.

"The symbol," she asked, "what is it?"

"Kau lua," he answered, sizing the bracelet to fit. "Ancient Mu hieroglyph." He removed a couple of plates and measured it again. "Mo' bettah," he said, fastening it around her shin and letting it fall into place. "Feel okay?"

She lifted her arch and touched her ankle just above the bracelet. Was it a gift? "Perfect," she answered. "Kau lua? What does it mean?"

"You wear it, its meaning will come to you." He rotated the clasp around to the back and patted her once lightly on the calf. "Let me know when you find out."

CHAPTER SEVEN

Morgan's bedroom door was open when Milissa arrived home that afternoon. The room was austere, full of antiseptic space. Milissa settled cross-legged into an empty alcove. "You should put a table in here," she said, "like a pedestal for flowers and things." Above her, hiding against the wall, she noticed a snapshot of a raw-boned woman with thin lips and clear blue, ingénue eyes, abandoned there years before when Morgan stopped using the niche as a midnight study. Milissa stood up for a closer look. "Who's this?"

Morgan came to her side. "That's Mazie. I'd forgotten it was there. We taught English together in south China." She took the picture down. "And this," she said, retrieving a miniature pixie doll from the alcove window sill. "I'd forgotten about it as well."

"Looks like Peter Pan."

"Mazie bought it for me – in Yangshuo of all places." She held the doll upright, her thumbs and forefingers pinched around each ankle. "My little Aussie. Too busy to keep in touch."

"Some relationships are situational."

"Time to say goodbye," she added, dropping the keepsakes in the basket by her night stand. "I was hoping you'd come home. Thought we might go out for dinner."

She had made reservations at the Kama Aina, a common eatery on the island, well know for its traditional "mahu aunties." The mahus were more frumpy than their drag queen, mainland counterparts, but less reactionary, exhibiting a more relaxed acceptance of their sexuality.

"Oh no, dear. We dress down in public," came the melodic, unsolicited response. "No like offend doze macho Stockmans cowboys, ya?"

"I'm sorry," Milissa apologized. "I didn't think you could hear."

"Not a problem, dear," six foot three, two hundred and twenty pound Manuko replied in perfect sympathy, touching two gigantic, delicately manicured fingers to Milissa's shoulder. "Dat's why we here. For you can look see. Isn't it wonderful? And how you, Morgan? Never see you."

Manuko moved gracefully to Morgan's side of the table. "Dis one good wahine," he continued, deepening his voice for emphasis, then adjusting back to contralto as he explained. "She went slap one sex discrimination suit on ol' Bunky for laying us off. Now dat Bunky went lose da suit, he t'ink he smart we staying on. We da main attraction."

"Pretty neat, Morgan," Milissa said after Manuko had gone. "Sticking up for these people. I'm having second thoughts about working for Stockmans."

"Because of Manuko's cowboy remark?"

"Every time I hear about Stockmans it's a negative. I spent this morning with a man from Maunaloa. Oh, I meant to show you. He gave me this." She showed Morgan the ankle bracelet. "Actually, a very attractive man. Keoni Mikala. You know him?"

"Linda's brother or cousin."

"He's gonna fight eviction. We really connected. What do you think of him?"

"I don't know him personally. My guess? He'll lean on you if you let him."

"Why would you say that? He seemed so sure of himself."

"Because of who you are, more sure than the rest."

"Maybe too sure. He's such a hunk." Milissa sighed, rolling her eyes to heaven, missing in that libidinal instant the small, enraged animal that swallowed Morgan's face.

"Responsibility for outcomes is vested in you," Morgan replied, her tranquil gloss instantly regained.

It sounded like a daily horoscope. Milissa twinkled and squinched her nose. Morgan's giving advice, she thought.

"Be circumspect," Morgan cautioned, shutting down with a velvet smile.

"Some things are worth telegraphing," Fidel said, sitting on the edge of his chair in John's cramped living room, chest out, the butts of his hands jammed against his knees – masking his delight that John was willing to play the martyr. "It'll serve as an inspiration to the tenants. But what we don't need is blustering. Everything you tell her will get back to X."

"What blustering?" John frowned, embarrassed by his pact with Milissa on the pending arrest. "She came by and asked what I was going to do. I told her. You mind if I cover my ass?"

"I'm suggesting we leave it at that," Fidel replied, satisfied that his plan to undermine Stockmans was on track.

Fidel came to the fight in Maunaloa a victim of Stockmans' orchestrated discredit. Bent on retribution and looking for a weakness, he saw immediately that X had overreached. In his rush to make his project a reality, but with no realistic prospects for future occupancy, X had emptied and razed the south side and then began to chew away at the small north section, discounting its virulence, never guessing it would become Fidel's route to recovery.

Fidel had arrived on the island three years before, scheming to make it the Hawaii of unfulfilled promise. Molokai, in his mind, tainted by the leprosy image, the rugged terrain, and dangerous coastal waters, was a fertile anomaly to Western progress – the pariah of the island chain, still holding to the hunting, fishing, and farming traditions of its original inhabitants and, through these practices, still retaining authentic strains of traditional Hawaiian spirituality.

His radical clarion, muted by reaction but attuned to circumstance, eventually struck a chord in Maunaloa. But elsewhere on the island, where the situation was less desperate, the imported piety of plantation workers and Midwestern entrepreneurs had formed a groundwork of political indifference. The Adventists, the Saints, the Witnesses, and the other New World denominations, the stock of Molokai's devout, neither condemned nor applauded Fidel. They simply looked away – perhaps unaware, certainly unconcerned – while Stockmans blackballed him with impunity.

Fidel's reputation upon arrival had earned him a byline in the *Sentinel*, the most liked of the island's three newspapers. His past practice had been to build a political base before making practical moves, a reasonable gambit on the mainland where economic diversity insured a fair hearing.

He pictured an island with homes built only in select, ecologically appropriate locations, and landscaped to compliment the natural surroundings. He advocated foresting of the dry western end of the island as a way of attracting moisture, an alternative to the current drawing off and desiccation of eastern mountain streams. He allowed that the effect of foresting would take years, but claimed that extant laval aquifers would eventually unclog, making the west arable and more temperate. He popularized the idea of wind-powered distilleries to draw upon abundant brackish water deep underground.

When he encouraged cooperative wholesaling by the island's small farmers as a way of gaining greater market share, his column, initially seen as a harmless stimulant, became a source of irritation. His next major suggestion, an island-wide cooperative community, got an abrupt response – a letter to the editor from a wealthy landowner who advertised her grocery store in the *Sentinel*. No "outsider with communist leanings" was going to tell her who she could deal with.

Following this salvo, others, predominantly Stockmans, began to complain that Fidel's byline was giving him an inordinate voice in the community. The *Sentinel* was in the grip of local advertisers. Fidel's apologia, in which he explained that cooperatives are voluntary organizations regulated by contract, was found on the Op-Ed page in the midst of letters from his detractors. Fidel, the editor explained, was not above the debate.

After his decline in the press, Fidel found it impossible to buy enough property to begin the kind of development he had in mind. The negotiations he had in the works mysteriously fell apart. He faded for a month, casting around for a way to go before deciding to challenge a Stockmans supporter for her seat on the county council, a knee-jerk response that revived the "communist" accusations in the next edition of the *Sentinel*. He withdrew from the race the following day. After more sleepless nights, he fixed on a plan.

He had been aware of murmurings about the redevelopment of Maunaloa but had always considered his project a superior alternative. Now that he was shut out he began to see Maunaloa as his only choice. A quote from a flyer announcing the first meeting of the Maunaloa Tenants' Association had been rattling around in his head: "cooperative preservation of indigenous culture and habitat." It sounded like something he might have written. He showed up at the meeting with a proposed agenda, and a hand-out detailing his approach to the *crisis in Maunaloa* and suggesting a new name for the group.

His was a thoroughgoing battle plan – the more thorough and demanding, the more he would be looked to for its execution. He and other members of the renamed Maunaloa Crisis Committee would attend every official meeting considering issuance of permits to Stockmans. Every decision, whether private or public, that touched on issues relating to the crisis would be monitored for its harassment value. Every action would be calculated to effect loss to the corporation in time or money. MCC's official objective would be to pressure them into saving what remained of old Maunaloa. Fidel's unspoken design was to use the situation as a crucible for his ideas, but also, and more significantly, to defeat his nemesis on its own turf and, with that to his credit, to resume his initial course for island-wide domination.

He was counting on a continuing downturn in the Hawaiian economy. The water lines all along the expectant grid of roads on Molokai's western view property – evinced by one lonely hydrant after another – had lain virtually dormant for seven years. A year or two more of delay and Stockmans might decide to scale back or simply pull out. It wouldn't be the first time such a thing had happened. The American Sugar Company, before the turn of the century, had shut down after depleting the island's water supply. And seventy years later Dole had found it necessary to leave.

Now, two years after that first meeting, Fidel could see that he had held his own. Stockmans had not relented, but there had been no new demolition. The south end had been leveled and platted, and otherwise prepared for building. Two model homes had been put up. But then came the shut-down. His next move would be to embarrass X so severely that he might lose his job. The name Xavier Spitz would be trouble in the mouths of international investors.

"This isn't a sixties replay, is it?" Cory asked. "Stage a protest, everybody yawns, the issue dies from unbiased exposure?"

"It's a documentary. They're calling it The Enclosure Acts, all about people being forced off traditional lands."

"Doesn't sound like headlines."

"It'll be shown on PBS."

Fidel was used to tug of war with his small core of adherents. He knew they were policing him, but he played the game. They were his imprimatur, especially John, the only Hawaiian in the inner circle. "I need you on this one," he said. "For introductions."

"No problem wit' dat," John replied, "but people gotta make up deir own minds."

"Give it a positive spin. These guys are pros. They can take it from there."

"Who we talkin' about exactly?" asked Cory's brother, Stan.

"A fellow named Michael Teague out of Seattle. Works for PBS. He says the piece will be aired nationally. I'm providing airfare and lodging." He paused to assess their response.

Everybody but Easy indicated approval.

"How 'bout you, Aunty?" Stan asked.

"I no vote."

Fidel had not anticipated Easy's presence – she had been negotiating with Stockmans to buy a new house – but he couldn't openly exclude her. "Easy has a right to abstain. I believe she is here to observe. Am I correct, Easy?"

"Observing you," Easy shot back.

"Hearing no protest then . . ." Fidel paused like an auctioneer about to end the bidding, "I'll call Seattle tonight."

Stan shifted in his seat, ready to adjourn.

"One last item," John said. "What're we gonna do for people once dey get evicted?"

Fidel puffed up and leaned forward. "I've given this some thought. The best we can do is fight like hell to keep them in. If we promise assistance after eviction, we'll be helping Stockmans."

"A lot of people aren't as interested in winning this fight as they are in having a roof over their head," Cory observed.

"Dat's why Stockmans hired Keiki."

Anticipating John's direction, Fidel closed his book of minutes and prepared to leave. "Well, let her handle it then. And damn Stockmans if she doesn't."

"So if she asks, we gonna refuse cooperation?" John's question was for everyone.

"Cooperation?" Fidel snapped. "Keiki, Milissa, whatever her name is, her efforts are intended to undercut our initiative. *That's* why Stockmans hired her."

"Even armies accommodate the plight of refugees," Stan put in, always ready with the extreme case.

The issue wasn't going away. Best to soft pedal it, thought Fidel. Maybe this Milissa can be used. "Let's keep an eye on the problem. Nobody over here has been kicked out yet. Maybe we'll work it case by case, after the fact."

"Hey," Stan contended, flapping his hands, "if Mannie or Julio ask me for help, they're gonna get it. It's really not an issue."

"But taking it on as a project is," Cory said. "We can't make the evictions more palatable."

"I helping Keiki," Easy put in.

"Oh, wonderful!" Fidel applauded with enthusiasm.

Easy gave him a deep, heated look.

"No. I mean it," he said, full of haughty glee. "You help Keiki and we can concentrate on our priorities. A splendid solution."

CHAPTER EIGHT

X's secretary was seated at her desk. He was standing behind her, leaning over her, drawing her attention to some detail in a document, his left hand on her left shoulder. Milissa held back, waiting to be noticed.

He looked up. "Aloha, Milissa," he beamed. "Come in."

She walked behind the counter.

"Kini Aka." X gestured back with one hand, then forward with the other as he moved in Milissa's direction. "*This* is Milissa Dogherty."

Milissa was especially at ease. She'd changed into silk slacks and a white cotton camisole at the office and borrowed Linda's car to make it there on time.

Kini came to her feet in sync with X's introduction. "Aloha, Milissa."

"This could take a while," X told Kini, glancing back as he led Milissa down the hall. "We'll be in the sanctum."

The small Hina Conference Room was an ultra-modern, sound-proof chamber, indirectly lit and furnished with low, receptive, thickly upholstered chairs set around a large, lap-level octagon of thick plate glass, fashioned to accommodate the eight member board that met there once a year. Crossed, hand-carved fishing spears and canoe paddles decked the walls, and Hina, mother goddess of Molokai, was backed into the corner beside the portable bar. Milissa imagined herself trapped like Hina in some Polynesian cliché on the umpteenth floor of the Sears Tower.

"Tell me what you've been up to," X began, with a hint of stealth in his voice.

Milissa leaned forward conspiratorially. "All the intriguing details?" she asked, feeling a need to make light of the close, cushioned ambiance.

"The naked truth?" X covered his eyes. "Never! How about some homely gossip? I hear you've been visiting the neighbors."

If the unwanted and unexpected subject of her visit with John was important enough to be first on X's agenda, he was going to have to be less roundabout. "Sounds like you already have a handle on the scuttlebutt." She laid her job description on the table. "This is what I had in mind."

"So, how did you find Mr. Mikala?" X asked as he scanned the document.

She sidestepped, responding to the question's plain meaning. "His aunty took me to his house."

"Not, how did you locate him. How did you find him?"

"Who's on first?" Milissa asked coyly.

He looked and smiled. "Their home run man. Did he talk about MCC's plans?"

"Your informant didn't tell you?"

"Kini saw you leaving his house. Not hard to do, right across the way."

Milissa pointed at her outline. "No secret agent stuff in there. Just proactive ombudsman, like we discussed."

X began to read in earnest. "I'm sure this is right." He touched his place on the page. "But how do we get around their claim that the one-on-one approach is playing favorites?"

"We don't. If we favor those who need our help the most, we can't be faulted."

The two began to wrangle. Her feistiness attracted him. He was fabricating issues as much to spark her ire as to test her determination. He didn't have the authority to create so large a fund. She told him to take it to the board. He wanted to limit the cost to relocation expenses. She wanted to ease the transition in other ways, especially for the children.

Her demand for "broad discretion" was a more critical concern. Such a term, if included in their contract, would redound to him if things went wrong.

"This is your personal promise to me," she argued. "There's no way I can really hold you to it. You're signing the checks."

"And it's your excuse to quit if you don't get your way."

"And yours not to hire me in the first place."

"I can see we're gonna be haggling a lot. Maybe that's good." He wrote *$1,000 per week through August* at the bottom of the page, then signed and dated it. "I do like this police presence thing," he added, pointing to the reference as he handed her the paper.

She noticed the sum – ridiculously high for part time work – but decided not to comment. "Police readiness," she corrected. "The idea is to discourage intimidation, from any source."

"I'll put you in touch with Sheriff Nakayama. He runs the substation up here. You can work that out with him."

"There's nothing in here about liaison with police either. Besides, I already did my bit. Mikala says you'll have to arrest him to get him out. He promises no violence, but he won't leave on his own. That's as far as I go."

"Shouldn't be a problem," X said with marked indifference. "Let me know if you hear anything else. I'll pass it on."

When Milissa returned with Linda's car, the front porch of the office was overflowing with people. The Ono had been raided the night before. All tenants even remotely associated with the searched apartments were given notices to vacate. Linda and Leilani were busy doing intakes.

Morgan was on the phone. "Please hold," she said to her party, then covered the receiver with her hand. "May I help you?"

"May I help you?" Milissa replied.

"In the present emergency, I'm afraid not. There may be a connection between these evictions and the Maunaloa matter. I take it you're now working for Stockmans?"

Milissa nodded.

"Until I look at the situation more closely, Linda and Lani will handle the Ono clients." Morgan kept her hand over the receiver, waiting for Milissa to leave.

The Ono had been searched pursuant to a warrant. Nothing had been found in the targeted apartment, but a marijuana roach had been discovered in plain view through the window of an adjacent unit. All persons located in the common areas – a good number on a hot summer's night – were rousted into the courtyard. The owner of the roach was the only one cited.

"What's the connection between these evictions and Maunaloa?" Milissa asked Linda.

"Hoh, girl, was dat me bragging 'bout how slow t'ings are 'round here? Stockmans owns da Ono. Maybe dey trying to make room for Maunaloa tenants. Ono kine mo' bad dan Maunaloa. Most people want 'em off of da island. You see how dey coming running to Morgan. All of 'em charity cases, 'cept maybe da one who got cited."

"Any regular clients I can take care of?"

Linda went to the door and called for Pale.

The frail, ponytailed Pale Gutierrez – Morgan's early morning, rifle-toting intruder – donned a weak, suspicious smile as she deposited her sandals and followed Milissa to her desk.

"Are you not feeling well?" Milissa asked.

"Doctor say I got da hep. He giving me injections make me feel sick."

"Sorry to hear that," Milissa said, projecting pity.

Pale grinned as if Milissa had made a cruel joke. "You got one cigarette?" she asked, hoping to glean something tangible from Milissa's haole compassion.

"I don't smoke."

"Mo' bettah, da hep make 'em taste stink anyway."

After giving the basic intake data, Pale explained her problem. Welfare was threatening to cut off her baby's aid because Heraldo, the father of her child, had been living in the home.

"I got no choice. He one bully. I try call da sheriff, he whack me."

"I need specific dates and details."

"He stay every night last week because he working at da wharf. 'Cept Friday he get drunk and come home piss again about his rifle. Went kick my butt." She tipped sideways and exposed a large hip bruise hidden by her shorts. "I called nine one one and he left. Haven't seen him since."

Her voice took on a confidential tone. "He like get his rifle back." She paused and added a note of caution in her own defense. "Probation say he not supposed to have one."

"What's he on probation for?"

"Assaulting me, one t'ing."

"Good thing they took it away."

"Dey . . ." Pale hesitated. Milissa didn't know that Morgan had taken the gun. "Just tell Morgan he like get it back."

"If you think it's important, I'll put it in my report. Now, let's get back to you."

Pale took Milissa through the times Heraldo had stayed at her place over the preceding month. In each instance, coercion involving threats or beating was used to get her compliance.

"You were right to come in. We'll get back to you if necessary."

"Dey gonna cut my aid?"

"Unlikely. There'd have to be a hearing first."

After Pale left, Milissa wrote out her notes of the interview and put them in Morgan's box.

Pale's was a typical case. Despite repeated cycles of warnings, complaints, warrants, and restraining orders, the sheriff would somehow never be able to contact the errant father, who would continue to stay in the home at his convenience. Everyone knew the drill. Each agency did its part in documenting phantom efforts to bring the scofflaw to account. Either the complaint was too far down on the sheriff's list to be given more than token attention at roll call, or the assigned deputy – old school chum, hunting and fishing buddy, etc. of the husband – would neglect the order for apprehension.

It appeared that everybody but the police knew where to locate Heraldo. He would lay low in his shack at Halawa for weeks on end, drinking and surfing until his supplies ran out. During his short stints of longshoring or field work, he could be found at either Pale's in Kaunakakai or his grandmother's in Maunaloa.

"Keoni," Leilani said softly, "must leave your slippers on da porch."

Milissa smiled at John from behind her partition and returned to her work, spurred on by his unexpected arrival.

Morgan emerged from her office and met John at the door as he kicked off his sandals. "Mr. Mikala, can I help you?" she asked, blocking his return.

"Just came to say hello to Keiki."

A mean wisp of glee vanished across Morgan's face. "Milissa works from eight until noon. It's now three thirty." She eyed John expectantly, unaware that Milissa was listening from behind the screen. "She would, at any rate, not be available during work hours."

John "oh"ed silently, pressed the air with his fingertips, and took two steps back. "Tell her I stopped by."

"Telephone messages can be left with the front desk."

Milissa came out from behind the screen and nailed Morgan with a stare. Linda was already on her way to the parking lot to stop John from leaving.

"Milissa," Morgan said, concealing her surprise, "I'd like to see you in my office."

Morgan sat behind her desk, her display of certificates at her back. "You were . . .?"

"I could tell we were backed up, so I handled someone not involved with the Ono."

"Very thoughtful. In any case, the Ono matter seems to have resolved itself. I spoke with Mr. Cass, Stockmans' counsel in Honolulu. He has assured me that, with the exception of the man cited for possession, he doesn't intend to prosecute these notices. Evidently they were hoping for more arrests. The important message for you in all this is the high potential for conflict of interest in our close-knit community, particularly when you're working for Stockmans."

Milissa stood mute, still indignant at Morgan's treatment of John.

"Be circumspect," Morgan added, dismissing Milissa with demure, downcast eyes.

John was playing possum in his pick-up.

Milissa jumped in beside him. "Is this our first date?"

He came out from under his cowboy hat. "You hungry?"

"Did you know?" she continued, sliding to the center of the cab and putting her hand on the gear shift knob, "you have an Iberian profile."

"Sounds impressive."

She framed him with her thumbs and fingers. "Very handsome. I'd say post-Saracen by the shape of the nose." She turned the rearview mirror in his direction.

He brushed back the sides of his hair. "You can call me Juan."

They spent the afternoon parked on Molokai Drive-In's hot, grease-blotched blacktop, harmonizing memories against the backdrop of the noisy Kam. It was burgers and fries for lunch, ribs and rice for dinner. This time they arranged to meet again. They would picnic at Kalaupapa Lookout, Wednesday afternoon.

That evening at home, Morgan and Milissa maintained a casual distance. Morgan mentioned food. Milissa wasn't hungry. Milissa's expression of relief that the Ono problem had been settled didn't invite an answer. Neither acknowledged the strain in their relationship. Milissa was preoccupied. Her stay on Molokai would be short. Her cultural distance from John was considerable. Their involvement was imbued with an evanescence, a heartachey, Cinderella quality that made it all the more impassioned from the start.

Before turning in she called Easy.

"Hoh, Keiki, you never came by. We had one MCC meeting. I like you to be dere."

"I'm avoiding the political stuff. Too much straight work to do."

"Fidel get piss when I tell him we working together. He say Keoni shouldn't talk to you."

"Tell him not to worry. We leave our work at the office."

"Easy t'ink you got enough trouble already, ya?"

"Trouble?"

"Keeping your minds on da job when you're apart."

"You think so, huh?"

"You like know what Easy t'ink?"

"No. Not now. After this afternoon . . ." Milissa cut her comment short.

"What? Tell Aunty," Easy cajoled.

"I need you to take me around tomorrow."

"Hoh, you no going to tell? I find out anyway."

"I'm sure you will. Can you help me? About twelve thirty?"

"Sure. You come over. Got just da kine."

CHAPTER NINE

"Kamali'i makou o Kualapu'u," Easy sang, strumming her ukulele as she watched Milissa cross the lots that separated her place, and John's next door, from X's office and warehouse.

"What's the song about?" Milissa asked, joining her on the lanai.

"A bunch of mokes from da old days t'umping deir chest 'cause dey Molokai cowboys. It's telling how deir ropes made music when dey twirled 'em to t'row da lasso on da bipi."

"Bipi?"

"Da cows. We never had 'em before da haole come. So we hear 'beef' and call 'em bipi."

"Strange, Hawaiians casting themselves as cowboys."

"Not strange." Easy hushed her voice and glanced around as if the old time "bipi" boys were still alive and listening. "Molokai men been paniolos more dan seven generations. Dey very proud, very macho." After a moment of reverie, she yawned, expanding to her feet. "Grampa usta sing about da time before da bipi. Was one about a chief made love in Hina's cave. And one about da Phallic

Rock tells how Nanahoa leered at one wahine – got so stiff his pecker turned to stone.

"But all dat nonsense faded plenty quick, once da bipi come." She stretched her arms to the side, extending her reach with each syllable, the ukulele dangling like a bauble from her muted fist. "Next come sugar, den pineapple, now maybe plenty houses, ya? Cannot stop 'em."

"These people in Maunaloa, are any of them cowboys?"

"No more cowboys Maunaloa. Cowboys living in Kualapu'u, drive up here everyday. 'Course dey work da horses now dat Stockmans come. Dey do mo' bettah dan da Maunaloa kine. Most here left over from plantation days. A few moved in to fill da vacancy when pineapple went bust. We got one Samoan family. Come, I take you dem."

He accepted Milissa's hand reluctantly, nearly smothering it between his thumb and first two fingers. The breath from his nostrils breezed down across her face.

"She like talk wit' you mom 'bout when you gonna move," Easy explained.

"She not home. Dey all down da pool Kaunakakai. Come, can talk wit' me."

The teenager stooped as he entered the house. Milissa followed close behind, undaunted by his size.

"Can you speak for your family?"

He positioned himself on a heavy koa dining table set against the wall. Its legs had been shortened slightly so he could lift to his feet with ease. "All Tuiasosopo speaking for each other."

"You are aware that Stockmans is planning to redevelop this property?"

"We know we gotta move. We going Beeg Island. You da bouncer, ya?"

"You need bouncing?"

Tiny tittered. Pleasure whispered from his pouty eyes, lighting up his huge immobile face.

Milissa held her silence.

"Where you from?"

"Seattle."

"Everybody from Seattle so beansie? You like one hobbit. Maybe you one wind-up doll."

He rocked back, whopped his thigh, and emitted a series of wheezy huffs as Milissa settled to the rug like an obedient child.

"You ever been to Seattle?" she asked.

"Got one nephew in Seattle."

"Maybe that's the guy they locked up."

Tiny peered down with feline intensity. "Why dey lock him up?"

"Too big," Milissa replied in a wee voice.

She paused to let the inference settle in, then stood quickly and put her hand on Tiny's knee. "He was scaring all the people. Bumping them off the sidewalk. Eating all their chickens. How soon are you moving?"

"Mama say September," he answered. "Dis moke in Seattle, what's his name?"

She wrote her number on a slip of paper. "Have your mom call if she needs help."

Tiny held the scrap up like a butterfly about to be released. "Dey call him Tito, ya?"

Milissa took the number back. "Ya, that's it," she answered, moving toward the door. "Tito, Tony, something like that. Too big. Scaring all the people. You coming, Easy?"

A squeal of delight eked after Easy as she caught up with Milissa in the lane.

"Tiny went catch on," she chuckled, padding out ahead.

"Keep one eye out for da cockaroach," Easy cautioned, skidding open the half-hinged gate. "Plenty trouble dis place."

A generic, slung-tit dog emerged from under the house, barking enigmatically, trailed by a passel of untouchable pups, candidates for euthanasia. She slinked and circled, too leery to elicit fear.

Easy climbed the steps and looked in. "Anybody home?"

A bare-bottomed two year old pressed his tongue against the inside of the rusty screen.

"Spacy, go tell Mama, Aunty Easy here."

The screen door rattled angrily as Spacy pushed away and scrambled down the hall at the rear of the living room.

"Lemme see what dis," Easy said after a long silence. She held the door for Milissa and stepped inside. "Somebody home, ya?" Her question echoed through the house.

A middle-aged crone emerged from one of the rooms along the hall. "Who you?" she asked as she ducked out of sight.

"What you mean, 'Who you?' You know Easy. Where you tita?"

"She sleep."

"Tell her one lady from Stockmans is here."

The living room was unfurnished. Its walls were a patchwork of missing paper and water stains. Its floors were warped, bowed up in the middle and pulled away from the baseboards where light seeped in from the adjoining rooms. Blankets and a pair of men's shoes were pushed into one corner. The furtive creak of floorboards could be heard overhead.

Twins, a girl and boy in grimy boxer shorts, appeared heads and hands first from the top of the stairs at the end of the hall. Grinning at each other and gawking at Milissa, they inched down the stairs and entered the room with their backs to the wall. Spacy tagged behind.

The woman who had shied away from Easy straggled in. "Aloha, Aunty," she said, clipping Spacy with a careless foot. "Party plenty last night. We just getting up."

Mistaking the woman's statement as a cue, Spacy placed his unattended bottom on Milissa's bare, sandaled foot and wrapped his arms around her calf.

"Gee up," he ordered.

"Spacy humping," the little girl snickered.

"Gee off," Milissa replied, setting him aside. "We'll play horsey later."

"Horsey," Spacy parroted, attempting to remount.

"Et, et," Milissa scolded. "Go to Mama."

The woman pushed him away. "He no mine," she said. "Shoo, shoo."

Milissa put Spacy on her hip. "Mrs. . . .? I'm sorry, I'm Milissa Dogherty. I work for Stockmans Inc. I didn't catch your name?"

The woman pursed her lips. Milissa was standing too close.

The little girl took a handful of her mother's robe. "She Salome."

"Salome. And your last name?"

"Sacramento," the girl answered again.

"Mrs. Sacramento, I take it that you're aware this house is scheduled to be torn down soon?"

Still no response.

"Where's your husband?" Milissa asked in frustration.

Salome sluiced her palm with laughter.

"He long gone," Easy answered. "Salome, where you tita?"

Salome pointed to a room at the bottom of the stairs. "She get piss you wake her up."

As they passed Salome's empty room, Milissa caught sight of a man in cowboy boots sprawled unconscious on the floor. Salome lagged warily behind. Easy and Milissa, followed by the children, continued down the hall.

Easy beckoned. "Salome," she whispered, "come wake her up."

Salome answered with a rancid, shifty grin.

Easy knocked softly. "Anybody home? Got one lady here from Stockmans."

Milissa glanced back. Salome's door was closing. She switched Spacy to her other hip and stepped in front of Easy. "It's gotta be two thirty," she said, turning the knob. "I'll bet these kids haven't eaten."

The small room reeked of wasted breath. A man in his late teens and an older woman with her face in his back were passed out on a mattress in the corner. Batik, tacked to the wall and hung from the ceiling with fishing line, canopied their heads. At the foot of the bed, sitting neatly on an orange crate, was a Bible bookmarked with a three-by-five of Jesus. On top of the Bible was a finely woven basket. The jaw of a tiny shark embellished its lid. A pot pipe, a cookie sheet spilling over with smoker's trash, a package of cigarette papers, and an empty Tokay bottle lay within reach amidst hardened pools of candle wax. Clothes were draped around the room. Beer cans were left where they'd been emptied. A soiled poster of the blue baby Krishna stealing honey from a pot was hanging on the closet door.

Spacy pointed at the mattress. "Mama," he said.

"Can let him wake her," Easy suggested slyly. "Mo' bettah like dat."

"Mo' bettah," Milissa agreed.

Spacy wriggled out of Milissa's arms and scurried across the cookie sheet, trailing a mess behind him as he climbed onto his mother's back. She grunted, bucked reflexively, and tumbled him away. As he pulled himself to his feet, he dragged the Bible from its perch. The shark's tooth basket overturned, dumping its contents into the swath of butts and ashes on the floor.

Milissa rattled off the evidence tongue-in-cheek. "One three-pack of disposable syringes, one clear plastic envelope containing suspected narcotic substance, innumerable cigarette butts." Easy picked Spacy up and pried his fingers from the Bible's tattered binding. "One clear plastic envelope containing suspected marijuana," Milissa continued. "Four, five, six Department of Human Services check stubs listing dependent children: Wia Ana, Wia Ui, Wia Kepa. Wia . . . !" She looked more closely at the woman whose face was now buried in the young man's back. "Ewa? Is that you?"

Easy winked at Milissa as they picked up and put everything back in its place. "Must be one drug induced coma, ya?"

The hall was cluttered with children. As Easy moved ahead, guiding Spacy with her hand, he sucked her finger in and bit down hard, then bolted out the front door. In hot pursuit of Spacy, she left Milissa behind to deal with the twins, who were crowding against her, outdoing the others for her attention. Four of Ewa's children – a girl and three boys, all bigger than the rest – huddled around a secret at the bottom of the stairs. The oldest of the four, a man-child in his mid-teens, moved quickly in behind Easy and blocked Milissa's way. Salome looked on from the top of the stairs.

"Looks like big brother has captured us," Milissa told her escorts as they reached the entrance way.

The young man pressed his back against the door jamb, allowing room for passage. The twins guided Milissa ahead single file, one on each hand. Halfway through they locked onto her wrists, responding like a Chinese finger puzzle to her sudden flex, restraining her for an instant while big brother secured her hips and rubbed his crotch against her thigh.

"Capture her! Capture her!" they cried, as if the competition had begun.

She twisted her arms free and pried herself loose from big brother. "Get off!" she shouted, gagging from his shitty smell. "Get the fuck away!"

The twins shot halfway up the stairs and stopped, hugging each other to embellish the fun.

Milissa glared at big brother. He smirked and gave his sister, Ana, a nod.

She took his cue and rounded her other brothers in. "Capture her!" she said, putting one at the end of each arm to form a cordon.

Milissa tried a tone of waning patience. "Enough," she cautioned. "No more play."

The trio stood their ground, glancing back at their leader for support. Ana sported hands on knees, waiting for the signal to begin. Lion, the youngest of the three, pouted, toeing in, wondering why the lady was so mad. The middle brother, Meek, postured defiantly while the other children filed in and formed a quiet ring around the entertainment.

"I said that's enough," Milissa repeated. "Now get back. This is not a game."

The hungry pack, prepared to risk a blow to the head if the reward were great enough, gauged their prey.

Milissa jutted the heel of her hand toward the forehead of a boy who was angling for her ankle bracelet. "I said get back!"

"I say get back," big brother aped and jumped into the room in grappling stance.

"Get back. Get back. Get back," they all began to chant.

The metallic taste of panic coated Milissa's tongue. As she turned to look for Easy, the projectile, a beer can tab, bit into her rib, bounced off the wall, and skittered away. All eyes were on it as it came to rest.

The circle went slack at the sound of Easy's voice. "What dis?" she growled through the door, still panting from her chase.

As Milissa backed onto the porch, big brother hocked a gob of mucous on the screen. Unaffected shrieks and heartfelt profanity blasted from inside. Her mind completely blown, Milissa sleep-walked toward the gate. There was a distant yapping at her feet. A windblown Hau bush teased the picket fence. She heard the rumble of retreat as Easy reached inside and sat the baby on the floor.

"Dat Kepa – da one who spit – he loko 'ino," Easy lamented, joining Milissa outside the fence. "One bad boy."

"Kepa not bad, Aunty. He only caught in Satan's trap. He be da best when he get free."

"Ui!" Easy exclaimed, "where you stay?"

"Going summer school, Aunty," the girl answered, displaying her uniform and looking wide-eyed at Milissa.

"No, I mean where you stay right now?"

"By da bush." Ui pointed to her hiding place. "Could hear da racket."

"Hoh, I no see you. You so quiet. You like come have juice wit' Aunty?"

"Cannot. I babysitting Spacy."

"Bring the baby," Milissa said.

Easy showed Ui the tooth marks in her finger. She buried herself in Easy's muumuu with a goodbye hug, then skipped into the yard. "I love you, Aunty," she called back. "I'll come by sometime alone."

"Dat Ewa's Ui," Easy explained after the girl had gone into the house.

As she and Milissa walked home, Easy unraveled Ui's curious tale. Three years before, the entire family had been "saved" at a camp meeting sponsored by the local Body of Christ Evangelical Church. Ui was eight years old at the time. Within weeks of the event all except Ui had fallen away. Despite routine abuse at home, she had continued her involvement with the church.

Evan Swan, the host of the original camp meeting and pastor at the Body of Christ, had kept an eye on Ui from the start. He was known to drop by the Maunaloa house at all hours to see how she was doing. Eventually he had her enrolled, tuition free, at Molokai Christian Academy. It was common knowledge that the church had made inquiries with family court to have her removed from the home.

Milissa, too down at the time to see the hope in Ui's plight, fell into Easy's overstuffed chair and stared through the window toward the two story house. All she could think of was the children in the hall – how they had blessed her by taking her hands, and then walked her straight into hell.

Easy put her finger to her lips. Milissa was asleep. She had been curled up in the chair for three hours, sapped by her ordeal.

Linda frowned suspiciously when she heard what had happened. "How dis come down?"

Easy faltered when she got to the part about going into Ewa's room.

"You da aunty!" Linda insisted. "Why you shamed? If you telling it right, Ewa gave up her privacy, she let Spacy run free like dat."

Easy shushed and pointed to the living room.

"Hoh, dat Ewa, you should know she junk." Linda hurried to her room then out the back door.

Milissa awoke to the reassuring sound of cookery. Easy looked in when the rice was done. "You hungry?" she asked. "Dinner almost ready."

Milissa sat up and combed her fingers through her hair. "What time is it?"

"Manini time," Easy sang out as she tossed the fish into the pan.

While Milissa stared blankly out the window, Linda tiptoed in from behind, slipped a lei around her neck, and kissed her on the cheek.

Milissa lifted the purple flowers to her nose.

"No scent," Linda observed. "Bougainvillea was so beautiful, Pele went steal her perfume."

Milissa's eyes glistened. "They're lovely. Where'd you find them?"

"Picked 'em in da yard. Dey climbing da Ohia tree."

"You just made this?"

"Got pikake out dere too, but some girls never like too much da smell pikake."

Milissa arranged the bougainvillea just so, and leaned back to maintain eye contact. "Pikake is intense."

"Too rich if you feeling sad, huh, tita?"

Milissa looked down again, leafing through the blossoms. Quiet tears released into her lap.

Linda sat on the arm of the chair. "Mo' bettah you no blame da keiki. Ewa and Salome, dey egg 'em on. Turn 'em loose on haole social worker types. You not da first dey chased away."

Milissa burped up a little laugh. "That's good to know."

"Aunty gave you da bad news first. Dey da worst case in town."

Easy brought in the food. The manini, served with sauteed onions, carrots, and zucchini, was nestled on a heap of steaming rice. Easy described its preparation for Milissa. "You gut 'em, cut 'em twice each side for da skin no pop, season heavily wit' salt and garlic, and fry for two, t'ree minutes in a quarter inch of olive oil. You burn 'em if da oil smoke. And watch out you no stand too close. Da sizzle sting. Next time, Easy walk you t'rough it."

"Like she did at Ewa's today," Linda put in. "You no see da oil smoking, Aunty?"

"Hoh!" Easy responded, "oil never smoked. Keiki just stand too close da kine."

It occurred to Milissa that Easy might have intended the day as boot camp. She had to know the history of social worker forays into Ewa's house. She had cautioned Milissa at the gate. But Kepa's sexual assault – she couldn't have anticipated that. The thought of Kepa humping her leg, his smell, it made her seethe inside.

"Confection for da gods," Easy announced, setting out papaya and three small cups of Muleskinner coffee to complement the after dinner story time.

Talking story, a folk craft long supplanted in most parts of the world, still thrived on Molokai. Like the local songs, local stories – homely accounts with refined twists of pathos and humor – tended to evolve from one telling to the next. Subtle embellishment was the license of the teller, a way of being part of the truth. But the change had to be imperceptibly gradual – how else to build a myth? – and part of the fun was in not getting caught.

"Dat ain't da way I heard it," Linda broke in. "Last time you said grampa put da fire out in da kitchen. Now you got him running t'rough one burning house."

"Same t'ing," Easy protested with a wry smile.

"Not!"

"Hokay, but he pulled me outta da fire like I said. Went risk his life for Easy only t'ree years old. Girl, you on Aunty's case tonight."

By nine o'clock, Linda and Easy had done their best to recharge Milissa with their images. "Why you never tell a story, Keiki?" Linda asked, as Easy made a bed for her on the couch. "You usually talking story all da time."

"Tonight it was my turn to listen. Catch me tomorrow, I'll tell you all about today."

"How you feeling now?" Easy asked, after she and Milissa were alone.

"I've been in worse scrapes," Milissa replied, allowing Easy to tuck her in. "Thanks for being there though. It hit me pretty hard."

"You ready to go out alone tomorrow?"

"Tomorrow? You think I should?"

"T'ink you will. Remember, stand back dis time, especially when you see da smoke."

Milissa lay awake in the quiet house. Easy and Linda's aloha had helped, but a residue of regret, an unfamiliar scepticism, had survived the day's events. What John had inferred, about her being out of her element, seemed to be proving true. Her mind turned to the mainland.

Milissa and Lindsay had sublet their apartment to Tiago, a medical intern from Madrid attending an institute at the university. Lindsay had arranged to stay at her mother's house for the summer, but chances were better than even that she could be found at the apartment with Tiago. It was one a.m. in Seattle, a weeknight. Everyone would be in bed. The greater intrusion would be to wake Lindsay's mother to find that Lindsay wasn't home. Milissa slid off the couch and took the phone to the lanai. What a gas it'll be to catch her at the apartment, she thought. She made herself comfortable in Easy's rocker and dialed home.

"Hola," said a sleepy male voice after a single ring.

"Tiago?"

"Yes."

"This is Milissa. You know, your other landlady? Sorry to call so late. I've been trying to contact Lindsay."

"Milissa?" Tiago sat up in bed.

"Milissa?" came another voice from the background. It was Lindsay.

"Milissa, the absentee landlady," Tiago handed her the phone.

"Missy?"

"None other," Milissa replied. "I knew I'd find you there."

"You bugger. You didn't call my mom, did you? What time is it?"

"So the Mountie, if you'll excuse the expression, got her man."

"We have our ways."

"I'm listening."

"You got a few hours?" Lindsay took the phone to the other room. "Missy, we miss you."

"We?" Milissa responded. "Maybe *you* miss me. Maybe."

Alerted by her best friend's melancholy tone, Lindsay changed positions and switched the receiver to the other ear, bracing for bad news. "Of course I do. What's the problem?"

"Some little animals treated me like an animal. I can't tell you how it brought me down." Milissa's account of her scrape at Ewa's prompted Lindsay to bring up memories of other close calls. They compared and contrasted for awhile, and by the abrupt end of their conversation they were laughing at each other's foibles, secure in the intimacy of a time-tested relationship.

"Saint Milissa of the righteously indignant," Milissa conceded, referring to her zeal on entering Ewa's room.

"And master of hyperbole," Lindsay added for Milissa's dramatic flair.

"Me, exaggerate? I almost left a relic on their living room floor."

Something hit Easy's window. It made a small metallic click.

"You remember that cab driver in Spain? When you said your bladder was bursting?"

"Ambulancia! Ambulancia!" Milissa mimicked. "Guy damn near had a heart attack. Ouch! God damn it!" A second something had hit Milissa on the knee.

"What is it?" Lindsay asked.

Milissa recognized the children's laughter as they ran. "That does it. I'll call you back."

She called nine one one and told them she would stay there as a decoy till they arrived. While the operator was urging her to go inside, Kepa appeared at short range. This time he grazed Milissa's temple, drawing blood.

"We've got a deputy coming up the Kam," the operator said. "Don't hang up."

Milissa dropped the phone, hurtled over the railing, and ran directly at Kepa, bowling him into the dust as he backed away off-balance, laughing at his tiny foe. She moved up his body while he lay there giggling, resisting as if she were tickling his ribs. In quick successive moves she jammed her thumbs into his eyes and kneed him in the groin. The lowness of his gangster style pants protected his crotch from her knee, but a paralyzing pain shot through the left side of his face as the sight went out of his eye. Milissa dug deep into the moist tissue, fleetingly amazed at the ease with which her thumb had entered in behind the eyeball.

Kepa threw Milissa off and got to his feet. He could hear the other children laughing at him from the darkness. He began to feel his way home, one hand in front, the other over his injured eye, disoriented but aware that he needed help, without a second thought for Milissa until she landed on his back and locked her forearm against his windpipe.

It was then that Milissa realized that Kepa was, in fact, a small man.

The advantage of surprise had passed. Her feet lifted centrifugally as he flailed and spun with the ferocity brought on by suffocation. As he loosened her grip she sank her teeth into his ear. He screamed and let go, groping for her jaw, jamming his fingers into her nostrils and clutching at her throat.

She felt a sharp burning sensation under her arm, but almost simultaneously Kepa cried out, "Fuck!," grabbed the side of his head, and sank to his knees. "No mo' da slingshot, Meek. Went shoot me in da head."

Someone else was on top of her, pulling her hair. Dizzying slightly, she closed her eyes, clamped down with her jaw, and tightened her grip, prepared for the onslaught.

Large hands lifted her from the ground. Lights were flashing.

"Keiki." Was it Easy's voice? "Keiki. Let go."

"Let him go, Miss Dogherty," urged a gentle male voice. "We've got it under control."

Kepa waited patiently, like a man caught under a wreck. "She went tear my eye," he whimpered softly. "Can get da bitch off me?"

The man's voice took on a stern edge. "Keiki."

Milissa hesitated.

A mild tug sent a measured shock into her shoulder socket. "Let him go."

Milissa released her hold and stood up over Kepa, too weak to move away. She cranked her neck and yawned as if to reset her jaw. Kepa sloughed her aside as he came to his feet and staggered into custody. Blood was oozing from his closed left eye. His hair was matted with blood.

Easy caught Milissa and held her up. "You all right, Keiki?"

She clung to Easy's muumuu and lowered herself to the ground. "Much better," she answered, daubing at her face for blood. "Guess it needed settling."

That night at Molokai General, Milissa received two stitches in her temple wound. There were two nasty marks on her back from the other slingshot hits. Her knees were scraped and cut. But she was released without complications.

CHAPTER TEN

The mid-island heat had slowed the morning to a marathon of lazy chores – filing, copying, scheduling. No clients till noon on Wednesdays. Morgan hadn't come out of her office. Everyone was lying low.

"The truth?" Milissa replied, talking to Lindsay on the phone. "I'm satisfied."

"No compassion?" Lindsay asked. "Sounds like you hurt him bad."

"I'm not filing charges. That's enough."

"Good. Best to let it fade. And be more circumspect from here on out. I don't wanna have to come over there and rescue you."

"Morgan's word."

"Huh?"

"Morgan said be circumspect."

"You do tend to barge ahead."

"Gotta hang up. I mean, no rush here, but break is over."

"Keep in touch, Missy. We're looking forward to getting you back in one piece."

Milissa stayed in her cubicle for the rest of her shift, anticipating John's arrival for their picnic, tickled at how he might react to her battle scar. At noon Morgan called her into her office.

"I spoke to Sheriff Fitzpatrick this morning. He told me you'd been assaulted."

"You should see the other guy."

"So I understand. I need to know if you're able to work."

"Oh, sure. A little stiff. I'll be better by tomorrow."

"Have you been looked at?"

Milissa detected an ogle lurking behind Morgan's sweet deadpan. "By professionals?" She pulled back the bandage on the side of her forehead. "You see the stitches."

Morgan's eyes widened as if her question hadn't been answered.

"You'd like to see the rest," Milissa remarked, unbuttoning her blouse.

"Oh, not . . ."

"It's only these welts." She had turned and exposed her bare, strapless back. Her blouse was draped below her waist, her forearms still inserted in the sleeves.

"You were out working for Stockmans when this took place?"

Milissa pulled the blouse up over her shoulders, allowing an innocent glimpse of breast as she turned and spoke. "No." Her voice was soft and matter-of-fact. "Under any circumstance, there's nothing improper about defending oneself. The little bastard's lucky I didn't have a gun."

A pang of kindred rage shot down from Morgan's heart into her groin. The color left her face. She appeared for an instant to be haggard. Her expression hadn't changed, but darkness lingered around the eyes. "Perhaps there are things that can't be overlooked. Try to take care."

"Oh, I will," Milissa replied, shrugging off the grip of their encounter. "Are you okay?" She walked around the desk and rested her hand on Morgan's shoulder. "Sometimes I think you could use a break. Maybe we'll take a little trip."

As her head listed toward Milissa's touch, Morgan caught sight of John through the window, pulling into the parking lot.

Milissa retracted her hand. "It's Keoni. Gotta go. You think about that trip."

Just a hug, initiated by Milissa and welcomely received by John, who kept his arm around her while he tipped his head back to appraise her injury. Neither spoke. A trace of amusement crinkled in the corners of his eyes as he started the engine.

She curled her feet up and faced him with her arm stretched receptively across the back of the seat, waiting, patient and light-hearted, as he wended through the lunch time traffic between the office and the Kam.

"Dey say you kicked some butt last night," he finally said. "You okay?"

"Who says?"

"Everybody. Dey calling you one hell-cat."

The characterization caught Milissa off guard. "Oh, great." A rush of unwelcome elation caused her to look away. "Are they making fun?"

John's laugh lines all but disappeared. "Fun? You didn't hear? Kepa lost his eye."

Milissa was unsure of how to feel. The jolt of pride evaporated, leaving only a stubborn, unfulfilling sense of justice. "How do you feel about it?"

"Dis was a long time coming for Kepa already. Question is, how do you feel? But dat's between you and yourself. You alright wit' me."

As they approached their destination, they entered a distinctly temperate zone. Unlike tropical Halawa on the east; high, dry Maunaloa on the west; or the arid lowland savannas, cragged with lava fissures and etched with haole koa and mesquite; the environs of the lookout were densely forested with ironwoods and other cool evergreens.

The road came to a cul-de-sac. Off to her right, Milissa saw a sign pointing to the lookout. Another one below it showed the way to Phallic Rock, Molokai's ancient fertility shrine.

"Dat t'ing aint worth seeing," John remarked. "Just looks like one big ol' blunt upside down pecker wit' a little puddle of muddy water under where da puka's supposed to be. Can go dere if you like."

Milissa grinned at John's repugnance. "Sounds fun. Maybe Linda and I'll go some day."

John got the lunch basket from behind the seat and led the way into the woods.

Milissa peeked under the napkin. "Mmm, gingerbread. What else?"

"Never looked. Easy brought it by dis morning."

All around were Norfolk pines, set apart among the taller ironwoods on a common bed of leaves and needles that worked, together with the sun-starved light, to limit undergrowth to, here and there, a glimpse of vivid color. The Norfolks' boughs, frond-like displays with long, segmented needles, diminished up their slender trunks in evenly spaced tiers, each tree the incarnation of a Bali temple tower, its wintry essence mirroring the island's tropic gist.

A wind that seemed to come from nowhere cautioned that the forest was about to fall away. As she stepped into the shallow clearing, it occurred to Milissa that, were it not for the awesome updraft, one might be tempted by the lush, gradual slope that cloaked the overhang. *Sixteen hundred feet*, read the sign. *Kalaupapa Lookout. Highest sea cliffs in the world.*

The wind grew constant at the stone, waist-high wall that bore the reader boards depicting and describing the history below. To the east, at the bottom of the dizzying 95 degree drop-off, Milissa could see the flat, isolated Kalaupapa Peninsula – product of a small, distinct eruption that followed the formation of the cliffs. The tiny Kalaupapa leper colony, centered around a glistening, thumb-sized, steepled church, was situated on its western shore.

At Milissa's fingertips was the face of the colony's most famous resident, Father Damien de Veuster, a Belgian-born Catholic missionary who, in 1873, at the age of 33, landed on the peninsula alone and unannounced.

In the time before Damien, by decree of King Kamehameha V, suspected lepers – men, women, and children of all ages – were tossed overboard from cages into windswept Kalawao Bay on the southeast shore of the peninsula. Awaiting the ones who didn't drown were predators – reeking lepers who raped the innocent and savaged young and old for their possessions.

So great was the boatmen's fear of contamination that Damien himself was forced, upon his arrival, to debark into the water. For the next sixteen years, he ministered tirelessly to the sick and dying, building their shelters, feeding them and cleansing their wounds, and finally contracting their disease. His last words were thanksgiving for the privilege of dying like the rest.

Milissa and John stood close, warming each other's space against the chilling wind, but not embracing – looking down at the peninsula and then back at the picture. Staring up at them was Damien before he arrived on Molokai, a boyishly handsome man whose wide, deep-set eyes haunted the observer with palpable compassion.

"He looks almost mentally disturbed."

John examined the photo. "He's wounded by what he sees."

"But there's no blame or self-pity."

John shook his head in quiet awe. "Makes me feel small."

Milissa contained herself with folded arms and touched the side of her face to John's shoulder. He reached behind her back and pulled her close, securing their affection. They stayed that way it seemed forever, gazing at the settlement below, bonded by their shared humility.

"Come by when you t'rough," John said, depositing Milissa at the entrance to a road resembling a shallow flood-formed arroyo, carved into the heart of Maunaloa by repeated recourse around the potholes and jagged asphalt wrack of the original street.

A short distance in, she heard the surges of a four-by-four, bucking and swerving from behind. It was late afternoon and she had just begun. Pressed to make a connection, she climbed quickly out of the way and waved. The driver passed without responding and pulled up next to his house. As she approached he jumped out and hurried into his garden.

"All these houses gonna be torn down?" she asked, standing on tiptoes and craning to get his attention.

He clamped his pliers on the chewed up spindle of his water tap and twisted, showering them both. "Was supposed to rain today," he said. "God damn da weatherman. My babies gonna shrivel up an' die." He stroked the leaves of his pepper plants, picked a couple of radishes, washed them off, and popped one in his mouth. "Ya," he answered, leading Milissa off his property and into the road, handing her the other radish as she came, "all of 'em coming down."

The houses in this part of town were more uniform than the ones Milissa had seen near Easy's. Apparently part of a single project, they were all squat, one and two bedroom, wood-framed structures with short, tin, quarter-sloped roofs. Each had a smudged and faded red or yellow ochre paint job, a three foot deep lattice-enclosed crawl space to ensure good ventilation and protection from the living earth, and the usual rusty screen door.

"Stockmans already cut back some dis side. You seen dat big, open space across from the warehouse?"

Milissa nodded. "The lots next to the deli."

"Was all workers' houses, like deze."

"Do these streets running through here have names?"

"Used to," the man said, deciding not to feed her curiosity with extra detail.

"Like what? Like what was the name of this street?"

"Main Street."

"Main!" Milissa stared at the rugged cut. "Incredible. And the rest?"

"Second, T'ird, Fourth. Like dat." He troweled the dirt with the sole of his boot to signal his impatience.

The sun was about to set. She felt that she was keeping him. "I work for Stockmans Inc."

"Hoh," he said, touching the side of his head in the location of Milissa's stitches, "you da kine."

"They hired me to find out what you people need to ease your move."

He forced a smile through his frown. "T'ought you was from da welfare."

"So we can talk?"

He gestured toward his modest stoop.

"You work for Stockmans and don't know deze places coming down?"

Milissa sat on the second step. "I knew." She gave a cutesy smile and bit into the radish.

He hunkered easily in front of her, giving her the elevation. "You were setting me up."

"No, just trying for an unaffected response. Your name?"

"Julio Garces."

"Milissa Dogherty," she said, shaking his hand. "Let me start with some questions about the people here."

"Let me make one observation first, ya?" He winked to prepare her for his admonition.

"Sure."

"When you say 'you people' . . ."

"I said, 'the people,'" Milissa broke in.

"When you say Stockmans hired you to find out what 'you people need,'" he began again, "what you t'ink Julio hear you saying?"

"What?"

"Can I clue you in?" He scooted forward deferentially, looking up into her face, coaxing her to take her medicine.

She nodded reluctantly.

He looked away. "I hear one haole girl saying brown skinned people all one kine."

"But I don't think that."

He continued to look away as if he were appraising some object in the distance. "It's not somet'ing you t'ink. Otherwise, you'd never say it in da first place, ya? Dat's why it's such a pisser."

He let the ensuing silence linger, then sat back, making himself a target for her reaction. "Ask yourself, would you say da kine 'you people' if I was a white guy wit' one tennis racket in my hand?"

"Are you saying this haole girl's a racist?"

"We all got da weakness."

Again she was silenced. He kept denying her traction by absorbing her points.

"But you on Molokai now, land of brown skinned people. Local people not gonna have patience wit' your lack of perception." He winked again. "Best you start out t'inking we all different. Mo' bettah for you like dat."

"Is this practical advice?"

"At da very least."

A child toddled out behind her, followed by a teenage girl who carried it back into the house.

"Can we start over?"

"It's on you."

"I understand a lot of people in Maunaloa are on welfare."

"Most people here on welfare."

"And what do they plan to do about moving?"

"No plan, only wait and see. Maybe Stockmans gonna help 'em pay da fare."

"Where'd you get that idea?"

"From you. Besides, it stands to reason. How else dey gonna get us out wit'out more fuss?"

"How about you? Your plans?"

"I like buy dis house." It sounded faintly like a plea. "Like buy a new one, but . . ."

"Have you applied for a loan?"

"To tell da truth . . ." Julio's eyes sank. "T'ought about it, but no use. I'm just waiting it out like da rest. I guess we all da kine. Like you figgah'd coming in."

"I figured wrong," Milissa reacted, angry that Julio should so quickly abandon his high ground. "You backing down from your advice?"

"Apply for a loan. How you expect Julio to get a loan? He don't even have a steady job."

"Never know unless you try. What sort of work do you do?"

"Fry cook . . . A, let's see . . . Longshore. Done a lotta field work."

Julio was married, the father of two boys ages six and eight, both recipients of welfare. His wife's teenage sister, also on welfare and pregnant with her second child, was living in the home. The boyfriend came and went. Neither Julio nor his wife were employed full time, but both were available now that the boys were in school. He was filling in as a packer at a nearby farm. She was working in the field.

He had come to Maunaloa as a boy, sent from the Philippines to stay with his grandparents. They died fifteen years after his arrival, leaving nothing but the pick-up that he traded in to buy his cherished four-by-four. "Dis used to be all pineapple," he said, standing up and waving his arm over the surrounding valley. "Maunaloa was good times den. Everybody making money."

As Julio's story unfolded, old Maunaloa came alive. Even through the closing dusk, the ochre walls had shed their tarnish overcoats. There were gardens like Julio's at every stop on the street and front yard parties into the night, especially after the harvests – cock fights and children, chickens and children everywhere.

"We lived for da now and da hereafter. Nothing in between. Paved streets in town and everybody had a pick-up. Now, half da families on foot."

"This was your neighborhood."

"Still is." He stepped quickly past her, opened his front door and flicked the switch for the lamp at the top of the stairs. "My family live dis house for fifty years," he said, turning to come back down. The light blinked twice and died. He joggled the bulb inside its rusty sconce and tried it again. This time it stayed lit. "Bad connection," he explained. "Mo' bettah," he added, switching it off and on with undiminished pride.

She thought of the volume control on John's TV, but held her tongue. The parallel seemed funny as a caricature of the average Maunaloan, but smacked of stereotype. Typical Irish humor, she thought, turning the joke on herself.

She gave him her number. He recognized it immediately. "Dis for Stockmans. Dey never call back."

"You leave a message for me. I'll get back. Meantime, no more wait and see."

"I need a job."

"Understood. I need some time. No promises as yet."

His eyebrow lifted cynically. "So you only taking notes right now, ya?"

"Ya, and I've taken note of you."

She'd made six stops since Julio's, all typical cases of involuntary decline since the days of pineapple, local people who had seen better times. At each stop she was reminded of Julio, adjusting to the fitful, wavering life signs of a failing legacy – taped cracks in window panes, the rattle of loose rungs, loose shingles tattling in the wind, tiny harbingers of aftermath.

She met Stan on his way to the deli, a welcome guide through the dim-lit, dog-infested neighborhood. The irony of Stan's status as a recipient of disability benefits, from a society which he shunned, had not escaped him.

"Half the guys in the Haight were on SSI. You told the Feds you were hooked on stuff and they signed you up. It was as easy as getting farm subsidies, or tax breaks for the corporate rich, or bankruptcy. Life is full of contradictions. Recognizing them is one thing, letting yourself get snared in their duality is another."

Stan was Cory Adler's brother. He had made a home in Mannie Santiago's garage. Right next door to Cory's house. He slept in the bed of the old man's truck which, at Mannie's age, was seldom used. He shaved and bathed at Cory's twice a week. Otherwise, his shower was Mannie's hose. He ate often at the deli, so they allowed him bathroom privileges.

"You . . . uh." Milissa was having trouble keeping up. He knew the path by heart. "You have any skills?"

"Living."

She laughed. "Credentials?"

"Masters in Semantics. San Francisco State. Under Hayakawa."

"So you can find work?"

They had reached the front steps of the deli. "Work. Indo-European root, 'werg.' Old English, 'weorc,' an act, deed, or" – Stan whispered – "actual work. The Greeks, on the other hand, believed that all good work was play. Same 'werg' root, leading to 'ergon,' for '-urgy' as in liturgy, and organ and orgy."

"What sort of play do you do?"

"My camcorder. Other side of the brain."

"Where will you go? If things don't work out here."

"There you go with that word again. Hell, who knows. Can't go back to the Haight. Maybe Amsterdam. Stockmans could pay my airfare."

Milissa looked across the open lots. John's lights were on.

"I wonder," she responded absent-mindedly, "if you could ever readjust."

"You're the one who's caught up in the karma."

She pulled down the corners of her mouth and nodded.

"Aloha," Stan said, turning up the stairs. "Gotta grab some eats."

"Aloha."

I'm starved, Milissa said to herself as she made her way across the unlit, irregular surface of the field. Hope Keoni has something to eat. She felt a light clitoral surge in anticipation of seeing him. I have to go slow with this guy. He hasn't made a single move. Too tired anyway.

No one was home. Strange, she thought, upset at not being welcomed. He told me to come by. "Oh well," she said aloud, returning to the darkness, "scratch him off the list."

She followed the dirt road in front of John's house around the west side of the field until she came to the main drag. John, who was entering the same dirt road on the east side of the field, saw her in the lights of an oncoming truck, sped up, swung past his house, and approached her from behind.

"Keiki, Keiki," shouted Maria as she bounced around the cab of the pick-up.

"Like one ride?" John asked, opening the passenger door.

Maria leaned into Milissa and hugged her around the neck as she got in. "Keiki, where you going? We got huli huli chicken."

"I came by, but no one was home. Thought you forgot."

"You supposed to just walk in," John said. "Was down checking da crab pots."

"You big Keiki. I li'i Keiki," Maria announced with unabated delight.

John reached around behind Maria and massaged the nape of Milissa's neck.

Milissa sniffed a laugh at her pouty self. "Big baby's more like it."

After dinner Milissa and Maria played POGs, a game in which the POGs – replicas of old-time, tab-type, milk bottle tops – are stacked and "slammed" by one's opponent, who keeps the upturned pieces. Tiny Maria was experienced. Her knack of releasing her slammer POG at the last instant effected such an impact that Milissa's supply was gone after only a few turns. Eventually, Milissa caught on and Maria suggested that they play for real. A hard-fought hour later she cashed in for a bedtime story and a promised roll of POGs to account for Milissa's loss.

When Milissa returned from tucking her in, John surrendered his place on the couch with a chivalrous bow. She threw herself down and plumped the pillow around her head.

"What's on?"

"A PBS mystery. Otherwise, junk."

He changed the channel and sat beside her on the floor. It didn't take long for her to fall asleep.

When she woke up the house was quiet and the lights were out. "Here goes, Lindsay," she said, throwing off John's patchwork quilt, tiptoeing into his room, and climbing fully clothed into bed.

"I don't sleep alone when you're around," she whispered, snuggling up to his back and wrapping her arms around his naked body. John pressed into her, but didn't reply. That night they slept.

CHAPTER ELEVEN

Milissa was up at dawn. She didn't wake John. She wanted to leave him contemplating the intimacy of their inviolate slumber. Nothing like a morning after to dispel the nimbus of that first nocturnal bliss.

Taking the quilt from the floor in the living room and placing it neatly folded at the foot of his bed, she threw a silent kiss in his direction and set out, intent on jogging home in time to catch a ride to work with Morgan. She was considering a shortcut down across the fields when Loka pulled alongside.

She climbed into the van, somehow not surprised to see him. "Right on time. On your way to the airport?"

"Kaunakakai," Loka replied, re-entering the highway from behind his ominous shades.

"I met Sea," Milissa put in after a mile of silence.

Loka nodded.

"What is that guy's story?"

"Long story." He turned left onto Kaluakoi Road, the only public access to the west end resorts. He knew where she was going.

"How did you know?" she asked, quavering her voice, playing on his penchant for second guessing.

"You look like you need to get home and cleaned up for work."

She gave the situation another minute of silence. "I am curious about Sea."

Loka was slow to respond. Was he thinking? It was hard to tell and he preferred it that way. He turned down Akaka Road toward the condominiums. "You're curious 'cause you got an affinity. You da kine. Most people never care, never even notice him. For now, probably best it stay like dat. Dis your stop."

"You bugger! How did you know where I live?"

"I going all da time up and down da highway, everybody jabbering 'bout da Keiki kine."

Seeing that Milissa's imagination was not appeased, Loka set the brake and pushed his shades to the end of his nose. "Some people like call me" – he widened his eyes for dramatic effect – "da living grapevine. Mo' bettah?"

Milissa popped her head into the kitchen on the way to her room. "Morning. I'll be ready in a minute."

Her bed had been made. Clean clothes were folded and stacked on her nightstand. Her way of stressing my absence, she thought. While you were gone I tidied up your room, etc.

"I fell asleep on Keoni's couch," she called out as she hurried to the bathroom. "You and I were going to talk. Sorry I didn't phone."

"Perhaps tonight," Morgan said in a voice modulated for close, melancholic conversation. "We don't have much time left."

"We don't?" Milissa stepped under the shower, out of Morgan's hearing, and parroted her quoth-the-raven tone. "Why's that? You have a dread, melodramatic disease?"

Within minutes, Milissa appeared in the kitchen, clean and eager. "Okay, my friend, let's perk things up. You're seriously in need of a jail break, all locked up in there."

Morgan pushed her plate delicately to the side. "If you expect to find excitement beneath this drab exterior, you're making a mistake."

"Not drab, demure – very afraid of anything but stuffy. Actually, your shyness, your childlike peeking between the robes of justice, is your most endearing quality. Did you know that?"

For an instant Morgan blushed, looking exactly as Milissa had described her.

Milissa knuckled her gently on the arm. "Can't hide from me. Wanna come out and play?"

Morgan's helpless expression hardened a bit. She always felt a hint of rage at the ease with which Milissa could strip her of her cover.

"Let's go to Waikiki."

"When would we have time?"

"This weekend. I'm strapped too. We'll make time."

Morgan came slyly out of herself. Not since she was a little girl in her father's arms, before her horrible discovery of womanhood, had she sulked and gotten her way. "This weekend?"

"We'll leave tomorrow night." Milissa spun in a circle and leaned with both hands on the edge of the table, fixing her smiling eyes on Morgan. "We're gonna have a ball."

Morgan returned Milissa's look, amazingly clear eyed and convinced.

"One condition," Milissa said, cupping her hands together as if the vacation were inside, about to be released. "On Molokai you're the boss, but once we're on our way I call the shots, at least until I see you loosen up. Deal?"

Morgan flushed again, but this time more prudently. "I'll make the reservations," she said, carrying her dishes to the sink.

On their way out, Milissa noticed the light on the answering machine. "Is that for me?"

"From Mr. Spitz. I didn't listen past the introduction."

Milissa played it back. X wanted to see her at five thirty that evening for an update.

The high noon sun bleated silently above the Body of Christ, the only tranquil feature in the bone dry town. Milissa stopped suddenly and turned back. She'd hardly noticed Ui standing in the shadow of the trellis at the entrance to the church yard. "Ui. Is that you?"

"Aloha, Keiki," Ui replied, peeking out and then pulling back from the exposure.

"Sorry about your brother. How is he?"

"Kepa's my half-brother. T'ink he lose one eye. Pastor prayed for him at services today."

A round little man with a shiny brown face walked up behind Ui. "Dey holding him in juvie on Oahu. Probation violation."

Ui tugged the man's sleeve. "Dis Keiki."

The man chuckled warmly and cupped Milissa's hand. "I'm Pastor Swan. You da one who put da wrath of God in Kepa. Ui say you helping people for da Stockmans, ya?"

Milissa looked at Ui and back at Swan. "I think we have something to discuss."

"Where you going now?"

"Hitching up to Maunaloa."

"We going Ho'olehua. I dropping Ui off at school. Can take you Maunaloa after dat."

They walked to the pastor's pick-up. Ui got in and closed the door.

"You like help Ui," Swan asserted, walking Milissa toward the back of the truck so that Ui couldn't hear. "You da one we praying for."

Milissa nodded. "You must be right. That's what I had in mind."

"We like send Ui to one Christian boarding school on Oahu. What you t'ink?"

"Can I ride back here?"

"You betcha."

Milissa climbed over the tailgate. "Let's drop Ui off. Then we'll talk."

Milissa had read it in an almanac endorsed by the Bureau of Hawaiian Affairs. Eighty five percent of Molokai's residents were on welfare. She had passed it on in conversation, but always with a modicum of doubt. You read a lot of things. Her home visits that afternoon and the day before had given substance to the claim.

Most heads of households in Maunaloa were women – single, separated, or divorced, with children and grandchildren on public assistance. Their family histories were remarkably alike. As pineapple began to phase out, fathers would leave home to find work off-island, officially abandoning their children, allowing mothers to qualify for aid. Eventually the daughters of these families would bear children, in most cases out of wedlock so that the welfare connection could be maintained, and the young mother would cleave to the parental home. The men who stayed on-island or returned unemployed, redoubled their hunting and fishing efforts, ably supplementing their family's income, but remaining out of the income loop.

Men, many presumably fathers, were present during Milissa's rounds, but none of them, unless they were caught unawares like Julio, presented willingly as householders. Normally, the women would answer the door and deal with her just as they would a welfare worker. The men would hang around, sidling in and out or listening from the other room. Their women were married to the state, and their children answerable to the counselor, the social worker, the teacher, the policeman, and the judge.

In Milissa's mind, though they were due any benefit flowing to the men, the women were closer to the pulse of things, less alienated and less in need of redemption. To the extent that men were stripped of status in the family, their children, despite the public surrogates, remained at risk.

She arrived at Stockmans early to type up her report. She had removed her bandage and fixed her hair so that the stitches were out of sight. The statement outlined a plan in its formative stage, but set forth Julio and Ui as candidates for help.

"Mr. X called." Kini laid the message beside her. "He's sending Harry to pick you up."

Milissa continued to write. "I need a few more minutes. It can't be five thirty yet."

"Not quite. I'll let you know when he arrives."

At exactly five thirty, Harry, an extra lanky, total Texan from the top of his Stetson to the studded tips of his size sixteen boots, jumped down from the cab of his oversized Range Rover, strode around the back, and opened the passenger door. "Miss Milissa."

"Harry," Milissa replied, stepping up to the knee-high running board.

"At your service, ma'am. Like a hand?"

Disdaining Harry's offer, she scaled the hulking rig and buckled in. "I can manage," she said, extending her arm, but unable to reach the door. "I'll get it," she insisted with a shoo of her hand, unbuckling and moving to the edge of the seat.

Harry stepped back and watched as she struggled to leverage the door in toward her body, martyring herself for a moment in the noncompliant space.

"Oh, well," she said, returning to the cab with a reluctant grin, "better give a girl a hand."

Harry closed her door, got in the driver's seat, and headed across the open lots. When he got to Julio's he took a right and rumbled off the end of Main directly into the valley.

Milissa spotted X's estate perched on the other side. "Short cut?" she asked, bracing herself for the romp.

Harry picked up the phone. "Comin' across, Mr. X . . .Yep. Got 'er all buckled in."

The valley floor was stifling. Brooding stud mares grazed among the skeletal mesquite.

"All these trees dead?"

"Nope. Just inside themselves, mostly underground. They green up come December."

As they reached the top of the lower side, Milissa felt the let-down of a slowing circus ride. "Some day you gotta let me drive this prairie schooner."

Harry glanced down at her dangling feet. "Well, ma'am, maybe with a few alterations."

She slid forward and touched her feet to the floor, leaning her forearms against the dash.

He heaved his giant toy over the edge of the plateau and parked it by the company helicopter.

Hessie, the Spitz' sixty year old Filipino housekeeper, met them on their way to the house. "Aloha, Miss Milissa. Come, I take you Mr. X."

"You got 'er, Hessie." Harry tipped his hat and turned back.

As they walked along the path, Milissa noticed Renee at a distance, working in one of the flower gardens along the perimeter of the grounds. Her children were playing croquet on the lawn. Renee stood to stretch her back and looked blankly in Milissa's direction.

She doesn't recognize me, thought Milissa, waving to get her attention. Renee slapped her gloved hands together to remove the excess dirt and returned to her weeds.

"What was that?" Milissa whispered.

"T'rough here," Hessie motioned, leading Milissa to the pool.

X was laid out in his bathrobe under a wind-tormented canopy. He straddled his lounge chair and took a sip from his drink. His eyes rolled up in irritation. "God damn thing's gonna fly away." He had a swagger in his voice. "Still trying to figure out this wind. Maybe higher walls."

"Pretty high already. Don't wanna block the view."

X put an empty tumbler on the low, tile-surfaced table at his side and pointed to the cooler. "Like a drink? Got margarita or tequila, lemons and salt. Lemons and salt. Hessie!"

In an instant, Hessie was at the entrance to the patio.

"Some lemons and salt for Milissa."

"A beer," Milissa suggested to ease the moment. "Mr. Spitz and I will split a beer."

"No mo' da beer," Hessie apologized. "Can send Harry you like."

"No beer for me. I get tired of that piss. Bring Milissa some lemons and salt."

Milissa sat on the other lounge chair and sorted through the cooler. "You have any pop?"

"Rule of the house," X said, waving Hessie off, "don't call me Mr. Spitz. Hate the name. Nothing refined about it. It's one of those names like Butts or Butkis. Brings entirely the wrong image to mind, don't you think? If you have to call me mister, call me Mr. X."

Milissa filled her glass with ginger ale. "I don't have to call you mister anything. I just thought . . ."

"I'm on my way down, you know. That's what Renee says. 'You're on your way down,'" X whined as he lay back in his recliner. "My problem is I'm human. How 'bout you, Milissa? You human?" He sat up suddenly. "Here." He added a slug of tequila to her drink and took a shot straight from the bottle. "Join the party."

Milissa slid the drink aside and put her report in its place.

X ignored it. "You doing us right up there?"

His tone had shifted. It sounded like resentment. She thought of Renee in the garden. Were they angry? Maybe it was Kepa. "Is anything wrong?"

"Depends on how you look at it. What'd you have in mind?"

They stared at each other for a moment.

"Oh! You mean the ass kicking you gave that little gangster, Kepa," X said, exposing himself for an instant as he swung his legs over the side of the recliner and brought his sandals down with a slap. "Sheriff Fitzpatrick called me about that." He picked up his drink and stared into it like a tea reader. "I asked him if I should fire you for assaulting the kid." He drained his glass, set it blindly down on Milissa's report, then leaned across and put his hands on her shoulders. "He told me that if I let you go, he'd hire you."

"You're kidding."

X laughed a whiskey laugh and pitched Milissa back on her recliner. "Kidding?" he said, standing up unsteadily and tightening his robe. "That's the best PR we've had in years. You're one tough little cookie. Whoops!" He picked up his glass and daubed the report against his robe.

Milissa was stung by X's horseplay, but even more by his delight in Kepa's injury. She recalled her remark to Morgan – "The little bastard's lucky I didn't have a gun" – and felt a pang of regret.

He leafed through the document. "Too bad you didn't bring a swimsuit. Five pages. Too many. Give me the gist."

"I've got a couple tenants – good prospects. Helping them will help your image."

"I like the image part."

"There's a man named Julio."

"Garces. He pays his rent."

"I want you to hire him. He'll need at least ten an hour to rent one of our new units."

"Doing what?"

"Working on the project. He hasn't done much, but he can follow directions."

"We're not gonna hire just anyone at ten an hour."

"Well then, you're gonna nitpick these really needy guys out of gainful employment and give the jobs to somebody's son. Isn't that the way it works?"

"Damned if I know. I don't do the hiring. That stuff's all in the construction contract."

"All you have to do is give the contractor a call."

"Not according to the contract."

"I'm sure they want the next one. They'll bend."

"Okay, okay. I'll give 'em a call."

"And tell them we'll be giving first option on labor jobs to the men of Maunaloa."

X sat and stared into the space between his feet.

Milissa didn't wait for a response. "And then there's Ui. Ewa's daughter?"

"Little Saint Ui," X muttered.

"That's the one."

"Pastor Swan's wife brought her to one of Renee's garden parties. Leaves quite an impression, according to Renee."

"Pastor Swan has asked us to send her to a boarding school on Oahu. I told him to get back to me with the figures. I'd like to guarantee at least one semester tuition and supplies."

X lobbed his head up and dropped it back down as if he were fighting a stupor. "Go with that one. And make sure the media's involved."

"I should be leaving."

He held his hand up to stop her. "We're going to Waikiki."

"What's that about?"

"In two hours. A dinner meeting. Couple of the guys from

Australia." He stood up, swaying badly from the booze and hyperventilation. "I've gotta get some sleep. You sit tight. I'll have Hessie bring you something to eat."

"At your service, ma'am," Harry said, reaching down to offer his hand.

"What's a girl to do?" Milissa replied, locking wrists with Harry and allowing herself to be hoisted through the hatch.

"Wind died down like we expected," X said, readily accepting Harry's arm.

The sudden and accelerating woof, woof, woof, the distant sound of Harry's voice clearing takeoff with air traffic control, the vibration of the cockpit, the shroud of darkness all around, flooded her with giddy apprehension. X, who was seated in front, looked back and trembled his hand above his head with the razzle dazzle of a minstrel's tambourine. "This is always a thrill to me," he shouted over the now fierce whine of the blade, turning forward to examine a financial statement at the instant that the aircraft sprang into the sky.

"Wooeee," shouted Milissa, her emotions releasing with the sudden lift.

X looked up for a second and returned to his accounts. Harry closed off with the tower and craned cautiously to examine the air space around them as they climbed to cruising altitude.

"One of the reasons I brought you along," X said, as he joined her in the cramped space behind the seats, "was to introduce you to our principals. I'd like to think you're gonna be with us in the future."

The statement surprised Milissa. And he said it so sincerely. Who is this genuine fellow sitting next to me? she asked herself. Some transformation.

X was stoked. "Now, for the substance of the meeting," he said, all shiny and smelling of aftershave. "The Stockmans, as you know, are from Australia."

Milissa nodded.

"Old man Julius is the major stockholder and Chairman of the

Board. They started out with stud farms, so that's what they're known for, but they have hundreds of holdings and investment interests. That should tell you something about Stockmans Inc. of America."

"We're expendable?"

"A fact that should never be stated as a question. A decision that could be made by eight men between quiche and key lime pie on any afternoon. My mother's part owner, but they have the clout. We'll be dining with two of 'em, Abbot and Bisk, in . . ." he looked at his watch. "In about forty minutes. I'll start by briefing them on our financial condition company wide – lickety split, a piece of paper and a few figures – and then we'll focus on Maunaloa, the first fee simple subdivision on Molokai, the first of many to come on Stockmans' property, blah, blah, blah. Oh, yeah," he snapped his fingers, irked at having to interrupt himself. "It's a pity, but it comes up every time. One of the drags on the entire operation is Molokai's notoriety. For starters, I mean, God bless Damien, but who wants to live with a bunch of lepers. Are you listening?"

Milissa was observing. X appeared to be on the verge of rambling. His delivery was speeding up and beginning to grate. "I'm right here, X," she said, putting her hand on his forearm.

"One of the first things that'll come out of their mouths'll be, 'Do you lot still have that leper colony over there?' They know the God damned thing is there, but the standard explanation is required. You know, isolated location, Hansen's disease, no longer communicable, Father Damien, historic interest, the lookout. You've been to the lookout?"

"Yesterday."

"Good. You're still impressed. You can explain. I'll count on you for that. I think they put me through it just to goad me. So . . ." X paused as if he'd lost his place. "So next, I'll lay out the plan. I'll start with the north section. That's where the big money is. Three hundred thousand dollar lots with houses built to order. Right away they're gonna want to know about the people still holed up there – how we're gonna get 'em out without an incident. This'll require some finesse. Abbot does his homework. The first time it comes up, I'll gloss over it with some good news on the south side – two house and lot packages in escrow. They'll like that, but they'll be itching to get back to the tenant problem. That's what they're really here for. They know it's the linchpin. That's where you come in. I need you to explain the transition. I assume you've given it some serious thought."

"Did you read my report?"

"Have I had time? Two things. Remember your audience. These guys are not bleeding hearts. And trust your intuition. You're at your best on your feet. Any questions?"

"When do we eat?"

X balked.

Milissa put her hands on her chest. "How much time do I have to get my act together?"

X moved abruptly to the front and buckled in. "You've had since what? Last Friday? Half an hour and counting."

Better in the end, he said to himself, looking down on the eastern shore of Oahu, that Milissa be thought to have innocently misrepresented the situation, than for me to make a claim that I can't deliver.

"Malcolm Abbot. Willy Bisk. It's my pleasure to introduce our future in-house counsel, Milissa Dogherty."

"Gentlemen," Milissa said, taking in the decor of the venerable Hotel Moana. "Please excuse my Molokai attire. X whisked me away without notice."

"How cavalier," Abbot replied.

"But, hey. You lot up here are known for dressing down," Bisk added, giving Milissa a supportive touch on the arm.

Milissa was relieved. "Let's try that one on the maitre d'."

Bisk and Milissa paired up right away, walking sprightly ahead, leaving the other two to hedge around the fringes of international finance in search of the door to Maunaloa. After the party had been seated, Bisk began asking Milissa questions about herself.

Always most at ease when in the spotlight, she gave considerable detail about her background, inevitably including travels with her parents. When she mentioned a trip down the Oregon coast during which she and her mother had surveyed the remains of Native American fishing camps, Bisk told her about a cash of crude paleolithic cutting tools his wife had discovered while foraging along the eastern shore of Vancouver Island.

"At first I was skeptical. But when Ethel laid them in a row from the smallest on up, they looked quite credible."

"That's always the thing. It's hard to believe they're not just broken rocks."

"We took them over to UBC and had them authenticated. Since then I've been an enthusiast. Seems we do our best in bays and estuaries where the tide isn't too extreme."

"Mom and I went to coastal towns and asked around for places the Indians used to fish. Sometimes you can see their names squiggled in small print on road maps – names like Indian Maw or Indian Inlet. You wouldn't know it until you were right on top of 'em, and even then you couldn't be sure. There's always this undercurrent of disbelief until you find a spearhead or a shell hook or something definitive, and then it's like a color-blind test, where the color-blind person sees numbers other people can't. Suddenly there are cutters and scrapers everywhere in relief."

By this time, Abbot and X had tuned in on the conversation and were exchanging conspicuous looks, signaling their wish to get on to more important matters.

"Did you know," Milissa continued, after a mischievous nod from Bisk, "that they found Clovis artifacts near Corvallis, Oregon?"

"A significant challenge to the belief that Clovis people came down through the corridor of glacial thaw east of the Cascades," Bisk replied. "Don't you agree, Mocky?"

Abbot reached for a witty reply. "Thaw me out when this is over?"

"We'll all be artifacts by then," X added.

Bisk turned to Milissa. "Mocky thinks we're in town on business."

Abbot elbowed X. "That's what Willy told our wives."

"Right you are," Bisk replied, straightening around. "So, what's on the agenda?"

Milissa leaned toward Bisk and placed her index finger flat across her lips. He turned to her attentively. She was thinking of a recently discovered adze quarry near Kaluakoi. X and Abbot pivoted their heads in her direction. She glanced at them and settled back. “Only teasing,” she said, wrinkling her nose.

“Save that thought,” said Bisk. “There’ll be other occasions.” He wrote *Ethel and Bill* on a cocktail napkin and, below that, their telephone number in Sydney. “Give us a call,” he said, placing it in her hand. “So, Xavier, how are things progressing in Maunaloa?”

X presented his planned remarks without a break – not even for the standard leper inquiry – ending with his announcement of the two houses in escrow.

“That’s a start,” Bisk admitted. “But things haven’t gone as planned. Mocky and I have discussed this. Do you suppose it’s because of all those families we’re displacing?” The question was rhetorical. “Isn’t that the crux of the thing?”

Abbot unfolded the front page of the *Star Bulletin* he had tucked in his pocket and laid it in front of X. The headline read *Three Fourths Opposed to Hawaiian Independence*. “Things have changed since you sold us on the redevelopment.” He put his finger on the article. “That this is even an issue is distressing. Means there’s a big chunk of pissed-off natives out there.”

Bisk re-entered as if the next line were his. “What we don’t need is our little town becoming a cause célèbre. There are several Maunaloas festering in these islands. The spectacle of third world refugee types living in cars and spilling into campsites is bad for business. How many people left in Maunaloa?”

X’s mouth was fuzzy despite a continuous flow of alcohol. He was coming down again. “Two fifty, maybe three hundred.” He glanced at Milissa for help, then snapped his head around in reaction to Abbot’s sharp reply.

“Three hundred can look like a thousand given the wrong press. What’s your plan to keep them from blowing back in our faces? Is there any room left in that housing project?”

X looked directly at Milissa. “The project is full. The few openings they had were taken by our first vacancies. We plan to move our diehards into our new rental units. We brought Milissa on to ease the relocation.”

Milissa hunched forward, elbows on the table, huddling up with the boys. "I would concentrate on the problem of moving our tenants to the south side and use that section as a pilot project. If we break even and succeed in carrying off a humane transformation of the town, we will have done something unheralded, something that will benefit the people and Stockmans. The south side can be a cornerstone, a centerpiece around which future, more profitable subdivisions are built. If we mess this one up . . . you know, forced evictions, violence, bad press . . ."

"A bunch of welfare bums in four hundred and fifty dollar cracker boxes hardly qualifies as a centerpiece for future development," Abbot interrupted. "I mean, just possibly the abodes will be of decent quality, but the tenants won't keep them up. By our reckoning they can't even afford the rent. Xavier?"

Abbot had seen the books. He knew the current situation. X tapped the tips of his fingers together, continuing to look at Milissa. "It's a difficult situation."

"Go easy, chums." Bisk held his hands up in Milissa's defense. "Milissa's offered us a way to go. Maybe a bit naive, but . . . How would you accomplish your little miracle, Milissa?"

Milissa dove back in. "I'm proposing a cure for a cycle of poverty. But we'd have to set aside the greed. That would be the miracle." She paused. "Is this really worth discussing?"

"I think it is," Bisk answered.

"Mr. Abbot?" Milissa asked.

"Yes, of course," Abbot replied dryly, miffed at being required to confess his interest.

"One facet of my program deals with employment. I've convinced X to guarantee the fathers of Maunaloa first right of refusal on labor and carpenter helper jobs." She had X in a bind. He wouldn't dare back away at this point in the pitch, especially after that bit about moving everyone into new rentals. "As each man hires on we arrange a one year lease. That's part of the deal. What we're doing here is training a work force for future subdivisions. We have in mind developing a work-study program through the local community college."

"I take it this thing is still in the planning stage?"

Milissa looked to X for an answer to Abbot's question.

"We've hired one man already, a Filipino named Garces. He promised to help us recruit."

"Good PR if nothing else," Abbot conceded. "Of course, some'll say you're hiring people to dig their own graves."

"Or to build their own futures," Milissa insisted.

Taking X's Julio fiction as a go-ahead, Milissa presented her case in its best light. "I've had discussions with church leaders about opening an after school daycare." She'd talked to Pastor Swan just once, merely hinting at the quid pro quo she was now presenting as a near fait accompli. "Its primary mission will be to benefit the children of Maunaloa, but we also see it as providing mothers time to find and keep full time jobs. Stockmans and the church community will form a non-profit corporation to run the daycare and develop children's services – nutritional supplements and advice, counseling, tutoring, and scholarships."

"We're sending one of our at-risk children, a very deserving little girl, to a Christian boarding school," X chimed in, riding up the manic flux of mixed intoxicants. "The child is high visibility because of her extreme devotion."

"How long have you been aboard?" Bisk asked Milissa.

"A week?" She looked at X for confirmation.

X nodded.

Abbot belched an appreciative laugh despite himself.

"Heard enough?" Bisk asked.

"Enough," Abbot answered as he reached across the table to take Milissa's hand. "Milissa, I'm encouraged. If half of what you say pans out, we'll all have done our jobs."

"Maybe we'll have to take a bigger bite out of the profit than we planned," Bisk said to X. "We'll consider it an investment."

"One caveat." Abbot held an instructive finger up to X. "Don't lift a shovel until you've settled the present dispute with your tenants. Get it out of the way before we start pumping money back in. Try your damnedest to avoid evictions, but if it comes to that, do it quick and clean. Profit motive has no conscience. Our investors can decide to put their pennies elsewhere if this thing starts to stink. I know I can. Now, for god sakes, let's eat. This booze is pickling my stomach."

X excused himself to use the bathroom.

Despite his drunken condition, X insisted on giving Milissa a ride home that night.

"Willy was being protective. Very sympathetic. The old guy's got a thing for you."

"You're crossing the meridian."

"Oops." X adjusted his course. "I'm definitely taking you if they call me down there." He looked at Milissa for a response.

Milissa looked up suddenly and then out the back window. "You missed Kaluakoi Road."

X skidded to a stop and backed up toward the cut-off, swerving the width of the highway until he came to a stop, killing the engine and rolling slowly backward into the intersection. "I got it part right," he said, slumping over the wheel. "Where now?"

Milissa got out, walked around the car, and opened his door. "Scoot over."

"My date's driving me home."

"I'm not your date," she said, turning an aggressive U and heading down to the resorts.

"You at Paniolo?" X asked when she took a right on Akaka.

"I'm staying with Morgan."

"Morgan Zarins, the bane of the common business man. She jumped on that Ono thing."

"I suppose you know about that." She pulled into the parking lot. They sat for a moment in silence. "I hate to abandon you in your condition, X, but I've got a long day tomorrow."

"I had it in the back of my mind that you'd invite me in – helpless as I am."

"You what?"

"Think I can make it back?"

Milissa handed him the phone. "Call Harry."

X fumbled with the key pad, made a couple of unsuccessful attempts, and handed it back. "Five two two. No. Five five two seven three three two." He watched her punch the number in.

A female voice came on the line. "Is Harry there?" Milissa asked cautiously.

"Harry?" answered the voice. "Who is this?"

"This is Milissa Dogherty, one of Mr. Spitz' employees."

"Don't call me Mr. Spitz," X said, grabbing the phone. "Harry, God damn it, I'm drunk."

"Xavier, this is Renee," said the voice, followed by a dial tone.

"Shit. It was Renee. Let's see, five five two . . ." He entered the rest of the number and looked over at Milissa. "Sorry."

"Um hum."

"Harry? What time is it? Come get me. Panilolo, ni, niolo . . . Yes. The parking lot." He looked at Milissa again. "It's like that ho'opono shit. Too many oh ohs."

She couldn't help but laugh.

He dropped the phone and lurched back against the door. "I think I love you."

Her laugh became a gentle scoff. "You're drunker than I thought."

"Right. Maybe it's just the hots." He started to walk his fingers across the back of the seat.

"Don't you lay a hand on me, or I'll tell Harry." She kept a smile on her face.

"Oh God, not Harry. He'd snap me in two. And Morgan would get me for sex harassment." He looked through the window, concentrating as if he'd spotted something moving in the bushes. "You do know I'm attracted to you, don't you?" His voice was surprisingly sober.

"I do not!" She punched him in the shoulder. "Now stop the nonsense. You're married."

He threw his head back, let out a high-pitched howl, then brooded for several minutes, making Milissa uncomfortable with his silence.

"Jeez," he finally said, "where the fuck is Harry? This is getting nowhere."

Milissa detected a hint of anger. "Don't get pissed at me."

"That's it! I gotta take a wiz." He rolled out of the passenger door. "Like a race horse," he wheezed from the darkness.

She could hear a steady drumming against the rear quarter panel.

Harry pulled around the corner and caught X in his high beams.

"Shit, Harry. Good timing. Caught me in mid-stream. Here, check it out."

Milissa heard Harry's door whomp shut. "All clear?" she asked. "I'm coming out."

"You're safe," X said, fumbling with his fly. "Big Harry's here."

She stayed by the driver's door while Harry boosted X into the super-truck.

"You all right, Miss Milissa?"

"Oh fine. A little tired. Take care of Mr. X."

"That's what I do. See you down the line."

She waved as Harry pulled away. X's keys were in her hand.

John looked out the deli window in the direction of Stockmans' office. "Sounds like X was using you for cover."

Milissa flashed in anger. She had described the meeting with confidence, sure that he would approve. "You think you have to tell me that. Like I can't fathom X's game?"

"Chill out, Keiki. Dat's not what I mean."

"That's the implication. It's not the response I expected."

"Sure you right. Tell you what. You keep tabs on my funky attitude. I keep you from going over da top."

"Agreed," Milissa said, receptive to his hand against her cheek. "Sleep well last night?"

"Mo' bettah da night before."

"The night before," Milissa fluttered. "I meant the night before."

"How about you?"

"Mmm, hubba nubba."

"Hubba nubba? What's dat mean? Why you blushing?"

Milissa grinned. "Me? You're the one. That's the language of love."

"No can be," John kidded. "Hawaiian language never have one 'b' like dat hubba nubba. You mean . . ." John leaned across the table and pulled Milissa gently toward him. "You mean ho'oipo," he whispered. The syllables exploded softly in her ear. He brushed her cheek with his. "Ipo," he repeated, kissing her parted lips.

She sat back without a word, disarmed, no translation necessary, content to look into his sage and mirthful eyes, amused at herself, unable to rebound.

Following the kiss, there was a subtle air of self-congratulation as they lingered at the table, sipping their espresso, sharing everyday thoughts, silently amazed at the newness of things.

"You know I gotta work this afternoon."

"I'll walk you down da street and let you go."

When they got outside, Milissa noticed that X's car had been moved into the office lot from where she parked it on the street. The horny mental residue of X's pass the night before had lost its sting. She dismissed her impulse to return the keys.

"You coming by tonight?"

"Going to Waikiki with Morgan for the weekend. We leave at six."

"Uh. I'm lonely already."

Milissa put her arm around his waist and they practiced their first syncopated strides. She hesitated when they passed a tiny boutique beside the road. It reminded her of a large toll booth.

"Dental Booth Boutique," John said, pointing to the sign in the window. "Used to be one dentist's office. Doctor flew in once a week. Everybody had to wait outside. Cash register was right inside da door. Got no bathroom, so da keiki gotta shishi 'fore dey get dere. Lotta times dey pucker deir okole all day long, den cry how bad dey gotta go so dey can lose da place in line."

"Bet little Keoni never did that," she said, smiling at John's facility for flowing in and out of dialect. He never spoiled a homespun sentiment with standard English or sacrificed a complex thought to the local patois. "Tell me about the good old days."

"Plenty ordinary stuff. Less see. Libby started up 'round here in da early twenties. Den other companies came in – Del Monte, Dole, like dat. Whole t'ing came and went in fifty years.

"By da time I was born, Maunaloa was at its peak." John led Milissa up the grassy slope between the warehouse and Maunaloa

Road and looked across the bottom of the north section. "All down here a lotta Filipinos, some Chinese, and a little bit Portugee/ Hawaiian mix. Japanese straw bosses lived up dat way." He pointed south, up the mild gradient leading to the top of the mountain. "And da haole headman, way up past da rest."

"Your parents. You never mention them."

"My papa was part Portugee cowboy, part Hawaiian. He worked da range till I was born, den hired on wit' Libby. Mom stayed home. We lived right dere." He nodded at his house across the empty lots. "Same place. Aunty Easy right next door da whole time."

"How far do your people go back on Molokai?"

"Two, t'ree hundred years. Before dat, who knows. Nobody's really from Hawaii. People haven't been here all dat long. Not too far back, geologic time, deze islands didn't exist. Pretty soon dey be all gone."

"You think so?"

"Check out da constant wind up Kalaupapa Lookout. Check out da muddy reef along da southern shore. Add on da global warming. Molokai's going home."

"Where are Mom and Dad living now?"

"Both passed away in deir fifties. Hawaiians are like Hawaii, ya? Going, going, gone."

John glanced at the high wall behind him. "Dis warehouse been here since I can remember. Libby used to keep da hand plows stacked inside, hundreds of 'em. We'd steal 'em and use da wheels for making 'wheelbarrels,' den race 'em down da back side of da mountain. Mama gave us plenty whacks for dat.

"You like one jaw breaker?" John beckoned for Milissa to follow him down the slope and across the parking lot. "Come," he shouted, disappearing through the swinging double doors of Maunaloa General Store. Milissa peeked into the dimly lit interior. The stock was arranged on the shelves to make less look like more – all pushed to the front and evenly spaced. She could hear John's footsteps knocking against the rubbed-raw, wooden floor.

"No more jaw breakers?" John asked in a loud voice, knowing the truth. The old Chinaman at the counter didn't look up. "No penny candy for years," John said, joining Milissa on the porch and pointing up past the deli. "Jason Dinn's kite shop used to be a chow hall for da summer hands. Teenagers like me who work da summer break ate lunch dere. Plenty work. Good food."

They went back and sat in front of the warehouse. "Could never tell back den, but t'ings already on da down slide. Union was plenty strong. Too strong for da kine. First sign of trouble, dey stopped replacing old-timers when dey quit. Everyt'ing come mechanized, dey say. No need so many hands. Nineteen seventy two, Libby sold it all to Dole. Claimed da union priced 'em out. Dole right away started laying people off. By seventy five everyt'ing no mo'."

"Did the union price them out?"

"Organized labor in a competitive economy reacts competitively – just one more commodity. Prices get shoved up by wages and da company can't compete."

"What's the answer?"

"Today Molokai, tomorrow da world." John laughed at himself, then paused to consider. "T'ought you lawyers had all da answers."

"Actually, lawyers have all the questions. What was the problem? The union got greedy and spoiled healthy competition?"

"Problem is dat labor can be converted into capital and controlled by individuals. Control of da pocketbook made it possible for Libby, Dole, da big kahunas, to dump deir labor force, take da cash equivalent, and find someone somewhere else who'd work for less."

"You hold Libby and Dole responsible then?"

"Now you back to answers."

"Take a stab."

"Everybody who has power is responsible. Da companies, da union, da state, da bosses, da workers who side wit' da company to keep deir jobs."

"Society's responsible."

"Don't you t'ink? Dat's why we got affordable housing ordinances, unemployment comp, social security, public assistance, t'ings like dat."

"Be more specific. Why is Stockmans responsible for what happens to the people here?"

"Stockmans' problem comes wit' da land. Da first inhabitants here were part of da land. Dey didn't own it. Nobody really owned it in fee simple."

"But surely the chiefs had rights. Codes of ownership."

John waggled his head ambiguously.

"Maybe not codes, but some conception."

"Da chief, call him da ali'i, was da master. Nobody challenged his right to take what he liked, especially if he on da scene. Some places were taboo for common people. But some of deze people were his ohana. Not some cold legal connection. Over here one great aunty who fell from grace. Over dere his ipo's husband. One kahuna. One sorcerer. He try to uproot everyone, he take a chance he get his butt kicked. Whole way of t'inking was more fluid. Lot of ali'i come and go."

"How do you explain the current reality?"

"By-n-by, da haoles lit an artificial light in da ali'i's head. Told him he could alienate the land. Promised dey would back him up wit' guns. Dis was a revelation. At first he only sold t'ings off da land, mostly all da sandalwood. Den one day he sold da ground itself, da mother of us all. And wit' each successive turnover, da new owner bought da ancient trespass. Like Stockmans bought a run-down town full of welfare recipients, tail end victims of da pineapple bust. How you t'ink it ended up dis way? Was all passed down from da start when da haole convince da ali'i dat people no come wit' da land."

CHAPTER TWELVE

John handed Milissa a grocery bag. "From Aunty."

She looked inside as he drove away. Facing up was an envelope with *Muumuus for Morgan* scrawled across it like a smile. She hurried into the house and tucked the dresses in her grip.

Morgan was already home, still in her stuffy uniform from court that day, looking agitated. "Out of that," Milissa ordered. "Sandals and something plain to start with. We'll add some color when we get there."

That was the problem. Morgan hadn't been able to make up her mind. Milissa headed toward Morgan's room, determined to find something less restrained. Morgan blocked the door.

"Okay. You can wear the straight jacket, but only till we get there. I'll be a minute. Meet you at the car?"

The car was running. Morgan was in the driver's seat. Milissa opened her door and put two hands on the steering wheel. "Scootch," she said, nudging Morgan with her hip. "I'm driving."

Morgan's vest torqued around her midriff as she scooted in.

"And loosen that thing up," Milissa added, gleefully attacking

Morgan's buttons. "Now breathe."

The trip to the terminal was tenuous. Morgan was silently phobic – blotched and sweaty. Milissa made a few innocuous comments, hoping to get into the air before a reason could be found for turning back.

As she headed down the airport access road, John passed her in his pick-up going the other way. Something in his look, straight at her but without apparent recognition, told Milissa not to wave. Fidel was close behind. Both had passengers with pale complexions.

Milissa remained subdued throughout the boarding process, giving Morgan not the slightest excuse to reconsider. But as soon as the plane left the ground she resumed command. "Nyt, Nyt," she said as Morgan removed a law journal from her carry-on. "No paraphernalia."

Morgan tucked the journal into her seat back pouch and unveiled her best little girl eyes. "You'd rather I stare into space?"

"Right, better to sit there and bat your eyes like a toad in a hail storm." The analogy was apropos, but inappropriate. "I mean . . . nothing personal. My dad has all these sayings."

Morgan smiled faintly and stared straight ahead, trying not to blink.

"Like whenever it got real cold out he'd say, 'Gonna freeze up . . .'" Milissa leaned over to finish in a whisper, "'. . . tighter than a bull's ass in fly time.'"

A nasty grin quivered Morgan's lips as she reached for her journal. Milissa snatched it from the pouch. Morgan's hand followed as Milissa lifted it first above her head, then out into the aisle, then back again. "The slightest trace of frost," Milissa went on, still playing keep away, "and Dad'd say, 'No books tomorrow, Missy. Snow'll be ass high to a tall Indian.'"

One final lurch and Morgan laughed out loud, not at Milissa's figure of speech, but her audacity. She wasn't used to being toyed with. As she sank back in her seat, it occurred to her again how much like Mazie Milissa seemed to be.

"He'd roll these things out deadpan," Milissa continued, "like they were original. That's really what made them so funny." She was having trouble reading Morgan's expression. "He didn't mean any harm. Politically incorrect, huh? About the Indian? S'pose you're right."

Morgan let the false impression ride. She thought it might help to tone Milissa down. But no. Without particular regard to rough edges, Milissa persisted, apologizing if necessary, but hammering nonetheless at Morgan's closet door.

"The decor is included in the price of the swimwear," Milissa whispered, steering Morgan into a lavish dressing room. "We should order out and spend the night here."

Morgan's eyes slid silently across the floor in the direction of the exit, pleading to be left alone. Milissa handed her a bikini and took a seat on a hassock in the middle of the room. "I'd prefer a one piece," Morgan complained, pulling the skimpy bottoms on beneath her slip.

"Waiting," Milissa said.

Morgan removed her skirt and blouse, hiked the slip up to her waist, then hesitated, agonizing over whether to expose her back or belly first. Milissa stood quickly and examined her like a weight trainer.

"Okay, small butt, firm legs. Good. Now, are you showing us your wading technique or can we see the rest?

"Uh huh," Milissa continued as Morgan stripped down to the thong. "Tummy needs trimming. That'll take time."

Morgan looked at herself in the wall-length mirror as though she'd made a mess. Her body hair was pervasive, feathering away from her areolas, radiating from between her buttocks into the small of her back, extending down from her navel to the insides of her thighs.

Milissa placed her hands on Morgan's shoulders and looked into her bleary eyes. "Girl," she beseeched, "have you never used a depilatory?"

Morgan covered her breasts with the top.

"Some cultures prefer body hair on women," Milissa commented, retreating to the hassock.

"I've never paid the slightest attention," Morgan said.

"No, of course you haven't."

"I know I'm hairy."

"Do you like it? Do you like the hair?"

"No." She could see that Milissa found it unattractive.

"Well, get rid of it then. I'll get some stuff. We'll take it off tonight."

The long silk shift hung free from Morgan's shoulders, cataracking colors down the spectrum from its sweeping, deep purple neckline to a wash of faded blue along its ankle-high hem. It was a gift from Milissa. The waiter at the Buccaneer commented on its elegance as he led them to their table. "Exquisite, madam," he said. "Such a regal gown." Morgan glanced at Milissa for assurance and nodded her appreciation. Throughout the meal, Milissa remained low-key, subtly buoying Morgan's fragile self-esteem.

It was dark by the time they got back to their room. Milissa took the hair remover from her bag. "Your skin'll have all night to acclimate."

Morgan went obediently into the bathroom and began to apply the cream. As she stroked her thighs, she thought of Milissa's smooth, supple limbs and was reminded of the girls who had shunned her in her childhood, of the hours she had spent alone with her dolls, playing with their tight little bodies – opening their legs, cleaning them, adjusting them in mean, awkward positions.

"Rolly polly, Daddy's little fatty," she murmured, "eatin' bread and jam all day." Her father used to sing it to her when he helped her undress for bed. "Rolly polly, Daddy's little fatty, never goin' out to play." She hadn't thought about that song for years.

"How we doing?" Milissa asked through the door.

Morgan snapped back to the present. "Almost done."

"Well let me see, deary," Milissa kidded in a witchy voice, peeking in, the first to see her completely nude since Mazie. "Don't forget the underarms."

After showering off, she modeled her bathing suit. Despite Milissa's urging, she'd chosen one with a skirted midriff.

"It's wonderful," Milissa fibbed, thinking now she might have preferred the shameless flopsy mopsy of their snorkeling trip, then turned suddenly, as if in response to a voice in her head, and pulled back the curtain from a window that overlooked the courtyard. "I hear ukuleles."

Morgan withdrew to the couch and placed her hands in her lap like a child awaiting permission. "I had hoped to do some reading."

"Can you hear?" Milissa opened the window. "They say if you walk the beach there's a different trio for every hotel. They play out on the terraces."

The thought of not reading herself to sleep disturbed Morgan. She was addicted to her solitude. She had all the society she needed with Milissa in the room.

Milissa looked out the window again. "It would be a shame to waste the opportunity. There's only now and tomorrow night."

After a moment of silence Milissa added, "I could go alone."

"No fighting you," Morgan said, rising meekly from the couch. "I'll wear my silk."

As they walked along the hotel strand, Milissa in bikini and blouse, Morgan in her rainbow shift, they could indeed hear the crooning of Hawaiian tenors accompanied by guitar and ukulele. They bought an order of roast duck and pineapple at a take-out stand and picnicked near the shoreline on tatami mats.

"The surf's so quiet."

"It's quite far out," Morgan replied. "A hundred yards from shore, sometimes more."

"You saw it from our window?"

Morgan's look was coy.

"You've been here before. Why didn't you say?"

"It wasn't important."

"Well how . . . Why were you here?"

"I got my law degree at UH. I came here frequently. My place to be anonymous."

"You never talk about yourself."

"Outside of school and the law, there isn't much to say."

"I can't believe that. You must be pushing forty. Did you ever have a boyfriend?"

"Milissa . . ." Morgan looked out toward the sound of the surf, unable to frame a response.

"Oh, I know you don't have men friends. But have you ever had one?"

"I had one friend. A Dominican Brother. I met him at a Newman Club function during my senior year at Chaminade."

"You're Catholic?"

"No. I got a scholarship there. It was smaller than UH, less intimidating to start out."

"So Brother . . .?"

"Kerin."

"Brother Kerin at the party, he found you attractive?"

"That wasn't the idea. It was a reception. I went there thinking the presence of clerics might make it more neutral." Morgan's smile admitted the folly of the assumption.

"How did the good brother show his interest?"

"He took me to movies and we attended mass."

"Mass. Sounds exciting."

"Not being Catholic, I couldn't take communion. He'd leave me kneeling in the pew. This was meant to inspire conversion. There's this feeling one has . . . When there's supposed to be love and there's not? It's worse than hate – more empty. Sexless is the closest word."

"The way you wanted it, right?"

"Absolutely. That was the revelation. I had to rub my nose in it to be sure."

"But you and Kerin must have had some laughs, some closeness. Everything isn't sex."

"I love the feeling of silk." She laid her cheek against her shoulder, embracing herself and rocking back and forth. "There was one time I suppose. We were babysitting. The child of a parishioner. Chip. Such a winsome little creature, so patient with his condition. He was in a body cast, all except for his arms, his legs, and his face. He'd broken his back in a fall at Diamond Head.

"I know we both adored him. We took him to Ala Moana Park and played cat's cradle. He loved cat's cradle. Kept the string around his neck when he wasn't playing. He could go on and on without repeating. He and I got into a marathon. At one point I mentioned that we'd never get back to the beginning and he said, 'Trust me. There's no beginning.'

"The idea seemed so funny coming from a six year old. My concentration faltered. I remember Kerin crouching down and putting his hand on my back. He and Chip guided me through the moves. I became the focus. The conduit for their energy. They were keeping the game alive through me. For a long time I stopped thinking and trusted that they were right. When I started to think for myself again, we struggled a bit and Kerin took control. His first move, the cradle fell apart."

Morgan began to trace a pattern in the sand. "We all laughed, of course. It was okay that Kerin missed the hold. I gave him a hug. But that was it. A moment of abandon in the midst of child's play. It was really all for Chip."

She paused, then went on reminiscing. "Chip laughed so hard he tipped over and got stuck on his back. He looked like a little broken soldier, his arms and legs pawing at the air."

"How about women?" Milissa interjected. "What was her name? The one in China?"

Morgan continued to trace. "You like my creation?" she asked after a moment.

"Is it an enigma?"

Morgan's answer was an enigmatic smile.

"I have a close woman friend," Milissa said as if to justify her interest.

Morgan scattered her design, whisked the sand away between her fingers, and examined them for cleanliness.

"Well, not that kind of close," Milissa responded, waiting a moment while Morgan shook off her mat and resettled. "We got kidnapped, sort of. Did I mention Lindsay?"

Milissa and Lindsay had met in Madrid at an open air café. While waiting for resort agents to sweep through in search of seasonal help – a common practice in southern European cities – they struck up a conversation and decided to stick together. That afternoon, three men took them to a dude ranch forty kilometers out of town, promising them a cash advance and two weeks work. "Stupid girls," Milissa said. "It didn't dawn on us until we saw there wasn't any water in the pool."

The plan had been to frighten them into submission. "Bone Face," the largest of their escorts, led them to a moldy kitchen and gave them some potatoes, promising that when they finished "peeling," he and his friends would come back and "whip" them. "And he didn't mean the spuds."

The short chase that followed ended in a field adjacent to the empty stables. Milissa and Lindsay held their ground, kitchen knives in hand, while their would-be captors debated bloodshed. When a neighboring farmer intervened, Bone Face accused the girls of stealing the knives. Playing on the irony, the farmer confiscated the knives as a reward and led his thieves to freedom.

"You have a friend who'll die for you," Morgan sighed, her moonlit face imbued with pathos verging on morbidity – reminding Milissa of the stricken Father Damien, staring from the reader board above Kalaupapa. The same precarious gaze, except with Morgan the pity was focused in.

"Well, not all that extreme," Milissa said, standing and stretching. "I doubt that we'd walk into a pit of vipers to prove our love." She bent down and looked Morgan in the eye. "You okay?"

Morgan nodded contritely, brought to heel by Milissa's light disdain.

"Good then, let's go have a drink."

She lay awake, still tipsy from her drink, the first in years, too dazed to read, feeling a mixture of pleasure and resentment from the emotional rolfing she'd received that day. For thirteen years, since losing Mazie, her only solace had been the dopamine-inducing hours of legal calculus.

She took no delight in helping her freeloading clients – the service for which she was so often praised. They were broken objects, dangerously in need of regulation. Her dominion over them, the deference she commanded, was the gauge of her own self-hate. Her way of remaining blind to this connection was catharsis – perverse abasements of her inner child that cast her back among the lepers and intensified her need to shun contamination, escapes so schizoid that they were either disassociated or simply scabbed over with shame.

As she traced back over the events of the day, she recalled the experience in the dressing room and how later, there in the hotel room, Milissa had seen her completely undressed. Her face grew hot against the pillow. She lifted herself quietly and looked. Milissa was asleep beside the still-lit reading lamp.

She'll go back and have a laugh about my beasty body with her friend Lindsay or that monkey John Mikala, she said to herself. She's really very cruel. She has a tomboy look. I wonder if she's ever had sex with Lindsay. Everybody has some kind of queer action in their lives.

She sighed inaudibly and slumped back down on her pillow, rolling on her side to keep her eyes on Milissa. With hypnotic ease, she began to imagine Lindsay and Milissa having sex. *They were following her directions. She was ordering them to stick their tongues into each other's butts and pussies. They didn't like it at first, but then it started to feel good and they began to moan each other's names.* She became wet and began to masturbate, lying very still with her thighs pressed together, working with one finger so as not to be apparent should Milissa wake.

I'll have to finish it now, she thought, or I'll be up all night. Her image shifted to *Mazie demonstrating clitoral stimulation with her legs spread and draped over the arms of a wooden chair.* This was Morgan's favorite fantasy, the one she would usually come by. Mazie had taught her to masturbate in that chair, the only decent piece of furniture in their one room house in Fuli Town. They laughingly called it the throne. Mazie had initiated her with that position. She would always get powerfully stimulated when Mazie showed her how. But this time, *Mazie let Milissa have the chair. It was an easy transition. Milissa was good. Better. More real.* Morgan gave out an uncontrollable groan as she came, turning quickly toward the wall, muttering in her throat as if she were merely disturbed by a dream.

To maintain the sense of levitation that followed her release, she kept her finger inserted snugly between her labia and imagined herself gliding above the clouds. As she fell asleep, *Milissa joined her in the air, cautioning her that if she became too self-conscious she would come down. "You can be aware that you are flying," Milissa said, "only don't look at your body at first or you'll start to doubt." She pointed through a separation. "Look down there at the people. They recognize you. They love and respect you. They know that you can fly and they can't.*

"Did you know? The more you fly, the better you get? Watch." Milissa lifted her shoulders toward her ears and shot ahead. By simply tilting her head, she was able to swoop about in any direction. "I've gotten to where I can look at myself," she said, coming back alongside, "without getting that sinking feeling. The idea is to not take yourself too seriously. But you shouldn't try it yet. Too soon." She put her hands on her chest. "See my little titties?"

Morgan looked over, embarrassed now. Milissa had no mounds, only small, plump nipples, pinched tightly between each thumb and forefinger. Morgan glanced at her own chest anxiously. Her breasts were snaking through the clouds, hauling her toward the surface like retracting cables.

"Try this," Milissa exhorted, pumping her legs in and out of Mazie's lewd wooden chair position, jacking herself three or four feet up with each thrust. "It's a good one for beginners."

As Morgan sank into the haze, she looked up and caught a final glimpse of Milissa performing her bizarre frog leaps, grinning and aiming her bottom in Morgan's direction each time she drew her legs back.

When Morgan came through into the open air on the darkened underside of the cloud cover, she saw that her breasts were connected to the ground. They were scoping slowly in as she descended.

She looked up as her feet touched. The overcast had followed her. It hung like smoke, a foot above her head. Lowering again as she lay down, it blanketed her body, smothering out the last infernal flicks of her exhausted mind.

"Rise and shine. Hit the deck."

Morgan blinked an eye, then slipped into the amniotic glow beneath her sheet.

Milissa came to attention at the side of her bed. "You've gotta get up. You've gotta get up," she sang, holding a tray of hot buttered croissants, blackberry jam, and coffee.

"What's that lovely tune?" Morgan asked facetiously, still fat with sleep inside her bay of filtered light.

Milissa whistled the remaining bars. "Revelry. You know, the Bugle Call. 'You gotta get up. You gotta get up. You gotta get up today.' I used to hear it every morning – well almost."

"Reveille," Morgan corrected, coming out of her limbo. "Your father, no doubt." She propped herself against the headboard and woke up her face with her hands. "For me it was a World War II cartoon – Bugs Bunny at Boot Camp, something like that."

"Morgan," Milissa laughed. "Cartoons? So that's what you did when you weren't studying." She put Morgan's breakfast on the side table.

Morgan was touched. "I'll try not to gush. I know it puts you off."

"No, go ahead. Let it out," Milissa expanded her arms and twirled toward the window, opening it wide and launching into an early fifties travelogue. "Today we sunbathe on the lovely strand of Waikiki, unique in all the world for its exotic splendor. Here, where the Valleys and the Crosbys courted Sweet Leilani from their luxury suites at the grand Hotel Moana, where Western opulence is couched in pure Hawaiian bliss . . ." She broke off and picked up a brochure from the coffee table. "Did you know that where we now stand there used to be a swamp? Here it is. 'Reclamation of Waikiki swampland began in 1921.' They got the sand from west end Molokai."

Morgan held up her croissant. "This," she said emphatically, "is pure Hawaiian bliss."

"Pure bliss," Milissa announced as she opened the refrigerator and took out a thermos. "Behold, the elixir. One quart pre-mixed pina colada."

"Swamp juice," Morgan declared.

"Morgan, you scoundrel. I think you have potential." Milissa looked at the container. "Waikiki swamp juice. Now, get your suit on, girl. We've gotta stake out a spot in front of the hotel so we can hear the music."

"Can't we order out and spend the day up here," Morgan wheedled, borrowing from Milissa's repertoire.

After a painful bout of coaxing, Morgan pulled herself from bed and retreated to the bathroom. Her distress, played out on the toilet, was a post-traumatic bow to Field Day, the day in middle school when everyone put on shorts and tank tops and presented themselves for athletic competition. Each year, Morgan would hide in a bathroom stall until she was found and marched into line to the snickers and pouty, puffed cheeks of her classmates, mocking her exquisite shame.

"Morgan, are you ready? I have a surprise."

A long shower later, Morgan stepped into the hall, wrapped from the neck down in a large, cherry red towel, all the more vivid by contrast to her bloodless face.

"I take it there's a swimsuit under there," Milissa remarked, sticking to the program despite Morgan's obvious anguish. "Here's some sunscreen. And here." She handed her Easy's surprise. "There's a note inside."

Morgan removed the muumuus carefully from the bag and stacked them, still neatly folded, on the coffee table. She dealt with the note in the same meticulous way, examining and reading the envelope before opening it, then setting it carefully aside and turning her attention to the message, which read: *Dear Morgan, from one big girl to another. Big is beautiful, only more to go around. Instructions: take off at shoreline and plunge self into water. Aloha, Easy.*

She put the note in the envelope and set it on the stack. "You've discussed me with this woman?"

"How do you mean? You do come up in conversation."

Morgan looked at the envelope with disdain.

"What's it say?" Milissa read the message. "What a lovely sentiment. Is there a problem?"

Morgan began to sulk.

"You do recall Linda saying Aunty could loan you a bathing suit. How is this so different?"

Morgan looked around as if the answer might be lurking in the room.

"No," Milissa went on, "as a matter of fact, I did not discuss this with Easy." Her disbelief had changed to irritation. She sat on the opposite end of the couch and leaned forward with her forearms resting on her knees and her hands clasped. "This was entirely her idea. Keoni gave the package to me when he dropped me at your house."

Morgan scooted away from the dresses, haughty with contempt for their defilement. After a dizzy silence, she saw the ire of personal insult rising in Milissa's face. Realizing that she'd forced a breach, she placed two fingers on the gift, undergoing John's contamination as a sign of her remorse. "Please," she pleaded, "do not discuss me with the others."

Milissa cooled off immediately, measuring her response. "You are a big part of my life. My mentor in the law. I am going to discuss you. It comes with the territory."

"Oh, please," Morgan continued, still clinging to the essence of her appeal. "Be kind."

"You have to trust that I will. Read the note again."

"It was a nice thing to do," Morgan conceded. "I really don't deserve it."

"Of course, you're right. Everybody knows it. They see your car already in the lot when they're on their way to work. They see your office lights on every night. They know you're up to something undeserving. Why do you think Easy gave you the muumuus?"

Morgan unfolded one of the dresses. It was patterned with the leaves and pompoms of the ohia. "Because I'm your friend," she answered, putting it on as if the discussion hadn't taken place. "It's a bit too large, would you believe."

While Milissa arranged the beach towels and set up the umbrella, Morgan sat in the sand toying with her drink, trying on a tiny pose beneath her extra large muumuu. Two Japanese girls to her left were wiggling their butts, adjusting their G strings to cover the essentials. Their boyfriends, all sleek and hairless in their purple shades and marble bags, busied themselves applying sunscreen.

"So, about your friend in the picture?"

"The only true friend I ever had," Morgan answered, masking her inflamed libido with a wholesome take on Mazie. "A very special lady."

"How about Linda and Lani?"

"Acquaintances. Mazie was my chum. We drank rice wine in the evening. I was able to share my feelings. I once saved her life." Morgan paused and watched Milissa stretch out on the towel. "But then she rejected me."

Milissa jumped up and put her hands on her hips. "Last one in's a sissy," she said, putting a cork in Morgan's pending ooze.

She pointed at Milissa. "That was Mazie. Always ready with the challenge."

"Well, on your mark then. And remember Easy's instructions."

Morgan downed her pina colada and lifted herself to a lineman's stance, knuckles in the sand like a child learning to walk. "Take it off at the shoreline and plunge in," she wheezed. "At the shoreline," she repeated, lurching forward, barely able to keep her feet as she followed her headlong motion down the slope and directly into the water.

"It was the only way," she said, remaining submerged from the neck down, suffering the kindly waves to bounce her on the sandy bottom while Milissa helped her out of the muumuu and laid it in the sun. "I never could have made the breakthrough in the open air. Impossible."

"Let's go out some," Milissa suggested. "It's shallow like at

Murphy Beach."

As Morgan paddled cautiously away, Milissa dove down, grabbed her by the ankles, then sprinted ahead, kicking up a wake to avoid retaliation. Morgan, frightened by the prank, turned back toward shore. Seeing what she'd done, Milissa swam back and went under again, hoping to play the apologetic jack-in-the-box several feet in front. But Morgan felt her slither by and pounced on her like a bear at a salmon run, then held her struggling beneath the surface.

Milissa came up sucking air. "Oh, you wanna play rough," she said, splashing weakly in Morgan's direction, taking heed of the ferocity behind her placid, paste-on smile. She doesn't know how to play, Milissa mused. No practice. Tries her hand at rough-housing and damn near drowns me. She searched around for a distraction, an excuse to call it quits without revealing her chagrin. "The band," she shouted as she headed in. "They're setting up."

Morgan tagged close behind. "Milissa," she simpered, "could you bring me my muumuu?"

"No way, tough guy." Milissa's smile was tainted with comeuppance. "You're on your own. Look there." A Samoan man was wading nearby with his wife and child. "He's twice your size. And check out his cupcake. You half again." She towelled off, slipped into her new designer T-shirt, and disappeared into the crowd on the terrace.

Morgan searched along the shore for cover. She noticed the three Samoans rejoining their extended family. The adults were obese, so bloated that they breathed habitually through their mouths, yet agile and self-contained as they frolicked with their young ones. Put to shame by their ponderous ease, she shed the sea and marched up the slope, her hands raised in surrender.

After sloshing down another drink, she put her sunglasses on and lay back in the sand. From behind closed eyes she separated out the laughter of the children. If one is very quiet on any day, she thought, one can hear that sound. The melodic prattle carried her back to the first down of pubescence, the surcease of small bliss, when her mercifully chubby body began its unwanted change.

"Oh God, how could you," she whispered aloud, *as she lay in the dark in her child's bed, listening to her mother in the other room. "I can't do it," her mother said. "She's your daughter. You're the one she favors. If I hadn't seen her come out of me, I'd swear they pulled a switch. None of my family looks or acts like that. Anyway, she'll do what you say. She'll just look at me and whine. Tell her to take a bath and put this in her panties." Morgan lay very still, dreading her father's footsteps,* phasing the memory of her mother's words into the ukulele strum that filtered through the voices on the terrace.

"Some light reading," Milissa said, throwing down a fashion magazine. Morgan didn't move. Milissa could see that she was crying. "You're letting yourself get burned." She removed Morgan's sunglasses and mopped the tears from around her eyes. "Let's try some sunscreen. A little on the forehead. And here on the bridge of the nose. And those ears. The ears always get it the worst. Now roll over."

Morgan dozed off as Milissa's small powerful hands massaged her back and shoulders. "There," she said with a pat, "you can get the rest. I'm going in." Encouraged by the kick-in of the booze, Morgan came awake resolving to return Milissa's attention. She pulled her muumuu on and stepped into her sandals. Not since her "slippers" of childhood had she felt so weightless on her feet. She walked across the terrace with an unaccustomed ease. Damn those heavy pumps, she said to herself as she entered the bar.

The bartender was all smiles and accepting of her ebullience. Morgan had embarked upon a separate act. She had become a graceful, worldly divorcé.

"I presume you like your ham on rye with Grey Poupon," he joked.

"Oh, you naughty boy," Morgan responded, not recognizing the catch-phrase.

He touched himself high in the middle of the chest as if to say, *My dear, you couldn't be referring to me,* and caught the cocktail waitress' eye. "It'll be a few minutes. Farah will get you something to drink if you like."

"Gin and tonic," Morgan replied. She had never had a gin and tonic. It just seemed like the thing to say. This was her third drink in less than an hour. By the time the sandwiches arrived, her system was humming. The bartender handed her the bag. She thanked him and walked away.

"I'm sorry," he called after her, "but even without the Poupon, you must pay."

She labored for precise enunciation. "Now, you are a nice man," she said. "Obviously not a woman hater, or I'd be the first on your list." She paused to steady her thoughts. "Pay?" She had forgotten to bring the money.

"Where are you staying?"

"The Moana. That's here, isn't it?"

"The Moana. Yes, you're in the right place. Sign the tab and put in your room number."

A helpless look told the bartender that Morgan didn't know the number.

"Sign here, dear, we'll figure it out."

Morgan wrote in a twenty dollar tip and signed.

"Thank you, Mrs. . . ." He looked at the signature.

"Morgan," she replied, dropping her disguise.

"Morgan," he said with genuine recognition. "Call me Barney. Would you believe it? A handsome guy like me with a name like Barney."

Morgan touched her nose, pointed at Barney, and winked. "Thanks, Barney. That's a nice name. Better than Harry or Hank. Know what I mean?"

Barney gave her a knowing nod, though he didn't really know, and excused himself to tend to another customer.

Milissa was snoozing under the umbrella when Morgan got back. She woke to the harrumph of Morgan landing beside her. Morgan was attempting to remove a sandwich, mauling the bag while mumbling about her conversation with "a male type called Barney."

Milissa took the bag and offered her the ham on rye. She fanned it away with a pucky grimace and waddled into the water.

Milissa watched her slop about – flopping back spread eagle and capturing air beneath her muumuu, then coming aright and squatting down to create a hilarious bust-on-a-tuffet effect.

When she tired, Milissa helped her out of her dress and led her to their room. There she slept a dreamless sleep, rising only at Milissa's insistence that she not miss the sunset.

"Feeling any better?" Milissa asked, fresh from the shower. "You must be rested. Sit there. I'll be right with you."

Morgan assumed a tidy posture in front of the vanity. "I'm not used to the alcohol. Still a bit woozy. Hungry."

"Good," said Milissa, pulling on a modest knee-length frock. "I've made reservations downstairs. And after, there's this amazing place Linda told me about.

"Now, don't blink," Milissa ordered, applying a touch of mascara to Morgan's eyes. "This will complement your outfit."

"I did make a fool of myself, didn't I?"

"If you did, nobody noticed but you. Well, maybe me, but that doesn't count. Don't freeze up on me now. We've got a full night ahead."

"I'll need your help tomorrow. I'm going to buy some more new things."

"Clothes are expensive in Waikiki."

"I can afford it. I've been frugal all my life." Morgan tried out her lashes in the mirror. "I want to look nice for my special friend, Milissa."

"Well, I should say. And for your special friends back home."

The Tahitian Lanai stood at the end of a torch-lit lane lined with tiny bamboo bungalows. As Milissa and Morgan entered the approach, they heard the waft of distant chanting, choral gusts reminiscent of a Berlin beer hall or a Baptist church down some Saturday night, dead end road in rural Alabama. But soon they recognized the assertive huffs of Polynesian glottal stops. And once inside the open-air saloon, they were over-awed by a packed house of mostly tourists, all singing in Hawaiian.

A large electrified pump organ, replete with rows of levers and switches, was at the center of the room. A small, diligent man in a black suit and no tie sat behind the console, looming his music in solitude while self-ordained song leaders, regulars at the bar, moved among the tables, tutoring the novices for beer and tips.

The most conspicuous of these conductors, because of his size and haole cast, was Jense Hoiness, a big, barrel-chested Scandinavian, waving a mug above his shaven head, showing off his gold incisor with each enunciation, constantly scanning the crowd for marks. As soon as she joined the row of faces at the bar, Morgan's fey expression caught his eye. Middle aged, ample build, looking vulnerable, he said to himself. She needs me.

Encouraged by Milissa, Morgan, who was already conversant in Hawaiian, indulged the big man's flattery with keen participation in the lyrics. He stayed several feet away at first so as not to abandon his following. But he returned again and again to his objective, giving Morgan reassuring looks and gradually shifting his neophytes around to face him in her direction.

No sooner had he arrived at her side than she turned away to coach Milissa. He commandeered the stool next to her and draped his arm across her stocky shoulders. More out of plight than participation, she put her arm around Milissa. Milissa laughed and hauled her in.

The three began to sway, and as their circle closed, the audience lost interest. One glance from the proprietor at Jense's nearly empty mug prompted him to disengage. "She's an expert already," he bellowed to Milissa over the music. "You follow her. Boss wants me to mingle." He strode away, a parody of the student prince, lifting his mug and leaning in – the better to display his tooth.

Morgan looked at Milissa for her impression.

"A character."

"A bully," commented the guy who'd had his stool jerked from under him. "He outta be put away."

Neither Milissa nor Morgan knew what the man was talking about, only that he was angry, which was enough for them to move away.

Jense came up to Morgan at the break. "You know Hawaiian, yah? You're quick, but not dat quick."

She nodded demurely.

He grinned. "Where you from?"

"We're from Molokai," she answered, bringing Milissa into the conversation.

"Molokai." Jense offered his hand. "I'm Molokai. Jense Hoiness.

I own a house up Maunaloa."

Morgan turned to Milissa to avoid Jense's touch.

Milissa shook his hand. "Milissa Dogherty. This is Morgan Zarins. You bought one of the new places?"

"No way," he bombasted, looking around for attention. "I own one a da old plantation houses on da north side. Used to live up dere with my sweetie pie."

Milissa eyed him with subtle scepticism.

"Till she left me for some rich guy," he added, aiming a wink at Morgan.

"I thought that property was all Stockmans'," Milissa said.

"Not this place. I got the lot and house for life estate. Got it in writing. You ever been up dere, you can see it from da main drag. My nephew and his mother stay dere now. Gunner and Hilda. Ever hear of dem?"

"Stockmans is redeveloping. The way I got it, they're tearing everything down."

"I heard dat too. Sent 'em a letter to keep deir hands off."

"How'd you come to own the place?"

The organ began to play.

"When you folks going back?" Jense asked Morgan.

Morgan looked at Milissa.

"Tomorrow," Milissa answered.

"I was planning a trip over next week to check things out." His comments were directed at Morgan. "Maybe we'll run into each other." He gave her shoulder a squeeze. "Gotta get a beer before dey start. Throat's dry."

Morgan's eyes followed him to the end of the bar. He looked back and slammed her with another wink, then grabbed up his refill and walked into the crowd, mouthing the words to a song.

The songs and chants, interspersed with inspired solo renditions of English and Hawaiian standards, continued unabated. By the time the inevitable *Danny Boy* had come and gone, Milissa and Morgan had found a table in the darkened restaurant section from which they could observe unnoticed. Eventually, the crowd thinned out and a chorus of regulars coalesced around the organ.

"You asked about Mazie," Morgan said, finally able to hear herself speak. "I've really never discussed her with anyone."

Milissa responded with the merest of receptive looks. After her vicious dunking that afternoon, she was leery of a deeper confidence. But she had this coming. Her constant drilling of Morgan up to then compelled her to abide.

"You remind me so much of Mazie. Your bodies, not your faces. You saw her picture in my room." Morgan's eyes glossed. "Dear Mazie," she sighed. "She was very homely. But she was an angel."

"Your angel," Milissa replied, pressing Morgan to own the relationship and not inject it into their own.

"My angel," Morgan agreed. "But I was saying how much you two are alike. You don't want to hear about that."

"Oh, I think I can take it. Sometimes I blurt things out to keep the conversation honest. Mazie was your angel. You were in love with her."

Morgan gaped half-smiling and propped her forearms on the table. "That was Mazie. She would just say things that were true. She wasn't tactful, but she knew how to keep things in the open. She was like a chiropractor. She'd catch you relaxed and snap things into place. And always after she would say, 'There, mate. Better now, eh?'

"Did I tell you?" Morgan went on, feeling the imprint of Mazie's remark as if she were in the room. "We lived in Fuli Town. In China by the river Li."

Milissa nodded. "You mentioned China."

"It was before Deng Xiaoping died. People were still wearing those pajama outfits. We lived in a one room, cinder block house. It had a water pump outside the front door and an outhouse in back. Actually, a bamboo blind in front of a hole in the ground.

"She never let up. Helping me discover who I was, she'd tell me." Morgan's face registered the bittersweet memory of her struggles with Mazie.

"Who were you?"

"Then?" Morgan put her hand over her mouth to hide her embarrassment.

"It's alright, Morgan," Milissa said emphatically. "We all have feelings."

Morgan gave Milissa an eerie, injured look, as if Milissa somehow knew and was deriding her with Mazie's sentiment. Milissa reached out to console her. She brushed her hand away.

"No," she said, "as much as I like your touch, it won't help." She didn't want to be treated like a victim. In this she was sincere – that was her mistake with Mazie – but she was also working Milissa, trying to tie her in by coming clean.

"I'm right here," Milissa reassured.

"At first we were pure pals. We did everything together. Cooked. Washed dishes. We bathed together in the front yard. We'd hang a blanket up in front of the pump, get sudsed up, and pour water over each other. We slept in the same bed. It was either that, or one of us on the floor.

"I remember my first night there. She'd been there six months already – it was her place. I started to make a bed on the floor and she insisted that I sleep with her." Morgan laughed inside her grief. "I spent several nights fully clothed on top of the blankets.

"She was the dominant one. But that was alright with me. I'd held my own in law school. This was to be my six months' hiatus before beginning practice. I was exhausted with competing. Besides, it never was my forte. And here was this spunky little sprite who was all over me when it came to real world know-how. She was like you. She had a courageous heart and she knew how to handle people. She certainly knew how to handle me."

Morgan turned her head from side to side, nodding in the specters of her tale. Her face darkened as she pressed her fingers to her temples. "And when she finished playing with me, she left me somewhere. I'm not sure where. She just forgot to take me home." Her fist hit the table with frightening force. The few remaining patrons stopped singing for an instant and looked in her direction. Milissa looked back, relieved to see that Jense was not around.

Morgan put her head on the table, weeping. "We got . . ." She peeked up in a contorted appeal to Milissa's understanding. "You know . . ." Her whining was out of control. "Involved."

"I know," Milissa said. But how could I know, she thought, feeling inadequate in the presence of such pain.

After a long tortured while, Morgan continued, sapped of emotion. "We said goodbye at Guilin Station. She was flying out of Canton. I was flying out of Beijing. We promised to write and planned to see each other. We exchanged one letter. I talked to her by phone about a month after I got back. She seemed distant. I never heard from her again. I wrote two more letters and called. Her phone had been disconnected with no forwarding number. After that, I threw myself into my work and closed myself off from the world like before.

"When I think back on the evenings in that house, especially near the end . . ." A little crazed and having nothing more to hide, Morgan decided to flaunt her self-disgust, maybe to test Milissa's tolerance, maybe to ascertain her appetite. "She'd do a few things to get me going and then she'd start manipulating me. Putting things in me. Making me take positions."

"Making you?" Milissa reacted, disguising her disgust with incredulity.

Morgan uttered a crude, mocking laugh. "You can see it, can't you? I know you can. Not so bad with a couple of cuties, but little Mazie and me?" She entwined her fingers, thumbs erect. "This can be our secret."

This was the part that gave Milissa pause – allowing herself to be entrapped in Morgan's remake. "This isn't you and me against the world," she protested. "We're not stuck in God-forsaken China. And I'm not Mazie!"

"Those bikinis," Morgan bedeviled, "can we look at them again?"

"Did you hear me?" Milissa insisted. "Damn! You're always somewhere else."

Morgan brought her face in close, treasuring Milissa's tiff.

Milissa quieted her breath. She'd been so taken back by Morgan's imagery that she'd missed their reversal of roles. She pressed her away to arm's length and held her there. "You caught me looking," she admitted, smiling and shaking her head. "Pretty slick."

CHAPTER THIRTEEN

After John dropped Milissa off at Morgan's place with Easy's gift of muumuus, he drove directly to the airport where he and Fidel met PBS reporter, Michael Teague. To avoid alerting Stockmans, Fidel had booked Michael and his cameraman, Smitty, out of Oahu on a commercial airliner, but arranged for their equipment to be shuttled over separately and delivered in an ordinary shipping crate. Given these precautions, one can understand John's empty stare when he passed Milissa on the access road as she was leaving for Waikiki. Hailing one another in the midst of Fidel's stealth could only have been seen as flaunting their friendship, a budding source of resentment on both sides of the battle line.

Michael and Smitty were taken first to visit Hiroyuki Nishimoto, a one time trucker for Dole who'd been scraping out a living as a blacksmith since they left. Stockmans was his major source of business, but their subdivision cut the other way. His income was sixteen thousand a year, little more than enough to support his wife and son and keep his equipment in repair. The higher rent would be beyond his means and he, like all the rest, was hard pressed to find affordable housing.

"We'll get by," he said, leaning stoically against the fender of his Chevy pick-up. "Maybe not here, but we'll stay on island. Couple years, my son'll be pitching in." Smitty panned to his right. Scrolled neatly across the driver's side door in English, Japanese, and Ilocano script were the words *Hiro's Horseshoes, Heart of Maunaloa.*

Hiro's parents had lost their California fruit farm during the Japanese internment. After the war they moved to Maunaloa, where they rose quickly through the ranks to middle management. Twenty five years later, his widowed father, heeding insider reports that Dole was shutting down, passed the postal worker's exam and found a job in Honolulu.

"Sorry you didn't go with him?"

"Not a question of sorry. I made my bed wit' Dole, driving truck and shoeing horses. Was banking I'd get transferred to Lanai. Dis here's my consolation." He patted his prize possession on the hood. "Dis and my tools. Dey sold it all to me for seven fifty and tax. Da last man dey let go.

"Besides, dis Maunaloa is my home. Keoni left for a while in da seventies." Hiro signed the shaka to John, who was standing off camera. "Hang 'round here long as me, you see all da young bucks back on da rock. How you, Keoni?"

"Hokay, Uncle," John replied.

"Keoni used to steal da company hand plows for make race carts."

John laughed. "Wheelbarrels, Uncle. Was you who'd look da other way."

"Come, Keoni," Hiro smiled, luring John into camera range. "Brah," he continued, taking a tight grip on the back of John's belt, "you remember dat gift you put by da super's door?"

John tugged to the side, eyes lit up and mouth agape, laughing at the end of Hiro's tether, betraying his complicity in the fabled case of the laxative brownies.

Hiro gripped his hood ornament with his free hand. "What you put in doze brownies, brah?" he asked, then let John fall away. "Guess

Keoni no like talk story on TV.

"Was mostly work for me back den," Hiro went on, erasing the glee from his face. "Made my first side money wit' da horseshoes. Afternoons, I'd volunteer at da company stables, picking up pointers from da livery man. He quit da operation early on. Doze in da know resigned a year or two in front. So I stepped in. By da time da plantation shut down, I had customers. Just a few, but Farley Chisolm took me on. Now I'm hitched up wit' Stockmans. You seen my place?"

"You work for Stockmans?"

"No work for dem. I get one contract. I do deir horses. Dey give me a space in deir warehouse and piece work – so much a trim, so much a shoe, like dat."

"Are you with those who think that Stockmans is wrong for putting people out?"

"Not a question of who's wrong. It's a natural disaster. How dey do it, dat's another t'ing."

"Not what they do, but how they do it."

Smitty filled the frame with Hiro's face.

"It's da haole management. Dey weak. Full of guilt. Dey work up people's hope, den do a switch. Don't wanna be seen as bad, cannot be good. It's a sickness."

"How would you do it differently?"

"Would have said what it was and stuck by it, den go 'round quietly assisting people who need help. Much better."

"What's your viewpoint on the demise of pineapple?"

"Da union went push too hard."

"The company is absolved?"

"Did I say dat? Was good dey had a lot of people working. But den dey snuck away. Well, not snuck. Just kinda walked out backwards. Covering deir ass. It's da haole t'ing. A sickness."

"What are your immediate plans?"

"To wait for my eviction, den find another place." Hiro could see the end in Michael's eyes. "Now I have a question."

Smitty pulled back to include Michael in the shot.

"You here to make trouble? What's your movie about?"

"People being evicted. We're documenting the effect of major financial decisions like the demolition of this town. Our format is historic. We start with The Enclosure Acts and move forward."

"How about we document a minor financial decision."

"What would that be?"

"How much you pay me for being in your show?"

"Before using this footage, we'll need a signed release. We'll talk compensation then."

Hiro craned into the camera lens. "You get dat part, Smitty?"

The walls were draped with tapestries, interspersed with dried leis, wreaths, dream catchers, and posters of the historic avant garde. Wallpapered to the ceiling were giant prints of Dali's *Don Quixote* and Van Gogh's *Starry Night.*

"Stan liberated that from X's wrecking ball," Cory remarked as Michael caressed the surface of her large, solid oak dining room table.

"Original Victorian," Michael observed, gesturing for Smitty to focus in. "Must have been shipped over."

"The rest," Cory went on, pointing out the futon, the handmade spring-rocker made from motorcycle shocks, and the giant hooka in the corner, "we call it Nouveau Haight."

Michael began his questioning with an unwitting probe, unaware of its double meaning. "Fidel tells me you had an arrangement with Mr. Spitz."

"Hardly an arrangement." Cory walked off camera, adjusted a dream catcher, and stood back to check its alignment. "A promise to establish a historic district and an extension of our college."

Cory explained her negotiation with X, putting the onus on him for its collapse, and leaving out their touch with intimacy. "I was referred to X by his wife, a benefactor of the college, so we started out on good terms. We met, I'd say, seven times and developed a prospectus. He let me believe it was being cleared with his boss. Stan got his call. He called here in the middle of a work day so he wouldn't have to tell me in person. I'd already done considerable organizing, gearing up for an opening event. Lost a lot of credit with the locals."

"You've mentioned Stan."

She focused an eye on Michael as a sign of caution. "My mistake."

"He lives here?"

"Might as well be." She cast her voice toward the kitchen and added, "He eats all my food."

"Tell 'em I'm disabled," Stan shot back. "All broke down by years of sloth since I expatriated from the mainland. Or was I extirpated? Anyway," his voice trailed off, "I got the hell out."

Smitty moved to the kitchen entrance. "Sounds like you were expiated," he intoned as Stan mugged for the camera. "What're you watching?"

"A children's show," Stan answered, returning to the TV screen. "What're you watching?"

"Smith!" Michael scolded.

Smitty drew back into the living room. "Just trying to liven things up. I'll erase it."

"Erase the whole thing. Back to where she mentions you-know-who."

"Bet you guys are hungry," Cory said, already on her way to the kitchen. "At least bring out the God damn sandwiches," she whispered to Stan. "I'll get the coffee."

As she carried the coffee to the table, Michael signaled Smitty to restart. "Cory, we know you're disappointed, but it appears that Stockmans has made adjustments to accommodate the remaining tenants." He glanced at his notes. "Inexpensive new rentals. South side houses priced to fit low interest loans. How would you rate their present undertaking?"

"As an undertaking," Stan inserted, setting the sandwiches on the table. "Code for 'burial'."

"Maunaloans have bad credit and no credit," Cory said in reply to Michael's question. "It's cruel for Stockmans to call these accommodations. It's not that they don't know. They're weeding these people out. That's the tacit plan. Fidel's got the right idea. We have to save the town."

She turned toward the camera, bent on rehabilitating herself in the image of a risen Maunaloa. “Make it a national historic site. There’s nothing more American than Maunaloa. We’re a land of immigrants. For seventy years this town has been a gateway to the promised land. Pay for the renovation with federal funds. Compared to all the millions that the government is wasting, how much could it be? Employ the tenants as helpers, apprentices, carpenters, and landscapers.

“Stockmans is gonna build a museum.” Cory shook her head as if the idea were clawing at the underside of her brain. “They’re gonna remove the present from its spiritual mooring and display it in a museum. You can’t preserve a culture in a museum any more than you can an animal in a zoo. Have you seen the old equipment in the storage sheds?”

Michael shook his head.

“Each piece customized. Each machete honed concave to fit the wield of the guy who used it. Each plow with its grips worn down and its beam initialed by the same hands. If these instruments could speak” – Cory looked straight into the lens, daring incredulity – “they’d ask to be given to the children of the people they served.” She turned back to Michael. “Ideally, if they were displayed at all, it would be at the families’ discretion, on their walls or in special locations around their homes.

“You know what a row Native Americans on the mainland make about their campgrounds and burial sites being ransacked by developers? This is no different. It’s exactly the same. I’ve got someone you have to meet. Let’s take a walk. Smitty, keep that thing rolling.”

Michael nodded his assent and followed Cory into the front yard. It had grown dark. The light on Smitty’s camera lit up the rutted alley leading to the house next door.

“Mannie,” Cory called out in a husky whisper as she rang the rusted bell on his gate.

A yellow bulb, drowned in the illumination of the camera, came on above the door. “Dat you, Adler?” a thin voice replied. “Turn off da fucking light.”

Smitty complied and a tiny man crept out onto the dim-lit porch.

"Who you wit'?" he asked, holding his cane up in defense, his intense eyes scanning the darkness.

"Our friends from the mainland."

"Come," he said, turning around with small robotic steps and shuffling back inside. "TV, TV," he peeped as he glanced back at the camera following him into the house. "Tutu been discovered, ya? Maybe we sign one contract."

Cory bowed slightly. "Mannie, we like see kupuna wahine."

Mannie held his hands in prayer. "Tutu one big star now, ya?"

Michael tipped his head, modeling himself after Cory's obeisance.

"Kahuna nui," Mannie said, identifying Michael as the expert, "come." He gripped him by the arm, pulled him through the kitchen into the unlit back yard, and dragged him down with unexpected force.

Not until he reached his knees did Michael see the white rectangle lying flush with the ground. He looked closer. "A gravestone," he said with astonishment. "Smitty."

Mannie reached back and whacked Cory on the shin with his cane to clear the way. Smitty's camera lit up the marble stone. Michael read aloud, "Tutu Api Pualani, died 1929. Moe . . ."

"Moe'uhane me Akua," said Mannie, "Sleep wit' God."

"This'll put a fucking crimp in their action," Cory snarled, still smarting from the whack.

Michael motioned for Cory to step back so that Mannie didn't feel upstaged.

A rosy gasp of pride permeated Mannie's parchment-thin skin as he sat in the eye of the camera, reeling in the past, his hand on Tutu's grave. He had cowboyed in the early years, from age fifteen until Libby came in 1923. For the next forty years he worked the pineapple, managing always to stay above the mud because of his skill with horses and machinery.

Tutu Pualani had brought Mannie up. His parents, a Portuguese laborer and a Hawaiian girl of sixteen, had died in the bubonic plague epidemic on Oahu in 1899.

At the time of her death, most people were aware that Tutu had been buried in the back yard. Eyebrows were raised higher up the mountain, but the solemnity of her passing muffled any serious protest. Though Mannie continued to tend it as a private shrine, general knowledge of Tutu's grave died out as those who could remember passed away. At ninety eight, Mannie knew he didn't have long, so he decided, with Cory's encouragement, to make the grave's existence public while preservation of Maunaloa's history was still an issue.

"Where will you go if you have to move?" Michael asked as they returned to the kitchen.

Mannie nodded back into the darkness.

CHAPTER FOURTEEN

Sunday morning was redemption in Maunaloa. Houses spilled into church yards, church yards into pews. The duty to atone, once coerced by threats of firing and worse, had become the right to yield, a respite from the spirit of disobedience that found itself miraculously renewed each Sunday afternoon, setting the pace for the week to come.

No interviews today, thought Michael as he looked out the window, listening to John's description of the small pilgrimage that was about to unfold.

"How best to capture the event? Is there a hill or a silo, some way to get an overview?"

"Da warehouse." John pointed across the clearing in front of his house to the long, tin-roofed equipment barn on the other side of Maunaloa Road. "South end is Stockmans. Other end is Hiro's Horseshoes. Can reach da roof t'rough Hiro's office."

Michael checked his watch as he put it on. "Church is at what?"

"Ten."

"Half hour. How do we get in?"

"I'll get da key. Meet you over dere, 'round back."

Hiro was reluctant. "I no own da God damn warehouse," he said, crossing himself.

"Dis for us, Uncle," John complained. "You gonna make me break in?"

Hiro pecked John on the chest. "You no bring my name in dis, I no bring you up for trespass. And be God damn careful you don't get caught. Now go away before I change my mind." He brought his arms straight down to his sides, fists clenched. "Now see what," he groused, crossing himself again as John leapt off the porch and ran for the warehouse, "you make me cuss on Sunday." He waited for John to stop and turn around.

"Uncle," John yelled back, "how I'm getting in?"

He strained to keep his voice down. "T'rough da window," he said, demonstrating with his hands.

By the time they reached the roof, the movement had begun. Off to their left, a small convoy of faithful were departing east on the Kam, heading for Church Row halfway down the island. Below them, a swarm of unwary children scrambled ahead of their watchful guardians. Hundreds more, caught up in the retreat, began to fill the narrow byways leading to the Christ Anointed service in the school cafeteria and Saint Vincent's on the other side of town.

"In da old times," John said for the benefit of the mike, "dis was a must. No church on Sunday, no work on Monday. Mama used to say, 'Father William worry you no come to mass. He t'ink you need t'ank Jesus for da kine job.' And Papa'd shoot back how Father was da company soul man."

A light blue van pulled off the road across from the grassy slope. Out stepped Kini Aka. She cupped her hands to be heard. "Excuse me, has Mr. X given you permission to be up there?"

"Hello, Kini," John shouted back. "X's secretary," he told Michael from behind his smile.

Keeping eye contact with John and company, Kini punched a

number into her phone and began to talk.

"No," John answered, loud again. "Just showing off da town to my Seattle friends."

"Think we'd better skedaddle," Michael said, backing through the hatch.

Smitty noticed a van like Kini's racing toward the warehouse. Behind it was a sheriff's car. He continued to shoot, ignoring John and Michael, who had left the roof.

Michael popped his head out of the hatch. "You coming, Smith?"

"We're already had." Smitty trained his lens on the approaching vehicles. "Might as well see what I can get. You go down and schmooze 'em."

John and Michael were received into the hands of the law as they wriggled, feet first, out through the tiny double-sashed window of Hiro's office at the back of the warehouse.

"You boys're under arrest," said the shamefully heavy sheriff, Norman Nakayama, still huffing from his walk up the slope. "Hands on da wall."

X stepped by John and looked into the window. "There were three. One missing."

"What's the big radical up to today?" asked Nakayama's deputy, a wiry little redhead named Rufus McKee, taking obvious pleasure in patting down and cuffing the two men.

"Keeping tabs on rednecks," John replied, flinching as Rufus grazed his testicles. "Hey! Cool it on the extracurriculars, Ruf. What, you got no home life?"

X checked the padlock on Hiro's door. "Rufus, get the key."

"I'll go in and get him," Rufus said, moving toward the open window.

"Get Hiro," Nakayama ordered. "We got no warrant. He's at Saint Vincent's."

"And you are?" X asked Michael.

"Michael Teague, PBS News, Seattle."

"Teague. Cute little name. Kinda artsy. Well, Mr. Teague, I should thank you. I was looking for a reason to run this guy out of town." X refused to look at John. "Too bad he didn't invite the rest of his low-life friends to climb up there with you."

"Friends? Who might that be?" Michael asked.

"Half of Maunaloa," Nakayama cracked, looking at X for approval.

Michael recalled Cory's words. "The tacit plan," he remarked for John's benefit.

"No plan," X replied. "Call it a windfall. What is this, Norman? Burglary?"

"Depends on deir intent. Maybe dey crossed state lines to foment riot, somet'ing like dat."

A few voice lessons and this guy'd fit right into Macon County, Michael said to himself.

Nakayama looked up and put his hand on his gun. "Get back wit' dat!" he shouted to Smitty, who'd been hanging over the eaves, recording their careless remarks. "Mo' bettah you come down before I send my boys up dere and t'row you off."

After disappearing through the hatch, Smitty tightrope walked the back partition of Hiro's ceilingless cubicle and swung out from a brace attached to the underside of the warehouse roof, stashing his videotape on top of a central beam. As he was about this perilous work, he heard X calling out Hiro's name.

Hiro yelled to John as he approached, "Keoni, what you do wit' da key?"

"Went lose it, Uncle," John replied. "No like wake you up last night. Deze guys so tired, I put 'em t'rough da window."

"You in your forties and still one bad boy. One second story man. Why you not in church dis morning?" Hiro turned apologetically to X. "Sorry, Mr. X, I gave dem da key to sleep in my shop. Not too smart, ya?" He glowered at John, keeping up the pretense but livid nonetheless. "My man Rufus say you on da roof. What you doing on da roof, Keoni?"

"Michael wanted a shot of Sunday morning Maunaloa, all da people going to church."

"No harm done," Hiro said to X, then nailed John with another frown. "Why you no say you going up da roof?"

"Creative spontaneity?" John asked Michael.

"No intent," Michael added, agreeing with John.

"Looks like creative spontaneity got your ass in one sling," Hiro came back.

"Creative bullshit," X glared. "These guys have expense accounts. They don't have to sleep in your dingy cell. Open the God damn door. There's another guy inside."

"Extra key's at home."

X retrieved a crowbar from the warehouse tool rack and handed it to Rufus. "I figured I'd find you guys out here this morning."

"Not out for da services?" Keoni jibed.

X ignored John, but eyed Michael, trying to size him up. Not sure how much he should offend. "We heard that you were in town. Didn't expect to find you on our roof."

Rufus snapped the lock and out walked Smitty, shooting on a new cassette. "You should have asked," he said, aiming the camera at X. "I would have come through the window."

Nakayama put his hand over the lens and removed the camera from Smitty's shoulder. "Rufus, take dis to da station."

Rufus grabbed it like a stevedore and trudged off toward his car.

"By the handle," Smitty growled. "That's forty thousand bucks. You bust it, you'll answer to me."

Rufus turned and scowled, beet red from one too many commands.

"Ruf," said Nakayama, "use the grip."

"Why are you detaining us?" Michael asked.

Nakayama looked at X. "Can ticket 'em for trespass."

"Where trespass?" John objected. "Uncle gave us permission to enter."

"Trespass on da roof?" Nakayama asked X.

"You gonna arrest me if I go on da roof?" Hiro put in, testing Nakayama's resolve.

"Naw, Hiro," Nakayama replied, dismissing the suggestion as if it were an insult.

"So my friends on da roof. Dat must be alright too, ya?"

"Let 'em go, Norman," X said begrudgingly.

"We're not going anywhere," Smitty said. "Not till I get my camera back."

"Take 'em to the station, give 'em their camera, and follow 'em out of town," X ordered.

"No stations," Smitty persisted. "Just give me my property and I'll leave."

Nakayama unsnapped his holster and stepped forward. "Young man, you coming wit' me."

Smitty held up his hands. "Am I under arrest?"

Nakayama looked at the ground, and then at X.

"Take the Harvard grad," X said, hoping that Michael would go peaceably.

"You're welcome to equal time," Michael offered while he and John were being uncuffed.

"I think not," X replied. "You appear to have a bias." As he followed Michael and the sheriff around the corner of the warehouse, Milissa came to mind. "Wait," he shouted, catching up. "Here's my card. Give me a call."

He thought for a moment after reaching his van, then telephoned the station and got Rufus on the line. "Rufus," he said, "unfortunate about the coffee you spilled on that video cassette. . . . The one we took into evidence. . . . Oh, that hasn't happened yet. . . . Uh huh."

While X was on his phone and Hiro was haranguing John, Smitty slipped back into the warehouse and retrieved the stashed cassette. A few minutes later, Michael returned with the camera and a pained expression. "The runt spilled coffee on our footage."

"Their mistake," Smitty smiled, handing Michael the real tape.

That afternoon, Milissa, just home from Waikiki, joined John and Maria for a swim at Make Horse. This time of year the surf on the west end came not in sets, but one breaker at a time, each wave containing its energy until it neared the shore, then slamming from a ten to twelve foot elevation directly into the steep, sandy incline.

Milissa followed John into the water. They let the back-tow pull them out beyond the single mighty slammer, far enough so they could rise with its cresting and set down gently as it toppled, crashing only a few yards from them onto shore. As Milissa watched, lifting and returning safely behind each crucial swell, John did acrobatics in their glossy, pent up apogees.

After several somersaults, he rode in on the tail of the last wave by and chased Maria up the bank. Catching her, he snatched her up and held her by the arms against the drag of the powerful, knee-deep flux. Each time the torrent returned she'd squeal with terrified glee. "Daddy," she'd cry, "no let go." And then, hugging him desperately around the neck, "Do more, Daddy. Do more."

"Do it to me, Daddy," Milissa dared.

"He not your daddy," Maria protested, squeezing him possessively.

Milissa embraced them both. "No, of course not."

She kissed Maria on the cheek just as another wave broke. John, who was nuzzling Maria too, but facing out, saw the thing belatedly. He took several backward strides, drawing Milissa with him far enough up the slope that, though the back tow knocked them off their feet, it left them sprawled above the edge of the roiling surf.

"Was that close?" Milissa asked in earnest.

"Not really," John answered, popping Maria into his lap. "Even if it pulls us in, dere's plenty time to get away before the next one. If we gotta fish around for keiki, den t'ings get tough."

"You kids having fun?"

John looked back in surprise. "Fidel," he said, scooping up Maria to avoid the next wave.

Fidel's boots sank into the sand as he approached. He was looking at Milissa.

"Fidel Monzón, dis Milissa Dogherty."

"Loka saw your truck parked up above," Fidel told John, shaking Milissa's hand and pulling her unexpectedly to her feet. "The Keiki," he observed. "I've heard a lot about you. I wish you had contacted me before Xavier."

"Loka?" Milissa asked. "The Hawaiian guru?"

"The kind," Fidel answered facetiously.

"Loka and Fidel are partners," John put in.

Fidel smiled, taking exception.

"My mistake," John ribbed. "Fidel is Loka's bwana."

Milissa looked puzzled. "Molokai Tour and Travel Service?"

"Small time," Fidel replied. "He drives. I provide the vehicle."

"You know Sea?"

"Sea the Sikh. Loka's pet project. I only met him once. I smell him every time I step inside the van."

"Strange guy," she observed.

"Aren't we all," Fidel shot back sarcastically, aiming his response at John. "Can we talk?"

"About dis morning?" John asked.

"Yes. Privately."

"Is it safe for Maria over at the tide pools?" Milissa asked.

"No problem. But keep her in da shallows, away from da swimming hole."

"Maria," Milissa shouted, "you wait."

"Da little fishies. Da little fishies," Maria yelled, already halfway there.

Fidel trudged off the other way, then stopped and faced the ocean, arms and legs bowed doggedly as if prepared to grapple with the surf. "I hear you got my guys kicked out of town."

John walked ahead a little. "I'd say we got a lot accomplished."

Used to intimidating people with his brawn, Fidel faced off in John's direction. John steadied himself, ready to either jump back or put one on the big man's nose.

"I," Fidel began, thumping himself on the chest with a punishing thumb, "have put immense time and money into this project. I'm not going to let some weekend radical fuck it up."

John looked over Fidel's shoulder toward the tide pools. "Not gonna let," he responded, remaining aloof as he contemplated his next move, burning inside at Fidel's contempt. "Sound's like you warning me. We supposed to have a conversation now?"

"Accomplished what?" Fidel snapped.

"Da kine footage, for one t'ing." John offered. "Have you seen it?"

"Da kine footage," Fidel groaned, scouring John's pidgin with disdain. "Don't tell me. You were the moderator."

John spoke softly, thickening his pidgin out of spite, requiring Fidel to listen carefully in order to hear him over the wind. "Da kine committee no choke wit' da local kine people, brah. Mo' bettah you no get so huhu wit' Keoni boy like dat. I bag out, you be pau!"

Of course, John was right about his value to Fidel. Without the Hawaiian in his inner circle, Fidel might well be pau – finished. He laid his meaty hand against his heart and looked at the sand in a gesture of self-control. "We're supposed to be allies, Keoni. I left the situation in your hands and now I hear the worst has come about. I deserve an explanation. Man to man."

"You talked wit' Michael yet?"

"You're the one to answer, not Michael."

John stepped around Fidel to rejoin Milissa. "Talk to Michael."

The tension in Fidel's body was palpable. He continued to stare at the sand. "I see you're in bed with the enemy."

"Me?" John said, still close behind Fidel. "You just da kine. All tucked in wit' da locals, but scared to fall asleep."

After a moment of tense silence, Fidel peeked back to find that he was alone.

Milissa had looked across the beach several times to where the two men were talking. She could tell by their postures and the careful distance kept between them that there was hostility. She watched as John came toward her, his hands stuffed into the pockets of his knee-length trunks, his arms tucked against his sides as if he'd been caught in the rain.

He picked Maria up and held her close. "How's my li'i keiki?" he said in a sweet, sad tone.

"Bonheur triste?" Milissa asked.

John looked at her quizzically.

"You sound both sad and happy."

He thought for a moment, looking at Maria. "Kaumaha hau'oli," he replied, translating the concept into Hawaiian. "Happy she so bright and beautiful. Little bit sad . . ." – he showed a small space between his thumb and forefinger – "because . . ." He looked at Milissa and shook his head, unwilling, in Maria's presence, to explain life's taint.

"Looked like you were having a problem over there."

John put Maria down. "He's only power tripping like the rest of us. Pissed about a run-in we had dis morning wit' X."

Milissa raised her eyebrows and nodded. "X left a message on my phone."

"One swell head," John remarked, looking up the beach to where he'd left Fidel.

"X? I suppose. Never got him angry."

"Him too," John replied. "Dey both the same."

"Fidel?" Milissa thought, then nodded matter-of-factly. "Not an easy read. When he lifted me off the sand as we were shaking hands, the ungradual force of the lift, not malicious just uncaring – like he was propping up a leg of lamb. I'm surprised to hear that Loka and he are friends."

"Not friends really. Fidel's never close wit' anyone. He exploits t'ings he has in common wit' people. Wit' us it's Maunaloa. He gets over wit' his money."

"With Loka?"

"Dey both utopians, I guess. He lets Loka run his spiel in da van."

"Loka knows his stuff," Milissa replied, a little defensive for her traveling companion. "We all have a touch of the blarney. And he seems to have a knack for seeing."

"So dey say." John was not impressed. Prescience wasn't his thing. He sat down beside her. "You like stay my place tonight? I mean . . . we don't have to do da ho'oipo." He put his arm around her and gave her a gentle squeeze. "Hubba nubba gonna do just fine."

Milissa looked to the side, hide-and-seeking for an instant, then pushing him onto his back. "I'll give you hubba nubba," she said, straddling his belly.

Maria, seeing the fun, abandoned her play and climbed onto Milissa's shoulders, bending Milissa forward onto John's chest and toppling into his waiting hands. As John held her above them, she chanted "Keiki plus Keoni, Keiki plus Keoni," arching her body horizontally, balancing on her hips, and winging out her arms.

She gripped his wrists and gazed into his naked face – his forearms, stiffed fist-first into the mattress, held up his head and chest, allowing him to play into the rhythm of her hips. It had begun as make-believe when he returned a second time from tucking Maria in and Milissa asked him to turn up the heat.

"Da heat?" he whispered. "You never noticed? No heat, da houses in Hawaii. Here, dis'll keep you warm." He unfolded his patchwork quilt.

She wavered. Was it meant to be her cover for the night?

"Move forward, girl, so I can wrap you." He sat down and put it over her shoulders, gathering it around her neck. "Dere, now you my Indian maiden."

"Come inside," she said, lying down on the couch and opening the blanket. Despite her boldness the last time she'd stayed over, the bedroom was too soon. That night had been a coup. Tonight her moves were in the open. "Let's pretend we're in the middle of a North Dakota winter."

"Brrr," John said, switching off the lamp and climbing in. "Can hear da wolves out on da prairie. Better stay close to da campfire."

"I hope there isn't one in my bed. I hope. I hope."

The couch was too small. John's back was exposed. He rolled over. "I'll keep a look out."

No sooner had they snuggled up side-spoon than "Daddy" issued from Maria's room. "Daddy, I'm t'irsty."

"Go sleep, Maria," John said, gruffing his voice. "Now you getting Keoni mad."

"Oh, Grandma," Milissa whispered in the silence that followed, "Now I know I got a wolf in my bed."

John put his hand in the small of her back and pulled her toward him, but she recalled how they'd been this way before – his back to her – and wondered if he was really interested.

She felt the drain of Morgan's emptiness when Brother Kerin left her in the pew, then "Boo," John flopped over and faced in. "You got a man in your bed."

She blushed and looked down. The sweetness of her breath filled the darkness between them. "Is this a chore?" she asked. "'Cause if it is . . . Well, sex isn't everything, right?"

"Come," John said, picking her up in the quilt. "We fix dis happy sadness. More private in my room."

She hadn't expected to be loved. She'd really never been. The others were boys. The hubba nubba, the ho'oipo, all of it was cute, so she thought it would be the same. She was willing to dispense with the foreplay. It was what she expected. A little pain at first. Nothing compared to the discomfort of intimacy.

But instead, he had opened her heart with patience. He joked her and stroked her and let her have her space, then cuddled her until she almost fell asleep. She lay on top of him, her bare breasts to his bare chest, still in her jeans, and told him about her first crush. They lit a candle and pulled the shade. Coyly – she could be modest now – she finished undressing and climbed beneath the quilt. He did the same, less shy but without pretense.

He kissed her, she touched his beard, ready for the morning shave – and then a free fall of ecstatic exploration. Years later she would realize what it had meant. His deep-dyed imprint on her self sublime. His scent that lingered in her mind. His taste that had become her own. His tone replayed in her soliloquies. Newborn depths of grace. Still undeciphered heights.

And now as light began to whisper through the shade, she cradled his hips between her thighs. Reaching around behind, she pulled him in with both hands, shortening his stroke, coming to him as she ascended. As she cried her final ecstasy, he cocked his lower back, almost coming out of her, then buried himself with a low unbroken moan. Spent, but still inquisitive, she reached back again and felt the root of his erection. Over and over it jerked as he unloaded. For an instant, he was in her but not with her. Each was sailing in a separate realm, she in the sea, he in the sky. When he came down, she surfaced, clinging to his chest, drowning in the thunder of his heart.

CHAPTER FIFTEEN

X was reading a report, slashing it with angry arrows, connecting margin notes to items in the text. "Milissa." He looked up long enough to acknowledge her. "Trying to catch up here."

She sat and waited. He was unshaven, looking dissipated. "This your new office?" she finally said, looking around the small staff lounge.

He scored a page so deeply that it ripped. "You know," he said, snapping his pencil and throwing the papers aside, "I have more to do than Maunaloa."

Milissa braced herself. "I know."

"Coffee?"

"No thanks. Too acid in the afternoon."

He fished a handwritten agenda from the scattered pages and propped his naked feet on the edge of the glass-topped table. "Everything hits at once. Someone took a sledge hammer to the water mains. Gotta be sovereignty stuff." He scanned his entries for a place to start. "The wife kicked me out," he added off-handedly. "Nothing new. Next thing, she'll take the kids to Maui and stay with my mother. Hedging her bets." He fixed on a subject. "PBS came to town a few days back."

"So your message said."

"The sabotage thing," he digressed, "that's not your problem." He peeked over the top of his list. "Neither is my trouble with the wife, though she thinks it is."

"She what?"

"It's complicated. Our blow-up centered on her suspicion that you and I are in the sack.

"Why would she think that? I'll give her a call."

"Hearing your voice on the phone again won't help."

"The call the other night. Did you explain?"

"I said it must have been a crank."

"A crank? You talked to her yourself."

"She reminded me of that. And then I explained. But it was too late." X hung his head like a naughty boy. "There's a lot more to this than one call. I've had a few liaisons over the years . . ."

"I don't want to hear it," Milissa broke in, sliding down in her chair and pushing the subject away with both hands.

"You're right," X conceded, stealing a glimpse of thigh through the tabletop. "Anyway, if I look like I just got up, I did. I slept here last night. Got my own apartment in the back."

Milissa shifted self-consciously and brought her knees together.

X took a ring of keys from his pocket. He singled out the key to the apartment and dangled it in front of her. "I know you have a place, but if you need some privacy, I'll be outta there by tomorrow. This other one is to the office. And this one's for the little Neon parked out front. It's nothing fancy, but it's new and it has a phone."

Milissa took the ring, removed the apartment key, slid it back to X, and kept the rest. "I'm fine at Morgan's. The car I need."

"No please." X picked up the key and offered it again. "You don't have to use it. Who knows, it may come in handy."

"Not a good idea," she said.

"Wouldn't want me stumbling in on you, huh?"

"I wouldn't put it past you. Now cut the crap. What about PBS?"

"My mistake they got so far. One of our tenants passed the word. I should have been out there as soon as I got the call. They found a grave in Mannie Santiago's yard. His grandmother. 'Tutu's grave' they're calling it. Fits right into their propaganda. First thing I heard when I got here yesterday morning. Tutu's grave. Tutu's grave.

"And then there were some remarks by me and Nakayama behind the warehouse. Bastard was shooting us from the roof. We took care of the tape, but they can attest to what we said."

"What'd you say?"

"Something about getting rid of the low-lifes. Guys like Mikala. Like that was our actual plan. It'll all come up tomorrow night, I expect. I've agreed to an interview. That'll be you. Six o'clock, here. Tell them what you're doing. Same stuff we told Abbot and Bisk. Their reporter guy gave me this on the phone." He handed her Michael's words. "His documentary theme."

It read: *Enclosure Acts Revisited, A Lesson Never Learned.*

"That's it from me." X checked all but the last item off his list. "You got anything?"

As Milissa leaned forward to make some notations on the back of the paper, X attempted another glance through the tabletop. "Jense Hoiness," she said, catching his look-away.

"Hoiness. You must have talked to Hilda."

"I talked to Jense. Ran into him by chance in Waikiki. He says he owns a house in our north section and has the papers to prove it."

"We know what he says. We got a letter from him a few months back. We have no intention of responding unless he takes action."

"What if he has a legitimate claim?"

"He'll have to prove it. And by then it'll be too late. His place is the next to come down."

"Just like that?"

"I've known about the problem since shortly after we came on. When I saw he hadn't paid rent for as far back as we could tell, I went to Hilda, the present tenant – his sister. She said that Farley Chisolm, the previous owner of the town, gave Jense the house. That's all I could get. Our counsel in Honolulu made a call to Chisolm's people and told me not to confront it head on. We're in the process of taking the place by adverse possession, if we ever lost it at all."

"What's his proof of claim?"

"He says he has a letter. No other details, except that it deeds him a life estate. Farley died last year and his family's not talking. But we have all the ducks. We've been paying the taxes. Always done that. We refiled our claim. His isn't on the books. To firm things up, I talked Hilda into paying thirty five a month."

"Thirty five for what?"

X laughed and gripped the nape of his neck.

"You told her it was a maintenance fee."

"She pays by check. We have it recorded as rent."

"Jense told me he's coming to town."

"Did you discuss the situation with him?"

"I didn't let him know that I was connected. He broke off the conversation when I started to delve. He told me he knew about the redevelopment. Said he was coming to check things out."

"See Hilda, will you? Ask her what her plans are for moving. She's got her boy there with her. Maybe you can devise some special incentive. And get back to me."

Milissa was intrigued by the plot, but not the part he wanted her to play. She didn't commit. "I had planned to stop by. I'm talking to everyone. Is there something under the table that interests you?" X had peeked again.

"Noticing your ankle bracelet."

Her disgust was tangible.

"No, really," he said, but broke into a smirk. "Well, I was looking around a bit. But the bracelet? Is it local?"

"It was a gift," she said precisely.

"A gift from an admirer." X knew who worked in silver.

"A friend."

"A close friend?"

X stacked his papers while Milissa churned.

"From Keoni Mikala. If it's any of your business."

"Keoni. The last time you mentioned his name it was Mr. Mikala."

Milissa shrugged. "What's your point?"

"That too close a relationship between Mikala and you is my business. I've had reports."

"Oh, I see," Milissa expanded her anger with calm. "A question of loyalty."

"I have a duty to our shareholders. The fact that you've apparently" – he gestured toward her feet – "warmed up to the opposition, gives me pause. Where emotions reign, secrets can be divulged, if only inadvertently."

"You're trying to block our relationship."

"I'm glad you grasped that."

"Why?"

"I told you."

"That's a ruse."

"My concern is legitimate. I need assurance to protect myself with the board."

"Assurance?"

"That you're not sleeping with him."

"X," she pleaded, her eyes merry with disbelief that he would state the obvious. "You don't need this." She felt like consoling him. She moved her hand in his direction, but then let it rest. "Well," she added after a pause, "I have work to do."

"Don't let me keep you," X said, crossing the last item off his list.

Milissa had knocked and waited and knocked again. She was leaving a note for Hilda when Loka pulled up in his van.

"Got what you looking for," he announced, opening his sliding door, "Alakazam." Out stepped the red-faced and testy lord of the manor. Back on his heels, Jense walked across the yard, a weighty satchel in each hand, his chin tucked into his neck.

Milissa advanced timidly. "Hello, Mr. Hoiness. Remember me?"

He exuded a sour whiskey smell and wheezed slightly as he held his keys at a distance to make out the one that fit. "Da girl at Tahitian Lanai." This was not the robust, self-confident man that she'd met in Waikiki. "Dey sent you over dere to spy on me, yah?" He tried the wrong key. "Your hack friend says you work for Stockmans Inc."

"Waiting for my fare," Loka said in a voice just loud enough to carry from the van.

"Hold on, boy," Jense squawked. "Son of a bitch," he mumbled, still fiddling with his keys. "Was hoping Hilda'd be here to cover da ride. Christ knows she owes me." The slam of Loka's door brought Jense up short. "You want to talk with me?" he asked Milissa, inserting the key and jarring the door, prepared to flee inside.

Milissa nodded.

"Give him his fare."

Loka met her halfway. "Dirty man," he cautioned in a low voice.

She handed him a twenty and turned back without her change.

Jense had left the door open. She did the same. She heard the toilet flush. The house smelled of boiled tripe. The windows were still weeping. Jense was at the kitchen table stealing a swig from his flask.

"Where's your chubby friend?" he rasped. "Hilda tells me she's a poor man's lawyer. She still got her cherry?"

"Are you poor, Mr. Hoiness?"

Jense's wet guffaw ended with a clearing of the throat. "I bet she does," he said, getting up and spitting in the sink. "I can tell. It's da baby fat." He plopped back down. "A poor fisherman. What you see here is all I got." He crowded the table with his arms. "But you know dat. You come to take it away."

"I came by to ask Hilda how to contact you."

"Thought you maybe could get da scoop on ol' Jense."

"You can't be that old."

"Fifty eight," Jense boasted, "old enough to be your fader. You like older men, yah?"

"This house is coming down. I thought Hilda could get you the message. But here you are."

"And what?" Jense asked, sucking his flask and squirrelling it behind his back. "And poor ol' Jense," he whined in mockery, "what can he do? You tell him you gonna tear down his place and he just tuck ass and go away, yah?"

"Is that what you'll do?"

"You God damn right dat's what I will do, if I God damn well please!" Jense snarled, dashing down another drink, befuddled by Milissa's misdirection. "But dis time I stay," he choked. "You think Jense some haole coconut, you're wrong."

"Perhaps," Milissa said with a distant air. "But I would hate to see you get involved in a lost cause at your age."

"What?" He leaned forward and jabbed at his shirt pocket. "You think Jense got no paper?"

"I think you should talk to your lawyer. Or get one."

"Son of a bitch, I will!" Jense said, almost tearing the button off his pocket to get at his claim. "And we get dis in front of da judge." He waved the soiled envelope in her face.

Her air of indifference had reeled him in.

"You don't believe me," he stammered, taking a fragile typewritten letter from the envelope and skimming through it for a line. "Here it is. 'To insure dat da child . . .' No, no. Let me see. Mmm huh. Mmm huh. Here we go. 'Da house is yours for life.'" He whisked the paper up and displayed it with both hands.

She reached out to take it and he snatched it back, almost gagging on his venomous glee. "You think Jense will let you touch his precious thing for nothing?" He tucked it away. "Maybe she got something to trade," he said, stretching his thick body back to relieve a surge of testosterone.

She held up her palms as if she might be game.

He drew out his flask and shook it next to his ear, then took a swig and handed it to her.

She pretended to sip, but pressed her tongue against the opening.

He laid the envelope on the table. "Can play dis like strip poker."

"One line at a time?" she complained. "How many lines?"

"Whew!" he pulled the envelope back. "You are a tricky one."

"I thought you liked bad girls."

"I bet you'd do anything to get your way," he said, licking his gold incisor. "You remind Jense of his ex."

Milissa unbuckled her sandals and sloughed them off beside the table. "Your wife?" she asked, tipping back the flask a second time.

Jense looked down at the sandals. "My common-law," he offered in return. "Da one dat got ol' Chisolm to give me dis place."

She let a little whiskey into her mouth.

"Dat a girl," he oozed, pleased by her reaction to its punch.

She stretched across the surface of the table. "How'd she get old

Chisolm to do that?" she asked, then recoiled from his reach and wrapped herself in her arms. "I just have to know."

He tapped the envelope as he spoke. "She got knocked up by his son-in-law. Den got him to give me dis house for claiming da kid."

"Where is she now?"

"Sitting in hell. We was only here a month and right away she's trickin' with da owners. I let her stay until she had da brat, den kicked 'em out and went to sea. Been fifteen years."

Again she brought the whiskey to her lips. "A very short-lived relationship."

"Naw, we was off and on for years before in Honolulu." He reached for the flask and grabbed her wrist instead. "Come sit on Jense's lap. I tell you all about it."

"Your change," said Loka, silhouetted by the lowering sun against the screen door.

Jense released his grip.

Milissa stepped into her sandals and moved quickly away. "Get a lawyer," she advised, her business concluded.

"You cracks are all alike," Jense shouted, standing up and spitting after her.

She squeezed past Loka.

"Lucky for her you showed up. I was getting set to pull her panties down."

"Predictably so," Loka said, sniffing the air. "Someone die in here?"

When Milissa got to the condo that afternoon, she found Morgan reading on the lanai.

"Left the office early?"

"I was hoping you'd come home. I wouldn't have been able to sleep. I was so pleased with the girls' reaction to my dress today."

Milissa sat on the end of Morgan's recliner. "The whole office brightened up."

Morgan smiled secretly. "Lani and Linda and I are having lunch at the Kama Aina tomorrow. You're the guest of honor. They want your report on our trip."

"I don't remember a thing," Milissa winked. "You'll have to refresh my memory. Actually, tomorrow's a bad day. I have a lunch appointment with Cory Adler. It's about my jobs program."

Morgan's smile died.

"Sorry. You wouldn't have me neglect my work."

Morgan returned to her book.

"Tomorrow night," Milissa perked, going to the phone. "Easy loves to entertain." She brought the receiver to the lanai as she waited for Easy to answer. "Easy. Milissa. I'd like to visit you tomorrow night. . . . With Morgan. . . . Like a little party, yes. . . . No. No Keoni. . . . No, just us girls. . . . That's the idea. . . . Six o'clock?" The time, she realized, conflicted with her TV interview, but Morgan was nodding yes. "Bless you, Aunty. See you at six."

Morgan marked her place. "At Easy's then. Six is fine."

CHAPTER SIXTEEN

As she was preparing to leave Morgan's office for her meeting with Cory, Milissa noticed Jense in the parking lot. Here was the conflict of interest that Morgan had warned her about. The fact that she and Morgan were friends hadn't dissuaded him. If he sees that I actually work here, she thought, maybe he'll reconsider. She made herself apparent when he came in, fussing around her desk and calling ahead to confirm her appointment. He reacted by doing his pompous best to offend the others in the room. She was tempted but didn't have time to play out the scene.

Her meeting with Cory was fruitful. Cory was not inclined to help Stockmans, but she had no choice. Hers was a public institution. She already had a landscaping program in place. The classes were taught via two-way television from Maui. The students were required to have sponsors for whom they worked in the area of their major. Past graduates had all been hired by the county to tend the public grounds in Kaunakakai.

"As for construction," she told Milissa, "our board expects us to expand whenever possible. If Stockmans agrees to sponsor, we'll arrange the curriculum."

Before driving up to Maunaloa, Milissa called X to clear some points she planned to cover in Michael's interview. In line with her pitch to Abbot and Bisk, a labor pool would be announced.

"A list of Maunaloa guys who'll have first crack," X said. "That's fine. But only at jobs for which they qualify. Have you come up with a response to Tutu's grave?"

"Not yet."

"Not yet? This is important."

"I'll think of something."

"Check with me first."

"If I have time."

Milissa was making house calls that afternoon along the perimeter of the north section, keeping an eye on the elementary school while she fielded her work-study plan. The idea of an after school daycare had germinated long enough. Tonight she couldn't simply repeat the unfounded assurances she had given the Aussies. She felt confident that Pastor Swan would cooperate – there she had leverage. But, to be at least convincing, she needed to assert some involvement with school authorities. She rattled the door to the small office building, but no one answered.

"Dey mostly go home after noon," Keku Reyes shouted from her front steps.

"No summer school?" Milissa asked, coming across the street.

"Just a short day in da morning. Dat place went shrink." The school's cracked blacktop, bent basketball hoop, and flaking jungle gym were old Maunaloa's final nod to child's play.

"Looks almost abandoned."

"Used to be one baseball field over dere. Had one keiki summer league back den."

The surrounding terrain, once a tempting maze of pineapple, and before that a never-never-land of ancient, untilled mystery, now sloped away in dry, chemically-altered escarpments. Close in, the housing project and the raw, weedy lots produced an eerie overlay of urban blight.

Keku detained Milissa on the porch while her husband, Kimo, eavesdropped from the living room. She wavered in response to work-study. "Got nothing against education, but not too good da pay." She feared that if Kimo went to work it might affect her benefits – with medical and food stamps she was bringing in more on welfare than he would make. She also hedged on the idea of moving into the new rentals. "Maybe dey no like my Kimo living dere. He no pay support."

"Da whole world's watching now," came Kimo's voice from inside. "Gonna have to take us out in cuffs."

"Stop talking lolo," Keku said, snapping him with her kitchen towel as he appeared. "None of my keiki gonna be in cuffs."

"You Keoni's squeeze," Kimo said. "She Keoni's squeeze."

"I know dat," Keku frowned. "Don't be disrespectful."

The sound of children scrapping drew them back inside. Keku caught the screen door as it closed. "Principal Sato," she said, pointing at a man walking toward the administration building.

"Excuse me," Milissa called, catching up with Sato. "I'm Milissa. I work for Stockmans."

Sato beamed his trademark, blissful grin. "Keiki, isn't it?"

"And you're Principal Sato."

"Someone's telling on me again," Sato said, radiating mirth.

"I'm sure you've had a busy day, so I'll be brief."

"Not really." Sato put his briefcase down. "It's intercession."

"In about an hour, I'll be talking to PBS about our building project."

"A big order," Sato said, blending a modicum of pain into his smile.

"I thought you might have some ideas about its effect on the children."

"If they're forced to move off island they'll have trouble adjusting. As bad as they get, they still have family here, extended family – nanas, aunties, and tutus. Elsewhere, say Oahu or Big Island, or God forbid the mainland, their first scrape and they're a number."

"How would you explain their predicament? I need something for the interview."

"Their predicament? They come last in the life of the town." Sato was no longer smiling. "If Stockmans and the committee had asked first, 'What will happen to the keiki if their houses are torn down?' they wouldn't be fighting now. This picture" – he pointed around the neighborhood – "would be different."

"Can you be more specific?"

"It's a universal remedy. Specifics issue from the heart's intent. You tell them Sato said, 'Consider first the welfare of the children.'" He weighed the air around him with his hands. "All else will fall in place."

Milissa had arrived at Stockmans' office late. What better way to hurry things along. John met her herding Michael, Smitty, and Fidel across the empty lots toward Easy's house.

"We're doing it at Aunty's," she told him, then ran ahead to prepare the scene.

Fidel groused behind as the four men entered the yard.

Milissa had Easy on the lanai, enlisting her to furnish background with her ukulele. "In your rocker," she instructed. "And you ladies," she hollered inside to Linda, Leilani, and Morgan, "pray through the windows. Pray.

"No upstaging now," she kidded, pinching Easy's cheek and taking final inventory of the set. "We'll do it here." She looked at Michael and pointed at the steps. "Right here."

"Whatever works," Michael responded, "but softly on the uke."

Easy nodded her compliance.

"Ground rules?" Michael asked.

"Introduce me as Milissa 'Keiki' Dogherty. Address me as Keiki."

"Anything else?"

People had begun to gather outside the fence. "Let them in and" – she prompted Easy to begin – "fire when ready."

Smitty put John and Fidel on crowd control. "Keep the space in front of the camera clear."

"Roll 'em," Michael shouted, enjoying the theatrics.

He began with a few rote questions. Where was she from? How long on Molokai? A little background. And then, foregoing an explanation of the crisis, he hit her with the substance of his inquiry. "What becomes of all these people when they're forced to move?"

"Evictions will be few, if any. We're giving everyone an opportunity to better their condition in the process of this change. We have programs that go a long way for even those with nothing but a welfare check." She outlined Stockmans' provisions for affordable housing.

"But surely these offerings fall short. They require either some initial capital or, at least, additional income. These people have no reserves. They can barely pay their current rents."

"Well intended, but ineffectual," Milissa conceded. "That's what I thought coming in."

"So you agree?"

Milissa had thought this one out beforehand, remembering Julio's lesson in traction. If you can't counter an assertion, don't fight it. Do what you can to turn it to your advantage. "I'd be foolish to completely disagree. Stockmans is aware that they've inherited a ghetto. This place is not amenable to pat solutions. That's why they hired me."

"You have some expertise?"

"I'm not an expert at anything. I'm an advocate. An ombudsman with a budget. On staff but not on staff. An in-house radical. Hired by Stockmans to challenge their conviction. Where their programs prove inadequate, I try to make up the difference."

"But there is a bottom line."

"We're a profit corporation, not a charity."

"An apt distinction. Primary motive profit, not public welfare. The nature of the beast."

Milissa sat more erect, held her shoulders back, and raised her angelic head. "This beast has a heart."

"That's you."

"That's me," Milissa granted without pause, moving immediately to Ui and Julio, to her job and daycare programs – not lying, but clothing each endeavor in vivid hope, directing her comments to the people behind the camera, lacing her presentation with respected names.

"'Consider first the welfare of the children,'" she said, touching Sato's maxim with an invisible wand. "He calls it a panacea." As she continued, she made out Jense's toxic face glowering in the penumbra of the camera light. "During my visit with Dean Adler, she showed me the Maui link-up. It has a life-size screen."

"She visited me," Jense blurted out. "Drinking my whiskey and peeking at my private papers." Smitty swung the camera around to catch Jense glaring at Milissa, challenging a reply. "Get dat fucking thing off me," he said, waving Smitty away and backing into the darkness.

"Do the work-study positions provide a living wage?" Michael asked, knowing he could edit out the interruption.

"A little above minimum. They're transition jobs. The wages scale up with skill level. The other jobs start at ten an hour."

Jense stationed himself at the back of the gathering, speaking conversationally to anyone who might listen. "Dat little slut came by my place yesterday and offered to trade ass for information."

The comment carried through the silent crowd. People bowed their heads and held their laughter as John sidled up beside the burly intruder and gave him a puzzled smile.

Milissa went on as if the remark hadn't been made. "We expect other agencies and organizations to pitch in. This'll be a community effort."

Jense brought his mouth to John's ear to share a manly confidence. "I tell you," he whispered, "she's a nasty little t'ing, you betcha."

Still smiling, John gave Jense a short, inconspicuous jab to the ribs.

Jense winced and emitted a deep, almost inaudible growl as he felt his ribs separate around John's knuckle. He lifted up his shirt to examine the location of the pain. Satisfied that he hadn't been stabbed, he brought his face down within an inch of John's. "You cock sucker," he wheezed, too much in pain to strike back, "I'll get you for dis," and then walked off, holding his side and cursing under his breath.

Fidel, who'd been moving closer to Jense the more obnoxious he became, was the only one who'd noticed this interaction. "You okay?" he asked John quietly.

"Okay," John replied as he turned away from the crowd.

"Who was that?"

"Not sure."

While Fidel and John were being distracted, Maria and Chase had climbed the unexposed side of the lanai and slipped into the shadow cast by Easy and her chair. Seeing them in the corner of his lens, Smitty zoomed in on Milissa and directed them off with his free hand.

The children giggled self-consciously.

"Maria," Milissa called out as they began to retreat, "you and Chase come sit with me."

Easy nudged Maria toward Milissa with her toe.

Maria crab-walked through the flood of light, blind to the extent of her exposure. Startled by the peal of careless hoots, she scuttled to Milissa's side and, keeping her head down like an army scout, she waved Chase in. Following her intrepid lead, several children filtered onto the steps, encircling Milissa. Smitty zoomed back to include them in the frame.

"This is what it's all about," Milissa said. "These and the old ones."

Michael took his cue to mention Tutu's grave.

"The grave of Api Pualani," Milissa replied. "Wonderful news." As she spoke she heard Jense again, griping out beyond the light.

"And how does Stockmans plan to respond?" Michael asked, also aware of Jense's voice.

"Our CEO suggests the plot be saved as a historic monument, a shrine."

"That's enough," Michael said to Smitty. "This is impossible. Maybe we'll pick it up later. Who the hell is that?" He looked back over the gathering. Rufus McKee and Jense were confronting John outside the gate.

"Mr. Hoiness has made a complaint," Rufus said to John. "And he has a welt on his side."

"You smelled his breath?" John asked. "Maybe he fell down."

"Whoops," someone said.

"Dat's gotta smart," came another comment, accompanied by sparse laughter.

Rufus removed his handcuffs from his belt. "It's my duty to take you in."

Kimo Reyes and several older teenage boys filed through the gate and circled the dispute.

"No need to take me in," John replied. "It's only a misdemeanor. I'll drop by and talk wit' Nakayama in da morning."

Concerned by the heat of the crowd, Rufus hesitated. "Step over to my vehicle," he said. "We can discuss it there."

John didn't move.

Jense eyed the ground and edged in his direction. "You little weasel," he said to Rufus under his breath. "Take him in." Before John could react, Jense had him by the collar. "What!?" he hollered to the deputy as he hoisted John to his tiptoes, "I gotta make a citizen's arrest?"

In the six-man struggle that ensued, John came out of his shirt, leaving it wound like a leper's wrap around Jense's forearm and fist.

"Dis one citizen's arrest," Kimo shouted, riding Jense full Nelson as the other boys restrained his arms and legs, one per limb, rooting him in place.

Rufus unsnapped his holster. "Enough," he commanded, "let him go."

Jense first untensed, then took advantage of the corresponding lull to fling the shirt in Kimo's face and shove him to the ground. "That's all?" he asked Kimo, inviting a response.

Kimo came to his feet and waved the boys aside, but John held him back. "Mo' bettah you let da bugger slide," he cautioned. "You got a family."

"Who's next?" Jense welcomed. "Come on boys, try me one at a time."

"Mr. Hoiness is it?" Fidel asked, stepping into the no-man's-land.

"Dat's my name," Jense snarled, slightly weakened by his adrenaline debt, breathing heavily and wiping sweat from his eyes.

Fidel put a casual hand on Jense's shoulder. "Why don't we settle this another day," he said, moving closer as he spoke.

Jense looked down and recognized on sight the prince of bullies, the pit bull for whom his breed had never been a match – shorter by three inches, but heavier, broader, more compact, quicker, and more cunning.

Fidel smiled softly, almost intimately, as he applied minimal pressure with his thumb to Jense's collar bone. "What say, old fellow? No reason to get hurt."

Jense clapped his hand over Fidel's and grinned like a chimpanzee. Fear refracted from the glitter of his vicious teeth. "Aye, Captain," he whispered as Fidel pivoted him away from the crowd, "had a bit too much to drink."

"Come on," Fidel replied big-brotherly, "I'll walk you home."

Rufus removed a pad and pen from his breast pocket and spoke into the silence left behind. "Now," he intoned officially, "I'll need you boys' names."

Amused looks were exchanged.

"Hmm, Keoni Mikala, and you Kimo . . ."

As Rufus continued his rigamarole, salvaging the appearance of authority by checking in on his radio and training his flashlight through the yard, the darkness emptied around him. "You'll be hearing from us," he said to no one in particular.

Morgan had been watching through the curtains. She was intrigued by Jense, devilishly repulsive – leaking lust in her office that afternoon – yet pitiable in defeat. They were riding him. She saw herself beneath them and felt she knew him better. Disgusted by prey and predator alike, drawn to their rooting by self-hate, compelled by loathing to participate, she'd singled out the soldier of her benighted heart.

Milissa came in and joined her at the window. "Sorry, Morgan. This I didn't expect."

"Isn't dat da haole who came in today?" Leilani asked, peeking over their shoulders.

"That's him," Milissa answered. "He and I had a run-in at his house."

"Dat's him," Linda agreed. "Herring choker!"

"Linda," Easy tisked, "no talk like dat."

"I hope dey bust him. Such a pig. What dey fighting about?"

The beam from Rufus' flashlight backlit Easy through the open door. She turned and shouted, "Get dat off my head you little pecker . . . wood," swallowing her second syllable, then nodding to acknowledge Linda's "Shame, Aunty, shame," and Milissa's appreciative laugh.

"Last time I do crowd control," John said, coming up the walk, tucking in his shirt.

Milissa gave him a hug as he stepped into the living room. "You all right?"

"First dey catch us on da roof. Now dis."

"What roof?" Linda asked.

"Naw." He waved his hand. "Tell you later."

"Out wit' it," Linda said. "You mess up again, brah?"

"Tell us about your manly exploits," Leilani cajoled.

"We're waiting," Milissa pressed.

"Hoh, you already heard X's version. You tell 'em."

"Keoni!" the women chorused, demanding a taste of mischief.

"It's Morgan's call. Dis her party."

Morgan smiled from her seclusion by the window.

"Hokay. We'll give Rufus time to cool off. Remember dat trap door, Linda? On top da warehouse?"

"Where we used to smoke da pakalolo," Linda answered.

John went on to tell the story in detail, including Rufus' randy frisk and Smitty's deft exchange of tapes. "Push came to shove, dey couldn't hold us. You know dat Hiro. All da time acting upright, but he still likes to cap on da haole man."

John looked at Easy with a question.

"Maria's at Chase's house. I told her she could spend da night."

"Hoh, Aunty," he moaned, "I'll be all alone."

Everyone but Morgan caught the innuendo. "Aw," they wailed back, "poor Keoni."

Milissa took him by the arm. "Poor boy. I'll walk you out."

Morgan, more at ease now that John had left, moved from the

window to the couch.

"A small glass of wine before dinner?" Easy asked.

A twenty second hole opened in the cheer while Morgan focused on the rustling outside the door.

"I'd love a glass," she answered, the instant Milissa came back in.

Easy poured the drinks and Linda handed them around.

"A toast," said Milissa, "to Morgan for her years of dedication."

"And her new dress," Leilani added as they all took a sip.

"How long you been practicing law?" Easy asked.

"Leilani and I started out together thirteen years ago. She broke me in."

"Hoh, Morgan," Leilani said, shifting to face her from the other end of the couch. "You so shy back den. I used to have to walk her to court. But now she cracking da whip."

Easy sat between the two, causing them to tilt in her direction. She put her hand on Morgan's. "Everyone knows Morgan. She got one ono reputation."

"Aunty," Linda said, "you embarrassing her."

"I like her to know," Easy said. "Everybody say she da kine."

Morgan sat red-faced, painfully aware of Easy's hand on hers and afraid to respond.

"Nana," Easy said, giving Leilani room to get up. "Can you bring Easy her uke? It's out on da lanai."

Easy laughed and pulled Morgan toward her as if the two were posing for a snapshot. "Lani no like me call her Nana," she whispered, girl to girl. "She t'ink I'm too old."

Morgan grinned helplessly in Easy's head hug.

When Leilani returned, Easy hefted herself the remaining couple of feet to the end of the couch. "Mahalo, Lani. Now let's see," she said, strumming the uke to tune her imagination. She hummed Morgan's name several ways but wasn't satisfied. "Tita, what's your middle name?"

"Marie," Morgan answered.

"Hoh, Malia, dat's easy." She serenaded Morgan with a medley of island favorites, fitting in "Malia" whenever a line permitted. "You part Hawaiian," she observed during a break in the lyric.

Morgan nodded cautiously, turning up her smile, but lowering her eyes.

"Mahi mahi," Linda said quietly, so as not to break the charm. "Enjoy."

Easy took some of the fish with her fingers while the rest was being set around. "Mmm, nice da mahi mahi. You like try some?"

Morgan didn't hear. She was searching for herself in some past time, imagining her Polynesian royalty, focusing damp eyes on her companions.

"I'm famished," Milissa remarked, coming from the kitchen with the sweet potatoes. "That interview drained me. Morgan, eat." A drawn, unconscious facet of Milissa's face, apparent to Morgan alone, cautioned her to drop her sappy mood.

"Here," Linda offered, "let me help you. A little bit of each. You like it, take some more. But gotta work fast to keep up wit' da aunty kine."

Morgan began to nibble at her food.

Easy responded between bites. "Linda poking fun at me. Mo' bettah she start eating she can keep up wit' da hula kine." She put her plate down and searched through her CDs. "We try dis one for da preview." She inserted the disk and readied to begin.

"Stand back. Tsunami coming," Linda announced.

Morgan tensed at Linda's mockery.

"Be kind to Aunty," Milissa pleaded.

"Aunty no mind. She know she ono."

Easy's undulation was amazing. It was impossible to subdivide as one might with a rumba or a waltz. It appeared to be empowered through gyration of the ankles. All from below, the waves expanded up her thighs and hips, exhaling through her wrists and fingertips.

"Wit' da hula," Leilani commented, "mo' biggah, mo' bettah."

Easy spoke without effort, transposing her meaning with her hands. "Big girls, we beautiful like da ocean."

"Dis is why dey call her 'Easy'," Linda explained.

"Come, Morgan," Easy said, keeping with the rhythm as she reached out from her Sea of Galilee.

Morgan hugged the arm of the couch.

"Oh, look dis little chicken," Easy bantered. She took Morgan by the wrist.

"Haole girls always scared to swing dey butts," Linda said in an aside.

Morgan allowed herself to be pulled to the edge of the couch, then hesitated.

Easy pouted. "You make Easy sad. Come, Aunty show you how to catch one man."

Morgan stood stiff-legged, riveted in place by the attention. Everyone was hovering.

"Clear some space," Easy ordered. "What you t'ink dis is? One faith healing?"

"She can walk. She can walk," Linda quipped under her breath as she lead Milissa to the corner for her lesson.

While Easy worked hands-on with Morgan, molding her movement and position, Leilani sat and observed.

"What you t'ink dis, Lani?" Easy asked, showcasing Morgan's rearview, mechanical hip movements. "Keep 'em up," she directed as Morgan began to flag.

Leilani held her laughter, took a closer look, and whispered back. "Morgan got no okole."

Easy put her finger in the air. "Gotcha," she agreed. "Tita," she said cautiously as she turned Morgan around. "When you bend your knees, no need tuck your tush like dis." She stepped away dramatically and thrust her hips forward like she'd been goosed. "Mo' bettah you stick it out like dis." She arched the small of her back and raised one heel, lifting her behind high above its normal plane.

An irrepressible leer seeped from the corners of Morgan's eyes as she tipped back her glass. She lifted a heel and bent at the waist as if she were angling up to a fire hydrant. "Like this?"

"Yes, dear," Easy answered, straining to keep a straight face, "dat's da kine. Now, follow me." She stood beside Morgan and moved side to side, nudging Morgan's hip with her own. "Dat's right," she encouraged. "Now keep dose buns up da sky. Dat's right."

To her surprise, Morgan's hips began to loosen.

"Dat's right," Easy cheered, "do da grind."

The others turned their attention to Morgan and Easy, who had begun to move in unison.

"Hele on!" Linda cheered, "Geev 'em up, Morgan."

Morgan stopped.

Linda put her hand over her mouth.

"It's okay, it's okay," Easy assured. "She got it now. It's like one rubber bone disease. She never be stiff again. Did you see, Lani?"

"Little bit," Leilani replied, avoiding the issue. "Was so busy watching Keiki."

"Keiki needs serious work," Linda remarked, taking the focus off of Morgan.

"I beg your pardon," Milissa answered, "I thought I was doing quite well."

"Let's show 'em what we got," Linda suggested. "You too, Nana."

Linda restarted the music and the three women, Milissa in the middle, began to hula. After a short while, Easy and Morgan joined in. The dancing continued, with raucous laughter and mini-solos, through a second bottle of wine.

"Time for da recital," Easy announced. Everybody sat quickly, expecting the others to go first. "Keiki and Morgan gotta do one solo."

"A duo," Milissa begged. "We can't make Morgan do it alone."

"You da one afraid," Linda kidded.

"How about it?" Milissa asked Morgan.

"I don't know if I can."

Milissa hussied to the middle of the floor, daring Morgan to follow.

Everybody waited.

"If you insist," said Morgan, mimicking Milissa's flounce, giggling, absolutely flustered.

"We got the rubber bone disease," Milissa said. She put her arm around Morgan and began to wiggle out of control.

"Dem bones. Dem bones," Morgan chimed in, writhing with Milissa as they fell out on the couch.

Humored by the rubber dance, but struggling to maintain her discipline, Easy clapped her hands and turned off the music. "Hula is an art. You do it, you gotta do it right."

After a quick review and some attitude adjustment, the two performed the rudiments of hula. Easy, Linda, and Leilani caught their energy, applauding and praising them just as it began to wane, about thirty seconds in.

Easy produced a ti leaf lei and placed it around Morgan's neck, kissing her on both cheeks.

Linda slipped a ring on Milissa's finger. "From middle school," she said. "My ring for sweet t'irteen." It was a silver band, very thin and unadorned. "Can keep it to remember me."

Milissa rotated the ring and wondered how to respond. "It's lovely. But not as sweet as you." She tugged Linda gently down beside her on the couch, to be near to her and separate from the rest. "I remember being thirteen," she said. "There weren't any girlfriends. My parents home schooled me. I had this crush on my dad's intern. I think he was interested. But he didn't dare."

"Was hormone alley in da lunch break halls," Linda remarked. "You never missed much."

Morgan sat next to Milissa, examining her lei, drifting into painful reverie.

Milissa jostled her to attention. "Where are you now? Always somewhere else."

"The classroom. I stayed in the classroom." Morgan yawned, tipsy from the wine. "Even ate lunch in the classroom."

"Lay on da couch," Easy said, shooing the girls and patting a pillow for Morgan's head.

"I shouldn't lie down. I have court in the morning."

"Will you relax," Milissa scolded, pushing Morgan playfully onto the pillow. "And give me those tired old feet." She took Morgan's feet in her lap. "We just got her out of pumps, you know. Imagine these little piggies in the hoosegow all those years. Gotta get 'em ready for tomorrow."

"Keiki went stay wit' Keoni," Easy put her hand on Morgan's shoulder to welcome her back from sleep. "You like stay da night?"

Morgan sat up, not quite awake, and began to brush herself off.

Easy joined her on the couch. "Otherwise, if you still groggy, but like go home, Linda can give you a ride. Keiki say not to worry about your car. She'll pick you up in da morning."

Morgan continued to primp but now more fastidiously – singling out invisible bits of lint, checking closely for contamination, then coming abruptly to her feet. "Not necessary. I can drive my vehicle. Your phone?"

Easy pointed to the end table.

"Your phone book?"

Easy handed her the book.

She trembled as she rustled through the pages.

"Can I help you?" Easy asked.

She entered the number, casting up an acid glance when John came on the line. "Ms. Dogherty, please." Milissa's voice was soft and drowsy. Hers was hard and dry. "You needn't pick me up," she said, smothering Milissa's reply in the cushion, her empty eyes scanning for the door.

"Morgan," Easy implored, startled by her absence. "You okay, Morgan?"

"Ready?" Linda asked as Morgan passed her on the lanai.

"Let her go," Easy said, catching Linda by the arm. "She still asleep. Having a bad dream."

Milissa confronted her at sunrise in the Paniolo parking lot. "It's just you and me," she said, stepping in front of her and blocking her driver's side door. "Come out from behind the face."

A child's bloated body buoyed to the surface of Morgan's smile and sank away. "You mustn't detain me. I have a brief."

It was Milissa's courage that bewitched her – the indomitable Keiki, braving the gates of her tormented soul. She turned and walked off, her stubby heels hammering the blacktop. Tears mixed with mucous at the corners of her mouth as she fought the urge to smash Milissa's head against the car.

"Morgan?"

She closed her eyes and dug the nails of one hand into the palm of the other.

"What do you want from me?" Milissa persisted, coming around in front, unaware of her peril.

Morgan opened her eyes. Her face fell out of form. "I want you to love me," she pleaded, choking on her shame.

"But that can't be. Not the way you mean. I'm a lover of men. I love Keoni."

"Do you give him satisfaction?" Morgan hissed, suddenly transformed by her enchantment, her features cinching with disgust. "When he's inside," she flicked her fingers toward her crotch, "does he say he loves you?" She put her hand up to ward off Milissa's response. "I know," she sneered. "He grunts." The chronic smile returned, lingered for an instant on the nasty thought, then lapsed into its fey dissociation.

Milissa stepped back, astonished by the change – familiar by now, but recognized at last for what it was. "I'll see you at work," she said as the episode faded from Morgan's eyes. "It wouldn't be like you to be late."

During their first few hours at the office, Morgan instructed Milissa in a couple of tasks without the slightest note of perturbation.

At eleven o'clock, Jense appeared in the waiting area.

"Pardon, Mr. Hoiness," Leilani chirped. "Must please remove your shoes."

He stuck his thumbs into his belt and bloated out his stomach. "Morgan ready to see me?"

"Yes, sir, but must first remove da shoes."

"You'd think we was a bunch of Japs," he said, always ready with his metal grin.

Alerted by his bombast, Morgan received him when he came back through the door.

"Away from da little snoop," he snorted, following Morgan past Milissa's cubicle.

Over the ensuing hour, his voice stormed several times through Morgan's walls.

"We got a deal den?" he said, turning to face her as she ushered him out of her office.

"Mr. Hoiness will return in two days," Morgan told Leilani. "Give him the needed forms and schedule him in." She filled out and signed their contract and handed it to Jense.

He signed and smiled his satisfaction at Milissa, who was looking on.

"Milissa," Morgan said with cybernetic cheer, "in my office for a moment?"

"Be right there." Milissa stalled for a couple of lines in her brief, waiting for Jense to leave.

Morgan was at her desk, backed up by her certificates. "A conflict has arisen that requires you to make a choice between employments. Mr. Hoiness has retained me to represent him in his claim on the house in Maunaloa. Since today was our second consultation, and since you have seen him once on behalf of Stockmans, this is not a decision that can be put off. I'll need your answer by day's end. We here, of course, hope that you will stay."

"What choice?" Milissa laughed. "The decision was made when you signed to represent him. I've already worked against his interest, which prohibits me from staying on with you."

"Of course, you're right," Morgan replied whimsically, surrendering the game.

"You wanted to see what I'd do if I actually had a choice."

"And what would that have been?"

"Now you'll never know."

A burst of disdain escaped from Morgan's nose. "Have your work space cleared by noon."

PART II

". . . all jigged out."

CHAPTER SEVENTEEN

Moke caught up to Milissa with the news. She quickened her pace to John's front door.

"Keoni's fishing," Moke said as she read the notice. "He was gone when dey tacked it up."

"Repeated unlawful acts. Ten days to vacate. Statutory period for week-to-week . . . I wonder." She headed for Jense's house.

Moke came quickly behind. "Da old man got one too."

"You're with me," she said, taking Moke's arm as they mounted the low open porch. "Scheduled for demolition." Her finger moved down the form. "Same period." She towed Moke to the middle of the field. "You must believe me," she insisted, stopping in the dusty heat, "I had nothing to do with this."

"Hoh, tita," Moke insisted back, "I no t'ink dat. But you at da crossroads, girl. You ride wit' dis, it's on you."

Her house calls that afternoon reflected the events of the past two days. Accounts of her PBS showing had inspired hope in some, while others who'd heard about the evictions were trumpeting Stockmans' betrayal. At most stops she didn't go in. Angry at X for not consulting her first, depressed about her falling out that morning with Morgan, she limited her inquiries to the tenants' plans and hedged when asked about jobs.

She got up at dawn the following day and repacked her duffle bag, stuffed on the run the evening before while Morgan was still at work. Her room at the Ono was just the four walls she had needed – back at the beginning it seemed. She had sat at its window half the night keeping pace with the moonlit surf.

Though Loka's belief that she was on a spirit quest kept constant vigil, she had never felt so incomplete. The heartache of putting an ocean between herself and John warded off temptations to run back to Lindsay. She thought of Morgan – who was, at that moment no doubt, suffering alone in her apartment – and of Easy and Linda as she twirled her friendship ring.

One thing certain, she would stay until law school convened. But where to live? Maybe with John, though it seemed a little presumptuous just showing up at his door. The idea of X's apartment was rejected out of hand. She could afford a place of her own, but self-doubt was creeping in. She needed companionship, not a set of rooms.

She drove to John's before daybreak and walked in unannounced, laughing to herself about the duffle bag secreted in her trunk. John and Maria were still in bed. "Keoni," she whispered, slipping out of her jeans, "you awake?"

"You never check your messages?" John asked. He rolled over and stretched out the sleep. "I called for you to come last night."

She got under the covers and climbed on top of him. "I've been so tied up with Morgan, I forgot to check. I see you got a message of your own."

"X found his excuse. You like see my ahi?"

"Your whaty?" she asked, laying her head beneath his chin.

"One tuna," John said, rolling her off playfully and putting his feet on the floor. "I caught it in Kaiwi Channel, down off Make Horse. Fifty pounds."

"You're not worried about your eviction?"

"My eviction? Not mine. Just a t'ing dat happen."

"What'll you do?"

"Gotta follow through with the plan."

"And after that?"

"Move in wit' Aunty till we find a place."

"I got evicted too."

"All broke down wit' Morgan, ya?" He slid his feet into his sandals. "Good. You can bunk wit' me."

"Not so quick." She pulled him back as he lifted off the bed.

"You no like see my ahi?"

"This is not a casual decision."

"You don't catch a fish like dis one every day."

"You don't catch me every day."

"I can relieve myself first?"

"And get your buns back in here."

John came back quickly and sat on the floor beside the bed, facing Milissa with his arm relaxed in the crook of her waist. "Dis is complicated stuff, huh?"

"It deserves discussion, don't you think?"

"You need a place to stay, Keiki. Who else you gonna stay wit'?"

"But it sounds so noncommittal." She brushed his hair back from his eyes as if to clear his mind. "If we decide to live together, it should mean more. More than a place to stay."

"I was gonna ask you anyway."

"Ask me what? To come shack up with you? Forget it."

John went into himself. He could see that she would leave if he didn't open his heart. For an instant, the only thing holding her was the weight of his arm. "Please come stay wit' me Keiki. I wanted you to from da start."

"That's what I needed to hear from my baby."

He pulled her close.

"I'm so down. Raw from lack of sleep."

Her silent tears began to wet his face. He held her while she sobbed. "Kisses," he finally said, smooching her around the mouth and letting her down on the mattress.

She rolled drowsily away and tucked her knees in toward her chest. “I love you, Keoni.”

He pulled the sheet over them and snuggled side-spoon.

“This time you’re in back,” she murmured. “Should I stay on at Stockmans?”

“We’ll talk about it later. Rest.”

He was engrossed in the last few minutes of her interview when she walked in. “Gotta hand it to you,” he said. “You pulled Tutu’s grave right out from under ’em.”

“As long as we follow through.”

“Fidel’s been blowing smoke for months.” He flicked off the monitor. “It’s our turn.”

Milissa ignored his deceit. She needed his okay on an article about her relocation plan.

“Draw it up. The *Sentinel* can print it as an insert. But let me see it first.”

She took out her final draft. “Sign here. I’m including our offer of employment.”

“It’s your baby. You sign. Put in that I’ve approved.”

“Ui’s check. That you’ll have to sign.”

“It’s in the mail. I talked to Swan this morning.”

“Good. There’s also this part on matching funds.” She pointed to the section in her draft that covered daycare. “And then I’d like to talk about the evictions.”

“What matching funds?” X pulled the article his way.

She’d talked with Principal Sato. He was making arrangements for use of school property. “So that’s a shoo-in, but we’ll need to carry the program till the grants come through. I’m notifying backers that we’ll match their contributions.”

“You have commitments?”

“I’m counting on Pastor Swan to fund-raise. He owes us. Hopefully his congregation will pitch in. You must have connections.”

“Right. You get the holy roller money first. If they come through, maybe I can squeeze my contacts for some matching funds. But no guarantees. Another thing. The parents have to be working before we enroll their kids."

"Fits hand in hand with our employment plan."

"Take on a hundred men to do the work of ten so we can babysit their kids? Some plan."

"Those not hired can use the time freed up to enhance their quality of life – job training, therapy . . . we'll need daycare volunteers."

X frowned. "Who do you think you're pitching? Nothing like a hit of crack to enhance the quality of life. That's how they'll use the free time. They're enhanced all the time as it is."

"I've called on half the people in town. No one seemed high to me."

"The ones that came to the door. The other half were zoned out in the bedroom."

"Do I take it you're rejecting the daycare? The board guys were impressed."

"But they're not here now, are they?"

"What was his name?" Milissa made a show of searching her briefcase for Willy Bisk's number. "Willy . . . Here it is. Bill and Ethel Bisk." She laid the cocktail napkin on the desk.

"I haven't rejected the daycare. I'm just not throwing money at it."

"Willy saw it as an investment."

"I'll bring it up next time he calls. Now, about the Mikala eviction."

"I'll bring it up," Milissa countered. "He suggested that I call."

"About the eviction." X took a copy of the notice from his drawer. "I'm sure you've read it. We see our car parked over there most mornings."

"Is that why you're evicting him?"

"No, but it's reason enough. The last time you and I discussed Mikala, my concern was confidentiality. It still is, but now there's scandal. He's being ridden out of town for law infractions and here you are bunking with the man. My God, he's almost twice your age."

Milissa smiled at X's duplicity.

"Consider this a formal warning. Cut it off or I'll have to let you go."

"Suppose I do. Will that change things with the eviction?"

"Not at all. It's my duty to separate these guys out. They're a danger to the community."

Milissa put Willy's number back in her case.

"About the matching funds. We'll guarantee ten K. If it's matched, maybe more." He returned the article. "And show this to me again before it goes to press."

"If you decide to fire me, be prepared for a counter charge."

"Your word against mine." X eyed her as she rose to leave. "I like you when you're hot."

"Poor fellow," she said, showing him her back.

In what seemed more than ever an empty performance, Milissa began to knock on doors, delivering her offers of employment.

"Pale?" she asked with surprise. Pale looked frail, even more down than on that day when they talked at the office.

"You Morgan's lady," Pale said, moving her out onto the porch. "What you doing here?"

Over Pale's shoulder, in the hall leading from the inner rooms, Milissa saw a man drying his hands and face on a towel. He quickly halved his body in a doorway, allowing one eye to peer back through the dinge. "Who's dat?" he asked in a low menacing voice.

Pale gave her brow a frightened lift.

Milissa stepped around her. "Milissa Dogherty, from Stockmans."

Pale looped back in front of Milissa. "We sleeping. Cannot . . ."

The man pressed between them. His scowl lifted to a sly grimace. "Dis Keoni's old lady," he told Pale. "Why you act so sneaky?"

Pale communicated her plea for confidence by looking at Milissa's feet.

"You're the head of household?" she asked him, following him into the living room.

He slumped onto the couch and adjusted his genitals. "Shit, girl. T'ought you was some kine of heat."

"Are you renting here?" she asked Pale.

"My tutu rent dis place," the man said.

"And you are?" she asked him, then looked at Pale.

"My husband," Pale answered.

"Husband." Milissa took a seat at the table and prepared to take notes. "Your name?"

He picked up his remote and clicked on the soaps.

"His name?" Milissa asked Pale in a half whisper.

"Pu'u Lima," the man broke in. "Why you gotta write it down? Pu'u means fist. Lima means five." He held up his hand, formed a fist, and tamped it into his palm. "Pu'u Lima."

"Maybe I should talk to Grandma," Milissa suggested.

Pale scurried toward the kitchen to get Grandma.

"Not!" Pu'u commanded, his eyes on the set. "Tutu busy wit' da keiki kine."

Milissa gave Pale a gentle, dissuading look. "I'll leave this." She placed a job notice on the table. "Positions at Stockmans, Pu'u. Look at it when you have time."

Pu'u came back with a threatening whine. "Pu'u never work for da fucking Stockmans Inc. Never. Tell you one t'ing 'fore you gotta go. Local brahs all plenty piss at Stockmans for evicting Keoni. Gonna be some shit fly over dis."

"You might want to check with Keoni on that."

He flicked the television off and stared at the empty screen, brewing a tantrum for Milissa.

Her chair stuttered as she pushed it in. "I'll find the door."

"Best t'ing you stay wit' Stockmans," Easy said. "Poo on X's warning. He let you go, he make one big mistake. Now Morgan, she somet'ing else. You gotta keep away from her. She one sick wahine. And I don't mean da gay t'ing. No shame for be gay. Everybody's got a little bit da kine. But she got ghosts – da kine like catch your body for keep 'em. I saw one looking t'rough her eyes da other night."

"Her haunted look," Milissa agreed. "But I feel like I led her on, playing the Polly Anna."

"So maybe you learned somet'ing. But too late to apologize. Gotta let it go."

The screen door slammed. Linda was home from work. She

plopped down at the kitchen table. "You got out just in time."

"What did Morgan say?"

"Hardly anything. It's dat Hoiness guy. He came at two, was still in her office when I left. I had to send t'ree people home 'cause he running over."

"He has her targeted. He was making moves on her that night in Honolulu and saying lewd things about her when I was at his place."

"You t'ink dey?" Linda smirked and signified by poking her finger into her closed fist.

"Linda," Easy protested, "you no be nasty."

"Naw," said Milissa, embarrassed at the thought. "But she can be manipulated."

"What happened wit' you two?"

"She was jealous of Keoni."

"Jealous?" Linda leaned forward in her chair and turned her head from side to side as if to check for eavesdroppers. "You mean Morgan got da hots for you, baby tita?"

"Can I trust you with this, Linda?" Milissa looked at Easy for help.

"No teasing, Linda. Keiki serious."

"Okay. Okay, but you know I'm aching to hear."

"She is seriously closeted. Deep, dark self-loathing. And like a fool, I tried to save her."

"And she went latch onto you."

"Took it the wrong way."

"Hoh, I always figgah she da kine asexual."

"She is, except for one little festering pocket of libidinal shame."

"Like one boil, ya? You bust it wrong, can make you sick all over."

"Why showcase Keoni?" Fidel asked. "X could have chosen a weaker link."

"Trying to break our will." Cory laughed at the thought. "What's left of it." She looked at John. "You still gonna fight the eviction?"

"Of course he is."

"Let him answer for himself."

"Just asserting his pledge. I say we build toward the event, draw power from his resistance, and bring the crisis to a head. What say, compadre? Time for a showdown?"

"Get the placards out?" Cory teased. "Throw ourselves under the bulldozers?"

"Why don't you do that." Fidel said, keeping his eyes on John.

Cory was disconsolate. "Again with the media schtick. I warned you guys about unbiased coverage. Milissa stole our best material the last time out. Tutu's grave. And then that bit about Dean Adler showing her around – shit! She made it look like I was cozying up to Stockmans again." As she got up and lit a cigarette, she caught John smiling. "You think it's funny. I bet you and Milissa laughed yourselves to sleep."

"It is funny," John admitted. "Little Keiki blowing everybody's mind."

"Seriously," Cory asked, "are our secrets safe with you? You seem to take this whole thing rather lightly. Otherwise," she looked at Fidel, "I don't know. I'm too busy to play games."

John reflected on his quarrel with Fidel at Make Horse. "Too much in-fighting here. Maybe I should step aside."

Fidel put his palms on the table. "Let's talk it out. One item at a time. Media. True, the news has become jaded. But today if you don't have their attention, you don't have an issue. It's all in finding the angle. PBS is a foothold. The private networks keep an eye on what they do."

"Fidel," John interrupted, infected by Cory's acrimony, "Why you never say where you coming from? Why you never say what's in it for you?"

Cory sat down and answered the question. "Fidel wants to be adored from afar. He's not at ease with being loved for who he is. It's his conditioning."

Fidel responded in a civil tone. "My motives are my own. I've championed causes all over the world. It's what I do."

"Try to remember, champ. You helping us. Not da other way around."

"I'd say it flows both ways. Are you the one without the ego? At any rate, I can't be faulted by either of you for what I've done."

Fidel palpated the table lightly with his fingers, looking away and listening to the sound as if it might divine the mood of his constituents. "We do make a good looking team – the noble savage, the academic, and the organizer. It would be a shame to let it fall apart. You're locked in, Keoni. Nine days from now and your number is up. More or less a constant. Of course you could always prevail. But I can play off of you under any circumstance, with or without your cooperation. I mean, I would need détente of sorts, but . . ."

"Got your hook right here," Stan shouted from the kitchen, inflecting like a pitch man, slapping the rolled up Landlord Tenant Act against his palm as he entered the room. "Heard you guys bickering and hatched it during the commercials."

"Keoni," he continued, ignoring their unanimous aversion, "always the most receptive." He handed John the pamphlet, opened to the part on remedies. "Read here." He begged for silence from the others as John skimmed the section.

"Tenant's remedy for repair," John read. "You can do da job yourself and deduct da cost from your rent."

"Provided that you've given the owner notice and he fails to have the work done," Cory added. "I've been badgering Stockmans to do repairs since they took over."

"You and how many others?" Stan asked.

"Some," Cory agreed. "Not sure. So get busy with the fix up. You owe me."

"Cory Anne," said Stan, "you miss the point." He pivoted his head from John to Fidel and back, gaping for effect.

"We wonder how many others are in a position to exercise the remedy," Fidel said dryly.

"We do wonder," Stan responded, "but does it really matter for our purposes? We simply claim that we've notified Stockmans, start fixing, and let them prove otherwise."

"Who wants to put the time and money in without the reward?" Cory asked as Stan's purport began to settle in.

Stan stared at Cory and pointed at Fidel.

Fidel scrunched his face in disbelief, but retained a glimmer of interest.

“The whole town you mean,” John said, bringing the thesis forward with amused anticipation. “Everybody starts repairing and claims compensation.”

“And X says, ‘Not,’ and tears ’em down,” Cory countered.

Fidel perked slightly. “If there’s compensable repair and X destroys the evidence?”

“He’s liable,” Stan answered. “Probably take the court months to separate out the legitimate claims and verify the work. They’d have to stop the wrecking to resolve the issue.”

“Got just da guys to help us start t’ings up,” John offered. “Nappy’s people on Oahu. Da Sovereign kine.”

Cory held out her hand. “There’s your angle, Fidel.”

Fidel demurred. “No amount of cabinet work and plumbing is gonna interest the media.”

“But a lot of bright, newly painted houses and a swarm of radicals might,” Stan rejoined.

“Might. And the cost to me?”

“Sixty, seventy houses. Materials. We’d have to feed everyone. Free labor.”

“And how does Keoni’s eviction factor in?”

“That’s the grabber, the thing that gives the project urgency. Initially the media will be attracted to the circus, but as Keoni’s eviction appears on the horizon their focus will shift. We pack it all into the nine remaining days.”

Everyone waited for Fidel. He shook his head. “I need a couple hours to think and make some calls. In the meantime, I suggest that you organize yourselves.” He closed his little minute book, caught John’s eye, and spoke to him as if they were alone. “The picture that is forming in my mind does not include Milissa. You two will have to break it off.”

John let out a gentle scoff.

“A couple hours then,” said Stan. “We’ll work it out.”

CHAPTER EIGHTEEN

The final approach to Halawa was a single undulating lane that felt its way, in and out of jungle, down the eastern sea cliffs. Milissa parked her car for a moment at the lookout above the bay. She could see a solitary figure meandering along the beach a quarter of a mile below. *When I was a girl, I watched the sea,* she said to herself, quoting some lines she'd written in her teens and never finished. *But now I watch what the sea brings in.*

Nothing was discrete, she added, beginning to improvise, *and I was everything. But now I see the pieces scattered on the beach, each one my heart, sometimes pulled back before it can be spoken. I recognize myself in little things – small, incomparable moments, evermore and gone.*

Unaware that he was being watched, John looked up toward Milissa. His eyes caught a frigate bird sailing above the cliffs. Lowering his gaze to the mouth of the bay, he followed a surfer along the crest of a wave and returned to his search for shells. He and his mother had combed this beach when he was a boy. She had introduced him to Hawaiian shell craft.

He thought about her as he scanned. She was a small woman like

Milissa. People used to ask if she had Filipino blood. He laughed to himself at how angry she would get, and then recalled how she would make a joke of it by walking with small steps, the way she said the Filipino ladies did. Racism was a way of life in the islands, an open and convenient source of humor to which no one was immune.

His mind wandered back to Angel. He had always chosen women like his mother, small and feisty. Even little Maria fit the mold. He laughed again, never losing contact with the thousand tiny objects in the sand. He picked one up – a perfectly round puka shell, a dime-sized disk with a peppermint stripe spiraling toward the hole in its center.

He sat down when he saw Milissa coming. "So nice, da east end surf. Maybe we should move down here. You like? Can hang out wit' da squatters."

"I guess I like," Milissa crouched behind him, her arms draped over his shoulders. "Did you see the scary sign?"

"Sharks? Dat's just to frighten off da haoles. Never no sharks here." John paused to amend his claim. "Well, was one a couple years ago dat bit one surfer dude. But long time before den, nobody get hurt."

"Bad bite?"

"Bad enough. Never found da body."

"All it takes is one."

"Dude coulda been a sweepstakes winner. Same odds. Some t'ings you never can prepare for." John pointed to a boy who'd fallen from his board. "Now he gotta struggle back. Heading out alone. Dat's da part you gotta like as much as when you catch da big one. Otherwise dere's too much time to worry if you gonna win da sweepstakes. Poised above da merciless unknown, dat's one t'rill you gotta love, or else you gonna dread it even when you riding high."

"Everybody's scared of the unknown."

John stripped off his clothes and ran into the water. He body surfed a couple of waves and came back in.

"Keoni," Milissa murmured, falling back in frustration, "I'm afraid. I need some therapy."

He took a handful of shells from the pocket of his pants and sorted through them. "Got all da answers hiding in dis shell. Just da t'ing for fear of da unknown." He handed her his peppermint striped puka.

"I'm serious," she said, examining the piece of symmetry. "Come sit." She rolled over on her stomach and patted the sand.

He pulled on his pants and sat cross-legged by her head.

She leaned on her elbows and assayed Linda's ring through the hole in his puka. "You know I've been riding the crest of things, feeling so special for not taking sides." She let down her props and looked up.

"Sounds like you took a spill."

"It's all come down around me."

"Not so easy heading out dis time."

"It would help if I knew you were with me."

John had asked Milissa there to pose a quiet-side arrangement, a way of escaping Fidel's demand – a proposal less than uplifting.

She sensed his hesitation. "It's ruined with Morgan. And things are all mixed up with X. He's insisting that I break it off with you, or else. I was embarrassed to tell you last night. Not the sort of thing you wanna bring up on your first night living with a guy. Especially after my fuss about commitment."

John stroked Milissa's hair.

"X says it's strictly business, but it's really about his ego and . . ." She frowned at the puka. "Well . . . me putting up with his remarks." She came to her knees, put the puka to her lips, and blew a tiny stream of air against his cheek. "Can you feel anything?"

He took the shell and hid it between his palms. "Truth is, we got da same dilemma. I keep seeing you, no more MCC."

She sat back on the bottoms of her feet. "Fidel's afraid I'm pumping you."

"X's afraid I'm pumping you."

She bowled him over. "Pump, pump, pump," she chanted as they laughed and tumbled in the sand.

He came out on top. "So what we gonna do?"

"You're the big kahuna. Ask your magic puka shell."

He searched around her quickly. "It flew away. How about we go to da chapel instead?"

"You're being quaint."

He stood and offered her his hand. "Come, I'll show you."

His thoughts began to open as they passed beneath the vault of ohia canopy. "You like I quit da MCC?"

Milissa pulled her head back in astonishment.

He knew the answer. "Course not."

"I love it that you're a fighter."

A fighter? He wasn't so sure of that.

She grabbed him around the neck and swung herself into his arms. "A fighter and a hunk. My hunk."

"Same way I love you," he said, hugging her to his chest. "Dat's why we gotta make it work da way it is."

They turned off the main road onto a narrow, rutted drag.

"It's like a doll's house," she exclaimed, dropping to her feet when the tiny, chalk-white chapel came in view. "Is it real?"

He opened the miniature gate. "Services twice a month. Open night and day."

"It's so teeny," she whispered as they entered the empty nave. The sign beside the door read: *Maximum Capacity 25. Dedicated Easter Sunday, 1947.*

"Built after da tsunami."

For a moment they sat close and quiet while Milissa sounded out the syllables of Our Father, written in Hawaiian, wall to wall above the lectern. Much like a boy seeking his first kiss in the dark of a movie house, John put his arm behind her and leaned in, about to unveil his plan when she saved him the pain. "Let's sneak around," she said. "I'll get a room at the Ono and we can rendezvous."

He loosened his grip on the back of the pew. "Just da kine? You're not offended?"

"It's only temporary. Until we see what happens with your eviction. I'm not gonna drop the ball with all these people. X would dump the entire program if I quit before it was in place. And then he'd put the blame on me."

"But not a room. Too conspicuous. You like camping out?"

"Hanging with squatters?"

"I got da equipment."

Milissa looked at her watch. "Back at the house?"

John smiled, shy from over-confidence. "In my pick-up."

After John and Milissa put up their tent, he drove directly to the airport. The night before, Fidel had returned to the meeting at Cory's and given his approval to the renovation blitz. Announcing that he had ordered a hundred gallons of paint per day for the duration, and that he was bringing in a media expert, he urged everyone to push for volunteers. Michael Teague, a KOHA TV crew, and a reporter from the *Honolulu Advertiser* were on hand with John at ten a.m. to greet the first contingent when they filed off the plane in traditional warrior regalia.

The airport staff's reaction was divided as the militants, all members of Sovereign Hawaii, paraded through the lounge toward the parking lot. While the younger workers signed the shaka and engaged their proud arrivals with the brothers' handshake, the older, war veteran, householder types stood back and smiled disapproval. But the spectacle had served as an opening event, an unexpected gauntlet in the face of Molokai's conservative community, a proto-patriot invasion, heralding the entrance of the world into little Maunaloa.

Fidel had spent his morning doing research. Those in the know had recommended Jock Bissell, the world's pre-eminent expert in attracting media to unsung causes. By the time he got Jock on the phone, Fidel knew who he was talking to. Jock's specialized career began in the late sixties when, after dropping out of ten years as a Madison Avenue pinstripe, he became a reporter for the *Bay Area Brief*, a San Francisco-based, counterculture magazine.

While at the *Brief*, Jock's backlog of national contacts had afforded him rapid access to the anti-establishment meteors of the day. When the magazine folded from an overdose of cannabis, Jock, never having been a smoker, joined with others to create the *Open Tome*, a slick take-off on counterculture sentiment, geared to the yuppie appetite for affordable freedom.

Following his bent, Jock arranged most of the celebrity interviews that established the *Tome* as a top rate national magazine. Not satisfied with rock star glitz, he reached out successfully to movie legends like Brando and Fonda. Ultimately the *Tome* became, under Jock's guidance, a coveted showcase for statespersons, authors, and educators. "Buckley's in the *Tome* this month," one was heard to say. "How cool. What money won't buy."

Over time, Jock became a back room advocate of humanitarian causes. "Attention in this world of ideas is half the battle for the mind," he would tell his staff. "Our goal is to attract national and world figures to the issues, to make something of what might otherwise be nil."

After a decade of leveraging against neutrality – the editorial staff had become increasingly wary of the direction in which he was taking the magazine – Jock outgrew the *Tome*. His freelance career began at age fifty three and he was now a vital seventy two, living in splendor on the cliffs overlooking Big Sur.

"Once the public eye is fixed on a given situation," Jock said, gazing out over the Pacific coastline, "by the presence of, say, a Robert Redford on an Indian reservation where the kids are dying of rickets, or the Pope visiting Cezar Chavez during a grape strike, the issue takes on a life of its own. Deserving or not, it gets the winning attention of homely conversation in every truck stop and espresso bar from here to Newark. Now right off, I know that Jimmy Carter's gonna be in Honolulu. Next week, I think. Some kind of symposium on children. That'll be his focus while he's over there. The idea is to get him up to . . .?"

"Maunaloa."

". . . up to Maunaloa to see the kids. How does tearing down the town affect the kids? Be objective."

"It puts them in the projects, most of them."

"Is that bad?"

"Children in projects, street gangs, inner city stuff. It's bad. It's also soft news." Fidel's personal designs hinged on physical preservation of the town, an outcome that might or might not square with the best interest of its children. "The harm done these kids by moving them will be a side effect, a significant but secondary result. Preservation of their community is the primary issue. My PBS people are looking at it more holistically. They see the displacement of an entire culture. Including, but not limited to, its children."

"The kids angle may be limited for their purpose, but, precisely because it's everywhere – filler on every local station – it's easier to focus on, timely and familiar. I like what Teague is doing, but it won't create the immediate effect you're asking for. Cultural displacement is truly soft. Old and soft. Practically speaking, as regards viewer appeal, it went out with the Indians."

"What if Carter doesn't grasp our concern? What if he decides the children would be better off in the projects?"

"Not likely. One of his goals is culturally appropriate habitat. We have an opportunity here to bootstrap your issue with his current interest in child welfare. You'll have to trust my intuition. You'd be damn lucky to get him up there."

Jock himself was a valuable commodity. Fidel knew better than to quibble. "I'll wire the money to your account this afternoon."

"I'll call Carter's people as soon as we hang up."

"See you late tomorrow, then."

"Can't wait to get there. Haven't worked in a month."

"Work has been slow?"

"No scarcity. It's like blackberries and women. If you don't discriminate, you get stuck."

Fidel imagined Jock being fed blackberries by a woman half his age. "I prefer grapes."

"No challenge with grapes. It's all in the picking. You spot a ripe one, you go for it methodically. The trick is to get in and get out without a scratch."

"Getting out . . ." Fidel left off intentionally.

"Can be more hazardous than getting in."

"Uncanny, isn't it, how the thorns can settle in around you once you've made your move."

"All the more reason to be sure. The attractive thing about your situation is the framework, the painting and renovation action preceding the eviction. It's all there. Time frame. Participants. Local hero. What's his name?"

"Mikala. Keoni Mikala."

"Yes. Well, steady ahead with all that, but nothing new until I get there."

"Right."

"Right then. See you on the ground."

On her way up island from Halawa, Milissa stopped by the *Sentinel.* Surer now than ever that X meant to drag the process out and use her as a shield between himself and the community, she decided to publish the tenant program unapproved. Though she hadn't finalized her understanding yet with Swan and Sato, the insert contained a generic daycare commitment, crowned by X's ten thousand dollar guarantee.

Next, she paid a visit to the Body of Christ. The tuition check had been delivered. Ui was covered for one semester's tuition – room and board at Christ the King in Honolulu. The following semester she would attend Kamehameha Schools, Hawaii's lasting legacy to native children. The admission and scholarship applications had been turned in.

"The sooner out of Ewa's, the better," Milissa suggested.

"Hoh, she already out," said Swan. "Gone Honolulu yesterday. Welfare went made Ewa let her go. Ewa got doze charges, ya?"

After allowing Swan to lower his resistance, gushing gratitude for all she'd done, Milissa drafted him to fund-raise and help run the daycare for its first six months. "I'm on my way to Maunaloa," she said as she closed the door on his agonizing smile. "I'll have X give you a call."

She found Kini alone at the office, typing up a job application form for the tenants. To Kini's credit, the document was simply worded, including a first-right-of-refusal clause, and requiring no more than a check mark and a name for its completion.

Milissa intended to deliver one to each family by day's end – not just to drop them off, but to make a personal appeal to every householder – to have the forms filled out on location if possible so that she could hand them in herself.

While she was still at the office, she took a call from the airport. The caller, an agent of Molokai Air, telephoned because "Mr. X asked me to report unusual activity. Was a dozen of 'em, all get up like warriors. Went drive away wit' Keoni Mikala. TV cameras, da whole bit."

"Headed where?"

"Never know. You like, I find out and call back."

"Not necessary."

Milissa had decided that today would be her last push in the field. The rest of her stay on Molokai would be dedicated to monitoring the progress of programs in place and tying up loose ends, not the least of which was getting the grant process rolling for the daycare.

"Kini, tell X to open the daycare trust account with Pastor Swan as co-signer. And tell him to call Swan. It has to be done today. I'll be meeting with Principal Sato tomorrow afternoon. I'd like him to know we mean business."

"Will do," Kini replied weakly. "Whenever he gets in."

As Milissa headed down Main toward Julio's – a comfortable place to start – she looked back and noticed John's pick-up pulling into town, bursting with brown skinned men in loin cloths and short feathered capes. They parked in front of John's and piled out. In T-shirt, boots, and jeans, it seemed as if John were the one in costume.

"And the sunglasses," Milissa whispered to herself. "He never wears sunglasses." Their agreement had been to avoid each other and to get together at the campsite every other night. His head turned in her direction. She knew he was looking, but he gave no sign.

There was a party at John's that night. Among the gathering were Puni "Nappy Kam" Kanikela, President of Sovereign Hawaii, and his Minister of Information, Alvaro Castinada.

Sovereign was a hard core vanguard of about a hundred separatists. Romanticized in the media for its confrontations with authority, it was the darling of the movement's under thirty set. Not all of those present were separatists, and many who were disagreed with the engagement tactics and militant rhetoric of Sovereign.

Their differences temporarily submerged, the enthusiastic participants sat in John's back yard in small, motley circles, eating, drinking, sharing an occasional joint, waiting for directions. Playing it close to the vest on the chance that X was listening in, Fidel didn't assemble them for orientation, but moved from group to group, laying out the ground work for the days to come.

"Shipments of paint and supplies will arrive here from Kaunakakai wharf each morning. Tomorrow we have three places ready to go. That allows us eight workers per house. We'll do three houses a day to begin with. The pace will pick up as our numbers increase."

"What? You da boss man?" Kimo gave Fidel a hostile smirk. "T'ought Nappy and Keoni be da kine."

Fidel passed over Kimo's comment like a cold wind. "Divide yourselves into crews. Each crew select a lead. Leads report to Keoni."

"You like me be your boss?" Nappy asked in confidence, taking Kimo aside.

"Mo' bettah dan one fucking haole." Kimo lowered his voice in response to Nappy's composure. "Dis about da people, brah."

Nappy put his hand on the back of Kimo's neck and pulled him gently forward. "You see me following Fidel's orders, ya?"

Kimo nodded.

"What you t'ink den? Nappy's just one dumb kanaka, let Fidel go suck him in?"

Kimo stretched his "No" and rolled his eyes, stubborn but subdued.

"I can be one lead," Keku said, tapping Nappy on the shoulder.

Nappy kept his fix on Kimo, not yet sure that he'd behave.

"I like be one lead," Keku demanded. "My father was one house painter. I done everyt'ing from scrape to trim." She moved Kimo and stood in his place. "Can also keep my man in line."

"Den get your crew together, tita," Nappy grinned. "We got da women's lib."

"Comes to hard work, all da brahs for women's lib," Keku quipped, stepping back to size him up. "You just da kine."

At the back of the yard, a haole boy in his late teens offered John and Fidel a hit of pot as they approached his little seance. John accepted the joint, took a drag, and passed it to Fidel, who received the lit end between his thumb and forefinger, crushed it out, and returned it to its owner.

Oblivious to its condition, the young man toked at the extinguished joint. "Uh . . . swww, swww . . . This is, uh . . . swww, swww . . . Olika and Denise . . . swww . . . and Dexter, I'm Dexter." He examined the compressed end of his creation, touched it to his tongue to make sure it wasn't lit, and handed it to Denise.

"Dexter." John went into a crouch. "I'm Keoni. Dis Fidel. We like brief you on da haps." He could see that the three were going to need some nursing. "I'll take deze," he said, looking up. Fidel nodded and walked away.

"For starters," John continued with Dexter, "you gotta put dat hair under a hat. Otherwise, you'll get 'em all t'rough wit' paint."

"No problemo, dude," Dexter replied, casting back his mane of sun-bleached hair. "I'll shave it off and start again."

Olika muttered out of his head-hung trance. "Brah, you one lolo white boy. You cut 'em off, you gonna burn your lily coconut."

John got to his feet. "I'll find you a hat. You t'ree wit' me. But Olika gotta bring his brain, and . . ." He watched as Denise lit the roach and sipped the last few wisps. "No pakalolo on da job."

"I like one hit," called out a weak, girlish voice, approaching from behind.

Denise held up a scrap on the tip of her finger. "No mo' left, tita."

Ewa snatched the tiny remnant, popped it in her mouth, and scurried back into the dark.

John followed with a cautious smile. "Ewa, you here for work?"

"What you t'ink?" she answered, shading her sunken eyes beneath the bill of a too large baseball cap. "You t'ink I no good for nothing?"

He put his arm around her and walked her to the steps of his workshop. "You off da shit den, ya? Cannot do da kine and work 'round here. Dis too important to be fucked up wit' a bust."

She leaned away. "No treat me like dat, brah. You know I used to be one revolutionary."

"Ain't no revolution, tita. Just hard work."

As she sank in his single-armed embrace, John realized how frail she'd become. "Hoh, you one walking clothes hanger, girl. Cannot work so sick like dat."

"I coming down from smack," she whined, shivering slightly, then reaching over and gripping his sleeve. "Gotta let me do dis t'ing for keep busy. Otherwise, no can stay straight. Jesus telling me to reach out."

John held her away. His fingers touched around her biceps. "Tita, you too weak."

Ewa growled and dug her nails into his forearms. He winced, surprised at her strength.

"Now I geev 'em one head butt," she said, feinting slowly in the direction of his forehead.

As John let go, she dropped her hands and pressed her palms against his thighs, bowing her elbows slightly in, playing the femme fatale. "Maybe little Ewa not so weak. You t'ink?"

"Hokay, you can work da kitchen. But I see one single lolo look, you out. And dis." He took the hat from her head and made a pocket in it like a catcher's mitt. "No hiding in dis hat."

She fretted with her hair. "Can keep da God damn hat. Got lotta funky hats."

"See you at sunrise den. My back porch."

CHAPTER NINETEEN

"Bacon, toast, pineapple, coffee," Cory called out as she and Ewa bustled through the back yard gate. "Keoni, something to set these trays on."

John produced a beat-up folding table from his laundry room.

Committed to the action that lay ahead, Cory had taken two weeks off from work. "Easy found Ewa on your front porch this morning. She's been requisitioned."

"I told her to meet me on da back porch," John replied. "How's she doing?"

"She's doing more than you right now. Ewa honey, get some cups."

John looked at Ewa sternly. "She's on probation. Id'nat right, Ewa?"

Ewa nodded contritely and looked at Cory.

"Go on back," Cory said. "I'll deal with the massa."

"She eat yet?" John asked as Ewa left the yard.

"Coffee. Says she's not hungry."

"Don't let her work without eating."

"This table," Cory fussed, setting out the food, "it's uneven."

The workers, up now for half an hour, started edging toward their breakfast.

"Can use da garden hose for clean up when you t'rough," John announced.

While they ate, John moved among them, assessing their readiness. "Gotta be prepared for anyt'ing." He directed his comments at Nappy, Alvaro, and the other dominant members of the group. "X might show up first t'ing. Just keep 'em working. No confrontations. No excuse to bring da sheriff in. We like dis t'ing to grow, so touchy touchy for da meantime."

"Listen to da man," Loka agreed, standing by the table, stacking bacon and pineapple on a piece of toast, broadcasting his advice to get John's attention.

"Loka!" John shouted, happy to see his old friend. The two whopped hands and tumbled through the three-tiered grip. "How you been?"

Loka put a piece of toast on top and crushed his sandwich to a bite-sized density. "Never see you down da Kama Aina anymore."

"Got da best of me, da night life. Besides, Maria rules da roost. She likes her papa home."

"Brought da supplies." Loka motioned toward the front of the house, barely missing Ewa as she moved around him with another tray of toast and bacon. "Dat Ewa? Hoh, everybody coming to da party, ya? Got my man Sea here too. He like eat before we divvy up da paint."

At the mention of food, Sea stepped forward, head slightly bent to mask his eagerness.

"Sea, dis Keoni."

Sea pressed his palms together.

With a corresponding bow and backward wave, John invited Sea to the table.

Loka prodded Sea with kind impatience. "Go, brah," he said. "You gonna waste away."

Sea pressed his palms more tightly and stared fervently at John.

"Go," said John, almost irritated by the man's timidity.

"Most kind," said Sea, selecting pineapple and toast from trays not yet defiled by bacon grease. "Shukria," he added gratefully, then hunkered by the gate, noticeably apart from the rest.

"Devadasi," Nappy said and sat down carefully beside him.

Nappy didn't know the meaning of the Hindi word, but getting no response and hoping to draw Sea out, he used it again, this time pointing at Loka who stood a short distance away talking with John. "Devadasi."

"I am truly surprised," Sea said with a smile. "Rather than involve ourselves in the pastimes of the sudra, perhaps you, your temple dancer friend, and I can while away the morning with the deeper meanings of the *Gita*."

"Gita! Da Hindu good book. I pegged you right, den. You from India."

Sea shrank into his crouch, hoping no one had overheard.

Noticing his discomfort, Loka entered in. "Hey, Naps. Howzit, brah?"

"Been conversing wit' your man like you suggested. He no like discuss da kine."

"Mr. Sea. Dis Nappy Kam. President of Sovereign Hawaii. He got friends can maybe help you down da line."

Sea maneuvered Nappy quickly through the handshake he had learned from Loka.

"Hoh, plenty facile wit' da motions, Mr. Sea. Whip it on me one more time."

Sea kidded softly as he reproduced the moves with cybernetic ease, "Sahib Kam, by Nappy I am understanding that you sleep a lot."

Nappy nodded, playing along. "Me and Smiley and da boys. We kick back plenty now da wicked witch is dead. How 'bout you? Loka tells me something's keeping you awake at night."

Sea looked at Loka for direction.

Loka huddled with the two. "Mr. Sea's a political refugee from da Punjab."

"One Sikh," Nappy blurted out, overloaded with delight.

Sea unleashed a slashing glance.

"Hoh, sorry," Nappy said, backing down his decibels. "I never meet one Sikh. Where's your head rag, Mr. Sea?"

Sea ran his fingers through his close-cropped hair. "Sadly, Sahib Kam, my kesh is now suspended for the sake of revolution."

"Reminds me of da sisters in Algeria – taking off da veil when dey planted purse bombs in da French cafés. Trying to look European. Un-hiding to stay hid, ya?"

"You are mistaken in this likeness, Sahib Kam. I am not a terrorist."

"So, why da incognito? How come you on da run?"

After Loka's reassurances that Nappy could be trusted, Sea revealed that he was Kumar Singh, a journalist sought by Punjabi authorities for information in the death of a Sikh official, assassinated for betraying the cause of sovereignty to pacifist conciliation. Sea had claimed in his daily column that the presumed assassins were entrapped by an agent provocateur who did the actual killing. Details in the article were seen as evidence that Sea had prior knowledge. When he ignored a summons to appear, a warrant was issued for his arrest.

Rather than face the prospect of providing evidence against his fellow Sikhs, Sea fled by way of China, eventually securing passage out of Shanghai with several Chinese dissidents in the belly of a merchant ship headed for Hawaii. While anchored beneath the northern cliffs of Molokai, waiting until dark to steal across the channel into Honolulu Harbor, the ship attracted the attention of the Coast Guard. Sea, the only one who couldn't pass as crew, was hurled overboard as she was being seized.

Three hours later he dragged himself, half drowned, onto the lava beds at Make Horse, where Loka happened to be fishing. After reviving him and getting some sense of his plight, Loka realized their mutual good fortune – the chance meshing of their interests – and the two made a pact. In exchange for safe haven, Sea would school Loka in the teachings of his faith.

Loka's hunch that he'd find help for Sea among the Maunaloa influx had paid off. Nappy promised his support and that of his attorney. "Anyt'ing else you need . . . Loka, you know Alvaro."

Nappy pointed across the yard to his second in command. "Put Sea in touch wit' him."

By eight, the crews were scraping and taping. Fidel had scheduled the most conspicuous work sites first. Two of the initial three were visible across the field from Stockmans. Julio had balanced his portfolio. Not only was his house at the top of Fidel's list, he'd also signed up for a south side rental, spoken to Kini about a job, and obtained an application for a home loan.

"Yellow on yellow," Keku called out as she headed toward the back of the house. "Just like you ordered. Come, you can lay on da first stroke."

Julio saw Milissa coming up the other side of Main – on her way to help him with his loan form – but he didn't want to miss the christening. He dropped a stack of old newspapers at Stan's feet and ran to join Keku.

"Learning a skill?" Milissa razzed, recognizing Cory's brother beneath his painter's hat. She watched him draw a yard of tape and fix it deftly to the newsprint tacked against the inside edge of the sill.

"It's an existential art form," Stan answered. "You fix things up about to be torn down." He finished covering the window and stepped away to join Milissa, pulling her toward the street for a full view of the homely facade. "Ever notice how windows look like eyes?" He sighted with his thumb as if to measure for perspective. "You take one out, the other stares right at you."

Julio appeared in the unmasked window.

Milissa waved to get his attention.

"I think I'll leave the sighted one uncovered." Stan went on, talking now to himself. "Let someone else finish the job."

"What's this about?" Milissa asked as Julio opened the front door.

"Dey painting my house. Fidel gonna fix my wiring. Put a handle on my faucet." He explained MCC's reimbursement scheme.

"Might work," she said, reflecting on how John had kept the secret. "I'll check the code. Where else are they working?"

"T'ink dey doing Mannie." He held his loan application out as if he had been caught with something stolen.

"You think you deserve my help?"

"Just following your lead, Keiki. Remember what you tell me? No more wait and see?"

"Memorializing Tutu's grave are we?" Milissa asked.

"Pau," announced the fibrous little man, stepping back and jutting forth his full, black beard – brush in one hand, rag in the other, both delicately aloft, preparing to affix his signature to the still wet sign. "Ka Lua Kupapa'u o Tutu Pualani. Tutu Pualani's corpse pit. You like?"

"Did X commission this?"

He moved to the lower right hand margin and stroked in *Jason Dinn*. "Nope," he answered, continuing to appraise his work. "You still with Stockmans?"

She recognized the name. "You're the guy who owns the kite shop."

He remained engrossed.

"It's nice. But we had something more durable in mind."

He finally turned and looked at her. "Then I'm your man."

"You'd work for Stockmans?"

"This town's my livelihood. Can't afford to be too partial."

Over the top of the sign, Milissa recognized Moke painting Mannie's downspouts.

A group of reporters came out of the house. "Your work?" one asked as Jason hurried away. They had rummaged through the neighborhood all morning, pitching in at work sites, running to the deli for refreshments, impatient with the tempo but hung up on the ground until their takeoff times. John had kept the genie in the jar, telling them the town was being renovated by default, but leaving out the legal implication.

Milissa had decided to stay out of it. Her urge to steal the limelight was muted by a waning sense of obligation to Stockmans. She could feel the stir of the impending chase. But like the rabbit who had set the pace, she sensed that it was time to leave the track. She held her hands up to the reporters, put off her impulse to pester Moke, and headed for the office to see if X had opened the daycare account.

"He left yesterday morning for Maui," Kini reported. "His mother's. His message said he doesn't want to be disturbed."

"Patching it up with the wife, I hope?"

"Afraid not." Kini looked at Milissa for a second to set her up for the news. "She's taken the children to the mainland. Her parents."

"Did he make the deposit?"

"Not according to the ledger."

Milissa looked out the window. The press had assembled in front of the deli. X caught sleeping, she thought. Doesn't want to be disturbed.

Jock arrived on the two p.m. out of Honolulu. Fidel was there to greet him. "Any press in Maunaloa?"

"A small swarm all morning. They're getting antsy. KOHA's packed it in already – at least their camera crew. They're outside in the parking lot talking to the charter guy from Sea Wings."

"Point them out." Jock keyed in a number on his cell phone and maneuvered Fidel toward the exit as he listened to it ring. "Vanessa," he responded, pulling Fidel to a halt at the curb. "Jock Bissell here. Any openings?" He scanned the lot while she was bringing up her boss's schedule.

"They're in a Neon," said Fidel.

"I count five." Neons were the stock in trade of the airport's only car rental agency.

"Over there. Dark blue."

"Park next to them. If they try to leave, block their way."

"Block their way?"

Jock returned to Vanessa. "Four hours sounds good. On Saturday?" He shooed Fidel away, then grabbed him by the elbow. "Those pictures," he whispered, covering the receiver.

Fidel handed him some shots of Maunaloa.

"We couldn't ask for more," he crooned into the phone, pointing at his watch and mouthing “three, three minutes,” to Fidel.

Fidel walked off muttering about being treated like a gofer.

“The Hilton,” Jock continued with Vanessa. “It has a helo-pad. . . . Of course, the ride’s on us.” He perused the photos while she cautioned that the four hour block of Maunaloa time was only penciled in.

“Understood,” he said, making his way into the parking lot. “Any idea when we’ll know for sure?” He spotted Fidel sitting in his pick-up. “Yes, it would be nice to see him too. . . .You have my number.”

He hailed Fidel in a loud voice as he approached. “Mr. Monzón? Jock Bissell.” He opened the driver’s side door and glad-handed Fidel unceremoniously from the cab. “Good news,” he projected, loud enough to be heard by the cameramen leaning on their car an empty parking space away, “Jimmy Carter’s interested in the Maunaloa visit. He has an opening Saturday afternoon.”

“Jimmy Carter,” Fidel replied, rocking slightly on stiff legs and tucking in the tail of his shirt.

Jock slouched against the fender. “Not so good news. Our counsel says the UN wouldn’t think of intervening. It’s out of their jurisdiction.”

“I knew that,” Fidel chuckled, warming up to Jock’s malarkey. “Internecine.”

“The Panthers tried it in the sixties.” Jock continued to play to his audience while he took his place in the truck. “They claimed the ghettos were virtual colonies. Here, you have the Australian thing – a quasi-colonial connection.”

Fidel closed his door on Jock’s line and pulled around to the baggage claim.

Jock kept an eye on the mirror while his stuff was being loaded.

“How much of that was bullshit?” Fidel asked as they headed away.

“That was Carter’s agent on the phone. I’ll know for sure by tomorrow. Here they come.”

The Neon pulled in close behind, tailing them as if they were in tandem.

Now more at ease, Jock began his update. In eight days, on the day following John's eviction, Carter was slated to attend the National Conference on Disadvantaged Youth in Honolulu. The event was a spin-off of the Felix v Waihee Consent Decree – a Federal Court, class action settlement awarding the "disabled" children of Hawaii millions of dollars, to be paid out by the state for rehabilitation. Included in the class were children who had suffered historic, societal neglect. Many kids on Molokai – "mostly up in Maunaloa," Jock conjectured – fell within the definition.

"No doubt," Fidel agreed, still wary of the emphasis.

"How's things on your end?" Jock asked.

"They should be applying final coats about the time we get there. The first three houses."

"Can't stress enough the need for full expansion of your project, up to and through the time that Carter's on the set. How many workers do we have?"

"Twenty four as of this morning."

"We'll need ten times that many by week's end. As soon as we get there, call the media together. I'll announce a Wednesday morning press release."

"This is it." Fidel turned left as the Kam tailed off into the rumpled, three block stretch of Maunaloa Road.

"Stop here."

They parked in front of the warehouse.

"Tell me about our hero."

"The mainstay of the resistance. All the young men look up to him. If it weren't for the radical edge, he'd be perfect for local office."

"A real shaker then?" Jock replied, taking in the town.

"Oh no. Underspoken, a kind of stoic, silent injun type until you get him going. Then he can be eloquent." Fidel tittered under his breath, amused at his own magnanimity.

"Sunday. Odd day for an eviction."

"Perfect really. A day of inspiration."

Jock put his arm out the window and waved for the Neon, parked a dutiful distance behind, to pull ahead.

The Neon passed slowly and stopped in front of the deli. Jock and Fidel watched as a woman of Japanese descent walked down the steps, spoke briefly with the driver, and looked back toward their pick-up.

Jock pointed to an unpaved area in front of Maunaloa Market. "Pull up over there. And don't get out."

"Mr. Monzón," the woman called, crossing the street and holding her mike to Fidel's unopened window. "Mr. Monzón," she repeated as Fidel let down a two inch space. "Did we hear correctly? Jimmy Carter's coming to Maunaloa?"

Fidel turned his head toward Jock. Jock leaned forward slightly and then, sure that he'd been made, reached across and lowered the glass all the way. "Sadako Shige, is that you?"

She framed her face in the opening and visibly switched off her mike. "Jock," she replied sedately, "you have something for me?"

Heedless of the cameras, Jock hurried around the back of the truck, picked Sadako up, and did a spin. "Whadda ya call that?" he asked, nodding sideways toward Fidel. "Nibbling around the edges? Shaking the tree?"

"Never go to the front office for a scoop," Sadako announced emphatically, quoting advice she'd received from Jock years before while interning at the *Tome*. Her pupils darted from side to side. They were surrounded by reporters.

"Where can we talk?" Jock asked.

She turned him around and aimed him through the re-creating wall of news hounds.

"Mr. Bissell," one reporter shouted, "what's in store for Maunaloa?"

Jock halted as they fell away and folded back around in front of him, blocking his access to the deli. Several questions came at once. He composed himself and waited for silence. "The Maunaloa Crisis Committee will have a press release on Wednesday morning. You won't be disappointed. Till then, no comment."

"KOHA," Jock remarked, settling at a window table to keep an eye on the press. "An NBC affiliate." He looked at Sadako dubiously. "Field reporter?"

"Anchor, Jocko. Anchor. Six o'clock. I've been out here ten years."

"So what's an anchor doing on a still emerging story?"

"I got a tip you'd be here. Thought it might be worth a special."

"A tip from whom?"

"What's it worth?"

"Not important. You've got more to offer than your sources."

Fidel came through the door and turned toward their table.

Jock pointed at the counter. "Be with you in a minute," he said, returning to Sadako. "Tell me about your special."

"You tell me," Sadako replied, showing him an usher's palm. "You're the ring master."

"Let's make this simple. I'll tell you what I need. You tell me what you need."

"You first."

"An hour special, prime time, after Carter's visit, before he leaves the islands. Daily prime time coverage for the next seven days. A daily briefing on national reaction to the Maunaloa crisis. 'Maunaloa Crisis,' that's our catch phrase. And you?"

"First crack at Carter. Even before the networks. An inside line on breaking stories and a reasonable lead over the other affiliates."

"Can we use your station's chopper? Here and back this Saturday?"

"We can."

"There's your interview. An hour in the air." He shook her hand. "Of course, this hinges on him coming. I should hear by tomorrow. Meantime, not a word. You'll be the first to know."

Sadako stood to leave. "My flight's at four. Tune in at six. I'll have a spot on Maunaloa."

Jock remembered Fidel. "Sadako, Mr. Monzón."

She patted him on the back as she passed the counter. "We know Fidel."

Fidel's head adjusted to her exit like the needle on a compass, an overly precise reaction to such casually transmitted praise. They didn't know him. But that was not important to Fidel. Important was that they knew *of* him.

"She can see me anytime," Jock said, lifting himself onto the stool beside Fidel. "But don't tell her anything without checking first. Okay?"

The waitress came with a refill.

Fidel watched the coffee swirl. "Are you ready to see the work sites?"

Jock smiled at his client's nonresponse, then swiveled and peered through the open door. "They're still out there."

The hubbub ebbed as he and Fidel stepped onto the portico. "I," he said, loud enough to blunt the ends of several blurted questions. "I," he repeated, in a tone of admonition, "am aware that there are rumors." He noticed that Sadako and her entourage were gone. "Don't be misled by your competition. You'll hear from us on Wednesday. Nothing's certain until then."

Jock glanced into the open lots as they drove along the lane in front of John's house. "Recent demolition?"

Fidel pointed the other way. "If I hadn't come along this would all be gone." A patch of yellow flashed between the shabby structures facing on the field.

"Let me guess. That must be our beacon."

They turned down Main and parked by a group critiquing Julio's new paint job for PBS.

"No trim," Jock commented as he stepped down from the cab.

"No way," Fidel replied. "They're just not done. Who's in charge here? Where's Keoni?"

"Julio's a no frills kind of guy," Stan was telling Smitty and Michael Teague.

"Pure yellow," Julio put in. "Like da sun."

"Where's Keoni?" Fidel repeated, then stomped into the thicket that surrounded Mannie's house next door. "No trim my ass. He knows better than this."

"Monzón," the old man called from his back porch the moment that Fidel broke through, "you step on Tutu's bones, she put a curse on you."

Fidel froze as if he'd stepped into a mine field.

"Saw what dey done to Julio's. Too shrill. Good t'ing I got dat scrub to block da view. Dis blue your boys put on is Tutu's favorite kine. You like?"

"Have you seen Keoni?" Fidel asked, cautiously retracing his steps.

"I telling everyone how I asked Stockmans plenty times to paint da last five years. Been bitching 'bout my plumbing too. Got no pressure."

Fidel abandoned Mannie in mid-complaint and backed into the bush.

"No suction in da lua," Mannie went on, laughing as Fidel receded through his cataracts. "Cannot flush da kine."

Milissa opened Easy's kitchen door. "You alone?"

"Only me," Easy answered, blowing back a floured strand of hair. "Maria went play da school yard. I making biscuits. How you?"

"Staying on the sidelines."

"What you mean, sidelines? Come. Can cut da biscuits. Lotta volunteers to feed. So exciting dis, ya? Everybody pitching in."

Ewa appeared behind Milissa. "More biscuits, Aunty. Dey 'bout ready to eat me."

"On top da stove," Easy replied, flouring her board. "Tell 'em plenty chili left."

Wriggling her shoulders to repel Milissa's haole taint, Ewa filled her tray and scurried from the room.

"Keiki, where you stay last night? I no see your car in front of Keoni's."

There was no answer.

Easy turned, her hands held up like a surgeon ready to be gloved.

Milissa touched her finger to her lips.

"Hoh, you keeping secrets," Easy whispered. "How you figgah dis?" she asked her giant clump of dough, rolling it out with kind attention. "Maybe Keiki and Keoni leading one double life? Bet you . . ." She punched out several rounds and paused. "Bet you dey got one love nest."

Milissa kissed her on the cheek. "Gotta go."

Easy put two biscuits in an ornate china bowl and covered them with chili. "Bring back da bowl and spoon tomorrow. Now go, before I put you to work."

The inner circle – expanded by Nappy, Alvaro, and Jock, but absent the impulsive Stan – pow-wowed over dinner in John's living room.

"Stan's idea," Cory told Jock. "He's predicting we'll be visible from the space station."

Jock chuckled. "Now there's an item for the news in brief."

Fidel didn't like the joke. "We're gonna mute the colors. Mix 'em up to tone 'em down."

"Oh, don't," Jock objected. "Make a statement. Knock 'em dead. What'd we order?"

"You saw it. Lemon yellow, barn red, and a kind of blue. I was with Stan on the idea of bright, but I wasn't expecting . . ." Fidel shook his head, admitting to himself that somehow Stan, expressly uninvited, had made it to the meeting anyway.

"What kind of blue?" Cory asked, knowing the answer, but tickled by Fidel's chagrin.

"Da can said *Jay Blue,*" Nappy answered. "Got one jay blue house already."

Loka could hear them laughing from the yard. He peered through the screen. "Was checking out da artichokes at Friendly Market," he announced as if he were already in the room. "Pastor Swan come by and say he got one cousin named Toma, a sheriff's cadet down Kaunakakai." He came through the door holding up the produce. "Can steam deze, you like," he said, commanding their attention with his nonchalance.

John took the artichokes to the kitchen.

Loka sat against the wall. "Toma let it slip dat Stockmans gonna bring da sheriff up tonight to collar Nappy on some traffic fines. You got tickets, Nappy Kam?"

"Parking tickets. Dey been saving 'em up to make 'em count. Stopped me plenty times, but never took me in. But dat's in Honolulu. Cannot arrest me here for tickets outta town."

"They can," said Cory. "Not usually done. Honolulu'd have to pay to bring you back."

Jock gazed inward as the rest debated Nappy's getaway. No use trying to escape by road. Their trucks were well known. Alvaro proposed hiking down the mountain and paddling to Lanai.

"We got my outboard," John offered, standing in the doorway to the kitchen, keeping an eye on the artichokes. "Maybe Moke's. It's stronger for the open sea."

"Too conspicuous. Paddling at night dey'll never notice."

"Da channel's too dangerous at night."

"Carpe diem."

Everybody looked at Jock.

"Dum de dum," came back Alvaro. "Jocko speaking in tongues."

"Seize da day," said John.

"Our break, not theirs," Jock went on. "We'll let them take him in. After a bit of hide and seek, after they've made a stink hounding him down for traffic tickets in front of the media, we'll pay the fine and march him back like Caesar from Pompeii."

"You'd do all dis for me, Jocko?" Nappy asked with a rueful smile.

"Let's say it's for the cause," Jock replied.

"You picking up da tab?"

"I am."

"You're on." Nappy pointed at Jock to seal the arrangement. "Last time I checked, da fine was creeping up around one t'ousand."

The room filled with the murmur of appreciation that follows a well-played poker hand.

Not pausing for the pain, Jock whipped out his phone and called Sadako. "Shige. Bissell here. Sheriff's coming up tonight to bring in Nappy. . . . Honolulu parking tickets would you believe. . . . First we'll make them look. Should be quite a show. . . . You're the only one. . . . Through the brother of a local deputy. . . . Yes, in confidence." He looked at Loka for assurance.

"His cousin." Loka nodded.

Jock fell silent while Sadako called for transportation. "We'll keep him under wraps," he said when she returned. "Morning? We need you tonight. By afternoon, assuming I hear from Carter, we'll have the networks up here. I want you to precede them. You're the harbinger, the reason that they'll come." He put his hand over the phone. "That'll get her in gear."

She asked to talk with Nappy.

"Only for a minute," Jock insisted. "Sixty seconds. We've got to get him out of here." He handed Nappy the phone. "Don't tell her anything."

"This is the first place they'll look," Cory said. "Mine'll be second."

"Mannie's," John suggested.

"Mannie's?" Jock asked.

John briefed Jock on Tutu's grave.

"Excellent. A perfect place to focus the attention of the press."

"All clear," Loka called out from the back porch. "Plenty dark."

While Nappy and Alvaro, led by John, made their way along the unobtrusive paths that honeycombed the town, Cory took the shorter, open route to ready Mannie for his house guest.

"T'rough here," John pointed, locating a childhood breach in Mannie's back yard fence.

"Sovereign's yours till I get sprung," Nappy told Alvaro. "Never know how long."

"You covered, brah," Alvaro said, giving him a hug. "Be consulting wit' you constantly."

Alvaro yanked away the thorny brush, clearing the passage for his chief. "Power to da sovereign kine," he whispered as Nappy burrowed after John.

"Power," Nappy whispered back, scuttling, hands and feet, across the old man's unkept garden patch.

"For Christ's sake, why didn't you call me when they first showed up?" X asked, talking to Milissa from his mother's place on Maui. "I've gotta get a call from the sheriff to find out what's happening in my own town? . . . Ya, the sheriff. . . . No, Fitzpatrick at the main station. The head fucking guy. He's on the other line. . . . No, I didn't open the God damned account. . . . I'll do it in the morning, if I have time. . . . You laugh? . . . No, you listen. This has priority. I'll talk to you tomorrow."

After he finished with Fitzpatrick, X called Harry. "Get a bulldozer out there. . . . Move a little dirt around the clearing, but don't disturb anything that's stationary. . . . Don't *do* anything, Harry! Just look busy. You're good at that."

The pilot hovered over the rubble-strewn ground, not daring to set down for fear of damaging his landing gear. Finally, at Sadako's insistence, he risked a fine and landed on the road in front of the warehouse, settling just long enough for Buck to bail out and catch Sadako in his arms, then springing skyward with a vengeance.

Jock ran up to greet them. "Good catch," he told the cameraman.

Buck picked up his camera and grimaced at the disappearing point of light. "Pilot's pissed. Sadako got him out of bed."

"Bed? It's only seven thirty."

"He wasn't exactly sleeping."

"My fault," Jock apologized, uneasy that the law had not arrived in search of Nappy.

"So where's the action?" Sadako asked.

"Nothing yet," Jock answered, guiding her across the darkened clearing toward John's house. "Watch your step. It's rained."

Sadako stopped. In every direction she saw rocks and bricks and bits of fence, chunks of concrete, cans, and non-biodegradable debris from leveled middens, all barely silhouetted by the distant inner light of houses in a row. "A little moonscape. You should see it from the sky. Over there." She pointed out beyond the warehouse to where the ground was graded for construction and then allowed through winter, spring, and early summer to erode. "It's like a thousand heads, all the little boulders peeking through the surface. What's the theme here, Jocko?"

"The dialectic of emergent and recessive forces."

"Give me that in pabulum form."

"When power is at its peak, the enemy is near. Your little army of misshapen heads were right beneath the surface, waiting for Stockmans to get bogged down over here. Watch the ruts." Jock took her arm. "Instead of shoring up their victory on the south side, Stockmans overreached, and now they're losing ground on both fronts." Jock left Sadako and Buck to set up in John's side yard and went back in.

Behind the house the volunteers lay awake, talking among themselves in anticipation of the sheriff's arrival. Alvaro urged them to get some sleep. "Another twelve hour day tomorrow. Never no mind da man. He come, I'll shake you out."

Flashlights appeared through the gate. Sergeant Kale Ford and six deputies were suddenly moving through their midst, quietly questioning men who approximated Nappy's description.

"That you, Mr. Kanikela?

"Not me."

"Identification please."

"Stand over here where we can see you."

"Shit, brah, we got no constitution?"

"You others just stay where you are."

"You got one search warrant?"

When a couple of look-alikes were taken out front for questioning, the rest of the workers followed, ignoring orders to stay behind.

Rufus stepped ahead of Kale and knocked on John's open door.

"Deputy Rufus," John intoned as Kale moved the little wire-haired impertinence aside.

"John Mikala," Kale said in an official tone.

"Eh, Kale," John replied, latching the screen. "What brings you here dis time of night?"

"Got one warrant for Puni Kanikela. He stay wit' you?"

"No Nappy here, brah."

"Mind if we look inside?" Rufus challenged.

"You like take one look, Ruf?" John moved his eyes from Rufus to Kale and pushed the screen door open so that Kale had to step away. "We let *Do Right* check, eh Sarge?"

Rufus put his hand on his holster and slipped through the opening.

John smiled at Kale through the screen. "Maybe you like me take Rufus hostage, ya?"

"Hoh, brah," Kale said, rolling back his eyes, then craning to follow Rufus' scrutiny of the premises. "You tempting me."

"Groovy gangbusters," Dexter shouted from the clutch of volunteers now hemming in the men assigned to Kale's back.

"Groovy?" Olika lifted his arm and put a space between himself and the sun-bleached haole boy, tipping him off balance. "You sound like one beatnik. Fifties ain't cool."

Raucous laughter pealed all around. "Groovy gangbustahs. Groovy gangbustahs," reverberated the phrase.

Kale's back-ups, Cadet Toma and another greenhorn, tensed and menaced by the coarse sounding laughter, braced themselves for action.

Alvaro moved to the center of the crush. "Everybody chill," he said, raising his hands. He gave Olika an impatient look and lowered his voice. "Why you pick on dis haole boy, brah? Bad guys come in all colors. Aim at da ones wit' da badges and guns."

Sadako stood outside the front gate. "The latest in the strife between Stockmans Inc. and Maunaloa residents," she said, turning from the crowded yard to face the camera. "The County Sheriff is out in force tonight on Molokai. Here to capture Nappy Kanikela, Hawaii's golden boy of nationhood. Nappy came to Maunaloa yesterday to help the tenants renovate their homes – a last ditch effort, we are told, to save the town. An offense to some, but not a crime. Our copy of the warrant cites Kanikela's unpaid parking tickets." A murmur came from the crowd. "Moments ago, a deputy entered the house you see behind us." Buck focused on John's front door. "He's coming out. He appears to be alone."

Rufus kept his back to the onlookers as he reported to Kale. "Not in there. Mikala acted like they knew we were coming. Playing a game. I'd say he's somewhere in town. Or the woods."

Kale stepped out of hearing range and radioed his captain.

"Everybody stay put," Rufus called out.

"We under arrest?" asked Olika's girlfriend Denise.

"You will be if you try to leave," Kale answered, coming back onto the porch.

"Hoh!" Olika shouted. "Cannot arrest us all for Nappy's tickets. Dis ridiculous."

"Listen up," Kale commanded. "We just received a telephonic warrant. We're seeking Kanikela now on Federal charges. Anybody hiding him or failing to report his whereabouts will be prosecuted. Alvaro Castinada?"

"Present," Alvaro answered.

"Mr. Castinada, over here."

While Olika and Denise were checked for warrants, Kale led Alvaro from the yard. Buck caught the scene on camera as Kale bandied briefly with Alvaro, then cuffed him and put him in a squad car.

"Sergeant Ford," Sadako said, closing in on Kale. "KOHA. We have some questions."

"Can only tell you what I told dem," Kale patted the trunk of the car as a signal for the driver to leave.

"That'll be fine." Sadako looked at Buck, who pointed, prompting her to begin. "We are talking to Sergeant Kale Ford of the County Sheriff's Department. Sergeant Ford, we understand authorities have raised the stakes against Sovereign's leader, Kanikela. Can you fill us in?"

"We have a telephonic warrant authorizing us to bring him in for harboring a fugitive."

"Can you give us more on the charge?"

"Only dat it's Federal. Da fugitive was being sought for tax evasion."

"Any success in locating Nappy?"

"He's not where we t'ought he'd be. We t'ink he's still on Molokai."

"Why did you arrest Alvaro Castinada?"

"Obstruction. He'll only give us his name – keeps citing da Geneva Convention."

Sitting on the couch with his equipment – a two-line speaker cell phone and voice communication laptop FAX/PC – Jock was watching Sadako on TV. As she finished with Kale and did her closing, her voice, heard faintly through the window, marched ahead of its echo on the screen.

"The authorities have responded decisively to Sovereign's sudden presence in Maunaloa. One of its leaders is in custody, another is being sought. The impact of this reaction, how it will play out over the next several days, remains to be seen. We'll keep you informed as things heat up on Molokai. Sadako Shige, live for KOHA Late Breaking News."

Jock had been calling the networks since Nappy left, trying to bring them on board. But now, should Nappy decide to run from the Federal count, the coverage might actually compete with Maunaloa, drawing attention away. John had Nappy on the speaker phone, about to broach the issue when Fidel walked in.

"This is not traffic tickets," Fidel snarled, hearing Nappy's voice. "The man is charged with a crime. If immigration hears that I'm involved they'll terminate my visa."

"Visa?" Jock laughed, "They'll have us all behind bars."

"Can't let dat happen." Nappy answered, never in doubt about his intent. "Look plenty stink for Maunaloa if I split. So, how we gonna turn me in?"

Jock switched off the speaker and finished with Nappy one-on-one. They agreed on a simple plan. As a condition of his surrender, Nappy would be to allowed talk to the press before being taken away. Nappy's lawyer, Gary Spence, would make the arrangements. "Have something prepared. Not about sovereignty. That's already out there. About Maunaloa." Jock wrote down Spence's name.

"We can't let this slow us down," Fidel complained, taking a seat on the couch, impatient for Jock's attention.

Jock clicked off the phone. "Pick up Nappy's lawyer at the airport. Here's his name."

Fidel stuffed the slip of paper in his pocket. "Did you hear that they arrested Alvaro?"

"Did you hear me on the attorney?"

Fidel took out the slip and examined it, still not focusing. "Some of our guys are threatening violence." He looked at John. "Loka wants to talk to you. Give him this." He handed John the name. "He said that Sea went over the fence out back. Something about warrants."

John found Loka leaning against his van, still in his glasses, staring at the night sky. "About my man Sea," Loka said, letting John hang on the fragment.

"Ain't gonna talk to you till you come out of doze shades." John transferred them from Loka's face to his own and handed him the note. "Your bwana asked me to give you dis."

"Hoh, da stars too bright," Loka joked, shading his eyes to read.

"Nappy's lawyer," John said. "Pick up and delivery. Now, what about da mysterious Sea?"

"He needs a hideout."

"He in trouble?"

"He's here illegally. A political refugee. Wanted in da Punjab for conspiring wit' separatists."

John returned the glasses and made eye contact. "Don't shit me, Loka."

Loka held his hand up in an oath. "Swear on da haole Bible, brah. Been letting him stay in da van since he showed up, but Fidel no like da smell."

"Da smell?" John laughed. "Get him some deodorant."

"Dere's one more t'ing, brah. Actually, more to da point. Before Nappy went into hiding he set Sea up with Alvaro. Alvaro was supposed to put Sea in touch wit' dis guy." Loka read the name on Fidel's note. "Dis Spence guy can help Sea with his case. But I been listening. Alvaro's not so stable on his own – too loose with his talk about guns."

"You'd like to break da connection."

"Wit' Alvaro, ya. He and Sea been getting pretty tight. Just hope it's not too late. We can find him an attorney later on."

"Have him come see me. We'll get him tucked away."

"Where?"

"You don't have to know."

A second all-terrain vehicle, identical to the one already following him, pulled into John's rearview as he headed down the darkened tail of the Kam. From the lookout he caught the glimmer of Milissa's car, parked near the trail to their campsite. At the bottom of the grade, the tiny bone-white church loomed larger than itself beneath the full moon glow. Passing it and circling back behind a clump of trees, he came around to join with his pursuers as they crept, lights out, into the opening.

After sighing to a stop, the deputies, one in front, one behind, got out and shined their flashlights through his windows. "What's up, Keoni?"

John recognized Tobias, his old school chum.

The other man, whom he hadn't seen before, brought his head down close to John's, peered out through the windshield in the direction of Milissa's car, and nodded. "Someone waiting for you, Mr. Mikala?"

"My ipo."

"Step out da truck."

John complied. "We camping."

"You and Mr. Kanikela sharing one tent?"

John looked at Tobias, who was standing back observing. "Dis your trainee, brah?"

"Dis Titus Rizzo. Deputy Rizzo."

"Let me guess." John sized Rizzo up. "Desert Storm."

Rizzo took John by the back of the arm. "Let's have you put your hands against da car."

"No need," said Tobias.

John reached back and countered Rizzo's grip, leveraging his arm against the deputy's in preparation for a struggle. "Still lolo from da toxic fumes, eh Rizzo?"

Tobias stepped between the two. "No need," he commanded, prying them apart. "Cuz," he said to John while backing Rizzo away, "I like meet your ipo."

John, heart pounding, acquiesced with a faint nod and allowed Tobias to move him toward Milissa's car, but froze as Rizzo began to follow.

Tobias turned and lowered his hand. "Stay by the vehicles. In case we gotta make a call."

While Rizzo stood where he'd been stopped, refusing to retreat, the other two approached and tapped on Milissa's window.

"She's probably sleeping down below," John said.

Milissa sat up in the back seat.

John reached through and touched her as she rolled the window down. "Keiki, dis my . . . Dis my cousin, Tobias." He kept contact with Milissa, but leaned back so Tobias could see in.

Milissa got out. "Thought I'd wait up here. Too creepy down there alone last night."

Tobias shined his flashlight into the front and back seats.

She laughed nervously. "Your cousin's shaking us down."

Tobias crouched and traced his beam beneath the car. "Like see in da trunk."

She looked wide-eyed at John.

"Tobias t'inks we got Naps in da trunk."

"Naps in the trunk," Milissa groused, unlocking the lid. "No Naps in here. Too small. Too much junk." The trunk was crammed with her belongings.

"We camping, brah. Like I say, no Nappy here. You like come see?"

"Naw. Ain't searching t'rough da woods at night for no one."

"Who's Nappy?" Milissa asked as Tobias walked away. "So much for sneaking around."

Their tent was set back from the strand, wedged into a thicket of kiawe. John built a fire in the sand and explained the recent saga to Milissa, including Nappy and his whereabouts. Reflecting on his breach of confidence, he looked back at their den, certain that his trust in her needed no assurance. "You cut away some branches."

"I caught a thorn." Milissa's fingers stroked the tiny puncture in her heel, then wandered to her ankle bracelet. "Nice fire."

"Comes a little bit cooler dis time of year."

"The luster of mid-day on objects below," she quoted, capturing the glint of the moon in her anklet's silver plates. She tipped one of its petroglyphs in his direction. "This was our first connection – a symbol of our unity."

"Kau lua."

"Kau lua. The meaning of the design. Unity? That's it?"

"Man and woman. I said it would come to you."

She laid her head in his lap and held his hands against her heart. "Christmas," she said, turning on her side. "You can come to Seattle on Christmas. I'll be aching for you by then."

"You'll have your nose in a book all da time, ya? Make me feel like a house stud."

She swatted him playfully on the chest. "I'll strap you to my big brass bed."

"Sure, I'll come see you for da holiday. But we got to get it down mo' bettah before den. Long time between September and . . . What? When you graduate?"

She sat up and faced him, moved by his resolve. "June."

"You coming back to Molokai in June?"

"Whatever it takes." Her outward enthusiasm didn't wane, but she was not convinced that Molokai was her place to be. A subtle distance paused between them, come and gone so quick that it was felt but not remembered.

"I know what it takes. It takes family. You and me? Can we be family?"

"You're asking my opinion?"

John laughed self-consciously and shifted to his knees. "I'm asking for Maria, too."

She knew he was serious. But too serious. She didn't want it this way. She had to mix it up, to pull the question from his heart. She drew him forward and wrapped her legs around his waist. "I wasn't sure," she said, her straight arms pressed against his shoulders. "Thought you wanted to knock me up right here."

"You like make babies in da rain?" he asked, feeling a sprinkle on his neck.

She began to work his buckle.

"I love you, Keiki," he said, as if to let her know that sex was not a condition.

"Just fuck me," she said, unbuttoning his fly.

Turned on by her aggression, he helped her out of her shorts and positioned her legs, one over each of his arms.

"Let me put it in," she whispered, taking it out, cupping it in her hand to get it hard, then wetting it with her saliva. “Let me rub it here some.” She gave out a little cry as she stroked the head across her clitoris. “There it goes. Now push. Oh God, yes. Like that. Like that.”

The rain came harder. They didn’t notice.

He held his climax, moaning as if in pain.

“Oh God, I love that moan.”

He moved more rapidly.

“Yes, yes,” she pleaded, almost in panic as he emptied.

“Ahhh,” he unloaded. “Ahhh.”

They lay entwined until the rain began to chill.

“I bet it’s warmer in da water.”

They rose and entered without speaking, embracing as they lolled outside the gentle surf.

CHAPTER TWENTY

Jock had been up most of the night, dozing between communications. He'd faxed and telephoned the major networks with the Federal warrant update and chatted it with several prominent newscasters. As of six a.m. the Independent News Service, promising a freelancer from Oahu, was the only taker.

Gary Spence had made his way to Mannie's undetected. From there he negotiated the details of the surrender on Jock's terms. Everything was set for early afternoon.

Work began at seven. By eight, big Tiny Tuiasosopo and some of Kimo's teenage sidekicks had joined the effort. The crews had been instructed to form a cordon between Nappy and the press when he appeared. Otherwise, they were to stick to their normal routines. As John moved from site to site, cautioning against reaction to the taunts of rent-a-cops now stationed about the neighborhood, Loka and Sea showed up in separate vehicles loaded with supplies.

"No deliveries today," came the command of a young officer.

Loka produced a business card, then doubled his effort to unload, winking in help from Moke. The officer took the card to his sergeant, who was badgering Sea a few houses away.

"Aina Mano, Governor's Liaison," the sergeant read aloud. "We'll see about this." He rebuked the officer beneath his breath as they returned to Loka, already back in the driver's seat.

"Sorry, Mr. Mano," the officer said. His sergeant reached over his shoulder and handed Loka the card. "We're under orders. No deliveries today."

Loka put the card in his breast pocket, looked to the empty ground behind his truck, and headed for Keku's, his final stop. In the interim, Sea had finished unloading and left the area.

The sergeant and his junior marched to Keku's driveway, gathering reinforcements along the way. "Confiscate the supplies," he ordered. "They can claim them at the office. And Mr. Mano, or whatever your name is . . ." Turning to take back Loka's phony card, all he could see was Easy's sweaty, moon-shaped face, inches away and twice the size of his own.

"You on my property," she said, tipping up his badge. "And you ain't no police. Dis one trinket." She loosed the shield with disdain and chested him into the arms of his advancing men.

Weakened by a sudden change of chemistry, he drew into his radio. "We've got a situation," he reported. "Send a deputy." All the while, Keku's crew was furiously unloading the truck.

"You come strutting 'round my place," Easy warned, emanating Kali's rage, "mo' bettah you bring one army."

She hadn't moved, but somehow she'd increased. He felt alone beneath her wrath. His men had propped him up but kept themselves in check. He took out his gun and backed into their spongy space.

"Go ahead and shoot." Easy brandished the knuckles of her right hand. "I bust your coconut like Captain Cook." No one moved. "Dey send you out to capture Nappy Kam? You pissants haven't even got da nerve to capture me." She noticed Nakayama hot-footing it in her direction. The crew circled around in front of her, creating cover and confusion as she slipped through Keku's yard and wound her way back home.

"Where's da woman went accost dis man?" Nakayama asked.

"Dat's me," Keku said. "Dis patty ass went bump me when he

came up to da truck."

Nakayama waved abuse, then targeted the sergeant. "You say she big. How big?"

"Big, big," replied the sullen, beet red leader of the pack. "I think she's in the house."

His men, standing at a distance, choked back their laughter at the still fresh image of their sergeant cowering beneath the lady samurai.

Milissa had Sato on the line when Easy came through the back door. "The cafeteria will work," she assured him, pouring hot water into her cup, the receiver tucked beneath her chin. "A place to come in from the rain. . . . The grant forms? . . . Oh God, yes. I appreciate the forms. Wouldn't know where to begin. I'll stop by and pick them up."

She put down the phone, only glancing as Easy passed through into the living room. "Just can't get a decent cup of coffee where I'm staying," she called after Easy. "You like a cup?" She stuck her head around the corner. Easy was sitting on the couch, her face in her hands.

"Oh, Aunty." She ran across the room. "Aunty, you okay?"

Easy looked to where the ceiling met the wall, placed her index fingers to the inside corners of her eyes, and swept the tears away, then buried her face again in her hands. Her body began to heave. Milissa held on for the ride, consoling her until she finally stood and shook her blubbery arms to loose the crying spell. "Typical wahine," she spat, scolding herself as she peeked out through the curtains. "Hoh, I so piss," she added, huffing down on the couch.

"Pissed," said Milissa, "I thought someone had . . . well, died or something."

"Piss at myself. For pretending I can cash in wit' da haoles. Now X went hire plenty jackboots. Protecting me. So I can get my piece of da pie."

"Jackboots?" Milissa walked to the window.

"Security guards. Dey try take Loka's paint." She accented her complaint with karate chops and sank deeper in the cushions. "I pushed da head man." She wailed in disbelief. "Da sergeant. Damn near got shot. Now dey never let me buy one house." She joined Milissa at the window. "T'ink dey looking for Easy."

"You think! Did they call the sheriff?"

"Hoh, I got to clean up. Cannot let Maria see me like dis." She patted her hair and walked toward the bathroom.

"Did they call the sheriff, Aunty?"

Easy hummed to herself as she splashed water on her face and straightened in the mirror.

"Easy?"

"Saw Nakayama coming 'cross the lots." She turned to leave. "I go talk to him."

"Let me. I'll stop by on my way to Sato's. You pushed the guy?"

"Went bump him like dis." She demonstrated.

"No hands?"

Easy nodded her head.

"May not be as bad as you imagine."

"T'ink dey lock me up?" Easy asked, following Milissa to the door. "Ah, who cares." She stopped and contained her fright. "Easy been one goody goody sitting on da fence too long."

Milissa looked back on her way down the steps. "Yes, haven't we."

"You tell 'em Easy waiting."

"I hear the neighbors had a brush with our security."

"Bunch of greenhorns," Nakayama muttered from behind his desk.

"This isn't to be acted on without X's approval."

"For da record, we don't take orders from Mr. X."

"Of course, but considering the propensity of these scab types to act unprofessionally . . ." Milissa paused to let the qualifying terms sink in. "We'd rather not stir things up."

Nakayama returned to his work. "I saw her."

There was no response.

"Can tell her Norman never even filed a complaint. Sergeant didn't wanna live it down."

"You saw the suspect?"

He looked at Milissa impatiently.

"I'm sure Mr. X will be pleased. Top of the morning then."

Despite the annoyance of security, renovation carried on apace. Toward noon, the media began to trickle in. To Jock's inexpressible delight, the boyish Adam Brighter, NBC's west coast man, had made a final connection the night before and arrived in time to join Sadako on her flight to Molokai. "They called me from Honolulu before the Federal warrant thing. Said you were here. I wanted to come then. My bags were packed, but I couldn't get authorization. When New York got your fax and saw Sadako's scoop, they woke me up."

"We're on in less than an hour."

Adam looked at Jock for a few seconds. "It's an honor to meet you."

Jock's eyebrows raised uncertainly.

"Father of the media event."

"You've got my number then. Tell me. You think I put this thing together?"

"I know you didn't swing the Federal warrant."

"You're a bit of a trailblazer yourself." Behind the veil of small talk, Jock was figuring how best to use young Brighter. "Coaxing NBC to come to you instead of risking the Big Apple, that's a first. I hated it back there. That's why I moved out west."

"Bess and I are happy in Seattle," Adam said, brushing back his forelock.

"How can I accommodate you?" Jock asked, settled now on his approach.

Adam answered calmly, without hesitation. "I want Nappy before the arrest."

"You'll be here for Jimmy Carter's visit?"

"Not sure. Have I missed something?"

"Not yet." Jock picked up the phone and dialed Nappy. "But we've gotta move quick. Where's your cameraman?"

"Gavin Dunn. On loan from KOHA. He's waiting in the car." Adam took out his cell phone. "Can I make a private call?"

Nappy came on the line.

"Nap," Jock replied, "one second." He held the phone aside and pointed through the kitchen. "Try the bathroom. And not for publication on the Carter visit. Saturday."

Adam nodded and left the room.

"I'm sending you a guy from NBC," Jock continued. "Adam Brighter. . . . Put him on. . . . Gary. . . . Right through the front door. . . . Oh, I doubt they'd barge in on a network interview. We should be so lucky. . . . Okay, you're the legal guy. . . . It's not an issue. We'll slip him through the fence."

Jock hung up and hurried to the back yard.

Maria and Chase were playing POGs on the slab at the base of the steps.

"Maria, get your dad. Tell him I've got a news man here. There's a quarter in it for you."

She looked at Chase.

"One dollar," Chase counseled.

"A dollar?" Jock protested. "We used to do things for a penny."

"A penny?" Maria squinched her nose and snickered.

"Okay. Okay. Everybody wants it their way. Run."

They squirted around the corner of the house.

"I'm timing you," Jock yelled after them.

"We'll have someone here this Saturday," Adam said from the kitchen. "Probably me. Depends on how big they see it."

"Nappy Kam? Unusual, even for a nickname. How'd you come by it?"

"In elementary school dey called me Nappy 'cause of my African hair. Had plenty fights 'bout dat until my fifth grade teacher told us King Kalakaua, a distant in-law of Kamehameha, was maybe fathered by a black coach driver. Teacher said Kalakaua had a woolly head like me, and after dat dey all went call me Nappy Kam."

"It has a certain ring."

"Studies show da Polynesians got black blood along da way from where we came. Can see it in da race. Not so bad da Nappy Kam.

Shows my roots." Nappy did a Groucho to concede his pun. "Plenty people got da African don't even know it. Maybe you, Mr. Brighter."

The camera closed on Adam's fair complexion, soft brown hair, blue eyes, and high bridged nose.

"Possibly. Does it make a difference?"

"Not to me. It's what's inside dat counts."

Adam created a pause by checking his notes, setting up his next question. "You're coming out of hiding. Why?"

"Surrendering da body. Uhane staying underground in Maunaloa."

"Uhane?"

"Spirit. If I run, I take uhane wit' me. Everybody looking for dat rascal Nappy Kam. Never mind da Maunaloa crisis."

"Explain the crisis."

"Outsiders tearing ohana from da land."

"Ohana? This is?"

"Ohana is family. Uhane, God's breath, is da spirit of family."

"Most would argue that this is Stockmans' land, to do with as they please."

"Land and ohana all one t'ing. If local people choose to leave, dey take da spirit wit' dem. Expel dem and da spirit stays behind. Very stubborn da kine."

"You're saying these families here are somehow invested in the land?"

"You got it turned around. Land – aina we call it – is invested in da families. Aina, da source of life, is deir first mother. After dey get born, game, plant food, oxygen from da plants, da forest through da eyes, permeate dem, tie dem in."

"Their detractors say they're merely tenants – recent, rent subsidized immigrants."

"Some are recent. Every year, two, t'ree Filipino children cross da sky to Maunaloa. But people mostly go back four, five generations here, and all mixed in wit' old ohana. All da brahs like claim ohana even wit' one drop Hawaiian blood."

Adam looked at his watch. "I'd like to move on if we can. We have very little time. About the harboring charge. When you took this fellow in, did you know you were breaking the law?"

A look of selfless gravity came over Nappy's face. "All men are family, born of da same mother, connected by God's breath. Da essence of God's breath is wai ola, fresh living water. It pervades all space and nourishes all creatures wit' da power to live in harmony. When dis power is abused, wai ola begins to wane, ohana comes apart, and man falls into self-predation. Easter Island monoliths? Dey looking for wai ola, da essence of uhane. Fish float in da sea, but life itself floats in da living water of God's breath. Uhane, spirit of da family of man. Dat's da law I wasn't breaking when my friend came 'round to visit me."

"But you knew he was being sought? In another jurisdiction, so to speak."

Gary waved the question off emphatically.

"I knew he was a tax protester. Did not accept dat da U.S. owns Hawaii. Just like people here do not accept dat Mr. X can outright own da mountain."

X arrived in front of his office at noon, all decked out in cowboy boots and hat, chauffeured there by Harry in his monster truck, with seven brown skinned paniolos in the back.

"Mr. Spitz, Mr. Spitz," came the din.

"Mr. X," Sadako said correctly, meeting him as his feet touched the ground, "Sadako Shige, KOHA. A few questions."

X took Sadako by the wrist and gathered in his burly retinue. "That's why we're here."

"Your reaction to the self-help renovation?"

"A political tactic instigated by outsiders. If you inquire of those involved, you'll find that nine out of ten of them don't live here. Never did."

"I wouldn't point fingers," shouted Stan, who had been invited by Smitty into the crush of cameras and reporters. "Stockmans is owned by outsiders."

Jake Jacobi, one of X's hands, muscled his way toward Stan. Stan put his camcorder in Jake's face and backed away. "Howzit, Jake? Gonna kick my ass on national TV?"

Jake saw Smitty's lens in his periphery and slinked back to the truck, looking small and silly as he sank into its wheel well.

"Six houses and counting," Sadako continued. "We hear they're billing you for the work."

X put on his generous smile. "They have our address."

"You intend to pay?"

"We'll make a decision."

"Do not evade or quibble," Stan broke in, his eye still in the viewfinder, feeling his way forward with the splayed fingers of his empty hand, hips preceding shoulders. "Will you pay?"

"We know the public sometimes requires simple answers," X said to Sadako, "but the dynamic here doesn't lend itself to a fixed response. We'd like to have a whole new town, but wealthy interests undermine our efforts. Ask yourself who's paying for this latest stalling tactic. The paint. The supplies. You think it's the tenants?"

"Not the tenants," Stan chimed in. Buck, Sadako's cameraman, shifted to include him in the frame. "They can hardly meet their current rents. But you know that. That's why you'll be charging more in your new places." Stan knelt down and aimed his camcorder up at X. "Let's try this angle. Makes you look taller than the rest."

X gave his back to Stan and rolled his shoulders forward. "Let me say this. These people were given notice months ago that their houses were coming down. This so-called renovation is done with full knowledge of that happening." He moved to put Buck's camera between himself and Stan. "Now, I'd like to introduce the benefactors of our enterprise, Stockmans' employees." He gestured expansively along his row of cowboys. "They're on the range all day. In the gulches and on the slopes. Mending fence, clearing mesquite, keeping our horses off the public lands. Don't have the leisure to play politics."

"Until now." Stan side-stepped along the chorus line of cowboys, recording their expressions. "You boys on the clock?"

X continued. "Some of them will be purchasing homes right here in this section." But his voice weakened as people began to peel away.

John was standing across the street, talking to Nappy on his cell phone, hailing the reporters to follow him.

"Which only goes to show," Stan persisted, "that Stockmans is building another company town on top of the old one. It's like the punch line to a cosmic joke."

"Sorry to cut this short," Sadako called back to X as she caught up with the pack. "Nappy's about to show."

X climbed onto the roof of the truck to get a bead on where Nappy might come out. He saw John some distance ahead of the rest, turning down the narrow ingress that led to Tutu's sign. "Mannie's," he shouted as his cowboys sprinted past the crowd now laboring behind its cordon of paint-spattered volunteers. Halfway across the field, the cowboys joined a plain white van that followed on their heels to barricade the car-width, hedged-in lane and cover them as they converged on Nappy.

Before being pushed aside and held at gun point, John had given warning. Nappy struggled with his captors out in Mannie's yard just enough to spice the scene for Gavin, who was filming for Adam Brighter through the window.

Gary watched over Gavin's shoulder. "Jock was right," he said, reflecting back on Jock's remark about the opposition barging in. "We should be so lucky."

The barricade was quickly manned by Stockmans' security. "Step aside, step aside," Rufus demanded as he waded through the tangle of workers and reporters.

Sheriff Nakayama, with papers in hand, strolled leisurely behind. "Where's Mr. Kanikela?" he asked, entering the relative calm of the turn-around in front of Mannie's house.

"He stay inside da van."

"Hoh," Nakayama curtsied, "no like keep him waiting."

When word filtered back that Nappy was in custody, Olika ran into the open lots and grabbed a two-by-four. He held it up to Kimo. "Can break da windows in da van."

"Cannot, brah. Dey make one asshole in your forehead."

"Fuckers," Olika shouted as he pressed into the crowd.

"Drop it," Fidel said, grabbing him by the back of the neck and jerking his head back and forth like a dust mop when he refused to comply. "Drop it," he repeated with inquisitorial patience, clamping down harder, doubling him over and holding him at arm's length, squeezing out the last drop of resistance, then deftly catching the board as it fell.

All around grew quiet, amazed and horrified, but not prepared to fault Fidel's intervention. They stared at the ground as he strutted a few paces off and hurled the board across the unfinished field. Denise knelt down by Olika and reproached them with her eyes for not stepping in.

Nakayama came to the back of the van. "Cannot allow it," he said to reporters demanding an opportunity to talk with Nappy. "Situation's way too volatile. Look dis." He pointed at Olika, who was getting to his feet, obviously in shock. "Got one incident already." He looked around, a curious twinkle in his eye. "You like make a complaint, young man?"

"Fuckers, fuckers," rose the protest as the van backed through the gathering and sped away, rooster-tailing red dust in the faces of the children who were pelting it with rocks.

"Nappy was supposed to have addressed the press before surrendering," Sadako said, approaching Nakayama. "Chief Fitzpatrick gave my station manager his guarantee. Any comment?"

"We understand you folks supposed to get a crack at him," said Nakayama. "No one told us when. Chief Fitzpatrick only tell me pick up Nappy Kam."

"Who's behind the vigilante action?" someone asked. "Why didn't the FBI do the arrest?"

Nakayama pointed at the cowboys. "Deze men are Stockmans' security. Brought in for crowd control. Was one fracas just before I got here. Rightly so, dey took da problem in hand."

While hostile questioning continued, John and Moke began to move the workers back to their jobs. John teamed uncles up with hotheads, keeping Olika for himself. "Cannot let 'em t'row us off," he exhorted. "Dis bullshit only make 'em stink mo' bettah."

After finishing with Nakayama, the reporters (all except for Michael, who remained outside the envelope) took their turns in front of Tutu's sign. Each recounted the maneuvers that kept Nappy from the press, but one among them was outspoken. "While it is true that the sheriff's primary duty was the peaceful arrest of Nappy Kanikela, it was obvious to everyone present that a plan orchestrated by Stockmans Inc., with the apparent complicity of local authorities – a plan to keep the public from hearing Kanikela's side of the story – was successfully executed here today. Sadako Shige, KOHA Evening News."

"Uncle," Kepa called to John, sidling abreast of him, hands stuffed into his low, baggy pants pockets – head, neck, ears, and brow covered in a tight watch cap. "I can work?"

John continued toward his job site. "T'ought dey went lock you up."

Kepa shrugged and did a little skip to catch the rhythm of John's pace. "One month dey let me out. T'ink dey sad for me I lose one eye."

John stopped. Kepa pulled up a couple steps ahead and faced him. The empty socket, sunk beneath a heavy roll of watch cap, was leaking slightly in the corner.

"Why you no keep it covered?" He took Kepa by the arm to steady him for observation. "Should get one eye patch. You like, I make you one."

Kepa's biceps tightened at John's touch. "No like one sissy eye patch."

"No like one pirate patch? Wahines like da kine."

"You t'ink?" Kepa grinned and pulled the cap over his dead eye.

"Get one earring, you knock 'em dead."

Kepa returned his hands to his pockets and pivoted a couple penguin steps away. "We like work," he said, nodding over John's shoulder.

John turned and sighted Kepa's hard core band of gremlins, his brothers Meek and Lion, sister Ana, and some hangers-on, spy hopping between houses in the distance. He rounded them up, retrieved some tarp and scrapers from behind his shop, and walked them to their house.

"Like dat," he demonstrated, uncaking paint from the ancient two story structure. "Kepa's boss man. Responsible for keeping track of da equipment and making sure da work gets done.

"No work, no pork chops," he added, cutting short a whine of protest. "Supper's at six."

Kepa captured John's arms to his sides, hugged him with the adulation of a five year old, then turned to the others. "Meek," he shouted, trying to impress as John opened the gate to leave, "you my bitch."

John recognized the turn of phrase. It was a prison hand-me-down, one of a lexicon of sexually demeaning terms like "fatty backs" and "single barrelled broads." He bridled his disgust, noting that the gate was hanging from a single hinge, then walked silently away, hoping to repair the damage at a more propitious time.

Harry was busy doing nothing in the open lots. Milissa motioned his bulldozer to a stop, then walked around in front of the loud, idling machine and pointed at some ground level foundations, forming an imaginary buffer with her hands to ward him off. He yelled out a response, tipped his hat, and backed away. She continued across the field, concentrating on her footing, not seeing John until she'd reached the porch. Her voice was distant, without delight. "X told him to go through the motions but not disturb anything."

She faced away and spoke into the drone. "Maintaining a presence. Like us, huh? Acting like we're only crossing paths. Did you mean it, about being family? It's hard to tell out here in the real world."

John could hardly hear.

She projected her voice back in his direction, "Anyway, we don't have to pretend." And then she aimed it out again. "This shit. The cops and cowboy show this afternoon. I'm quitting."

John came down silently behind and put his hands on her bare arms. "Keiki, will you marry me?"

She turned, studying his face with her fingers as if she were blind.

"Keiki?"

Intent on her scrutiny, she kissed him in select places around the neck, cheek, and forehead. "Yes," she answered, and then, "Yes!" again, breaking from her trance.

He took out a silver band, etched with filigree, and put it on her finger.

"Oh, Keoni," she said, holding him like her dearest friend, "it's perfect." She examined it privately. "How did you know my size?"

He took her other hand and touched Linda's friendship ring.

"Linda. She knew?"

"Told her I was laying for you from da start."

She pressed her forehead to his chest. "We should tell someone."

Their thoughts in sync, they looked across the field and headed in Harry's direction.

He saw them coming, stared intently over his blade, and rumbled away, pretending not to hear their calls. They had to separate to corner him.

"Hold up," Milissa yelled. "We have something to tell you." Harry killed the engine. "We're getting married." Her words embossed the silent air.

Harry's Adam's apple jumped ahead of his "M'gosh." He dried his hat band with his handkerchief and looked inside. "Little pardner," he said, blocking its crown and plopping it on the back of his head, "you sure got a mind of yer own. John Mikala's gonna have his hands full."

They laughed at his far-reaching grin and then at how his long, angular face, framed against the ample brim, caught up with the immodest implication of his words. "Well," he said with a blush. "I mean . . . No disrespect intended." He removed his glove. "Congratulations to ya both."

Milissa had to mount the tread to reach his hand.

"John Mikala." He seized John with a mighty, heartfelt grip. "You got the prize."

He sat back in momentary thought, then started his engine. "Mr. X'll surely be surprised."

Milissa cupped her hands to be heard as he jolted forward. "You can surprise him for us if you'd like.

"Nice man," she added quietly, watching him jostle away.

John didn't disagree. She could see his mind was back on the job.

"I'd like to help. Did I tell you I can paint?"

"You never!" John kidded. "Anyt'ing you never do?"

Milissa was embarassed, even in front of John, to suggest that she might join in after siding with the enemy. "What do you think? Pretty awkward, huh?"

"Can you do da scrape?"

"The scrape? Can Michelangelo do the fresco?"

"I'll put you out wit' Moke dis afternoon."

The tired, hungry workers filled the yard as John delivered the announcements. There was Adam Brighter's coverage of Nappy's bust, set to show on NBC the following night. Alvaro's return was expected sometime before the program aired. Nine houses had been completed, three ahead of schedule. And most pressing – the thing that drew the most applause – Easy's pork chops baked in sauerkraut and applesauce, and a pony keg of beer were waiting in the wings. Milissa had given John the gist of a recruiting plan that she and Moke had hatched while on the job. He had promised to bring it up. But first, "a hand for da new guys."

Tiny, Kimo's friends, and most of Ewa and Salome's brood came to their feet.

"Kepa?" John insisted. "You no work today?"

Kepa rose reluctantly. His head, still butch from his last prison haircut, was wreathed in a black silk bandanna, pulled down on one side to cover his injury.

. "Hoh, Long John Silver," came a remark from the crowd.

The ripple of involuntary laughter silenced everyone it touched.

Kepa's sighted eye stabbed from one offender to the next.

John took Milissa's hand. "Let's hear it for Kepa."

Ewa pointed her chin through the applause. "Dis Keiki bitch went tear out Kepa's eye."

"Shush, tita."

She jerked away from Easy's touch. "No tell me shush. She behind me losing Ui too. You went bring dis devil in my room when I sleeping. She went t'row my Jesus on da floor. You shame."

"Shut up!"

Ewa flinched at the bite of Easy's command.

"You poison Kepa wit' your stink talk."

Kepa located Milissa in his shallow field of vision.

John hugged Milissa to his side. "Ana," he said to Ewa's daughter, "why you no stand?" He pulled Ana gently to her feet and held her close as well. "Ana and Keiki. Anyone left out?"

Milissa felt annoyingly like John's little girl. He had her tipped off balance. She couldn't move her arms. The faces all around her were impersonal at best.

"Keiki has a plan," John announced, releasing her so suddenly that she did a stutter step to keep her equilibrium.

Kepa's cackle of contempt shattered in the ears of those around him.

"Uncle," Milissa whispered to John, pretending to be peeved, "too tight the squeeze."

"Listen up," Moke shouted as people clustered away from Kepa, distracted by their need to disassociate. "She went bust her buns for help you already. Give Keiki some respect."

"She working for da Stockmans," Kimo countered.

"Went quit Stockmans," Easy shot back.

The devil moaned in Ewa's throat.

Milissa spoke softly. "I did notice that there weren't many women. I guess most of them are at home with kids. Maybe uncomfortable with men's work. There aren't many of us, men or women. What? Maybe thirty. Moke and I are putting together a phone tree. Statewide. If your wives and girlfriends can't be here, they can help get others out. After dinner, give us your numbers. We'll take care of the rest."

Jock, who'd been watching from the porch with John's dog, Ché, glided up next to John while Milissa was talking. "She's right," he said so everyone could hear, prompting a bark from his companion.

Jock was hard to classify on sight. His appearance didn't spur the enmity aroused by the beefy, high-pectoraled, northern European types most commonly perceived as haole. He was slight, Mediterranean, more easily mistaken for an Asiatic mix. To add to the enigma, his racial distinctions had eroded. Age had drawn him closer to the aboriginal man.

He spared no one his impartial scowl. "About the need for more people, Keiki's absolutely right. I don't know about the rest. I know this thing'll fall apart if you don't . . . Well, first if you don't stop fighting. The two go hand in hand. People won't stay if you're all ugly like this. Whatever divides us, we have to set it aside. That's how we overcome."

He spoke more quietly to John. "Where's Fidel?"

"Loka," John shouted. "Where's Fidel?"

"Out on da edge of da world."

"He lives down Mo'omomi," John replied. "Likes to be alone."

"Ah, well. He's missing all the fun." Jock raised his voice again. "Jimmy Carter, ex-President Carter, will be visiting us on Saturday. Tomorrow morning, on schedule, I'll notify the press." He lifted his hand to quiet the hoots of approval. "Tonight we party. This whole week can be a party if we work together. Later, when the dignitaries and TV cameras are gone, when the party's over, if it's still in you, you can fight."

Easy put four glasses around the surviving pitcher of beer. "We co-conspirators now. Partners in da revolution."

Linda poured. "Hoh, dat X. He somet'ing else, bringing in doze hooligans."

"We'll get our revenge," Milissa responded. "You being a master spy and all, if we ever need to get the goods on him, like his shoe width or maybe his ring size," – she examined her engagement ring – "we can call on you."

Linda whooped with delight. "You asked her! Tita, let me see."

Milissa put out her hand.

"Aunty, Keoni and Keiki getting married. Come look."

Easy held her arms up like a cormorant drying in the sun. A tiny treble fluttered forth, astonishing in contrast to her size.

"What you t'ink, Aunty?" John smiled. "Partners in love mo' bettah, ya?"

She smothered him with hugs, embarrassing him as she had

when he was a boy. "Mo' bettah," she replied, coming away already moist around the eyes, looking at him as if she were the one he'd asked. "I so worried. T'ought you'd never pop da question. Hoh, Keiki, let me see." She pulled Milissa onto her lap. "You one lucky girl."

Linda couldn't keep it in. "Morgan'll be jealous when she hears."

"Linda," Easy clucked. "Sometimes you never grow up."

Maria shuffled from the bedroom and laid her upper body over Easy's knee.

"Poor Morgan," Milissa said, letting Maria take her place. "Is she okay?"

Easy gave Maria to her father and retreated to the couch. "Enough about da kine."

Linda followed with a testy look. "She acting kinda crazy like she coming loose. Spending plenty time wit' Jense. Wore dat purple muumuu yesterday."

"Keiki," Maria said, nestled in John's arms. "Where you stay?"

Milissa stroked Maria's hair. "Camping at Halawa, pepe. I missed you."

Maria snuggled more deeply, reluctant to forgive Milissa's absence. "Like go home."

"Too much noise at home," John said. "You stay wit' Aunty."

"No," Maria whined, clinging to his shirt.

Linda put her feet up on the couch. "You guys use my bed. I'll sleep here."

John puckered Maria's lips. "Go climb in Aunty Linda's bed. Me and Keiki be in soon."

"Come now," Maria insisted.

Milissa stood. "I'll tuck you in."

Maria considered the offer, then looked imploringly at John.

He set her on her feet. "You and me den. But you walked in, can walk back out."

"Yes," Maria exulted, leading the way in triumph.

CHAPTER TWENTY ONE

"A show of force followed by a show of pussy," X observed, looking at Milissa as if his words were meant for her. He scribbled out and handed her a note while his sergeant, on the other end of the line, gave his rendition of Easy's assault. "Bullshit," X broke in. "You should've blown her knee caps off. Well," – he smiled at his own bravado – "at least squeezed off a couple rounds."

Your ass was crossed out and replaced. *Your fine ass*, the note read, *is fired. My condolence to the lucky man.*

He hung up the phone as she slid the latest *Sentinel* across the desk. Inside was Stockmans' insert, locking him into his pledge.

"I honestly thought we might get cozy," he said.

"Cozy?"

"Some kind of convenient understanding."

She wadded up his message and flicked it in his face. "Your cock sick fantasy."

Injured but aroused, he struggled with a self-defiling grin. "Cock sick? Dare you to say it again."

She felt like she'd tripped a cripple. "You don't have to put yourself through this," she said, queasy from his reaction.

He leafed through the insert and found the grant proposal forms she'd tucked inside. "Someone'll have to do these. We'll take the fee from your final check."

She let it pass, relieved that the job would get done.

He swiveled his chair and surveyed the north section through his window. "On your way out . . ." The growing patchwork of brightly colored houses caught in his throat. He pulled forward to take a better look. "Your keys, leave them with Kini."

She knew he'd be watching as she made her way toward John's, but who cared. She was rid of him. She ran into the open lots, hurdling Harry's freshly minted ruts, stopping to marvel at Mannie's bungalow. Bluebell, she mused, with dandelion trim. And Julio's next door, still seamless like the sun.

"Keoni!" she shouted, bursting through the door.

Jock was busy at his laptop. "Not here." He held up an item from the morning *Advertiser*. "Just had this faxed from Honolulu. You up to posting it?"

Milissa read the headline. "Carter to Visit Maunaloa."

"Makes it official. Tack one on the Tutu sign."

She had him run off extra copies and set about delivering them to work sites.

Tiny was unimpressed. "Heard dat last night," he said over the blare of his radio.

"Well, now the world knows. Here's a memento." She placed a copy on the canvas by his feet and passed one to Kimo and Keku.

"We're what's happening," Tiny teased, bending at the knees to paint the underside of Keku's eaves. "You pushing yesterday's high."

"Then why so sullen? You should be dancing a jig."

"One jig." To Tiny, the word was peculiar. He giggled. "Like see you dance one jig."

"You think I won't?" Milissa struck a squat Bojangles pose.

Tiny's mass began to shimmy with the titters.

"Say your name," Milissa challenged.

"Tiny," Keku answered.

"His real name."

"Matauta'i." Tiny mouthed the syllables succinctly, exploding on the "t"s.

Milissa reproduced the sounds exactly. "Ma-tau-ta'i. Enough right there to do a jig. You chant. I'll dance."

"No way." Tiny sobered and returned to his work. "Jig da radio."

Kimo was intrigued. "She cannot jig da rap song, brah. Do one chant for Keiki."

"Geev 'em," Keku urged. "Do Ma-tau-ta'i, like dat."

He turned his big, unsmiling body toward Milissa.

Kimo killed the radio.

"Ma-tau-ta'i, Ma-tau-ta'i," he began, still in opposition.

Milissa sprang into action. With arms hung motionless, she clogged and twirled, doubling his pace.

Spurred on by Keku, who was clapping time, he winced as if he'd caught a stomach cramp, then found the basic rhythm with his feet.

Milissa grasped his hands. Using them as leverage, she leapt in syncopation. "Ma-tau-ta'i Tui-aso-sopo," she exhorted, extending the chant to the giant's full name. "Ma-tau-ta'i Tui-aso-sopo," she exclaimed, bouncing up each time he hoofed the ground. "Throw me in the air."

Romping around them like children at a grown-up party, Keku and Kimo chimed in.

"Throw her, Tiny."

"Like da lady in da circus."

"Now!"

On command he took her by the waist, hurled her up, and caught her in his arms.

"Dah dah!" she trumpeted, pointing her toe and fanning out her arms to the ovation.

"All jigged out," Tiny puffed, putting her down and lowering himself against the wall.

"Me too," Milissa agreed, taking her place at his side, "all jigged out."

Alvaro had been held a couple nights for investigation and released. A group recruited through the phone tree travelled with him from Oahu. They arrived in time for dinner.

"Why you went work for Stockmans?" he asked Milissa.

"Just trying to help."

Kimo handed him the application Milissa had left with Keku a few days before.

"Dis you?" he asked.

"That's me."

"You still recommending deze positions?"

"Somebody's gonna take 'em. The south side's going up."

"Hoh!" The backs in the small circle straightened.

She had to think. Had it all been for naught. She glanced at John who was listening from the steps of his workshop. "I wouldn't encourage anyone to work for Stockmans," she added. "Not any-more. But I wouldn't blame them either if they needed to feed their family."

Alvaro folded the form and pressed it into his pocket. "You and Keoni getting hitched. Now you wit' da sovereign kine, ya?"

"My rite of passage?"

"How else you gonna qualify? You not Hawaiian. Not even a resident."

"I'm a universal citizen."

"You no like Hawaiian sovereignty?"

"Not sure what it means. Probably different things to different people. If it's tribalism, something you have to be born or married into, it's not for me."

"Where would you draw da line?"

"I wouldn't."

"We were tribal back before da haole took da land and outlawed our religion. Cannot be a Jew unless your mother is a Jew. Cannot be a Hindu 'less you born one. Maybe same da kine Hawaiians. We got a right to start where we left off. Can figure out da rest from dere."

"Race is a source of perfection. It deserves equal footing – a fair start. But the supremacist thing, the core tenet of tribalism or race religion, the idea that the root is more perfect than the tree – Aryan Nation, Nation of Islam, whatever. That I can't buy."

John joined the circle beside Milissa.

"You leaving us, Keoni?" Alvaro asked. "Marry your lawyer and move to da mainland?"

"What you t'ink, brah?" There was a hint of jurisdiction in John's voice. "Molokai my home. You in Maunaloa now." He looked at each of the newcomers, then returned to Alvaro. "You check out what we done? Fourteen houses done already."

"Been watching on da tube. Never looked around yet."

"You gonna stay and help, den? Must be plenty busy running t'ings for Sovereign now dat Nappy's down."

"Brah," Alvaro reacted. "Dis *is* Sovereign. Sacred land. Got sprung and came right over."

John got up and walked toward his back door. "You talk to Nappy in da slam?"

"Dey was keeping us apart." Alvaro turned to those around him to finish his response. "He no make da bail. Da judge set it too high."

A few moments later, John stepped onto his porch carrying his television set. "News Front," he announced. "Nappy's bust." He plugged it in and tinkered with the sound.

The segment opened with a pool-side appeal by X for law and order, interspersed with brutal stills of cowboys stuffing Nappy in an unmarked van. Adam then reported Chief Fitzpatrick's broken promise to the press, and closed with Nappy's uncut interview straight through to the abduction, allowing the betrayal to be felt first hand.

CHAPTER TWENTY TWO

The response to Adam's piece was exponential. By Friday afternoon, twelve new crews and a team of carpenters were in the works. Though the press had faded, Jock was keeping them pumped for Carter's visit. Part of John's back yard fence, torn down initially for added room, was resurrected as *Da Camp* sign. The rest was used to build a platform for the evening's celebration.

X drew hidden catcalls when he commandeered his dozer and paraded it before the row of houses facing on the open lots. But when he stopped in front of John's and ordered his sergeant to uncover the sign, "Cannot," Alvaro called out. "We keeping it a secret till da Bad Bones come."

"The Bad Bones?" X butted the structure with the heel of his hand and climbed back on his machine. "That's when?"

"Eight o'clock," Alvaro answered, looking down to fill his brush.

The engine's whine was followed by a snapping sound.

John ran out of his house. "The sign," he yelled back to Milissa. She followed him to his pick-up. "Keep him busy," he said, racing off toward Mannie's.

She stepped in front of the dozer and touched her toe to the wreckage. "You made a boo-boo."

"My mistake." X double clutched it into low and pulled back

over the debris. "Just getting the knack of this thing."

"You gonna pay for your mistake?"

"Was it a historic monument?" he answered, creeping forward.

She held her ground until John appeared on foot and signaled her to move aside.

X roared past John and burrowed headlong into Mannie's narrow cul-de-sac. Near the bottom of the lane he found John's truck, blocking access to the turnaround and Tutu's sign. He looked back. The way seemed less confining coming in. To make it in reverse would take some skill. A piece of hedge and several fence posts later he emerged onto the field, a length of chicken wire tangled in his grille.

As he retreated to his office, Tiny, Olika, and Dexter railed after him, then huddled for revenge. "Sugar in da gas tank," Meek suggested from the sidelines.

John overheard the comment. "Tiny. You boys. What's dis? Moke," he called, "help me here. We got some friendly butt to kick. Meek, what's wit' da sugar in da gas tank?"

"Just kidding, Uncle."

"He just running at da mouth," Tiny concurred, seeming very much a boy in the face of uncle power.

"We never," Olika stammered.

"Meek," John asked, "where's Kepa? Figgah he be right inside some stink like dis. Why you no working on da house?"

Moke took Tiny, Dexter, and Olika aside.

"Kepa never work," Meek complained to John. "Never stay home no mo'. Just come bragging now and den how he one big hunter. By-n-by we quit da house. Cannot do it all alone."

"Hokay. We'll get some muscle over dere. But you be ready for work in da morning. And no hanging wit' deze guys." He pointed at Tiny and the boys standing several feet away with Moke.

"If I ever!" Moke announced to his detainees, "I'll take you somewhere quiet and make loud noises wit' your heads. Just me and you. You like?"

Tiny couldn't control his silly laugh.

"And you." He took a piece of Tiny's side fat in his hand and dug in deep enough to let him know it could be torn away. "Can find you wit' my eyes closed."

"Sure you right," Tiny answered, suddenly contrite.

Bad Bones' "Check, ch, ch, ch. Check," crackled in the sunset as the workers cleaned their gear and hauled it in. By nightfall a new sign had been erected, and John and Easy's back yards, now combined, were overflowing with workers and guests. John estimated three hundred as he stepped onto the platform to introduce the band.

"Hana hou Maunaloa," he announced, "da Bad Bones wrote it 'specially for da fight we in."

The band launched into a reggae rendition of a familiar folk tune, with new words to fit the occasion.

Goin' up da road to Maunaloa.
Up da hill to do it all again.
Gonna stay dis time for save da old ways.
Here for build ohana wit' my friends.

Hana hou! my Maunaloa.
Hele on!
Here to build ohana wit' da kine.

Gonna see da stars in Maunaloa.
Mo' bettah dan da lights of Waikiki.
Gonna talk some story 'bout da old days.
'Bout how da mountain came out of da sea.

So familiar was the tune, that most were able to join the chorus the second time through.

Hana hou! my Maunaloa.
Hele on!
Here to build ohana wit' da kine.

"You," Cory shouted over the music, hugging Jock from behind, "are a fucking wizard. How'd you find these guys?"

Jock steadied himself to support her. "They found me."

"What? You just waited by the phone?"

"Pretty much. It's all in the material." He took her beer. She dropped her arms so he could drink. "You got your jelly bean houses, revolutionaries, good guys, and bad guys. A made-to-order drama in a small movie set town, on a small island, in the heart of – where else – Hawaii. I plop down in the middle of the action, run up my antenna, send messages, and field calls."

"Can't compliment this guy," she said as Stan appeared through the crowd.

"Too good for kudos, eh? Have you mentioned his cute mustachio?"

"Hey," Jock responded, raising his voice above the chorus, "the 'stache is another thing. For it," – he twirled the ends – "I take full credit. Let's go over to the side. Can't hear."

Stan followed them down the slope. "Not a saint. Just another narcissistic SOB."

"A wizard," Cory corrected.

"Maybe warlock," Jock wheezed, settling into the side of the mountain. "A simple, earthly practitioner." He pushed at the back of Cory's knee. "Sit."

"You too," he added, tugging Stan's pant leg. "I need your sister's help."

Jock outlined his objectives for the days to come. He cautioned against focusing solely on the event of John's eviction. "We don't wanna set ourselves up. What if they put it off? What if they succeed in taking him out? In any case, even if they capitulate, we maintain our momentum. Continue the renovation. Move on to new projects – grounds work, planting gardens. Whatever, we keep the cast in place and the extras in the field.

"That's for the long term. For now, we bring as much pressure to bear as possible on the showdown. We build on the numbers present and build again tomorrow. I project a couple thousand people between here and Stockmans when the papers are served.

"Keoni's image. We make him a colossus. He arrives with Carter. Walks with Carter. Leaves with Carter. By high noon Sunday, John

'Keoni' Mikala, President Carter's friend, will be answering the door."

Cory looked across at Stan. "The frog prince thing. A fucking transformation."

"Tomorrow I'd like you to address the press corps and act as Carter's host. College Dean. Maunaloa resident. Except for the cops, you're the closest thing on island to the state. But you'll have to clean up your mouth."

Cory pressed her lips in a half smile, irritated and bemused by Jock's provision.

Hearing no refusal, Jock went on as if the deal were closed. "Most importantly, you'll double as Keoni's advocate. A person of importance never fronts for himself. Keoni can't be seen to tout his own eviction. You're the front man. He's the presidential confidant. Get the picture?"

Stan nudged Jock privately. "We'll work through the night on her expletives."

"Fuck you, Stan," Cory snapped. "If your friend doesn't think I can separate venues, maybe he ought to try you."

"I'm sure you can," Jock came back. "Just wanted to see you in your fighting stance."

"Any of you don't know," Stan said to the crowd, "this guy's a hundred years old. Lived in Maunaloa all his life."

"Ninety eight," the old man rasped from his stage center kitchen chair.

Stan crouched next to Mannie, spoon feeding him the mike.

"Tell you about Pala'au town," Mannie began. Smitty's camera light came on. "We on TV?" Mannie asked, covering his mouth. He stood and took the mike from Stan. "You sit."

Stan hesitated.

"Sit. I like lean on you." He pressed Stan into the chair and held onto his shoulder. "Down da south shore, makai Maunaloa, was one fishing village dey called Pala'au. Dis before my time. Tutu say Pala'au had one giant man-made fish pond. Five hundred acres. Feeding plenty people. So how you figgah den? How you figgah

Pala'au she no mo'?"

"Da haole man," someone shouted.

Stan, always ready to steal the show, reached up for the mike. Mannie aimed it at his mouth, but whisked it away before he could speak.

"Boss Meyer," he said emphatically, looking at Stan as if he were a dunce. "He da head man back den, he got plenty bipi grazing on da mountain. Dey eating all da ground cover, make da streams come red wit' lava dirt. By-n-by da mountain choke da fish pond, and Pala'au eating beef.

"Boss Meyer had da town arrested when he found da bipi bones. All da mens got time. Five years each, cutting coral blocks to build da old Oahu prison wall. Ohana follow dem to Honolulu. Pala'au she went die.

"Tell you one more t'ing," Mannie went on, putting all his little weight on Stan to keep him in his place. "Da first mole in Kaunakakai harbor was made from one heiau. One rain temple. Da haoles trucked it in from Olo'olo up above da Kalamaula well. Half a mile of sacred stone."

A drum roll signaled the beginning of the second set.

"So dat's why we gotta keep dis haole down." Mannie nodded at Stan.

"Not me," Stan protested, slipping out from under his hand.

"You white ain't you?"

"Ya, but not Boss Meyer white."

Mannie looked into the audience and back at Stan. "We just play acting, brah. You cannot tell da difference?"

CHAPTER TWENTY THREE

"Dramatis personae," Jock announced, assessing his little troupe. "Mannie was right last night. Characters in the play."

John squinted and rubbed his morning stubble.

"The key," Jock went on, "is knowing who you are and your place in the production." He made room on the coffee table and clicked up a file on his laptop.

"Alvaro, you're the revolutionary. When we do the revolution, you can play the lead. Today you're doing back-up. Be on hand to answer questions. Otherwise stick to your assignment. You're here for depth." He put his chin in the crook of his hand and mimicked John's stubborn massage. "Keoni, why the face?"

"Just don't like shining people on."

"Of course not. It wouldn't suit you. Go deep. Say what's in your heart. And get a shave."

He scrolled ahead.

"Fidel, you're me. The man who calls the shots. But in appearance only. It's actually a troika. Any critical calls, consult with Cory and Keoni. I want Carter to see you. Just be there. He knows who you are."

Cory held some papers up.

"Cory?"

She handed them around. "Stan and I put this thing together. Everything Carter needs to know. Brief history. MCC's objectives. Worst case scenario for the keiki. Our plan to bill Stockmans. The provision in the Landlord Tenant Act. The blanks are for before and after shots. Any changes, tell us now. We figured five hundred copies."

Jock took out his pen. "Let him draw his own conclusions. If it's obvious," – he crossed out a line – "we don't have to tell him. If it isn't," – he crossed out and rewrote another – "we should state it as a fact. File down the barbs and let Keoni have a peek before you run it off. We'll need a couple thousand. Keep it to a single, double-sided page." He gave her his corrections. "Your statement to the press, before Carter arrives, that's the time to give 'em hell."

He pointed at Milissa. "The kids?"

"They'll be here."

"How many?"

"I'd say thirty."

"Good. Keep them in the picture. Running ahead, trailing behind, sans parents."

"Good?" Milissa teased. "I feel left out. Me too, Jocko. Chew on me awhile."

Jock softened to the humor in the room. "You're the one God judges. The rest of us, we've had our chance at innocence." He could see Milissa didn't like the separation. "Your thirty kids," he added. "Quickest way to lose control is scolding."

He paused, visibly letting down, looking at each of them as if for the last time. "Carter has his own agenda. He'll know exactly what he wants. Our job is to accommodate. Be flexible. Have fun."

Fatigue, held off for several days, had set in rapidly. He stood and hiked his pants up from inside his pockets. "I'll be in Keoni's room. Wake me if there's a fire."

He selected Trotsky's *Russian Revolution* from John's heap beside the couch. "I've had my eye on this one. Very dry." An afterthought crept in. "Fidel, you took care of transportation?"

"Stan's on that." Fidel looked at Cory for assurance. "Lined up a heavy duty jeep. A real classic."

John pulled a bottle of wine from beneath the cushions.

"You're a man of your word," Jock said, taking it and examining the label.

"Corkscrew's in da silver drawer," John replied. "Now go to bed. We got work to do."

The margin of the field was dappled red, blue, and green with rented Neons. "Ladies and gents," Alvaro said, as strangely familiar faces filled the yard, "dis Easy, your aunty for da day."

Easy removed a yellow shingle from a hook at the entrance to the lanai. "T'ink you got Alvaro scared. He forget to tell his name." The remark fell at her feet. Their attention was on their camera equipment and positioning for Carter's arrival.

"Food," Easy announced. Heads turned. "Hoh, now you listening. We got ice tea and two kine sandwiches." A few inched forward. "You stay. We bring 'em out. 'Cept you like come inside for use da potty, take dis here." She held up the yellow marker. "And put 'em back when you pau."

While refreshments were being served, Alvaro checked to see that the major networks were present, then spoke again. "Hokay, before I leave you in Aunty's hands, like give you some specifics. President Carter is expected here, dis location, around noon. Cory Adler, dean of da local college – she lives in Maunaloa – will be here to address you soon. We appreciate your patience."

Milissa took him aside. "They want you at the deli. There's a little hang-up."

"Hoh, tita," Alvaro said as they worked their way through the swelling crowd outside the fence, "da reporters, dey so real in da flesh. Robin Trent, she got one humongous backside, ya? And dat Bradley, he one righteous African. He look sorta haole on da tube."

When they reached the corner of the deli they looked back. The press was interviewing people in the field. With some chagrin, they noticed Moke holding court in front of *Da Camp* sign.

"Why we over here?" Alvaro asked as he hurried through the deli door.

Cory looked at her watch. "Stan's half an hour late."

"Cannot wait for Stan. Dey starting up already. Interviewing anyone wit' lips, eh tita?"

Not wanting to denigrate Moke, but concerned about his tendency to grandstand, Milissa merely raised her eyebrows in agreement.

"Cory?" Alvaro pressed. "We losing momentum."

"We've gotta go," Fidel said to John, then looked at Cory with chagrin. "Shoulda known better than to trust that bastard."

"A few more minutes," John urged, manning the eye of the storm.

Fidel took out his cell phone. "If he doesn't get here before Loka, we'll use the van."

"Shit!" Cory exploded from her chair. "I was counting on those flyers for my presentation."

They spotted Stan as they were leaving. He was parked down the street, across from the warehouse, sitting yoga style on the hood of the jeep with two reams of flyers in his lap, taking in the crowd as if it were his private audience.

"The handouts," Cory shouted, picking up the scent of pakalolo. "You're fucking stoned."

Fidel hurried ahead of John and got behind the wheel. "Key's in the ignition. Get in."

Stan raised his hands to heaven and howled, "Kundalini," as the hum of the engine traveled up his spine.

"Kundalini this," Fidel said, pulling suddenly ahead and skidding to a stop. "Geronimo!"

Stan unfolded in the air, elbows and knees akimbo, landing in a deep, ugly squat. He sat on his heels for a second, flaunting his uncanny touchdown, his packages nestled to his chest. "You'll need some of these for Carter," he said, hopping up and tossing a ream on the hood. "And, Keoni, keep an eye on Mr. Monzón. He's getting ahead of himself. Might actually hurt someone."

After they had driven off, he tore open the second bundle, gave a stack to Cory, Milissa, and Alvaro, and started mingling. Half-joking comments from the crowd about his MCC connections and "pull wit' da prez," sparked delusions of celebrity. When he reached the fence, he stopped to fan his fire with another hit of pakalolo, but when he filled his lungs and raised his hands again in praise of

Kundalini, the flyers tucked beneath his arm scattered in the ever-present wind.

"If you didn't get our handout," Cory announced to the group of reporters, "Stan, the one causing the stir, has just flown several in."

She held one up for the cameras. "Notice the picture on the front. That's our town a week ago. You can see the change for yourself." She pointed down the row of houses to her right and left. "We're calling this Anuenue Alanui. Rainbow Street. Your little cars came dressed for the occasion.

"On the back are some before and after shots. This one's La Hale, Julio's sun house. Here's Ula Hale. Milissa calls it Keku's Blushing Bungalow. We've been having fun. You should look around. We started with a handful of volunteers. How many now, Alvaro?"

"A hundred and thirty eight."

"Stockmans wants to put us out, demolish our homes, and replace them with ones we can't afford. We're determined to fix them up and rent them at present rates, maybe even buy them with low interest loans. Evictions are supposed to start tomorrow noon with our kupuna, our leader, Keoni Mikala, native Hawaiian, Maunaloa resident from birth. You shouldn't miss the fireworks."

"We be here, tita," someone shouted from outside the fence. "Geev 'em," shouted others. "Hele on."

"Keoni will arrive in a few minutes with President Carter. They'll go inside and settle on an agenda. Then we'll open it up for questioning. Anything I can tell you?"

"Will Stockmans be included?" asked Miss Trent.

"Not unless they make an effort to participate."

"Have they been invited?"

"One doesn't need an invitation to a public forum."

Adam waved his hand. "Cory, do you expect to stop the eviction?"

"We expect to prevail."

"But when?" Ed Bradley asked. "Do you have a timeline?"

"Timeline?" Cory thought. "Michael says it started with the Enclosure Acts." Every pen responded. "What century, Michael?"

"Eighteenth," Michael shouted from John's roof, where he and Smitty were shooting.

Cory spotted the President's jeep turning off the highway into town.

"Our viewers are concerned with the present," Bradley persisted.

"Tell them today marks a new beginning," Cory answered, taking a ti leaf lei from the arm of Easy's rocking chair and making her way quietly through the reporters.

The jeep pulled in behind Fidel, who was leading the way in his van. Jimmy, dressed in khakis and a floppy, broad-brimmed hat, climbed from the back seat, held the door for John, and went on with his observations as if they were alone. "That was fifty years ago. Homes near Pearl Harbor. Similar to these. Well," – he flashed his toothy grin – "not so vivid. Mostly muted tones. But the same bare bones look."

John took Cory by the arm as she joined them. "Deze places all went up before da war."

Jimmy turned to Cory. "You must be Dean Adler."

John stepped away but kept his hand in the small of Cory's back.

"Mr. President." Jimmy removed his hat to receive Cory's lei. "Welcome to Maunaloa."

Still detached from all but the immediate, Jimmy went on to question Cory about her students. Only eventually, when the heat of the day had finally sunk in, did he look around for shelter.

"Let's go inside," Cory suggested. "I'll introduce you to the host."

Samantha, Jimmy's aide, followed them across the yard, waving off reporters, then turned and waited at the top of the stairs. Stationed beside the porch was Fred, the President's bodyguard, the kind of guy one sees but doesn't remember.

"Aunty," Cory called through the screen door. "Someone here to see you."

Easy hurried to the living room, drying her hands on her apron. When she spotted Jimmy through her window lace she scurried out of sight, then reappeared with an enormous multi-flowered lei, wimpled up around her chin to tame her cheeky face.

"Come out here." Cory opened the screen. "This is President Carter. Jimmy Carter, this is our Aunt Easy."

"Aloha, Mr. President," Easy said, cheeks aflame, slipping her lei over his head. "Hoh, dear." She looked at Cory. "Jimmy has one dazzling smile."

"Mama always said God gave me teeth that made it easier to smile than to close my mouth."

She took his hand and lead him through the door. "Come. I made some presidential sweets. Sit here," she said, patting the cushion of her overstuffed chair and hurrying to the kitchen.

John felt suddenly incomplete. Easy had pulled the energy with her from the room. What does one say to a world leader while waiting for refreshments? On the way from the airport there was substance. Jimmy was asking questions, acclimating himself to new surroundings – now only curtains and crochet.

Jimmy sensed his unease, but didn't want to condescend with small talk.

"Mr. President," Cory began, ready to add anything to break the deadlock.

"If da sweets were out . . ." John had stepped on Cory's line. "Oh, sorry. You go first."

"No, no, go ahead."

"Just saying, if da sweets were out we'd be digging in, not trying to t'ink of something cute."

"Pressure's off," Jimmy said as Easy carried in a crystal bowl of sun-dried pineapple.

"So what kine t'ings you talk about?" John asked. "Cannot be all business."

"At home we talk about our projects. We talked more when Amy was around. Counseling of sorts. Mostly now, if there's nothing to say, I like the quiet. But times like this . . . Mmm, this is good! Times like this just now, while we were waiting, I never know what to say.

"When I was in office, I'd get stuck with these fellows – Sadat, Trudeau, whoever – and we'd have an agenda. Questions to be asked. Answers to be given. Not much room for chat. The royalty was especially hard to relate to. Nobody's fault."

"Dey stuck you wit' me to build up my image."

"Confessions are good."

"Preparing the world for my eviction." John laughed quietly.

"The world may well take notice." Jimmy pulled the chubby lei away from his face and put on his hat. "Samantha talked me into this hat. What do you think?"

John gave him a dubious smile.

"And this lei?"

Holding up his hand to signal a break, John left the house, obviously on a mission.

"My lord, this is delicious," Jimmy said when Easy returned with the coffee.

"Black. T'ick and black mo' bettah wit' da kine. Where Keoni stay?"

"He's getting something for the President," Jimmy answered.

Unsure of Jimmy's humor, Easy backed politely away. "Cory, I be in da kitchen."

Jimmy stood. "Please join us."

"Oh yes, Aunty," Cory agreed.

"Sit here." Jimmy gave her his seat and poured a cup of coffee. "I have some things to say. I'd like you on hand in case you have suggestions."

Easy sat forward in the chair, her cup and saucer on her knees.

"Sam," Jimmy called, "could you come in?"

John followed Samantha through the door and handed Jimmy a beat-up baseball cap.

Jimmy fitted the cap to his head, took a place on the couch, and looked around for attention. "My visit here demands neutrality. I've read your handout and I agree, but I can't be seen to be in league with the MCC. I need your cooperation. Disparaging remarks about Stockmans made by you, especially in my presence, will be attributed to me."

John looked at Cory and Easy. Both were acquiescent. "You're asking us to dummy down?"

"As you said, they stuck me with you to enhance your image. That I can accept. Can you accept a degree of restraint? We both have good works to do."

It sounded reasonable, compromising for the greater good, valuing appearance as reality, but it tasted like the stuff that Jock was dishing out – the right ingredients absent the essential spice.

"Let me unburden you," John replied, removing Jimmy's flower lei. "Tell you what . . ." He stood up and modeled it around his neck. "I have anyt'ing to say, I'll make it clear I'm speaking for myself. What you t'ink?" He turned to the side. "You like?"

"Too big," Jimmy beamed, "but you'll grow into it."

Cory and Sam moved the tight semicircle of cameramen back from the porch.

"Mr. Bradley?"

"Mr. President, you are recognized as a mediator of peace between nations and, at times, between factions of a single nation – Haiti being the recent case in point. What are we to make of your role in this essentially private dispute?"

"I am here as a guest and observer. In that sense, I've not departed from my role in Haiti."

"Do you plan to address the conflict between Stockmans and its tenants?"

"Not per se. My inquiry here is limited to the scope of Sunday's conference. I'll be looking at the impact this development is having on the children."

"Will you consult with representatives of Stockmans Inc.?" asked Robin Trent.

"I'm not a guest of Stockmans. It would be presumptuous of me to approach them with questions about their business. If we are unable to meet, it'll be a missed opportunity, but . . ." Samantha gave Jimmy a note. "I'm told we've received their call. We'll see what we can do."

Jimmy noticed Bradley's short-changed expression. "Yes, Ed, I know. I didn't really answer your question. To be honest, I had to give it some thought. I was recalling a comment Mr. Mikala made on our way from the airport. Your description of this dispute as private begs the question.

"Mr. Mikala's view" – Jimmy gave a nod to John who was standing behind him – "and one with which I agree, is that Maunaloa is an aftermath of colonialism. This seemingly private conflict was set in motion fifty to a hundred years ago when American corporations, with government backing and encouragement, began to invest in cheap land and labor here and elsewhere in Hawaii.

"This is not an isolated incident. It's playing itself out on every island in the state. Its scenario is familiar in other contexts throughout our nation's history. One pocket of residual poverty after another displaced by more affluent conditions. Whole communities swept aside, unable to participate in the bounty.

"I don't intend to give you a civics lesson, Mr. Bradley. I know you don't need one. Let it be enough to say – and this will end the questioning for now – that America has learned the pitfalls of exclusion well enough to make these once private issues public by law. In the case at hand, compliance with affordable housing statutes in exchange for cost saving waivers has made it so.

"And what have we here?" Jimmy stepped off the porch into the group of children that Milissa and Linda had packed into the opening in front of the cameras. "You were so quiet, I didn't even notice you."

"You *know* we appreciated that," Milissa added, only a little ruffled by her task. "Now who wants to talk to President Carter?"

Pepe pressed his shoulders in and looked at the ground when Jimmy crouched beside him. "Maybe this young man."

Milissa joined Jimmy and the boy. "No?" she asked as Pepe looked back to where his mother had been and, not seeing her, shrank toward the edge of the group.

"Pepe." Chase blocked his retreat. "You no like talk to da President?"

"I like," Maria said, touching Jimmy's knee.

"And what's your name?" Jimmy asked.

"Maria."

"Your last name?"

"Mikala."

"Mikala. That's a strong name. What's its origin?"

Maria compressed her face into a scowl, then turned around and placed her hands on Jimmy's knees, lifting her feet from the ground.

"Hawaiian," John coached from the top of the stairs.

"Hawaiian," Maria said, letting herself down and facing Jimmy with folded arms.

Jimmy caught John's eye, then returned to Maria. "What grade are you in?"

"Going second. What's your name?"

"This is President Carter," Milissa answered.

"Oh, duh," Maria came back. "I like know his first name."

"Oops. Sorry. Don't mind me. You're doing fine."

By now, the other children were crowding in.

"Good question. I'm Jimmy."

"I can read," said Chase, his spherical face propped cheek-to-cheek on Maria's shoulder.

"You cut," Pepe complained, trying to wriggle back in front.

Chase took Pepe by the shoulders and moved him back a few paces. "Be polite," he counseled. "Dis da U.S. President."

"Not," Pepe snapped, wiping his nose with his forearm.

Chase let out a quiet "tisk" and began again with Jimmy. "I can read."

"And you are?"

"Chase Kanawaliwali." Chase stepped around Maria and sat cross-legged by Jimmy's left knee. "It's Hawaiian too. Means gentle saint."

Jimmy lowered himself to a sitting position.

Chase framed his face in his hands.

"And what kind of material do you read?" Jimmy asked, with Maria now leaning conspicuously on his right shoulder so as not to be completely upstaged.

"Da kine," Chase said, touching the MCC flyer sticking out of Jimmy's breast pocket.

"Well, that's convenient," Jimmy remarked for everyone's benefit. "Could this child be a ringer?" he asked Milissa, grinning uncontrollably as he removed the flyer and handed it to Chase. "Master Kanawali, you have the floor."

"Kanawaliwali," Chase instructed. "Kana for saint. Waliwali, gentle, easygoing." He chose a passage. "Four days after our renovation began," he read, "Stockmans began to operate a bulldozer in da open lots between Maunaloa Road and da north section. You might ask why. Comparing da above picture wit' da field as it looks today, you will observe no change. Broken pavement and rubbish . . . rub . . ."

Chase glanced up at Jimmy, catching his own mistake. "Rubble, of course, not rubbish. See." He pointed at the picture. "And here's da bulldozer. And dis my house, teenie weenie behind da bulldozer. It's all fixed up and painted now. You like see my house?"

"Well, perhaps," Jimmy answered, showing hesitation.

Chase jumped up and ran through the cameras to the front of the yard. "Mama," he shouted, "President Carter said yes. He like see my house."

Feeling suspiciously programmed, Jimmy came to his feet, going along but looking around for a polite way out. As the hundreds present shaped and reshaped like a giant amoeba – with him, his child-strewn entourage, and the media at its core – moving across the field toward the Kanawaliwali house, he spotted Chase standing with his mother, who was herself circled about by an admiring clutch of housewives. "Mrs. Kanawaliwali?" he asked, his attention prompting those between to fold back, volunteering her into his presence.

She held her hands against her cheeks. "Dey say you coming visit me."

"Well, I'm not sure. When did they say that?"

"Last night. Dey say Chase going invite you over." Relieved by his apparent reluctance, she put her hand on his chest. "But we so shabby. Not one nice place to sit." Actually, the house was in good shape. Her real concern was passed out on the couch.

"That shouldn't be a concern. If you like, we'll drop by later and we can sit out on the stoop." He glanced at Cory, who was listening. "You let Ms. Adler know."

"Come back in a little while. Maybe I have some lemonade."

Jimmy caught up with John and ambled to a stop. "It's time to do some freelancing."

"We have to watch the time," Samantha put in. "Our schedule has us back on Oahu at four."

"Cory," Jimmy went on, "you and . . . the young lady with the children?"

"Keiki."

"You and Keiki arrange a quick visit with Mrs. Kanawaliwali. Just time for a drink of something and we're gone. She mentioned lemonade. Maybe Easy can help."

Jimmy asked the press to stay behind, then he, Samantha, and John (and Fred, of course) politely rid themselves of everyone and disappeared down Mannie's lane.

He wanted to see what work the crews were doing, check the condition of the houses, and perhaps have an impromptu chat with someone who hadn't come out for the hoopla. As they skirted Mannie's fence, John pointed out Tutu's grave and gave a little background on MCC's efforts to forestall demolition.

"And MCC's remodeling project? More buying time?"

"Was at first. We figured paint 'em and see what happens. But den, after Nappy Kam's arrest, skilled workmen started showing up. Now we doing serious repairs."

"My experience tells me some of these places aren't worth fixing." He cocked his head to approximate the cant of a red, two story structure nestled back from the road. "Now this place."

"Dis Ewa's place." John recalled his feeble intent to fix the gate. "Our only lost cause. Paint just made it more obvious."

Meek and Lion skidded their bikes to a stop nearby, sideslipping their rear wheels for effect.

"Yo, boys," Jimmy called. "What's up?"

Meek held his ground, but Lion sped away.

"Nice wheels," Jimmy said when he reached Meek.

Meek scanned his beat-up bike as if it were a body part, then glanced at Lion half a block away and took the dare. "You no president, huh?"

"I used to be."

"U.S. President?"

"United States President."

"Why you here den?" He looked suspiciously at Fred.

"To talk with you."

"Uncle, dis one president?"

"Dis ex-President Jimmy Carter," John answered. "Was President before you even born. President Carter, dis Meek."

Without acknowledging the introduction, Meek called back to Lion. "Come 'ere you little chicken boy."

Lion leaned forward, hugging his handlebars.

"He one gutless wonder," Meek apologized. "Who dis?"

"Fred. President Carter's aide," John replied.

"Not," Meek scolded, looking squarely at Jimmy and squinting for the truth. "Dis one narc."

"Secret Service," Jimmy answered.

"He got one bodyguard," Meek shouted.

"Shit," Lion squealed self-consciously, grinning and bucking his bike as if to hold it back.

"You checking up on us?"

"I'm here to see if the kids are being treated well."

"Treated well? You kidding."

"I'm serious."

"Whatchu mean? Cops picking on us? Like dat?"

"Do the cops pick on you?"

"Course dey do," Meek replied, as if anyone should know, then pinched his eyes at Fred. "What you t'ink?"

"If you'd all move back some," Jimmy said to his companions. "All includes Fred, the narc," he added for Meek's benefit. "Maybe down the road a piece."

Meek pushed his bike to Jimmy's side and helped him watch the others off. "You like take a spin?" he asked after a moment, leaning it toward the President as Lion squirmed with glee.

Jimmy tested the handlebar grips.

"Dis one dirt bike." Meek lifted his hands in presentation. "One trail bike."

"A little small," Jimmy said, hardly raising his leg to get on. "It's been a few."

"Wait up." Meek grabbed the back of the seat as Jimmy started away. Something in the old man's posture counseled caution. "Gotta be plenty careful wit' deze handles." He reached in front and took the brakes, then lurched the bike ahead and squeezed to demonstrate their sudden catch. "Dey front wheel. T'row you on your coconut." He put an attentive hand on Jimmy's shoulder. "Only go as far as Lion. Den come back. Keep out da ruts."

Sitting too far back with his knees bobbing above the crossbar, Jimmy lost momentum at the first rise in the road. As he pulled himself forward to lift up in the pedals, he mistakenly clutched the brakes. Unable to advance, the bike reared and leveraged out from under him. Meek caught his arm, easing his contact with the ground. The bike lay beside them, wheels spinning defiantly.

"You like try again?" Lion asked, racing up to intervene while Jimmy brushed his pants and checked for scrapes. "Mine's more your size."

"Actually," Jimmy said, a pain in his shoulder advising him to quit. "Actually, I think Meek's deserves another try." He saw Fred walking in their direction and waved him off.

Meek bolted to his feet and wedged his bike between the President and Lion. "Geez, Lion," he scorned, "Jimmy Carter's no quitter. How you t'ink he come President?"

This time Jimmy stood in the pedals until he reached a cruising speed, then sat forward, ready to rise. Meek and Lion ran alongside, cheering him to the end of the lane and back.

John watched with admiration while they stopped to talked. Jimmy leaned straight-armed against the handlebars, looking into the distance, concentrating on the appropriate phrase. The boys, increasingly at ease, appeared to vie, Meek interrupting Lion with a laugh or playful punch, Lion miming hoops to keep his rhythm while Meek held forth. Eventually, Meek invited Jimmy to take another ride.

"Like riding a bike," Jimmy announced as he pedaled over to John and Fred. "Once you learn, you never forget."

Meek worked him through the brothers' handshake. "You ono, Mr. C."

Jimmy widened his blessed grin. "You're pretty cool yourself," he said, then turned to Lion and held out his hand.

"One high five," Lion responded, slapping palms with the President.

"You see dat," Lion whispered as the three men joined Samantha in the shade of a nearby tree. "President Carter went high five me."

"Hoh, brah," Meek huffed, glancing over his shoulder at Lion. "Went ride my bike."

As he crossed the field to Stockmans' office on his way from lemonade at Chase's house, Jimmy talked with Sato on the phone. The principal had been watching through his window, enticed by the crowd's reaction as Jimmy moved about engaging in casual conversation, but unwilling to intervene without being summoned. Milissa, who was along for the meeting with X at Easy's suggestion, had arranged the call. Sato responded to Jimmy's questions categorically, opposing anything that took his children off the island. "It isn't as simple as moving from city to city on the mainland. Our culture is endemic to this place. Molokai is really all our keiki know. The break in continuity would be disastrous."

X came down the steps. "Mr. Carter," he said as Jimmy handed Milissa the phone, "good of you to come. And good to see you too," he said to Milissa, then turned his face toward the swarm of people entering the parking lot, a few of whom were waving crudely printed protest signs.

"I was hoping you'd make contact," Jimmy replied, shaking X's hand while they hurried in and down the hall.

Milissa noticed a certain ease between the two as she followed them into X's office. Financially self-assured, not the least distracted by material misgivings, it was almost as if they knew each other.

"My concern," said X, gesturing for Jimmy and Milissa to be seated, "is the spin the press might give your visit. Obviously we have a conflict." He took a binder from his drawer and came around his desk. "But it's not about the children. My family has always shown an interest in the island's keiki." He rolled his chair forward so that his knees were almost touching theirs and opened the binder. "This is Grandpa Spitz, back before the Second World War, dedicating the old Kaunakakai pool. And here's my wife, honored for our contribution at the opening of the new community college.

"Just this month we set up a trust account to finance our Keiki Cowboy After School Daycare." Ignoring Milissa's grin, X leafed ahead to the daycare's charter. "I'm sure these board members would be glad to discuss the project with you." He pointed to the signatures of Sato and Swan, entered in addition to his own beneath the bylaws. "Our way of helping Maunaloa's parents.

"This was Maunaloa when I first arrived." The shots were close-ups of loose fittings and termite infestation. "You may have noticed the newly graded land out back. Our south section. We took out eighty cottages, virtually uninhabitable. This is how we envision it." Milissa recognized the rendering. "Our new units. All done in plantation style, but decent places to live, and affordable."

"When was the area cleared?" Jimmy asked.

"A couple years ago. Thanks to our stalwart opposition, this has been a slow process."

"What happened to the people living there?"

"We moved some of them into the north section. They're waiting for the south side rentals."

"You moved how many?" Milissa interjected.

X winked at Jimmy, certain that he knew about her background with Stockmans. "Milissa knows all this."

"What? Two, three families?" Milissa persisted.

"I'd say more like five."

"And the rest?" Jimmy asked.

"Chose to move elsewhere."

"To off-island projects," Milissa offered, as if merely adding information.

"The south side was mostly the original bachelor units. The rent was peanuts. Families came and went. We were never sure who the occupants were. It wouldn't have been possible to track them."

"I noticed a few open areas on this side too," Jimmy responded. "The big one out front and a couple empty lots farther back."

"All houses that had to go. Beyond repair."

"And the ones left standing? They can be saved?"

"At a loss when you factor in the infrastructure."

"How many places did you take out over here?"

"I'd say a third."

"And those families?"

"Now they were a bit more stable. The whole process was more orderly."

"So you know where they went."

"I'd have to check."

"The projects," Milissa answered flatly.

"Milissa's the expert. She can tell you more about our work with the tenants than I can. She's the one who enlightened our approach. Because of her, those still here will have a better deal. Actually, I congratulate them for hanging on. Has she told you about our jobs program?" X handed Jimmy the binder, opened to the pages that contained Milissa's recent *Sentinel* insert. "For this we credit Milissa. It's her baby. We're committed to it one hundred percent."

"Stillborn," Milissa responded. "Especially the jobs part. I hate to admit it. I underestimated the problem. Not much risk in offering positions to people too disabled to work."

"Disabled? Not too disabled to paint a house or mount a demonstration." X rolled his chair back to give Jimmy a view of the field.

The number of people had grown. The rhythmic whoop of chanting had begun.

"True, most of them are imports, but some – Kimo Reyes, big Tiny, that haole fellow Stan, to name a few. Disabled?"

Milissa lowered her voice for Jimmy's benefit while X sized up the crowd. "There's a history here. These guys would no more work for Stockmans than join the Foreign Legion."

"Now there's an idea," X chuckled, turning back from the window.

"You never intended this to work." Milissa whisked the binder with the back of her hand. "When the dust of demolition settles, kids with designer jeans and shoes that fit will be in Mr. X's daycare. The rejects will be stealing starter jackets on the gangster playgrounds of Oahu. Seventy five percent of the tenants have already been evicted. Your count. A few able-bodied men, even if they'd stoop to work for you, are not going to turn this thing around. So much for the state's affordable housing policy."

Jimmy looked to X for a response.

"Some families will make the transition here. More, I think, than Milissa wants to admit. Some that have been evicted are still on island. We're set up to help them now. But some were too far gone to reconcile. There's a place for the chronically poor. We think it isn't Maunaloa."

"Keoni Mikala," Milissa asked, "is he one of 'the chronically poor'?"

"We've pressed Mr. Spitz far enough," Jimmy said, patting the head of an invisible child.

"Not a problem," X replied, affecting genteel dismay. "It's best that Mr. Mikala understand. He's been given legal notice and it's time to leave. You can see he's gone too far." He gestured toward the window. "His departure will defuse – is meant to defuse – further unrest among our people. The sheriff will be at his door tomorrow noon. We sincerely hope he's not at home."

Jimmy handed X the binder. "Thank you for having us."

"Thank you for coming," X replied, following Jimmy to his feet. "Feel free to call again."

Inspired by the first few ragged, hand-held signs, and put off by his limited opportunity for input, Sato had liberated staves and posterboard from the school's art supply and saw that they were distributed before the President presented himself to the press. The chanting tapered to a hush as Adam asked the first question. But when Jimmy began his reply – "The youngsters I have seen here today are more Hawaiian than Hawaii's general population" – placards shouting NAPPY and KEONI multiplied across the field like flowers in a time lapse video.

"Their historic isolation," he went on, not to be dissuaded from the subject of the children, "a factor in their cultural survival, has also brought about a potential weakness. Not having been exposed to the pitfalls of urban life, playing in the fields of child-sight far into their teens, they have maintained a deep, potentially deluding innocence that makes them less prepared to function in the wider world.

"Your second question, Adam, might be more aptly phrased, 'What *has* happened to the children?' The vast majority are gone. Since no one seems to know precisely where, I won't speculate. Something for you to look into. Next question. Brit?"

"Does your task here find common ground with MCC on the issue of affordable housing?"

"Good question. The Felix v Waihee Consent Decree, my guide in this endeavor, prohibits barriers to children's education. Does the lack of affordable housing constitute such a barrier? We'll look at the legislative record on fair housing to see how deep the mandate reaches."

"Mr. President."

"Ed?"

"Will affordable housing be available to these tenants under Stockmans' plan?"

Jimmy looked at John. "I'm skeptical. Mr Mikala?"

John stepped up to the mikes. "Dis all around you" – he pointed right and left – "is what we can afford."

"And if the new rentals cost the same? What then? Would you still fight the demolition?"

"It's more dan rents. Even if da rents weren't hiked, dey'd still tear deze houses down and put up new ones on a grid, looking all da same. Deir purpose is to skimp on space and regiment da neighborhood to get more profit *and* control. Dis town came up over time. Dat's why we got da winding alleys and da different shapes. All da places for da keiki kine to hide and seek."

"The keiki," Sadako asked John, "how do they see the changes going on around them?"

"Da little ones could care less. Dey use da south side lots for kickball. Da teenagers, dey're not quite so naive."

"Not as naive as President Carter has suggested?"

"President Carter called them innocent, not naive." John smiled at Jimmy, remembering his encounter with Meek and Lion. "He got in touch wit' deir better side. Dey can be little devils, but underneath it all, he's right, most of 'em are still undamaged."

"Naive, Mr. President?"

"I must confess an initial bias that these children would be less informed than, say, inner city or suburban children. I simply didn't expect what I heard from a couple of teenagers this afternoon. Someone mentioned the Enclosure Acts. I think it was one of you. There may be parallels, but be assured, these are not simple peasant children who consider their condition to be fated. Media exposure has alerted them to the difference between their lot and that of their peers across the country. Underpinning this recognition is their history of exploitation, preserved and passed along through stories told by the likes of Uncle Mikala here. They know about the strikes and the strike breakers. They know who took the good land and left the rest for those with blood enough to claim it. They have their own political heroes, past and present, and facts to back up their conclusions."

"What conclusions?" Stan shouted from the hood of the jeep, still parked beside the gate where it had been left when Jimmy first arrived.

"To put it in their words," Jimmy answered, as if the question had come from a reporter, "they think they're being ripped off. Robin?"

"Mr. President. You've spoken with Mr. Spitz, Stockmans' CEO. Can you summarize?"

"I'd rather not. Mr Spitz can make his case." Samantha lifted herself into the jeep and looked back at Jimmy – his cue to wind things up. "One thing is sure. Stockmans intends to move ahead with the development. I was told unequivocally that evictions begin with Mr. Mikala. Tomorrow."

"Any reason given for choosing Mr. Mikala to go first?" Ed Bradley asked.

"Another question best put to Mr. Spitz." Jimmy passed his eyes once more over the collection of reporters and stepped into the yard.

"Mr. Mikala," Ed called out as John, with Maria in his arms, led the way to the jeep.

John let Jimmy pass and leaned close to Ed, who was following him through the gate. “Can’t talk now. Gotta stick wit’ da man. You come by tomorrow. We’ll make it an exclusive.”

Maria scrambled into the back seat beside the President. “I going stay wit’ Aunty Lani,” she told him. “Daddy say he no like me be dere when Fidel go kick us out.”

“Not Fidel,” John said, getting in next to her. “Stockmans. Mr. X.”

“Chase say Fidel.” Maria jumped to her feet.

They had begun to roll, edging through the throng, suddenly enveloped in a mighty call and answer – the women chanting, “Hands off John,” the men responding, “Leave Keoni alone.”

Jimmy laughed despite himself. “I can see the headlines now,” he shouted to John, touching the hands in the crowd, accepting their approval. “Carter Sides With Separatists.” They broke off from the last well wishers and headed out of town. “You see why I have to be careful?”

“I see you going everywhere. North Korea. Africa. Big involvements. Why you figure little Maunaloa such a risk?”

“Your issue, especially with the twist of sovereignty support, is much closer to home.”

“Hoh, you mean a bigger economic threat.” John put his arm over the back of the seat and shifted to face Jimmy. “You got big business ties, Mr. President?”

“It’s not quite that simple,” Jimmy replied with a lenient smile. “We’re all connected. There are many concerns.”

John returned a testy grin. “You may be smart to walk da line. You already got a reputation.”

“What’s that?”

“You always see da light in everyone. Even bad guys. You da savior kine.”

“No.”

“Hoh, ya. You da kine.”

CHAPTER TWENTY FOUR

Jimmy's send-off was followed by a holding action. A cadre of captains was tagged from the large milling crowd, each to take twenty people in tow to keep the protest from disintegrating overnight. Food was brought in. Volunteers took to the phones and others were dispatched throughout the island to spread the word of the pending protest.

Televisions were blaring in and around *Da Camp*. Sadako's special – including intimate close-ups of Jimmy answering questions in the helicopter – coming on the heels of national news coverage, had riveted the state's attention. Though some reporters followed Jimmy to Honolulu, the majority stayed behind, and others, mostly international, were arriving by the hour.

By mid-morning the following day, a sizeable chunk of Molokai's population was crammed into the clearing in front of John's house. To add to the circus of color surrounding the field, hundreds of protest kites displaying the slogans FREE NAPPY and LEAVE KEONI ALONE, red on yellow, flitted against a cloudless sky.

A flat-bed truck and sound system was parked to the left of John's gate. All morning, one after another, the locals had come up to testify to Stockmans' abuse. To the right of the gate, Alvaro and Cory were manning a table, dispensing copies of MCC's flyer and a statement by Nappy, written for the event. Next to Alvaro sat sign painter, Jason Dinn, selling his three dollar kites.

Sheriff Nakayama and Deputy Rufus were stationed at each end of Maunaloa Road. X's private security squad ringed the perimeter of the field. A contingent of Stockmans' cowboys was earning double time, mingling intrusively with the crowd.

Milissa and John were still in bed. They could hear Jock banging around in the kitchen, and beyond, the drone of the loudspeaker as people took their turns. Though the words were muffled by the constant chanting, fragments reached the bedroom now and then.

Milissa played at recognizing voices. "You better get out there. That's Moke again, using up all the good lines."

John pulled the sheet over his head. "Do I have to? I scared now. Tell da sheriff come bring me my bedpan. Cannot get out of bed."

"Stage fright." Milissa jumped up and whisked the sheet away, leaving him naked and exposed. "Time to face the music."

"Cannot. Cannot," John pleaded from a fetal tuck. "Tell Nakayama dat Keoni got da flu."

"Coffee's on," Jock announced, leaning over his cup, still crimped from his ancient sleep.

Milissa glanced out through the front window as she hurried past the table. "Keoni," she shouted, finishing her sentence from the bathroom, "you gotta see this mob."

John pulled on his pants and padded out onto the porch. With the exception of his tiny yard, no patch of ground was visible in any direction – nothing but people, vehicles, signs, and kites. He dizzied for an instant and ducked back in the house. The town had been jubilant the night before. He thought the thing had crested. He'd expected a lighter turnout, not hundreds more. "Seen Alvaro?"

"He's out there somewhere," Jock replied. "Sovereign brought in the sound. They made their entrance on the flat-bed. 'Bout thirty of 'em. Quite a show."

John filled his cup and returned to the porch.

Alvaro and two men were consulting heatedly inside the yard. He saw John and broke it off, directing them back into the field.

"Dis you?" John asked him, gesturing toward the crowd.

"Dis everybody, brah. Some not so welcome. Stockmans' cowboys acting plenty huhu."

"I see more of your boys too."

"Gotta have our own security. Dey stationed all around da lot. Everybody plenty loose. Too loose. Dey waiting for da program from Keoni. Keoni dis, Keoni dat. Da big guy . . ." Alvaro pointed at Moke, propped against the truck, sucking down a beer. "He telling folks you plan on holing up. I keep correcting him, but he say he know Keoni."

The steady waves of chanting had begun to vie, scrambling into discord where their margins overlapped. Looking across the fence at John, perplexed by his reserve, the uncles tried to bring their younger men to bear, but they were caught up in the stir, climbing for a better view, jostling to the front, staking out their blankets for the bash. John turned away, touching Alvaro's left shoulder with his own. "Mo' bettah dey see what Keoni do. Dey never gonna listen anyway."

Alvaro placed his hand against John's chest. "Cannot refuse to speak."

John eased forward, testing for resistance. "You gonna wrestle me?" he asked, half serious.

"Brah." Alvaro's voice was vexed and breathy. "You only gonna let 'em haul your brown ass outta here, why you no just leave right now? People see you give 'em up like dis, no explanation, dey gonna be confused." The pressure on his hand decreased. "Why you do dis sit-in t'ing?"

"It's my way."

"Dat's all you got to say? What you t'ink? You Jesus Christ? Talking 'bout your *way*? How you expecting dem to understand your game, you cannot tell me? Walking outta here in cuffs ain't gonna cut it, brah. You like start one riot maybe wit' your zipped up lip?"

John stood awhile beside the mike, looking across the throng, waiting with intense calm for their attention. The resulting quiet was astounding. "Listen," he said, holding his hand to his ear. The silence held for several seconds before a distant, solitary yapping filtered in on the wind. "Whatchu hear?"

"Dat Ché's girlfriend down Paniolo Hale," Keku shouted. "She like him come visit." Laughter splashed away and rippled to the edges of the field as people passed on her reply. Ché ran into the yard barking at the repetition of his name.

Listening again, John pointed toward Kualapu'u town and waited for an answer.

"Da bells of Saint Teresa," Julio called out, looking at his watch. "Eleven o'clock mass."

"You step outside at night in Maunaloa," John mused, gazing down the seven mile grade to Mo'omomi and the sea, "can hear da breakers, can hear your heart beat. But let dis town become one Honolulu bedroom," – he took the mike in hand and set the stand aside – "no mo' peaceful nights. No mo' Maunaloa. Pretty soon dey got one mall. Next t'ing da chains and no mo' Molokai.

"Dis noon, I'm staying to make sure da sheriff does his job. Simple t'ing for me. Easy for him too. Just come and take me out." John paused and scanned the squints of disbelief. "So why da back-up, Sheriff Nakayama?" Four more patrol cars, brought up from the main station, were parked along the strip between the warehouse and the crowd. "You already got Deputy Rufus."

"Ruf, Ruf, Ruf," went up the scattered, mocking chant.

"Why all deze other deputies and rent-a-cops? All here to evict Keoni?"

John looked into the midst of the gathering. "T'ink dey here because of you. T'ings not so simple anymore. Dey try evict someone from Maunaloa, it's an event. Gotta bring da troops in. Tie up all deze resources. You making 'em do deir job."

"What," cowboy Jake Jacobi shouted, "you defying da law?"

"Resisting," John said softly. "Can evict us one by one. But da way it looks, dat'll take some doing. Dis afternoon, Keoni's moving in next door wit' Easy." He took the challenge to the crowd. "We all got neighbors we can stay wit', ya?"

"Damn right," yelled Moke. "You folks can stay wit' me."

"Me too," someone added. "And me."

"Cory," John said, "take names."

"Den we come swinging da la'au," Jake shot back, pulling out the billy club hidden in his boot. "Maybe you like dat?"

"Geev 'em Jake," another cowboy bellowed. "Whack 'em good."

"Jake," John replied, "you gonna whack us all?"

As Alvaro and company edged in on him, Jake spun around, anticipating an onslaught.

"We no like fight you, Jake," John went on. "We just curious about your anger."

Jake jabbed his finger at John and beckoned him to come down.

"Today," John resolved, disdaining the invitation, "we stop slipping away when da pressure's on. Today we turn and stand our ground."

A roar of approval washed over him. Alvaro jabbed his fist into the air and took another step toward Jake. Other fists shot up across the field.

"Whoa," John said, showing them his palms. "Da world is watching, brahs. Expose deze brutes by refusing to take deir bait. Open your hands." Arms fell. "No! Keep 'em up." He demonstrated. "Make 'em loose and wave 'em like da hula kine." Hundreds of hands began to massage the air. "You got it. Dat's da way." He gave Alvaro a wink and returned the mike to its stand.

Alvaro answered with a steely stare and turned away, gathering in his men while Jake paraded through the crowd, tapping his baton against his hand.

Before the press could respond to John's remarks, he jumped into his yard from the bed of the truck and hurried inside. Within minutes, Ed Bradley appeared at his door with a cameraman. Adam, Michael, Sadako, and their sidekicks were close behind. John invited only Ed and Smitty in.

Jock reported John's decision to the rest. Ed would do the interview with Smitty shooting. Michael would get a copy. There was no reason given. John wouldn't have it any other way. He promised to speak to Adam and Sadako after the fact. They could meet him at Easy's.

"Cold eggs and coffee on the table," Milissa said, giving John a departing kiss. "Meet you at the gate."

Wolfing down his breakfast, John turned on the TV without sound. "Just keeping an eye on da score," he said of the pre-season football game, then headed from the room. "Gotta shave."

"If you don't mind," Ed replied, "I'll follow along. Kinda like to loosen up. Get to know you some." He stood outside the bathroom door taking notes. "How about your background?"

"Not much." John looked at himself in the mirror. "Silversmith. Ceramic artist. Jeweler."

"Cultural."

"Hawaiian, Portugee."

"What's with the title?"

"What title?"

"Cory Adler called you Kupuna."

"She's hyping da media. A kupuna has da wisdom of da years. I'm just a Molokai hippie."

"How about your politics?"

"New left, Hawaiian nationalist."

"Elucidate."

"Like I say, a Molokai hippie. Got baptized in da San Francisco Bay. Came back and found da parallels."

Heedless of their time constraint, the two men shouted back and forth above the flush and splash and shower spray. But once the warm-up was complete, it took them less than seven minutes to do the actual interview. "My politics," John explained, sitting at his end of the couch, surrounded by his books, looking especially young in his still wet, slicked back hair and clean shaven face, "come from my tradition and a taste of what dey used to call new left."

In his early days he'd wondered what it meant. His tradition. He'd seen the heiaus, the ancient tapa with its intricate designs, the petroglyphs, the odd pen and ink renditions by the missionary folk. He'd heard the stories of the old ways. But none of this seemed palpably his. Something had intervened. Not until he reached the mainland did he realize that *he* was his tradition, that the answers were in him. In this new environment, he was able to distinguish the feelings that were handed down from those that were overlayed.

Open, receptive, non-possessive, non-violent. These words described his long-term heritage. Certainly there was a warrior legacy, predominant only in the final Aristocratic Period, and exaggerated by the present haole-centric world view. But preceding this, with low population density and abundant resources, there was little reason for combat. And traditionally, stretching back to Babylon, his people preferred to leave and seek new land than fight. This willingness to trust the unknown rather than resist lay deep in the Hawaiian character. "So you see, we come all dis way to get away from you and you found us anyway. Now we have no place to turn."

John's affinity with west coast hippie sentiment, an outlook that embodied many things Hawaiian, drew him immediately into the culture. There he discovered Gandhi's satyagraha and then, through the Vietnam anti-war connection, Marx's dialectic. This "new left" blend of enlightened protest and social science gave him a base from which to understand conditions at home.

He became a student of national liberation movements. He saw the common thread: the search for lost identity. He recognized the faulty rationale that replaced one master, capital, with another, Soviet aid. He realized that, particularly in Hawaii, it was not so much a matter of replacing as it was of casting off, of returning to a more sympathetic, less intrusive system.

"Maunaloa," he explained as he heard the sheriff's footfalls, "is da last and strongest gesture of Hawaiian sovereignty. We offer no alternatives. We just want to be left to do our t'ing. We may not have a plan, but that's our own concern. We know exactly how we feel." John jumped up to greet his nemesis. "Sheriff Nakayama, you like come in?"

"You like come out?" Nakayama stood with his back to the screen. "Two minutes till noon."

"Quickly then," Ed continued, "your sources of inspiration."

"Ghandi first for his non-violence. Trotsky for his theory of ongoing revolution and support for ethnic diversity. Ché Guevarra for his romantic bronze persona. Castro for his endurance. King for his oratory. The indomitable Nelson Mandela. Ben-Gurion. Arafat.

Ho Chi Minh. Rosa Luxemburg. All da forgotten women. And Nappy Kam, da first Hawaiian revolutionary."

"And your models for change?"

"All da national independence movements. From Ireland to Algeria."

"How about the atrocities?"

"I, myself, could not commit dem. But I don't stand in deir shoes."

"Is the Nation of Islam on your list?"

"It must be. I cannot side wit' forces dat oppose da black man. Sure, dey got a racist taint. I got a touch myself. It's like a disease. Whadda you expect after da ass kicking we all got. Everybody has a down side. Some say we're in a fallen state. I look for da redeeming qualities. Wit' da Muslims, it's da self-respect and dignity, da love dey cultivate among demselves. Hawaiian kine got something to learn from da Nation of Islam."

This time Nakayama tapped the screen.

Ed continued, assuming that the sheriff would step in. "Do you expect the tenants' passive occupation of the village to succeed?"

"Da great success will be da practice of non-violence. I hope someone out dere understood. Looked like dey were catching on. I like to t'ink dat we'll perfect its use for future confrontations."

"So your hope is high above your expectation of success in Maunaloa?"

"If da housing development is defeated, but my people miss da message of peaceful resistance, nothing will have been gained. What we're doing here today is one contraction in da rebirth of our nation. We struggle wrong, maybe we damage da fetus, maybe we never get reborn, or maybe we come out all pissed like da Middle East kine, destined to be our own enemy."

Tobias recognized Milissa from the night that he and Rizzo followed John to the campsite in Halawa. He held on to her while the rest of the crowd was moved back. "You his girlfriend. Can stay here by da gate."

"His fiancée," Milissa replied, turning to watch as John came down the steps and into the yard, his hands cuffed behind his back.

It could have been a branch, snapping in the wind. She heard it as she pushed the gate and stepped aside so John could pass. Everyone at the rear of the crowd looked up. A single kite, its string severed, floated to the ground. She let out a startled laugh as John hurled backward, performing an eerie Cossack dance to keep his feet, then slammed into the porch and toppled slowly onto his forehead, smacking it against the walk and collapsing on his back.

Shrieks of recognition ricocheted through the crowd. Some rushed up, some recoiled, some ran for help, some fell weeping. She burst past Nakayama. He was searching for his handcuff keys, still standing where John, rammed back by the force of the slug, had brushed by. John's chest was sopping red. His eyes were glassy. He was gasping.

She turned his head to the side, keeping her face close to his. "I love you, Keoni. You've been shot. Try to hang on."

Blood spilled from his mouth. "Mo' bettah," he said, able to breathe. He heard the squeak of leather as the sheriff knelt to free his wrists.

"Medic's on his way, Keoni. Dey say you gotta stay awake."

But the blood began to pool, pouring from his nose, pumping from his chest. "Keiki?" He searched the dizzy, fading light. "You come visit my Maria, ya?" He lifted his head, then sank back into himself, letting out a long, tapering sigh.

Nakayama reached to close his eyes.

Milissa came between, hunching over John as if to suckle him, taking in his empty stare, stroking back his matted hair until the medics arrived. When they covered up his face, she remembered how he'd hid beneath the bedsheet that morning, and reached to pull the shroud away. Easy touched her hand. "No need, Keiki. Keoni already gone. Come, I take you home."

A deep, emetic melancholy squeezed her heart. Caught up in Easy's arms, she was carried across the yard and into the house, passing in and out of consciousness, unable to tell if Morgan's voice, among the keens and moans of sympathy, was real or imagined.

PART III

"Question is, who's working who."

CHAPTER TWENTY FIVE

Milissa lay on Easy's couch, face down in a pillow, smothering her sobs as the helicopter lifted John away. Easy kept a hand on her until her breathing evened and she fell asleep.

She woke in the dark. Someone was stroking the small of her back. Assuming it was Easy, she closed her eyes. But when she felt the fingers trailing off along her backside, she flipped over and sat up. Her feet came down in Morgan's lap. In a surge of disgust, she kicked free and hurried to the kitchen.

Easy was at the table, her Bible beside her in the lamplight, her face buried in her hands.

Milissa sat near the window and watched their reflections fade, unable, in the shadow of John's death, to process her dismay at Morgan's presence.

"She followed us home," Easy confided. "All night just sitting in da big chair watching over you. I figgah dis no time to be unkind, so

I leave her alone."

She poured some brandy in the bottom of a glass and slid it toward Milissa.

Milissa touched her trembling wrist and set the drink aside. "Oh, Aunty. Poor Aunty."

Easy settled to the floor, her dress collapsing around her like a parachute. "Hoh, Keiki," she howled, tears gushing as she lay her head and arm across Milissa's lap. "My li'i Keoni. My only keiki kane. He gone. He no mo' in da world. Hope he's not lost like me."

Milissa hugged her body around Easy's head, rocked her for a gentle while, then sat up with a start. "Who did this, Aunty? Who would do this?" She patted the heavy arm, heavier now that the question had been asked. "Up now," she coaxed, slipping out from under and going to the sink. "Where'd they take Keoni?" She let the cold water run over the back of her neck.

"Gone Maui." Easy broke down again at the thought, lifting herself like a giant toddler back into her chair. "Dey got one crematorium. He always say he like me t'row his ashes in da ocean. Was like he knew he would go first."

"We'll have a ceremony." Milissa wet the corner of her towel and cooled Easy's face.

"Maybe we go Make Horse," Easy replied. "Can t'row 'em in da tide pool."

Make Horse. Milissa recalled the day that John pulled her and Maria out of the surf. "Does Maria know?"

"Cannot t'ink of how to tell her. She coming home dis afternoon."

"We can do it together. You and Linda and I. If that's okay."

Easy opened then closed her Bible. "Plenty people coming by. Better make some pupus."

"It's their turn for pupus, Aunty. Isn't that the way? You get some sleep. Where's Jock?"

"He's in my bed."

Milissa smiled faintly. "It's a king size, ya?"

"Queen."

"Whatever, don't let him get away. I'm gonna need his help."

She downed the brandy and headed through the living room.

"Up," she snapped, piqued by Morgan's cataleptic pose, still poised where she had left her on the couch. "We need to talk. I'll walk you out."

John's yard was cordoned off. In front, a deputy sat behind the wheel of his patrol car, his chin on his chest. Across the field, Rufus and the rent-a-cops were rousting hangers-on, mostly teenagers, who'd spent the night unseen between the houses. Inside *Da Camp*, a shaken yet substantial force of volunteers was just beginning to stir.

Milissa pressed against the yellow tape, straining in the half-light to see John's body outline on the walk.

"Anything I can do?" Morgan cooed from behind.

Awakened by their presence, the deputy opened his door.

"Try not touching me," Milissa answered, gesturing to get by.

"Officer." She held her ID up as she approached. "I'm investigating Keoni Mikala's murder. For his family."

He smiled with annoyance and pulled back his head, prepared to swat the license if it came too near his face.

"I need access to the yard. It won't take a minute. Did they retrieve the slug?"

He stationed himself in front of the gate and stared straight ahead.

She copied down his name, T. Rizzo, and stood beside him, mocking his wooden posture while she scoured the horizon, thinking back on the gun's report. It had a distant sound. There was a little rattle, an echo. Had it been close in, the percussion would've muffled in the crowd. Someone would have seen. She motioned Morgan to her side. "I was here when the shot was fired. Where were you?"

"I don't really know. I was coming from over there," Morgan pointed two o'clock from their position to where the highway enters town. "Everyone was rushing toward my car. I had to pull over and get out."

"You had to?"

"I couldn't go forward. It seemed the thing to do."

"So you just had to get out. Then what?"

"Someone shouted that the police shot John Mikala, so I . . ."

"Who? No, no, wait." Milissa moved Morgan away from Rizzo. "Who said that?"

"I don't know. Everyone was passing it around."

"Did you recognize anyone? Any of your clients?"

"Probably at the time. Nothing comes to mind. I was thinking of you. I came right here. That's when I saw what had happened."

"Thinking of me. Touching. You were here to see me."

"I was here on business."

"Not here for the killing, then?"

Morgan smiled softly. "I had papers for the sheriff."

"Serving your own process. A subpoena?"

"A stay."

"Ah, a stay of . . ."

"Eviction."

"Did you make service?"

"I did."

"When?"

"When I came through the gate. I gave it to Rufus McKee."

"Good timing. That was for Hoiness?"

"The house he occupies."

Trained at parsing truth, Morgan couldn't help being precise, even when attempting indirection. Milissa recognized the gloss. Not for Hoiness, but the house. Why the gap? The answer would be in the clerk's file.

Morgan saw the wheels turning. "Were you interested in what I did or what I saw?"

"Sometimes what people do can jog their memory."

"Well, there you have it then."

"Let's walk it through. You pulled over where?"

"By the corner of the warehouse."

They went to where the car had been. Milissa held out her hands as if it might appear.

"I moved it."

"To?"

"To Jense Hoiness' driveway."

"When?"

"While you were sleeping."

"So, let's follow your route when you first got out." She gestured for Morgan to lead. "Be there. What do you see?"

"People running in all directions."

"Anybody you recognized?"

"Mr. Monzón."

"Fidel. What was he doing?"

"Running toward John Mikala's house. Forcing his way. Someone told him the police did the shooting. Everyone agreed."

"Where did he come from? What was his path?"

"From behind me. He passed me on my right."

When they'd gone a distance into the field, Milissa stopped. "You parked at Jense's. Why not Easy's?"

"We'd planned to meet."

"Did you?"

"No. His lights were out."

"So you left the car there and walked back to Easy's?"

"I wanted him to know that I'd be by."

Milissa started off toward Jense's house, set in behind the others on the north side of the field. "Maybe he's awake by now." After several paces she pulled up. Morgan hadn't moved.

"We can't call on him together, unannounced."

"Why not?" Milissa shrugged, catching sight of Morgan's car backed into the driveway.

"It's not appropriate. What's my point in being there?"

"Maybe he'll need your advice."

"I suppose I have something to say about that. I take it you intend to question him. I'm not a criminal lawyer. Even if I were, I'd need time to prepare."

"Right." Milissa plodded past her, waving her off as she followed. "That's all for now."

"I do hope you and I can visit," Morgan simpered.

"So you can move in on my grief?" She heard Morgan gaining and turned around. "That's all, Morgan!"

Morgan took a couple of steps and froze, her saccharine smile patined with hate.

Easy, outside in her rocking chair, stopped rocking.

"You'll need time to prepare," Milissa called back, continuing on her way. "Your best defense is psychiatric." She halted with a matador's contempt. "And keeping away from me."

Jock looked out through Easy's kitchen window at the vacant house. He'd taken his equipment with him when the sheriff ordered them to leave. But his clothes and other personal effects, the keepsakes that he'd carried from the mainland – expired press credentials, an old photo of a younger woman, an engagement ring – reminders to himself of who he'd been, were still there, tightly arranged and accessible behind the couch. He thought of his chalet, bristling with technology, embedded in a cliff above Big Sur – all his but no one waiting. The gear, the house, the memories. Like Keoni's ashes, he admitted to himself, ready to be washed away.

"You think I'm out of my league?" Milissa asked as he pulled up to the table.

"Seems like it – just launching into this thing. You need time to think. Time to grieve."

"There isn't time. I'm doing what Keoni would do if it were me."

"You're not Keoni."

"Oh, right, I'm just a girl. We're supposed to fall apart. That it?"

He picked up her license. "State of Washington. They can't be giving these away."

"There's a test."

"Tell him 'bout da kine Seattle Sleuths," Easy put in. "She got experience, Jocko."

"I'll ask the questions." Jock mugged, flashing the ID. "You just keep my pencils sharp."

"Hoh, you see how he does dat, Keiki? He one natural, ya?"

"You could help me, Jock. I can't be everywhere."

"What do I know about investigation?"

"You were a reporter."

Jock felt a jolt of angst. He was seasoned. He should have recognized the signs. It was as if he'd scripted John's assassination. He looked at Easy. "You with me?"

"You wit' Keiki, I'm wit' you. She gonna catch da bad guy."

He placed the ID beside Milissa's saucer. "Maybe a little back-up here and there. Something in my range."

She looked at the card and then at him.

"And if I think you're off," he added, handing it to her, "I'll tell you. But you're the lead."

Easy got up wearily and put her hands on the old man's shoulders, squeezing them with reassurance. "Aunty going to bed now. Don't let me sleep past noon."

"Cardinal rule." Milissa straightened up, eager now to finish her last few bites of breakfast. "Confidential communication."

"That one I understand." Jock nodded.

She emptied her cup and faced him. "Maybe you do. I need you to talk to Fidel, to get his help with Hoiness."

"Hoiness?"

She filled Jock in on John's fight with Jense, and how Jense had kowtowed to Fidel. "What's important is that I interview Jense in Fidel's presence. Tell him I need his protection."

"I can do that."

"Does this mean you and Fidel will be sharing information?" Milissa asked.

"The question tells me no."

"Same thing with anybody else you talk to. We keep it to ourselves, right?"

"Understood." Jock paused to let her know her point was made, then added, "I have something that might interest you."

"What's that?"

"Smitty caught the action in the yard."

John's death throes tumbled through her mind.

"He says it's pretty bad."

"Has it aired?"

"No. He refused to share it with Ed. Claims their deal was limited to the interview. He and Ed came to me. I agreed with him."

"Why hold back?"

"Not sure. Maybe the angle. The others shot it from outside the fence. Their stuff was all over the networks last night. Big news following Carter's visit."

"Could be important."

Jock took out his phone. "Teague's on News Hour tonight. My guess is he'll show it then."

"Tell him we don't need a copy."

"Just a preview," Jock concurred, listening for his connection.

The curtain, lifted by a breeze, caressed Milissa's face. John's absence filled her lungs, shallowing her breath. Fidel and Jock, at the back of the encampment, seemed suddenly surreal, as if their gestures were the cadence of an undiscovered tongue. She tied her robe and walked into the sprawl of waking bodies. None, at first, were more convincing than the props around them or the backdrop of sea and sky. But when they smiled and spoke, her desolation turned to agony, then broke like a fever into spring.

Fidel was craning over Jock's shoulder, anxious that the work continue despite John's death or because of it – whichever motivation proved effective. He saw Milissa coming and looked down across the valley. "I've got three hundred people here. No time to play detective. Keoni would expect us to keep the pressure on."

Milissa moved around and stood below him on the slope. Her eyes were stern but full of grace. "He'd want us to cooperate."

"A perfect angel or a perfect bitch?" Fidel wondered aloud. "Either way you're a diversion."

She glanced at Jock for help.

"Why so harsh, Fidel? She'd prefer not to be alone with the guy. You can keep him in line."

"She's afraid? I doubt that."

"You might just make him honest," Milissa offered.

"He'd like to make you honest."

Fidel's half-parted eyes told Milissa that he knew.

"He says you gave him the scent." He chuckled at the turn of phrase, detecting a flicker of disgust. "Now that's more like it. You're best when you're pissed off."

He watched her warmth evaporate and sobered at the prospect of her acting on her own, then called out to Alvaro, who was helping Ewa unload take-out breakfasts from the van. "You have that draft?"

"Nothing to add," Alvaro said, returning Fidel's handwritten announcement.

Fidel passed it on to Jock without looking. "Fine tune this and fax it to Cory's office. We're having a memorial. It has to go out this morning."

"So, you're on board with Milissa then?" Jock asked.

"Things are backed up at the wharf," Fidel told Alvaro. "We'll need someone to help Loka. Our little Sikh has disappeared."

Alvaro didn't want to lose a seasoned worker. There were too few and each was vital for morale. "How 'bout you?" he asked with a testy smile. "You big and strong."

"I have to babysit Milissa. Ask Julio. He owes us."

"Julio won't work wit'out pay."

"How about Ewa's son?" Fidel brought Milissa into his line of sight, expecting a response but getting none. "In the spirit of cooperation."

"Ewa say some bugger smashed a beer can in his face last night. Cut his other eye."

"I bet he didn't see it coming. Five bucks an hour, then. Get Julio."

Alvaro scowled. "Whatchu mean, get Julio? Get him yourself. I no work for you."

Fidel turned to Jock. "You know where Julio lives. And, oh, the volunteers . . . Everybody in Easy's yard from now on. And down into the valley. Best to honor the eviction."

Jock looked at Alvaro for an opinion, but Fidel didn't wait.

Milissa had to catch up as he left. "I only need you with me," she said. "I'll ask the questions."

"Ya, ya," he shrugged, moving off toward the warehouse, "just call me Rocko." He held up his leather binder. "Gotta drop by Stockmans' office first. The renovation bill."

"Jense's first," she insisted. "Then, if you promise to stop being an asshole, I'll get you in a room with X." She'd read him right. The arrangement was symbiotic, joined by mutual distrust. He went along without a word.

Jense's driveway was empty, but heavy metal was blasting from one of the bedrooms. She thumped on the front door.

"Who's that?" came back Hilda's wiry voice.

Fidel reached past Milissa and pounded twice.

After considerable delay, a nose and a scruffy chin appeared behind the night chain.

"We're here to talk to Jense about the shooting," Milissa said, withdrawing her license before Gunner could focus in.

"Boy," crackled Hilda, "get away from that door."

"Fucking police," Gunner whispered over his shoulder.

"He's not here," Hilda replied, unable to get by her son.

"Does he have a rifle?"

"Sure he does," Gunner answered.

"Does it have a scope?"

"Can't hunt pig without a scope," he scoffed, then shouted, "God damn it," and backhanded Hilda for tugging at his shirt.

Milissa jostled the door to regain his attention. "Was he here yesterday at noon?"

He stretched the night chain taught. "You ain't no fucking cops."

Fidel reached in and clamped Gunner's immature goatee between his thumb and finger, holding him there while Milissa repeated her question.

"No," Gunner groaned. "He left way earlier."

"How early?"

"Real early."

Fidel rolled his thumb slightly forward.

"Six! Six or seven!"

"Where is he now?"

"The Kama fucking Aina, now let go."

"Looks like he's snoozing," said Milissa.

"Waiting for the bar to open." Fidel parked two rows back and to the right, avoiding Jense's rearview mirror. "You go ahead. We come up on him together, he'll just shut down."

Milissa cocked her head as if she had misheard.

"Go." Fidel pressed. "Get him talking. I'll surprise him from the other side."

She got out and settled her door ajar. "Mr. Hoiness," she sang as she came alongside his pick-up. "Can we talk?"

"'Bout what?" His eyes rolled in her direction.

"I've been hired by Mr. Mikala's family." She held up her ID. "To investigate his death."

He reached out, pretending to adjust the card, and twisted it away. "Who'd you screw for dis?" he said and let it drop to the floor. "Whoops. Looks like you're gonna have to sniff it out."

Fidel tapped on the passenger window.

Jense plunged his arm between his legs and groped. His look of inquiring fear, directed at Milissa, changed to terror when he heard the door unlatch and felt the cushion move.

"Maybe I can help," Fidel said, searching Jense's eyes for the impetus to strike.

Peeking down like a child who'd messed his pants, Jense spread his knees, raised his feet, and gathered back his baggy crotch to clear the way.

"Never wave your license in a bad boy's face," Fidel offered. "Private Detective 101." He caught the sour scent of panic as he grabbed the card and passed it across to Milissa. "Jense, Jense," he chuckled, "she just wants you to answer a few questions. As soon as we're finished I'll buy you a beer."

"You know I don't know anyt'ing 'bout dis stink," Jense pleaded. "You see I stayed away."

"You two have talked?" Milissa asked.

"Dat night. When you was interviewed by TV. He warned me off. 'Nat right, Captain?"

Fidel's eyes dulled and shifted to Milissa for relief.

"Where were you yesterday?" Milissa asked.

"Hunting," Jense replied, noticing the CLOSED sign being taken from Kama Aina's window.

"Of course. When to when?"

"Sun up. All day."

"Where?"

"Kamakou."

"Big mountain. Anybody see you?"

A man came out to sweep the walk.

Jense hit on a plan of escape. "Da pig," he answered, inching to his left, "but he got away."

"Hunting pig, how far do you shoot?"

"Far enough dat it can't catch you if you miss."

"Enough to need a scope?"

"Depends." He leaned on the horn. "Hey, brah," he yelled, honking as he jumped down from the cab. "You open, brah?"

Milissa cautioned Fidel. The man with the broom was looking their way, waving Jense toward the entrance.

"Say you come across a litter," Jense continued, hurrying to safety but pivoting every few steps to keep track of Fidel. "You bring her keiki down, might take an extra shot to drop da sow. You're too close, you're in trouble."

The waiting room at the main station was an eight foot cubicle with a bulletproof reception window and a remote control lock on each door. Inside the office, a deputy with his back to the glass was amusing the clerk. The clerk was at her desk, absorbed in his attentions. He looked down past his elbow to find the counter with the heel of his hand. T. Rizzo, Milissa said to herself as he glanced her way, then leaned back and blocked her view.

While waiting him out, her mind clicked onto Fidel. All was intuition at this stage. No one was immune. He'd led Jense home on a leash the night of her PBS interview. The story was well known. But now that she'd seen them together, the connection seemed less suspect. She checked her watch. He was at Cory's office, reworking the memorial announcement. Jock had refused to implicate the cops. She had less than an hour to finish her business.

She returned to Rizzo's khaki back and pressed the buzzer. He pushed forward and gave her a wink, keeping four fingers on the counter and turning sideways to finish his story. She knocked, but he continued unperturbed, eliciting titters and aw-go-ons from his admirer, who was crossing and recrossing her mini-skirted legs and snapping her gum.

The phone rang and Rizzo answered. The clerk got on another line. They didn't look her way, but their eyes were twinkling as if it were a ruse. Rizzo threw his head back laughing and paraded to the rear of the room. When he finally put the phone down and came to the window, Milissa wasn't there.

Outside, along the walk beside the station, she'd found a private entrance. Its double doors were hanging open, unattended. Inside, at the head of a broad receiving bay, she saw a corridor that appeared to run the length of the building – from the waiting room to her right, to Chief Fitzpatrick's office, she presumed, at the opposite end. Betting that once she got in and turned left no one would question her perky little secretarial presence, she ventured forth. Stoked by the potential for flimflam, she read the placards as she glided down the hall – Evidence. Men's Locker Room. Roll Call. Sergeant this. Captain that.

Kale Ford came out of the last room on her left. She continued to check the names but straightened her right arm to her side and cocked back her wrist, pointing her index finger in a delicate signal of distress. A few steps and he stopped. He recognized her from having pried her off of Kepa weeks before. She looked at his name plate, unaware that she'd been placed. "Sergeant Ford," she said, feigning her utmost naiveté. "I'm here to see the chief." He gestured toward the office from which he'd just appeared. Her hand shot out and took his as it dropped to his side. Rizzo had entered the corridor. He'd spotted her and was moving her way. "Milissa Dogherty," she added as if Kale had been expecting her.

Kale sensed her panic and identified its source marching down the hall. Enchanted by her fragile air, he chose to play her game. "Call me Kale," he said, returning her handshake and leading her toward the office. "He's waiting." He tapped lightly and stuck his head around the door. "Chief. Miss Dogherty here to see you."

Milissa, aware that Rizzo was standing behind her, stepped by Kale and entered the room.

Chief Fitzpatrick lowered his newspaper and peered over his reading glasses. "Miss . . .?"

"Dogherty. Milissa Dogherty." She placed her identification in front of him and sat in one of the armchairs facing his desk. Her sandals barely touched the floor.

His eyes lifted from her ID to the officers, hanging precipitously through the door.

"Anything else Sergeant?" he asked.

"Nothing," Kale replied and left immediately.

"Rizzo?" he went on, hinting irritation.

"Chief, you no mind . . ." Rizzo stepped gingerly into the room and gave Milissa a quizzical look. "Uh, Miss, I no see you at da window little bit ago?"

Milissa shape-shifted forward in her chair, gripping its arms, sticking her chest out, and lifting her chin. "Do you see me now?"

"Hoh, I see you." Rizzo moved slightly to his right in order to face her – the better to conduct his interrogation. "How you get here, Miss? You no check in."

"Is that your responsibility?" Milissa asked. "Checking people in at the window?"

Rizzo flushed. That this girl should presume to question him! And in front of the chief! "No," he said, befuddled by his own adrenal rush, "but da clerk, she no check you in too."

"T'ink maybe she too busy talking story wit' da kine," Milissa countered, mocking Rizzo with his pidgin.

"Chief." Rizzo pointed at Milissa. "She no check in. Yolanda no buzz her t'rough."

"Your watch, Mr. Rizzo?"

"First watch, sir." Rizzo came to attention, realizing that he'd stayed past his lunch break.

"And that was?"

"Up Maunaloa, sir."

"If you'd like, I can put you on hall patrol. You can keep an eye on Yolanda."

"Sir . . ." Rizzo began, prepared to conjure an excuse.

"Deputy!" Fitzpatrick warned.

"Yes, sir." Rizzo saluted and left the room.

"Keiki, is it," Fitzpatrick said, noticing her surprise at his use of the name. "Oh, we hear of you from time to time. Your work with Stockmans Inc. That incident with young Kepa." He took one last look and flipped the ID to Milissa's side of the desk. "Our haole private eye."

"Keoni's family hired me to investigate his death. I thought you should know."

"You could have gone through channels. We have a form." He got on the phone. "Yolanda, make a file on Milissa Dogherty and send it down."

They waited in silence until the folder came.

"Can't tell you how sorry I am about Keoni," he said, making note of her visit in the log. "You did right in stopping by. But I don't recommend your approach. How the hell did you get in?"

"After twenty minutes of Rizzo's back, I came through the employees' entrance. I guess that's what it is. Wide open. No sign."

Fitzpatrick hung his head and snorted. "I'll take it as a wake-up call. And you." He pointed. "Don't ever pull a shenanigan like that again."

"Yes, sir." Milissa straightened in her chair. "I was hoping we could cooperate. There are things I need to know."

"Oh, you're a wily one. You sneak in, then trade your trespass for the keys." He threw her a pad. "Make a list."

While Milissa wrote, he advised against embarrassing his deputies or offending the "wrong persons." He granted that he couldn't stop her from practicing, but let her know that if she crossed him, he'd make her work impossible.

"Aren't you back at school soon?" he asked, scanning down her column of requests.

"Might have to put it off. I owe this to Keoni."

"A couple areas I want you to avoid. We'll investigate our own people, including the private guys. We've already taken their guns for testing. Sovereign is under investigation by another agency, so leave them alone. I mean, don't question them directly." He reached the list across but tightened his grip as she took hold. "On the other hand, if they should let anything slip, anything you think we'd like to know, report that information directly to me."

Milissa nodded her compliance and kept her reservations to herself.

He let go. "Have Yolanda make a copy for the file. I'll introduce you to your contact. I just put him on the case." He took her down the hall.

"You know," he confided as he knocked on Kale's door, "if you hadn't whipped that Kepa so convincingly, I probably wouldn't be doing this. You're such a snip."

Milissa familiarized Kale with the background of the incident, her initial interviews, and her hunches – making it clear that she was merely following leads. Though he agreed with her tact of probing individuals with obvious motive first, he pointed out the animus of certain segments of the public against Sovereign and let her know that Sovereign itself was suspect because John, a proponent of non-violence, was a takeover threat. His abiding concern was that Homicide would take the lead as soon as he finished his work-up, normally restricted to three days. His aim, as always, was to solve the case before they could step in.

"Put everyt'ing in writing," he said. "Daily narratives." He stapled Milissa's requests for evidence and test results to the cover of the case file. "You'll see dis stuff as soon as I do. I'm short-handed here. We might as well work as a team."

Sunlight sliced through dampered, horizontal window slats, streaking the walls and floor of the dim-lit, formal board room with a brooding, early Bogart ambiance. X had Harry on the line. "And where the hell are you?" He cranked the louvers wide enough to peek, then lowered them again. "I want you in the hallway."

Fidel came in before Milissa.

"My appointment was with her," X complained as he got off the phone.

"Call it an intrusion," Fidel said, slapping his statement down beside the fifth of gin that marked X's place at the table.

Kini tapped lightly and looked in. "Process server." She nodded at the man behind her. "He insists on personal service."

"Mr. Spitz," the man said, "notice and petition for divorce." He gave X the papers and left.

X placed the notice next to his bottle, on the side away from Fidel's bill, and eeny-meeny-miny-mo'ed between the three until he settled on the alcohol. "I needed an excuse," he said, breaking the seal. "Or is it your presence that triggers my thirst? No matter." He swayed a little, still rummy from the night before. "One reason's as good as another. Care to take first crack?"

Fidel drank deep, then laid his invoice open, positioning the fifth across its crease to keep it from refolding.

"Whew!" X whistled, his mouth watering in admiration. "A man with an appetite." After matching Fidel's swill, he traced his finger down the paper to the bottom line. "Fifty three thousand. Almost worth paying." He cocked his head for a departing glance as he slid it back to Fidel. "But I think not. The part of the Act you're referring to says the cost is to be deducted from future rents. And it's meant to cover minor defects." He took a second, larger slug before finishing his point. "Not for unsavagable . . . sal-vedge-able . . . unsalvagable structures."

"The tenants are prepared to deduct for as long as it takes to clear the debt, and we'll be petitioning the court for an advisory opinion to protect our investment – that's just in case you decide to destroy their homes."

"Did you really think . . .?" X searched down and to his left, instantly forgetting where he'd set the gin. "I mean . . ." He latched onto the bottle. "I appreciate your gamesmanship. Quite an investment. But you misapplied the law. Even if you did go through the proper loop hoops . . . holes." He took another gulp. "Ooh, Mercy! There goes the good cholesterol." He swung his head abruptly toward Milissa, overshooting and adjusting back. "Milissa, about Keoni . . ."

"Your phone," Fidel interrupted, picking it up and making a call.

Still looking at Milissa, X groped in Fidel's direction, too numb to be sure, thinking it may have rung.

"Gary?" Fidel said. "Fidel here. . . . File the claim. . . . Says he won't pay. . . . Right here. . . ." Fidel turned to X. "Our attorney. He wants to talk to you."

X got on. "Counselor, how can I help you?" He covered the mouthpiece with his hand. "Milissa . . . so sorry about Keoni."

Fidel jerked the receiver away. "Gary. . . . Gary, it's me. He's not listening. . . . At the moment? Drunk. . . . Right, not a word. See you then."

X took another hit and thumped the bottle down. "Damn," he said after the kick had registered. "You're not gonna let up, are you?" He lurched to his feet. "Get the fuck . . .!" His chair tipped back. He grabbed the edge of the table to keep from stumbling. "Harry!"

Harry's face appeared near the top of the opening door. His hat was in his hand.

Milissa danced him quickly in reverse. "Fidel's leaving," she cajoled. "X is a little tipsy."

"Asshole," X shouted and flung the invoice at Fidel.

"Witness." Fidel smiled at Milissa on his way down the hall. "A propensity to hurl things at people who interfere."

X tried to steady himself with another shot, but shuddered instead, paling as the blood rushed to his stomach.

"Ah," he said, waxing silly again when the color returned to his face, "here we are, alone."

Milissa moved the fifth aside and prepared to take notes. "I have some questions."

"The couch treatment." X lowered himself to the floor and flopped onto his back. "It all started with the forceps."

She turned her chair. "Yesterday noon. Where were you?"

"I got a call from Fitzpatrick. He told me about your arrangement."

"Yesterday, X. Where were you?"

"Here."

"With?"

"You drag me into this thing, treat me like a suspect, I'm ruined."

"Were you with anyone?"

He sat up, head hanging, unable to clear his mind. "You can't believe I'm involved in this."

"You take a little nappy poo. I'll come by this afternoon with Sergeant Ford."

"Rizzo. God damn it. Deputy Rizzo and Kini."

"Doing what?"

"Just waiting it out."

"Why Rizzo?"

"I don't know. I guess he was assigned."

"What happened to the Hoiness eviction? I see he's still there."

"We dumped it."

"Dumped?"

"Settled."

"In writing?"

"Yes."

"Let me see the agreement."

"What's this got to do with anything?"

Milissa's eyes deadened. "The agreement."

He dragged himself into his chair. "Out. I don't have to talk to you."

"This afternoon, then." She got up to leave. "I'll come by with Kale."

"I won't be here."

"That's fine. We'll bring a subpoena. We can do it in court."

"Kini," he bellowed, "bring down the Hoiness stuff." He pleaded with Milissa while they waited. "I'm counting on your discretion."

"Count on nothing."

The file contained a promissory note, a quit claim deed signed by Jense two days before John's death, and a statement discounting Farley Chisolm's conveyance as *never taken seriously.*

"Five thousand then and five today. That should set you back."

"The company's money. I didn't buy the God damn house."

"Why the split payment?"

X leafed through the attachments. "He gave me this quit claim and this. It's a copy." He held up Chisolm's letter. "I wanted the original, so I held back. He's bringing it by at one."

Milissa shook her head, stunned by the symmetry of circumstance. "Five before, five after."

"It was late afternoon," X whined. "He didn't have it with him.

Who could have predicted?"

The letter was typewritten on corporate stationery and signed *Farley Chisolm, President.* At the top of the page was a logo with the words *Chisolm Villa Inc.* superimposed on a tiny village of plantation houses. In the upper right hand margin was a small-print list of corporate officers. The grant was premised on Jense affirming fatherhood of Cephas, son of Olive Strunk. The house was to pass from Jense to the child as a life estate when he reached twenty one and otherwise to revert to Chisolm Villa, its heirs or successors.

"Looks official enough," Milissa remarked.

"So did their bankruptcy. Chisolm made a big mistake bringing in his son-in-law, Mickey."

"Was Jense drunk the other day?" Milissa gave a knowing smile.

"Not when he showed up."

"So you plied him."

"Did I say that? What's there is there."

Also in the file was Morgan's stay of eviction.

"Looks like she got screwed," X remarked when Milissa noted that Morgan was entered as the plaintiff. "If we purchased first, it's ours. If she was first . . ." He flicked Jense's statement with his fingernail. "She bought an unenforceable claim."

"I'll take copies."

He gathered the papers in. "You'll tell them I cooperated?"

"I'll tell them you gave me the evidence."

Stan and Smitty had been buddies since the day of Nappy's bust when Stan, with Smitty's backing, heckled X unmercifully on national TV. So close were they that Jock had gone through Stan to get a look at Smitty's death tape. The tactic worked, but with a catch. The tape was shown at Cory's house with Stan as the MC.

When Stan spotted Jock and Milissa leading Kale up the driveway, he turned on his ceiling fans to clear the air. During introductions it was obvious that he and Kale were acquainted. Twenty years before, Kale had stopped him on the road from Halawa with a suitcase full of fresh-cut marijuana. In an act of lenience, typical in those hard times following the bust, Kale merely seized the crop and sent him on his way. After the statute of limitations had expired, Stan ribbed Kale about the status of the evidence and Kale kidded back by inhaling – an indelible mistake.

"Here to view the tape, I hope." Stan offered his hand like a dare.

Kale tucked his thumbs in his belt. "Tell you when I get inside."

Jock and Milissa lagged behind, staying out of the center ring while Stan showed Kale to the rocking chair. "Shock rocker," Stan jived, demonstrating the action of the springs, "has a tendency to take control. Sorry I can't turn you on. Just did up the last of my stash. You know Smitty?"

Smitty, slightly stoned, nodded from across the room.

"By reputation," Kale answered, remaining on his feet.

"Now, tell me true . . ." Stan continued. He held back a scampish grin as he inserted the tape. "About that pakalolo. You couldn't have smoked it all yourself."

"Wait," Milissa interrupted.

Stan pressed the start button. "Did you share?" he asked, watching for the image to appear.

"No. Hold it!" She rushed to the set and turned it off. "We're not just slapping this thing in and running our mouths. I take it we'll be watching Keoni's death."

Stan shrugged apologetically and reached for the rewind.

Milissa blocked his hand. "For now, Stan, you're an observer."

He turned to Smitty.

"If that's a problem," she continued, pressing the eject, "we can view this at the station. Kale, you guys have a VCR."

Kale moved toward the door.

"Not a problem." Smitty waved the sergeant back. "Keiki, you do the honors."

Milissa was relieved. She was leery of relying on Kale. There was still the issue of police involvement in John's death. "Look for the shooter," she said, restarting the tape.

The first few seconds were silent – as if the sound were out. John and Nakayama neared the gate, Milissa stepped aside and slid it back, a distant crack-ack-ack and the camera reflexed skyward, losing them beneath its lens, then levelling off to find the sheriff, alone and turning toward the house, not amused by John's apparent antic. Milissa, still behind the fence, reacted to John's slapstick dance with startled, girlish glee. Her squeal melted horribly. The camera followed her to John and watched her tip his head, emptying his mouth. Nakayama knelt and blocked the view.

"The rest is a blur," said Smitty.

"Why'd you jerk?" Milissa asked.

"The slug. I'm sure it was the slug. It hit the porch."

Kale took a note. "Run it again."

The second time through, knowing looks were exchanged when the camera jolted up.

"What?" She stopped the tape.

"Could hear da report."

"I heard it," Jock put in.

"That's it?" Milissa asked with patient disbelief. "You're too caught up in the climax."

Stan – chastened, but aching to rejoin the class – inched up his hand beside his ear.

"Did you see it, Stan?"

"The motion on the roof," Stan replied.

She backed it up and froze it where the camera's lurch had let a narrow band of blue into the scene, then ran it through the sequence several times to show a sudden, tiny disappearance from the roofline of the warehouse. "It's just a speck," she said, stepping it through frame by frame, "but see, it clearly goes away."

She was surprised when Kale took the tape and dropped it in a Ziploc. "We'll blow dis up. Get some idea what da bugger looks like."

Stan nodded at Smitty, praising his anticipation of the move. "Just da kine," he said, then turned to Kale. "Keep it. It's a copy."

Smitty whipped out his cell phone and dialed. "For the show," he said when Michael came on the line, "we think we found the shooter. . . . Check the roof of the warehouse. Stop it through. You'll see it. . . . Ya, right where we were that day. . . . Glad I caught you."

"You're gonna run it?" Milissa asked as he hung up.

"That's up to him. He's live from Honolulu at three thirty. Six thirty mainland."

Milissa and Kale talked on the way to his car. She noticed a couple of TV vans in front of the deli. They would have to be discrete. The reporters were already out, hawking for information. Kale needed at least an hour to handle the pressing business – a search warrant allowing access to the warehouse before the News Hour aired, and an arrest warrant for Jense. It was agreed that Jense would be picked up for fraud in the sale of the house. The victim, either Morgan or X, would be the second to have signed. Examination of the clerk's files and interviews of both would follow to establish a complaint. The objective was to keep all three on board for questioning in what was shaping up as a murder for hire disguised as a real estate transaction, an out of court settlement or, conceivably, both.

Kale posted his deputies at the warehouse, stopped by John's to retrieve the slug – imbedded in the porch – then sped off to meet with the chief. Milissa watched him disappear from sight. His candor had engendered a degree of trust, but their loyalties were not the same. At least for now, she would continue on her own.

"Stan," she said, returning to the living room. "You have a camcorder?" She knew he did.

Stan stretched his "Yes" across a knowing smile.

"Can we use it?"

"We?"

"Jock and I." She looked at Jock for backing.

"You like borrow Stanley's toy, no let him play?" Stan asked.

She waggled her head as if she were to blame.

"Why you no like play wit' Stanley? Why, Jocko?"

"You are a bit of a gamble, Stan."

"I can't loan it out. It's my baby."

Jock took out some cash and peeled off a five.

"Mon ami," Stan said and touched Jock's wrist, "you offend my artistic sensibility. You think I'd rent my darling easel for a fin?"

"I was thinking fifty."

"Two thousand." He held out his hand. "Or you let me do the shooting."

"We're trying to contain the investigation," Milissa objected. "Next thing, the whole town'll be involved."

"You're an elitist, an arrogant bitch. Keoni would have trusted me."

She stared at Stan, ready to respond in kind, but glanced at Jock, whose eyebrows were lifted in caution. "You're on," she said. "Get your camera. We're in a hurry."

"You need me with you?" Jock asked.

"I'm expecting Kale in an hour with a warrant for the warehouse. He's got men watching the entrances. I need you and Easy watching them."

"Them?"

"And whoever else. Can't hurt to be careful. We might be too late as it is. The place has been accessible since yesterday. Anybody could have come and gone."

Stan was hidden in a clump of haole koa by the Dental Booth Boutique. Milissa was across the street between the kite shop and the deli. Her view included Stan, Stockmans' entrance, and the grass in front of the warehouse. Stan scowled in her direction, tired of shooting the idle parking lot without knowing why. She motioned him to keep it rolling and pointed down past the deli. He shrank back. His lanky frame constricted to three quarters when he saw his target staggering up the street. Milissa crouched in silence, haunted by John's metaphor of keiki hide and seek, posed just the day before to the same reporters under whose noses she was now exploring his death.

Jense was on foot, struggling to keep to the center line. He crossed the parking lot, waited for Stockmans' steps to stop wobbling, then felt his way to the doorknob and turned it like the dial on a safe. No sooner had he crept across the threshold than Harry pulled up in his big wheels, lowered himself from the cab in one pivoting stride, caught the office door as it swung closed, and followed him inside.

Within seconds the two men burst into view. Jense threw a fist. Harry caught it like a line drive, smack! just over his right shoulder, and flipped Jense off the porch. Jense got up spewing fucks and sucks and spit on Harry's boots. Harry removed his hat, put on his gloves, and approached the problem like a piece of work. But Jense began to treat it like a game, slanting away and circling each time he found himself corralled into the street by the patient cowboy's outstretched, racket-sized hands. The shuffle ended with a kidney swat. Harry knelt, checked Jense's pulse, waited for his breath to start, and dragged him to the bottom of the grassy slope.

A patrol car darted from behind the far end of the warehouse, stopped and nosed onto the road, turned right, and stopped again. Rizzo was behind the wheel, giving Harry time to move away. Without looking back, appearing not to have noticed, Harry climbed into his truck and headed up the mountain. Rizzo pulled onto the grass and got out, his gun extended in both hands. "On your feet," he snarled, punching the barrel into Jense's ear.

"Deputy Rizzo," came Stan's voice from across the parking lot, "you're on candid camera."

Rizzo choked off his compulsion to react. Bile oozed into the back of his throat. He drew Jense to his feet as if the barrel were implanted and threw him over the hood, cuffing him while searching for a surreptitious way to cause more pain, but cautioned by the sudden presence of his fellow deputies and, most of all, the press who'd emerged from the deli, equipment in hand.

"You're under arrest." He stuffed Jense into the car. "Him too," he added, ordering Cadet Toma to collar Stan, still partially hidden in the bushes. "Obstructing."

Stan stepped out and trained his lens on Toma. Rizzo's lead, Tobias, looked at Toma and shook his head.

"I'll write dis up." Rizzo ducked into the driver's seat. "Dis'll mean your fucking jobs."

Stan came around to Rizzo's side. "Write this up," he said, capturing Rizzo's venom on video tape as he squealed away. "I'll send a copy to your boss."

Hiro was present to receive the warrant. With the media on hand it resembled an opening day. Nakayama was in charge of keeping them at bay. The only way to the roof was through Hiro's office. His door had been locked since Friday night. Out of respect for John, he'd taken Monday off. Kale and Milissa glanced around his grimy little enclosure. The back wall and the wall to the right of the door were permanent partitions, reaching up thirty feet to the level of the eave line. The front wall, containing the door and window, and the wall to its left were main structure, comprising the northwest corner of the building. A ladder, attached to the inside of the back wall, extended into the open space above the eave line to a trap door in the roof.

Milissa climbed and looked down into the warehouse storage bay. Kale left the office and came around beneath her to examine the outside of the partitions. There was no sign that they'd been scaled. Behind him were Hiro's anvil and tools and, further off, Stockmans' breeding stalls. Hiro, standing by, informed them that he and several employees had access to this common area.

"I'm going through," Milissa called. She lifted the hatch with her shoulder. Bracing the balls of her feet against the lower edge of the opening and stretching forward on her stomach, her head just cleared the peak. John's little front yard lay like a bull's-eye three hundred feet down angle. For an instant, stunned by the eerie sense of place and opportunity, she became the killer. Child's play, she thought, dropping her sights on Rizzo, back at his watch by the gate.

Kale's cheek brushed against her pant leg. She kicked as if she'd been caught.

"Whoa!" he said and held up his hand to protect his face. "Whatchu see?"

"You scared me."

"You afraid of heights?"

"No. It's just that . . . Well, take a look." She climbed down and hung to the side of the ladder so he could get by.

Kale too was taken aback. His steadiness against and behind the angle of the roof, with its ridge, a ready fulcrum to take aim, brought home the vulnerability below. "A pot shot," he remarked. "It's like a video game." He scrutinized the area of the hatch and, finding nothing, climbed in and closed the lid.

"Let me go down first," Milissa said with a touch of melodrama. "I'll be the shooter. Can't let anyone see me with the rifle. Gotta hide it before I leave. Check me as I go. Think what you would do."

Remembering John's account of how Smitty had stashed his tape, Milissa moved along the top of the partitions and looked for possible hiding places. "Not here," she said. "Not here."

Kale pointed into the warehouse. "Maybe he just tossed it."

"You think someone retrieved it?" she asked. "You see it isn't there."

"Either that, or he jumped."

"Thirty feet? Not likely. If he or she had help, the gun's well hidden – maybe gone by now." She needed the hope of a quicker fix to keep herself in character. "I say it's in the cubicle." She scrambled one-handed down the ladder and pitched herself from the third rung to the floor, darting to the right and depositing her imaginary firearm out of sight under Hiro's long, low supply bench. "Hmm, somebody's been sleeping in my bed," she quipped and crawled in for a better look. "And they've messed it all up." She pulled John's patchwork quilt out after her as she stood, dumping its contents at her feet.

"Don't touch it!" Kale placed his arm in front of her to keep her from mishandling the weapon. "And drop da blanket. We need to photograph it just like dat for chain of custody."

Merely looking at the cruel machine, still partly wrapped in the familiar comforter, filled Milissa with revulsion.

"On my front seat," Kale ordered and handed her his keys. "My camera. And get Hiro."

Kale checked the window while she was gone. The latch was broken. "Dis your rifle?" he asked when the two returned.

"No, brah," Hiro answered. He crouched down to take a closer look. "Nice piece. Nice scope. You t'ink dis kill Keoni?"

"The blanket?" asked Milissa. "It's Keoni's. Where'd you get it?"

"Never see it before."

"Was someone sleeping here?" Kale pointed under the bench.

Hiro glanced down sheepishly. "Keoni ask me can da Sikh sleep here. I say no, but tell him dat da window latch is broken. So, maybe he went sleep here anyway. You t'ink? Keoni always getting me in trouble."

"Da Sikh?" Kale asked Milissa.

"Sea. The East Indian. He's been helping deliver supplies."

"Hoh, da vagrant. Sneaky kine guy. We saw him wit' Loka at da wharf. Where's he now?"

"They say he's disappeared. You think he's the one?"

Kale rolled up the rifle in the quilt. "Gotta close dis area off. You like a ride home?"

Home? Her heart felt through the many rooms she'd occupied in her short life, searching for a refuge, a place in which to hide and work things out. Sea? It made no sense that such an innocent could do this thing. Could her intuition be so flawed? Had that been the problem all along?

Kale could see her absence. He wanted to console her, but held back, unsure of how she'd take it.

She put her hands on his shoulders, rose on one toe, and touched her cheek to his chest. "You finish up," she said, backing away as she turned to leave. "It's just across the street."

"See you in da morning, den." He followed her outside and secured the door. "Role call's at eight."

"At first she threw a fit," Jock told Milissa. "Running through the house yelling his name, calling Easy a liar, throwing herself on the floor. Then she started watching cartoons like nothing had happened. When she asked for him again, they took her for a walk."

"Where'd they go?"

"Out back. Somewhere down the mountain."

Milissa moved quickly through the volunteers. Fewer than a hundred had hung on through the day. The new ones glanced at her indifferently. The veterans smiled and flashed the shaka sign. Fidel, his boots resounding on the makeshift stage, was setting up a row of folding chairs behind the mike. Ewa was stationed at the serving table. Moke was tapping the keg. The banquet was ready, but the guests had not arrived.

"Keiki," Linda called, waving from an embankment some distance down the slope.

Milissa bounded straight in her direction.

"Dis my little hideout," Linda explained. "Been coming here for years. Used to be one heiau." They stepped into the Stone Age sanctum, surrounded by a wall of blackened boulders and hidden from above by the countless snow-white blossoms of a candlenut tree. Maria sat beside Easy on the ground, methodically tearing the fallen petals into smaller and smaller bits.

"Give Keiki a kiss," Easy whispered when she saw Milissa.

"Where my daddy?" Maria asked, glaring at Milissa, eyes welling with tears.

Milissa felt a pang of guilt. Recalling Easy's words that morning in the kitchen, she knelt and took Maria's hand. "Daddy's gone out of the world, sweetheart. I'm angry too. But it won't help. Nothing can bring him back."

Maria crawled to Easy's bosom and looked into her big moon face. "What happened to Daddy?" she asked with simple curiosity.

"Told you, baby. One bad man went shoot him – like you see on da tube."

"Did it hurt?"

"No," Milissa answered quickly.

"Just put him to sleep for he can go to heaven," Easy added.

Maria's face contorted. "Can I go home now, Aunty?"

"You stay wit' Aunty now," Linda put in. "Police are taking care of Daddy's house. Keiki's helping dem to find da shooter. She gonna put him in jail."

"Hoh, maybe he shoot you too, Keiki," Maria said, eyes wide with suspense. "Whatchu do den?"

"I'll call Aunty to protect me."

Easy growled and smothered the child in her defenses.

"Me too," Linda offered. "Call me too."

Milissa tipped her head toward the voices in the yard. "They've started. I've gotta go."

"Keiki hafta catch da bad man now," Easy said. "Give her a kiss."

Maria allowed herself to be hugged but didn't participate. Several seconds passed before she tilted back her head. "You one police?" she asked, dubious about the weakness in Milissa's tear-streaked face.

Laughter filtered through Milissa's grief. "You could say that."

"Like see your badge," she demanded, stepping back in anticipation of a miracle.

Milissa took the card from her pocket. "That's my picture."

"Looks like Daddy's driver's license," Maria responded, at first unimpressed and then brightening to an idea. "I can have one too?"

Milissa held her at arm's length, inspecting her as if she were a candidate. "Some day, I believe, yes. But you need to grow. And you must be good. You must be strong. Can you do that?"

Maria nodded rapidly and looked at Easy for support.

"I t'ink she qualify," Easy said, sweeping Maria into her arms and heading up the hill. "Going Maui in da morning for da ashes," she added in an aside to Milissa. "Reception's here tomorrow about five, den we go down Make Horse for t'row 'em in da tide pool."

Fidel had proceeded in the hope that John's murder would cause a groundswell of support and force Stockmans to capitulate. As it turned out, tensions kept in check while John was living took hold quickly following his death, and his memorial, meant actually to kick off Fidel's end game, was attended by only diehards, a handful of fresh recruits, and the ever-present press – a shortfall that was mocked by mounds of leftover food, an untouched cask of wine, and an unfinished keg.

Milissa watched from Easy's kitchen steps while he announced the hearing on his claim for reimbursement, set for the following day. "The court will state the law as it applies to our situation," he explained. "A favorable ruling will protect us if Stockmans tries to move ahead with demolition. Our objective, of course, is to hold things up in litigation for as long as possible."

"Courts are for da white man," shouted Pale's husband, Pu'u Lima. "Best t'ing for us is put up bunkers."

Pu'u's contagion had begun that morning when he stormed out of his house and picked an argument with Rufus, then joined a crew to push his hatred for the "haole pigs." From that point on, morale declined. Moke walked off the job, refusing to work with "scum." Olika allied himself with Pu'u to incite revenge against Fidel. Talk of race and violence quickly divided the ranks. More defections ensued. Most worked out the day and went home, not sure if they would return.

"You know da haoles gonna come in shooting," Pu'u continued, stepping forward and turning to the crowd.

"You right," said Kimo.

"Shit ya, he right," Olika chimed in. "We need guns."

"Who you t'ink dey aim at first, brah?" Pu'u asked, feeding on the sparks, spurred by the attention of the media. "You t'ink dey shoot Olika or Fidel?"

"Shut your rotten mouth," Keku snarled, ramming forward. "You ain't done shit 'round here. Now you come in wit' your hate talk. You too," she added and punched Kimo on the arm. "Tell you what." She moved people back. "Let's make a ring. We let Fidel and Pu'u work dis out."

The laughter revved, then died when Fidel sauntered off the platform. "Pu'u has a right to his anger," he said, putting his hand on Pu'u's shoulder, bathing him beneath an enigmatic smile.

"Don't get me wrong, Fidel." Keku stepped between the two. "You no hero here. You start pampering Pu'u, say goodbye to Maunaloa. He got a right to his anger, but he ain't right in da head."

"He's right 'bout one t'ing," Alvaro broke in. "Dey coming after us. Everybody hear what Jake say yesterday? 'Bout swinging da la'au? We stay here, we best be ready to protect ourselves."

Had the crowd responded with a rough hurrah, Milissa might have seen it as a temporary flux, a flash of anger subject to the sway of cooler heads, but the undoubting tone of acknowledgement, the deep murmur of recognition that simmered through them, brought her to her feet.

Fidel winked at Pu'u and nodded to draw him away from the rest.

Cory took control. "We need to talk this out." She offered the mike to the crowd. "Everyone's opinion counts."

Loka came forward first. The chairs behind him on the stage filled quickly. He cleared his throat, folded his shades, and tipped his head to the darkening sky, giving Milissa time to work her way to the front.

"Mr. Chairman," he finally said, "if I was a preacher, I wouldn't be driving cab. For me, mo' bettah one-on-one. Like Fidel out dere. You see him working, Pu'u? Question is, who's working who? But since I'm just a small town hack and wanna-be guru . . ." He hoisted Milissa up beside him. "I'll let my lawyer speak for me."

"Oh, you boys," Milissa Betty-booped, pressing a dimple and knocking a knee. "Bang, bang." She pointed twice and blew the tips of her repeaters. "Such a rootin' tootin' turn on with all your talk about guns."

Distracted by Milissa's tease, Pu'u broke off his parley with Fidel. "Hoh. Lemme get my pistol too," he shouted, fiddling conspicuously with his fly.

Milissa maintained a seductive tone as she walked along the front of the platform pointing at Pu'u and the few others who'd responded in kind. "These are the ones to keep an eye on," she told the cameras. "Point those things at them. They're hot for sex and violence."

"Aw, shit," Pu'u persisted. "You da one prancing around like you in heat."

"Just separating the men from the boys," Milissa replied. "How about you, Olika? You had an opinion. You wanna talk about guns? It's so exciting."

"Was talking about self-defense," Olika answered obstinately.

"Fucking right," Meek chimed in. "You just scared we gonna blow you away."

Milissa returned to the mike and spoke with quiet reserve. "You see how talk of self-defense inspires the young ones. How it releases the safety catch." She focused on the many sober faces, drawing them into her confidence one by one.

She noticed Moke standing at the edge of the crowd, having just arrived, and spoke directly to him. "See how it offers an excuse to cozy up to killing?"

"Now she gonna save us wit' da Bible." Meek laughed, nudging

Pu'u for support.

"Pussy," Pu'u hissed, smacking Meek with the back of his hand. "Don't rub up on me."

Milissa looked into herself and showed her palms so everyone could see. "What was it?" she asked, trying to remember. "What did Keoni say?"

"Not so much what he said," Moke offered in a loud clear voice. "Just dat he was so steady. Not pumping people's anger."

"You can't know now what you've accomplished here," Milissa continued, gripping the mike with both hands. "In ten, fifteen years maybe, when you look back and see how you've been emulated, how your work has spread, you'll understand. To Keoni this was an act of faith, a model of right action regardless of the outcome." She paused to drive home her point. "You can follow his example or throw his life away."

CHAPTER TWENTY SIX

Milissa hadn't slept. Slightly sick all night, she'd tried the big chair first and then the floor. When Jock woke up and offered her the couch, she refused. It was past her time of the month. Surely she would flow today. There would be cramps. Her queasiness, perhaps a touch of flu, would be an added burden. But morning was near. Too much else to think about. Too much to do. She had to prep her narrative for Kale and meet him at Morgan's office before it opened.

Jock microwaved some biscuits. There were dozens in the freezer from the week before. She made the coffee and they sat in silence, mulling the events of the previous day.

"Rizzo," Milissa finally said, recalling how quickly he'd arrived to pick up Jense. "I take it he was behind the warehouse."

"He delivered Hiro for the warrant."

"How'd he know Jense was out front?"

"No idea. He and the others stood off by themselves. We were talking with Hiro."

"Did Hiro say anything about Sea?"

"Not to us. He was pissed at Rizzo."

"About?"

"Being locked in the back of the patrol car on the way over. He said he was going to form a citizens' review board." Jock chuckled softly. "When Easy told him that she and I *were* the citizens' review board, he got all sleuthy and tried to eavesdrop on the deputies."

Milissa hung her head in disbelief. "You told him you were watching the police?"

"No harm. Easy and Hiro are old friends."

She groaned, bumping her coffee with an elbow as she laid her forehead on the back of her hands. "Shit!" She slapped the offending cup across the room. "Did we sit here yesterday, Jock – you and me and Easy – and talk about the importance of secrecy? You've jeopardized my tie-in with the chief." She pounded the table. "He specifically told me to stay away from his men."

"The cup," Jock said. It lay in pieces on the floor.

"Fuck the cup." She backhanded the air and bolted toward the door. "Fuck everything."

Easy appeared in the doorway. "Leave it," she told Jock, who was already on his knees. "Milissa's gonna pick 'em up."

Milissa opened her mouth to explain.

"Pick 'em up," Easy ordered.

"You don't understand," Milissa said, retrieving some fragments and holding them out as if to justify her anger.

"I understand." Easy's face was dark and unforgiving. "You one spoiled brat. T'ink you can ram around in people's life, just breaking t'ings and moving on."

"It's a cup."

"It's Easy's hard-earned china," Jock put in patiently.

"Easy," Milissa pleaded, trying to fit the pieces together.

"You t'ink everyone's a natural dummy except you. You da only smart one, eh? Only one wit' real feelings. Only one who misses my Keoni. Mo' bettah ask yourself why you so afraid of people dat you gotta be da boss of everyt'ing."

Milissa stuffed the shards of porcelain in her pockets and shifted into alien space. Jock and Easy looked suddenly unfamiliar.

Easy, unstrung by her own explosion, watched Milissa gather her things and leave.

"She'll be back," Jock promised, handing Easy the pieces left behind.

Milissa ran next door and threw herself on John's disheveled bed, clawing into the mattress, abandoning her body to his scent. The bones of sorrow in her pockets snapped and bit into her thighs. She writhed against them furiously, choking on her broken heart, then sank into the bottom of her grief.

With one blank eye exposed, she stared out on a world of grainy, elemental aspect, like the picture on a primitive TV. As she exhaled, the air grew oily and lost its charge, and the sheets took on the texture of her skin. She tried the lamp. The fire inside looked back with quaint familiarity. Sitting up, her feet came down on something firm. She felt it with her toes.

"Floor," she said, bewildered by the disconnect between the label and the thing. It didn't look like "floor." It looked like the mother of the table, the lamp, and the tackle box beside the door. The solid earth from which they'd sprung. The hasps on the box, the gutting knife inside, the hinges of her hand – call them what you will, they spoke their meaning with their form. And all these things, seen as if anew, were similar – her thumb caressed the inside of her wrist – made of the same basic stuff. She stabbed the knife into the table without thinking. It stood there quivering on its own.

Her spirit seeped across the room and darkened as it creased into the angle of the wall. Turning in fright toward the window, she caught the rising sun. It backlit her fingers, haloing their bones with blood light. Glancing down, she saw the digits shadow dancing on her chest. Correlations flooded in. At first mundane connections, but suddenly every dust mote had its source. Like the origin of planets, she guessed, blown away from star stuff. She slapped the bed and watched a heaven swirl in the shaft that cut across her shoulder.

Combining, building, verifying at the speed of light, she re-entered a world wounded with affection. Imbued with child-sight, she browsed John's unpretentious kitchen, noticing the imprints everywhere. Every simple design a conjuration. Every trademark a talisman, invested with the magic of its maker, transposed from the image of God. She showered, cleaned her mouth, and changed her blouse. God manifesting human in the matter realm, she thought, looking in the mirror to brush her hair.

She walked into the morning newborn. All things were themselves, naked and fit. The railing on John's porch was hewn from eternity. The steps forever worn. The sounds of her feet on the steps remained where they fell, like stones broken from boulders and smoothed by time.

As she drove east on the Kam in John's pick-up, the road created before her and disappeared behind. She smiled at the thought that it might decide to take her anywhere. CAUTION, CHILDREN PLAYING read the highway sign in front of Kingdom Hall. Sobering at the everpresence of death, somehow more poignant among the modest spires along Church Row, she pressed against the brake and broke the spell.

Morgan approached her office with blinders on. The thump of car doors sounded as she entered and clicked the safety lock. She waited for the footfalls, the rattle of the knob, the knock. Her broken eye appeared behind the cut glass peek. "Can I help you?"

"County Sheriff," Kale said with cheery satisfaction. He gave Milissa a wink.

"Can it wait?" The door opened a crack. "I'm preparing for the day." Milissa stood one step down from Kale, her frailty betrayed by a faintly lifted chin.

"You been bilked," Kale said, keeping up a jaunty tack to fill Milissa's void.

"Bilked?" Morgan closed the door and returned with pad and pen.

"Defrauded, cheated, swindled," Kale went on as she stepped out onto the porch.

"Theft by deception," Morgan specified, writing down the term. "By whom?"

"Jense Hoiness deeded the Maunaloa house to Stockmans on da same day he sold it to you."

While Kale and Milissa were showing Morgan the deeds and other items from the county files, Leilani walked unnoticed up the steps and went inside.

"By quit claim, Mr. Hoiness conveyed to me any and all interest he might have had in the house," Morgan explained. "I assumed the risk. It's possible that Stockmans was 'bilked' as you put it. I'll make copies of these and look them over this evening."

Kale took the papers back. "We'll need a statement."

"I'll write one up and send it over. Now, if you'll excuse me, I have appointments."

"We'll wait," Kale responded, prepared to follow Morgan inside. "We're holding Hoiness on suspicion. Can't keep him in wit'out supporting evidence."

"And you are exactly who?" Morgan asked.

Kale handed her his card.

She stepped back tightly and opened the door. "Please come in," she said, directing her invitation to Kale. "We'll talk in my office."

Kale guided Milissa before him as he entered.

"Nana," Milissa said and hurried to Leilani's desk.

"Hoh, Keiki." Leilani leaned forward, near tears, and took Milissa into her arms. "So sorry 'bout Keoni. So sorry."

"You'll have to hold my first appointment," Morgan interrupted.

"Kale and I are getting to the bottom of it," Milissa whispered to Leilani, patting her small, rounded back.

Leilani's eyes widened as she lifted her head from Milissa's shoulder and looked at Morgan, who was hovering for a response. "Oh, yes. I'll have dem wait. Mr. Hoiness called. He won't be in. He . . . Well . . ." She took the first call of the morning off the spindle. "He left dis message."

Morgan snatched the message and nodded for Kale to join her in her office. Milissa held back for a moment, murmuring John's passing with Leilani, then followed them in.

Morgan was sitting at her desk, her past on the wall behind her, her future frozen in a placid, bile-dyking smile. Kale was on the couch to her right, his knees above his belt line, his questions and documentation spread out before him on the coffee table. He switched on his recorder and placed it at the end nearest Morgan.

"Dis is Sergeant Kale Ford," he began, stating the time, the date, and identifying those present. "Miss Zarins is a witness, maybe a victim, in a fraud investigation involving Jense Hoiness. Dis interview is taking place in her office with her permission. Is dat correct, Miss Zarins?"

"Yes." Morgan stared straight ahead. "But please restrict your questions to the fraud."

"Da time is eight fifteen," Kale continued. "We're going off for a minute to check da sound." At full volume, Morgan's voice was barely audible. "Sit here," Kale directed. "Mo' bettah to pick you up."

Morgan perched on the edge of the couch, as far as possible from Kale. Milissa slipped quietly into a straight-backed chair, close enough to participate but not to interfere.

Kale switched on the recorder. "Hokay," he said, pianoing his papers for a place to start. "Eight nineteen. We're back on."

In response to Kale's questions, Morgan affirmed that she'd been representing Jense in his eviction and had filed a counterclaim based on Farley Chisolm's letter, asserting Jense's title.

"So, when you bought da place, you knew Stockmans' argument for ownership?"

"I made certain assumptions. We hadn't yet received their answer."

"Did you know dey'd been paying property tax?"

Morgan looked at Kale in amused disbelief. "Of course. I did a title search."

"Den you know Stockmans is da owner of record."

"I know they filed a claim several years ago to bolster their attempt to retake possession."

"X mentioned once that Hilda was paying thirty five a month," Milissa remarked. "Did Mr. Hoiness say what that was for?"

"Is Miss Dogherty working for the county sheriff?" Morgan asked.

"Under my supervision," Kale answered. "Did Hoiness tell you his sister was paying rent?"

"He characterized it as a maintenance fee. The receipts – I have them – give no description."

"Why not wait for Stockmans' answer before buying the place?" Kale asked.

"Twenty thousand dollars," Milissa put in. "Not like you to be in such a hurry."

Morgan slid back behind her barricade. "Mr. Hoiness was losing heart."

Kale held up the recorder to catch her voice.

"I wanted to be part of the fight," she snapped, reddening with anger, offended by Kale's pursuit. "Part of your fight," she added, suddenly sweet and unctuous, turning to Milissa. "Basically speaking, I bought the case. It has merit, don't you think?"

"What time was it?" Milissa asked.

"Time?"

"The time of day you committed this selfless act?"

"Morning. Friday morning last."

"Did Keoni come up in your discussions with Mr. Hoiness?"

Morgan's vapid smile resurfaced.

"Apparently Miss Zarins t'inks da question's out of bounds."

"Beyond the scope?" Milissa asked.

The smile disappeared.

"Hokay, da witness has stopped answering. For da record, I have to ask you not to leave da island. If you attempt to do so, I'll have you arrested as a material witness. Is dat clear?"

Morgan stood up stony faced and opened the door.

"Still no answer. Da time is eight twenty nine. We pau."

When he and Milissa got to the station, Kale found a message from the chief. Stockmans' attorneys had called. Any further questioning of X would be done by prosecutors. Morgan's story, uncontradicted, was plausible. If Kale couldn't pursue X, he had no fraud case, no way to keep Jense locked up and the other two in check.

Having decided the night before that Sea was his best bet, he took the setback in stride. The Coast Guard had already been alerted and deputies were stationed at the airport and the wharf. "All we had wit' Morgan and da kine was motive," he contended, arguing with Milissa. "Wit' da Sikh dere's a damning piece of evidence."

"Someone else put it there," Milissa insisted. "If you catch Sea you might solve a mystery, but it won't be Keoni's murder. Sea's too meek. Too kind-hearted."

Also in Kale's basket was a stolen weapons report. The seized rifle had been sourced to a local contractor who reported it missing from his house in early May. A note, *Heraldo Gutierrez, questioned and released – Halawa*, was in the space for possible suspects. But the report mentioned only a rifle. The one found in Sea's bedding had a scope. Gunner had told Milissa that Jense used a scope. Milissa suggested that Gunner might recognize the one in evidence. If not, at least Jense's rifle could be taken in for comparison.

Kale radioed an east end deputy to locate Gutierrez. "You do Gunner," he told Milissa. "I'll have Toma bring you up da scope."

"And you?" she asked.

"Gotta get my guys out searching for da Sikh."

"Where will you look?"

"Can start on da slopes of Maunaloa."

She could see that he was distancing himself, dismissing her theory of the case. She wanted to force the remaining issues. There was still Stan's tape of Jense's arrest, the efficiency of Harry and Rizzo's arrivals – too well-timed to have been by chance – and their ferocity in dealing with Jense. But she was still spaced out from her latest collapse and couldn't shake the nausea that had troubled her since dawn. Jock had been right when he said she needed time to grieve.

"I'll be in Maunaloa this afternoon," she told Kale. "If you haven't done it already, I'll talk to Gunner then. Right now, I need some down time." She had in mind the patch of grass behind the wall at Kalaupapa Lookout. How good it would feel just to lie there and absorb the sun.

The Kalaupapa view revived Milissa. No need to lie down. The wind in her face, the get-away of cool, crisp climes, reminiscent of her northwest Indian summers, took her back before her Keiki christening, back when she was a child by any name. Lost in reverie, her mind leafed forward to her first few days with John, pausing on the day he came to see her at the office unannounced. She'd just finished interviewing Pale. She remembered Morgan turning John away.

She pushed back from the lookout wall as if the stone had moved beneath her hands. "Pale Gutierrez!" she said aloud. "Pu'u Lima!" Pale had called him Heraldo. She ran to the pick-up and headed toward Maunaloa. As she raced along the Kam, she retrieved another fragment, less than a footnote in her memory. Pale had mentioned a rifle. Heraldo had wanted his rifle back. From where? From whom? "Tell Morgan," Pale had said. "She'll understand."

When she pulled into town she spotted a patrol car in the open lots. Cadet Toma was just closing the trunk. Hilda, Jense's sister, was treading briskly away toward home.

"Where's Sergeant Ford?" Milissa shouted, slowing to a stop.

Toma folded his arms, leaned back on the trunk, and looked in the direction of the deli. Kale, Tobias, and several other deputies were coming down the steps.

Milissa joined Toma against the car. "What'd Hilda have to say?"

Toma adjusted to attention as Kale and his men drew near.

"What's up?" Kale asked.

Milissa nodded toward the young cadet. "We ain't sayin'."

"You got a secret, Toma?"

"No, sir," Toma answered and opened the trunk. "Just t'ought you'd like to know first. Ol' Jense's tita went bring dis Winchester."

"Hoh, she changed her mind." Kale explained to Milissa that he'd been to the house only half an hour before, that Hilda had refused to hand over Jense's rifle, but that Gunner had identified the scope on the suspect rifle as belonging to Jense.

Tobias took the Winchester from Toma and checked the markings where the scope had been attached.

"What did Hilda tell you?" Milissa asked, intent on getting the cadet to answer her directly.

Toma returned the rifle to the trunk, closed the lid, and then, as if a little voice had prompted him, removed his notes from his breast pocket and read them to his sergeant. "Da lady say, 'Dis da rifle Sergeant Ford requested.' And she say, 'Any more questions 'bout where Jense was da other morning, ask da boy.'"

"I asked him," Kale replied. "She was in da room. He told me he didn't know. Just said Jense was hunting."

Toma stood ready. "Gunner left on foot when you was gone. You like me bring him in?"

"I have a suggestion," Milissa said, anxious to unload her bombshell now that Gunner had implicated Jense.

"We probably spooked him," Kale remarked, looking toward Jense's house.

Fed up with being invisible, Milissa walked around and opened Kale's door. "Get in."

Kale fired back a feisty smile. "Cannot. Coast Guard spotted da Sikh down Mo'omomi. Got a man hunt here. We just on our way down."

"Trust me," she said with conviction. "I'll tell you on the way to where we're going."

"I'll catch up," Kale told Tobias. "Keep in touch by radio." He got behind the wheel and leaned across as Milissa opened the passenger door. "Toma, keep an eye on the house."

"If he shows up?" Toma asked.

Milissa looked at Toma with faint disdain. "Detain him," she said, taking her place in the car. "And give us a call."

A couple of knocks and the yelling inside subsided. A long silence passed before Pale opened the door. She'd been crying.

"Mrs. Gutierrez?" Kale asked.

She swung the door open and disappeared through the curtain at the end of the hall. Milissa tried to move by Kale, but he blocked her with his arm. "Mrs. Gutierrez," he called, "we'd like to talk to your husband."

"'Bout what?" came Pu'u's voice from behind the curtain.

"Heraldo Gutierrez? County Sheriff. Dat you?"

"You got one warrant?"

"No, sir," Kale answered.

"You got no warrant," – Pu'u's pause was broken by a loud mechanical clack – "go away."

"Pu'u," Milissa shouted. "This is Keiki. Pale invited us in."

Pu'u stepped into the hallway, holding a shotgun across his chest. "Now you invited out."

Kale put up his right hand and located Milissa with his left. "Whoa, brah. Just a couple questions."

"'Bout what?"

"The Mikala case."

"Hoh, you like pin dat on me, ya?"

"Not really," said Milissa, squeezing sideways to get through the door. "Will you excuse me!" she snapped, forcing Kale off balance. "I know these people."

Before Pu'u could sort out his motivation, Milissa was in front of him, her fingers resting gingerly on the barrel of his gun. He looked at Kale and wheezed, laughing like a Mexican bandito. Kale's grimace vied with an embarrassed grin. Shirley Temple had imploded their machismo. Pu'u swept the gun beneath her chin, held it there for an instant, then reached it through the curtain and propped it against the wall. "Girl, you fucking crazy, walking up on me like dat. Let's take dis shit outside!" He strode in Kale's direction. "No pigs in Pu'u's house."

Kale followed him into the yard, incensed by his arrogance, smarting from Milissa's slight.

"Local people say it was Stockmans," Pu'u puffed, turning to face Kale, who was squarely in the path of his retreat. "So whatchu t'ink?"

"It's about a stolen rifle," Milissa answered over Pale's shoulder as she led her out the door. "What was it you told me, Pale? Something about Heraldo wanting his rifle back?"

Pale howled, anticipating pain when Pu'u raised his hand and moved in her direction.

Kale caught him from behind and brought his arm down in a hammer lock. "You're under arrest," he said, slipping him into a choke hold when he resisted. "Keiki, no more questions."

"Don't hurt him," Pale pleaded. "Da rifle no stay here. Morgan took it months ago."

Pu'u stabbed at Pale with his eyes.

"Son-a-bitch," she screamed, lunging at Pu'u in self-defense.

He grabbed her pony tail as she raked her nails across his face.

Kale had to cut his air off to keep him from snapping her neck.

When he came to on the ground, Pale, whom he'd dragged down with him, was at his side, coddling his choppy breath.

"On your stomach," Kale ordered.

The rest was drill for Pu'u. The feeling of the rusty clay against his cheek, the reading of his rights, the cuffs, the gentle pressure on his crown as Kale placed him in the car, he'd known it all before, all except the part where Pale was allowed to ride along, uncuffed and unadmonished.

On their way to the station Tobias came on the radio. "Just checking in," he said. "No Sikh, but we found his campsite."

Pu'u, as Kale had anticipated, immediately turned on Pale, thinking that his whisper would be drowned out by the raspy call. "Bitch," he hissed, "you like send me to da penitentiary? I told you to get dat piece back."

Pale recoiled against the door.

"Yo, Sergeant," Pu'u reacted, feeling exposed in the ensuing silence. "You holding me for what?"

"You get dat?" Kale asked Milissa.

"It's admissable," she answered. "I'll testify to what he said."

"Burglary," Kale told Pu'u. "Felon in possession of a firearm."

"What'sat gotta do wit' Keoni?"

"You tell me," Kale answered, following up immediately with a call advising that he was en route with a suspect in "Mikala."

"Dat's it," Pale said without prompting.

"How can you be sure?" Milissa asked.

"Dis one moose gun. Mo' biggah dan you see 'round here."

The gun's size, exaggerated by the small interrogation room, wouldn't be enough to set it apart as a positive identification.

"Anything else?"

"Dis leaf kine stuff." Pale traced the heliconia on the stock, following it with her finger to a divot in the fore-end. "And here's where Pu'u swung at me and hit da wall."

"Was dere a scope?" Kale asked.

"Nope," she answered, "just da kine," continuing to stroke the flower design while she recounted Morgan's confiscation of the gun.

Milissa glanced back through the tiny window while she listened. Jense, shackled and shrunken in his baggy prison garb, was entering the room across the hall. A hand extending from a polyester sleeve, Jense's lawyer she presumed, reached up to greet him as a deputy undid his cuffs.

Sensing opportunity, Milissa weighed the prospects. Morgan and the rifle. Jense and the scope. Their conveyance. Their motives. Enough to tie them in but not to pin them down. The crime lab guy, waiting in the roll call room to pick up evidence, had promised a preliminary read by late next morning, barely in time for Kale's report, due on the chief's desk by noon. Surely, after thorough testing, the gun's rifling would show up on the slug. Jense's prints might match those Kale'd lifted from the breech. His features might be recognizable on Smitty's tape. But the only real hope before the sergeant's deadline was Jense himself.

With Kale's leave, Milissa interrupted Jense's meeting and announced the added charges. "Think plea," she said as though Jense weren't in the room. "He knows who paid him. My guess is we can get it down to murder two. We'll pass it by the prosecutor after lunch."

Ray Kahaliwai looked up from crushing out a cigarette. He'd finished court for the day but was staying on to catch the afternoon hearing. "Tell me you're not part of this."

Kale glanced inside. The court was filled with friends of MCC. "We were looking for you."

Ray's office had received complaints that Milissa was running the investigation. He shook her hand, listened to Kale's request, then answered by the book. "Put your recommendations in your report. Homicide'll send 'em up to us if they see fit. Meantime, no deals."

"Dis guy's prime," Kale cautioned the prosecutor. "Give me somet'ing. Just a nod."

The bailiff came back to close the doors.

"I can't do that," Ray reacted, retreating into the crowd.

"Promise me you'll bring it up with your boss."

"Okay, okay. Call me in the morning."

"You coming wit' us," Linda said, surprising Milissa from behind.

Playing the captive maiden, Milissa looked back at Kale as Jock and Linda locked arms with her and marched her into the courtroom. She heard his radio crackle. "Dey winged da Sikh," he called after her. "Bugger got away." She resisted slightly, almost turning back as he disappeared down the courthouse steps, but Jock and Linda urged her gently on.

Fidel and Gary Spence were at counsel's table. Stockmans' lawyers were across the aisle. The front row on Fidel's side, where Milissa and her captors crowded in, was a showcase of MCC protagonists: Stan and Cory, Loka, Moke, Alvaro, Kimo and Keku, with Tiny and Easy holding down each end.

"You AWOL?" Milissa asked Linda.

"Hoh, girl," Linda answered, "we closed. Morgan got picked up."

"Arrested?"

"At da airport. Just now before I came over. Dey were still struggling when Lani called. Took four police to get her off da plane. She was going to Australia, tita. Lani say she had some kinda super grip on dis pixie doll. She say dey broke her fingers getting it free."

"All rise!" cried the clerk. "The Honorable Alan Shigazawa presiding."

As if on cue, Milissa leaned conspicuously forward – her cheeks puffed, her hand pressed over her mouth – then sat back swallowing, pale but dark around the eyes.

"Are we ready?" asked Shigazawa, smiling warily at Milissa while the crowd settled in.

Easy lumbered to her feet, exchanged seats with Linda, and laid her arm on Milissa's lap.

"Ready, your Honor," Gary replied.

"And the defense?"

Stockmans' chief counsel, Mr. Cass, was looking toward the door. "Ready, your Honor," came his second's thin reply.

Milissa convulsed again but kept it down. "I think it's premenstrual," she whispered and moved closer to Easy. "I wish my period would start."

"Premenstrual?" Easy said, louder than Milissa would have hoped. "Premenstrual is da headaches and some beginning cramps. You either sick or pregnant, one."

Mr. Cass rose from his chair. "If the court please, before we proceed we'd like a ruling on the cameras. Counsel was not advised that they'd be present."

"You object?" asked Shigazawa.

"Well, yes we do," Mr. Cass replied, cranking up his filibuster, "and we apologize to both his Honor and esteemed counsel for not objecting earlier . . ."

X popped out of the crowd like a fresh boutonnière. Milissa, preoccupied with Easy's revelation, thought she heard him say, "Good news," as he handed Fidel and Mr. Cass a statement.

"Your Honor," Mr. Cass said, looking at X for assurance before he went on, "there's been a change in course. We need a moment to consult. Perhaps a short recess?"

"Any objection, Mr. Spence?"

"None," Gary replied, concentrating on the details of X's missive. "I'd like a side-bar before we continue."

"Counsel in my chambers." The gavel clapped impatiently. "And bring your clients."

Easy hoisted her arm to the back of the bench behind Milissa's head. Her relaxation rippled down the row. "So you past due?" she asked below the hubbub as the parties filed out.

"A couple days, I think. I lost track. Did you hear about Morgan? There's too much happening at once."

The effervescent care one might have expected was absent from

Easy's smile.

"Sorry, Aunty."

"'Bout what you sorry, Keiki?"

"About the cup." Milissa felt her pockets. The shards were crushed beyond repair.

"Ah, pepe," Easy sighed, "you right, it's just a cup. 'Sides, whatchu worried 'bout one cup? You pregnant."

"You think?"

Fidel emerged from chambers wearing a seldom-seen grin. Gary came behind, his hand on his client's shoulder, his eyes still fixed on X's statement. Before the clerk could finish his introduction, Shigazawa was clearing his throat, ready to begin. X sat by the aisle and turned his chair toward Fidel. Mr. Cass and his aide adjusted to X's formation but kept their eyes on the bench.

"The defense has agreed to pay," said Shigazawa, signing the order and handing it down. "Court costs and fees are included."

The courtroom hummed with consolation. Stockmans' surrender meant defeat for Maunaloa. The goal had been to continue Stockmans' work stoppage while the issue was being litigated. Now nothing stood in X's way.

"There's more." The gavel slammed. "Mr. Spitz has asked me to make an extra-judicial announcement."

Shigazawa waited for quiet. "It has been decided, all the way from down under – after a well-placed call from a well-known peanut farmer, I understand – that the houses in the north tract will be remodeled and brought up to code consistent with the efforts already expended by their present occupants who, I further understand, will be allowed to remain." The silence exploded. "It has been a unique pleasure for the court to take part in this historic moment. We will be watching. Court is in recess until . . ." – Shigazawa raised his hammer and tapped it gently in his palm – ". . . until the racket dies down."

X gave Fidel a handshake for the press.

"We will enshrine our Tutu's grave," X said, upstaging himself with Fidel as the cameras angled in. "And the town will be renamed Mikala Maunaloa in honor of our departed friend."

"Dey taking Keoni's spirit," Loka told Milissa, as if they were watching a pagan rite. "Dis is why our ancestors hid deir bones. Da flesh was burned, but da bones were saved to keep da spirit safe inside."

"Dey trying to steal his fame," Easy corrected. "His spirit's safe in Easy's heart."

Stan glided from boulder to boulder, carrying the precious urn. Milissa, skipping along behind, matched him step for step. The others descended more cautiously. "Watch it," Jock laughed and caught himself on Loka's arm. "Some of these babies are loose."

The tidepools at the bottom, formed by an ancient lava bed that jutted far beyond the shore, swallowed up most of the surf before supplying John's half-full, childhood swimming hole. Easy found a place above the basin on a pillow of basalt, John's refuge when the tide was high.

"No like t'row your ashes in da ocean," she told him. "Mo' bettah here where I can come and sit." Stan handed her the urn. She cradled it like priceless wine. "Dis for you," she said, passing it to Milissa, "so you can tell Keoni's keiki kine for sure dat dis is where you said goodbye, and down and down like dat."

Milissa slipped into the pool and unsealed the urn. As she poured, the sea rushed in and swept her off her feet, dusting her face and hair with John's remains. Unabashed, she emptied the container, then plunged beneath the second swell and let it lift her to a perch above the water line. While she watched the influx drain away, she realized the urn was still in her hand.

Easy saw her question and pointed toward the open sea.

"Let me," said Stan, "You'll break it. You'll never reach."

"What?" Easy chided. "You t'ink da bottle is Keoni?" She waved Milissa on. "Go 'head, Keiki. Let it fly."

CHAPTER TWENTY SEVEN

The physical evidence – the suspect rifle and John's quilt, the slug taken from John's porch, the scope, Jense's rifle, and Smitty's tape – was at the crime lab. The witness interviews, officers' narratives, and papers relating to the sale of the house were laid out on the table in the roll call room. The wounded Sikh was still at large. Kale and Milissa sat across from one another compiling their final report.

Stan's tape of Jense's arrest was also in the mix. Kale was wary of including it for fear of overreaching. But Milissa pressed the question of Rizzo's motive for abusing the old man.

"If you didn't give the order to pick Jense up, who did? How did he know he was there? You saw the tape. He was looking for an excuse to blow the guy's head off. Given his proximity to X and the shooter on Sunday and his demeanor over the last few days, he should be questioned."

"I'll file a complaint with internal investigation. You wanna record your suspicions, put 'em in your narrative." He picked up the tape. "We'll pass dis on to Homicide as evidence of Jense's contact with X."

The phone rang. "Sergeant Ford," Kale answered. "Hold on, I'll ask." He lowered the receiver. "It's da lab. You see a mark on Jense?" He traced an arc below his eye.

"Dark circles, ya."

"Nothing," Kale said, returning to his party. "We're sure." He hung up the phone. "Da shooter got himself a Weatherby. Crawled too far forward on da scope."

"A Weatherby?"

"Weatherby half moon. Deze big guns kick. Musta smacked him hard – dey found some blood inside da eyepiece. That eliminates Jense. Only one left now is da Sikh."

"Not really. There's Jense's boy."

"Gunner? You're reaching. I saw him yesterday. Close as you and me. Not a mark."

"No, no, I mean . . . you're right, I am reaching, but it's about that thing his mother said." She leafed through to Toma's report and read the entry. "'If you want to know where Jense was, talk to his boy.' Why would she say that?" She paused to check her memory. "Anyway, that's not what Toma told us yesterday. Where's Toma?"

Kale called him in.

"What did Hilda tell you when she gave you the gun?" Milissa asked.

Toma reached for his statement, but she held it away. "What did she say?"

"She say, 'Dis da gun Sergeant Ford went ask for. If he like know where ol' Jense was, talk to his boy.'"

"'His boy,'" Milissa said, putting her finger under the words. "But when you reported to Kale in the field yesterday, you said, 'the boy.'" She turned to Kale. "And we automatically assumed that he meant the boy, Gunner."

"Da lady was talking 'bout Gunner," Toma insisted.

"How do you know that?" Milissa asked, squinting at the cadet.

"'Cause Gunner is Jense's boy!" Toma replied, mocking Milissa's squint.

"Gunner's Jense's nephew," Kale interjected. "But what's da point?"

"Exactly that," said Milissa. "If we want to know where Jense was the morning of the murder, we should be talking to his son, not his nephew." She took the Chisolm letter from the pile of documents and came around and showed it to Kale, reading over his shoulder. "Here it is: 'in exchange for acknowledging paternity of Cephas, son of Olive Strunk.' Let's pull up Ewa's AKA's. It's just a hunch."

Ewa had a long series of petty crimes. "Ewa Wia," Kale read aloud, scrolling through her history. "AKA Eva Via with da 'v', AKA Olive Strunk. I'll be damned. Da Strunks end in '79. Over on Oahu. Mostly prostitution." He returned to the letter. "Cephas is Kepa in Hawaiian."

Milissa pointed to the name, Miguel Villa, second on the list of corporate officers. "Pronounced Via, no doubt. Chisolm's son-in-law, Mickey. Gotta be Kepa's birth parent. The one that Jense stood in for."

"So, if we got dis right, Kepa might know where Jense was da morning Keoni was killed. Dat's something at least. We'll put it in da report."

"No," Milissa answered, quiet but emphatic. "We've gotta bring him in."

"Why? You think he was involved?"

"Up to his eyeballs." She swept her finger beneath her eye. "He's nursing one of your Weatherbys."

Kepa peeked through the rip in the shade that covered his second floor window. Kale and Milissa were in the yard. "We got Jesus," he heard his mother tell them. "You go 'way." He crawled into the attic space, his heart exploding in his eye. "He not Kepa's father," Ewa went on when reference was made to Jense. "He da devil himself, dat's what."

When no one came to his room, Kepa returned to his peep-hole. Two more deputies had arrived. Kale was sitting in his car with one foot on the ground, talking on his radio while looking up at the tattered shade.

"A warrant," Kale told the dispatcher. "Have the chief get back to me."

Tobias leaned in and nodded over his shoulder. "Sarge, we got visitors."

Kale turned off the radio and looked toward the road. Fidel and Sea were walking their way.

"Check his eyes," Milissa said as Kale positioned Sea against the hood. "No Weatherby."

After patting him down and reading him his rights, Kale put Sea in the passenger seat and examined his eyes. "No Weatherby."

"Your wound?" Milissa asked. "The deputies said they hit you."

"It was actually a slip. I reached out for the ground and as you can see . . ." He showed them the hole in his shirt where the bullet had passed beneath his armpit. "Nothing but scraped elbows."

"You wanna tell us how you got dat rifle?"

"He's a witness," Fidel protested.

"Gently." Milissa rested her hand on Kale's shoulder. "Sea, tell us what you know."

Sea looked up and pressed his palms between his knees. "It was Sunday. Hiro had said he would not be coming in. There was a great gathering outside, so I remained in bed beneath his workbench, perusing a catalog of farrier supplies. My solitude was interrupted by some rattling at the window. I next looked up and saw young Kepa slithering, head in front, over the sill, projecting the rifle before him, leaning it neatly against the wall, then tumbling to the floor, quite agilely indeed. As he rolled forward, I saw his face. How he did not see me, I can never know. His sighted eye was blank, his mind in another place. When he came to his feet, his view of me was cut off by the bench top. But his rubber thongs and hairless calves were no more than a meter from my nose. Quite naturally, I shrank into my covers in fear that he had come for me, never imagining his true intent. No sooner had he gone up through the roof than I was out of there, exiting where he came in and hot-footing it from town. When I reached the highway, I heard the gun's report."

"How did you connect with Fidel?"

"After three nights in the open, with no food and being hunted by your men, I took refuge in his place of residence, arriving yesterday afternoon. I wasn't sure how I would be received, but I had nowhere else to turn. Since then, I have remained in hiding, listening to the radio, timing the release of my account as leverage against extradition."

Kale looked at Fidel for an explanation.

"He was at my place when I got in last night. I hadn't been there since Sunday morning."

"Fortunate timing," said Milissa.

"Yes, that had crossed my mind. Had I discovered Sea sooner . . ."

"You would have lost your leverage with X. The pressure of Keoni's death fit right into your program."

"Unhappily so. I had an inkling it might happen at some point. But not like this. If anything, I expected a political hit. He was a natural for the part."

While everyone was focusing on Sea, Kepa had slipped out through the bathroom window.

"He's heading for the woods!" Toma shouted. "Behind the house."

Disregarding Kale's order to stay back, Milissa circled around the stand of pines at the rear of the house to where it opened on the southern slope, hoping to keep track of Kepa if he emerged. But he surprised her with a head lock and wrenched her to her knees, delaying long enough to pump a fist into her face.

She heard the huff of air escaping from his lungs when Toma tackled him. "Too tight, Uncle!" he cried as Toma pinned him with a knee and bit the cuffs into his wrists. "Aunty, Aunty!" he bawled to Milissa, who was staunching a trickle of blood from her nose. "Tell Toma to loosen da cuffs. I no like hurt you. Just trying to get away. Please, Aunty!"

"Toma!" Milissa yelled, causing the blood to gush, "loosen the God damn cuffs."

Kale broke from the trees, inserted his leg in front of Toma, and told him to step away.

"Sergeant Ford," Kepa whined as Kale read from his Miranda card, "why you chasing me?"

"'Cause you running," Kale said, ratcheting back the grips. "What happened to your eye?"

"Was one hunting accident." The eye was swollen to a slit.

"Hunting up on Kamakou with your father?" Milissa asked, her head tipped back to keep the blood in check. "Is that what he told you to say?"

"We heard dat someone smashed a beer can in your face," Kale added. "Mo' bettah you tell da truth. Maybe we can cut a deal."

"Deal for what? Never did nothing."

"Keoni's dead, Kepa." Kale knelt and spoke in confidence. "Aunty already put his ashes in the swimming hole down Make Horse."

Kepa opened his festering eye. "Cannot blame me for Keoni, Uncle." He looked directly at Milissa. "Dat's not what dis about."

Milissa was surprised by Kepa's certainty. Did he have information that would clear him. Suddenly the eye wound seemed less probative. His blood on the scope, if it was his blood, tied him to the scope not the rifle. There was also the question of motive. The why was obvious with Jense. Even Morgan. But if Kepa valued anyone, it was John. Was Sea telling the truth?

"Cannot lie to Uncle," Kale insisted, repeating his assertion like a shaman exorcizing the possessed. "Cannot."

"Cannot lie to Jesus," Ewa said, pointing at Milissa from the edge of the woods. "She da one. Da devil paid my boy to shoot dis haole bitch, but she stepped out da way and let Keoni take it in da chest."

EPILOGUE

"Kepa retained his juvenile status in exchange for testifying against Jense. Jense got second degree for admitting that the sale to Morgan was murder for hire. Was X involved? If he was, Jense kept it to himself, which would have been unlikely. Kale and I took Kepa's confession. He admitted that he'd pulled the trigger, but put the death on me for stepping out of the way."

"That had to hurt."

"I'd been through the guilt and grief already. Somewhere inside, even before Ewa blurted it out, I knew I'd brought it on. Actually, for an instant, I felt lucky. But what hit me . . . When he said it in the interview, I sort of snapped and drifted off. Like in those near death simulations on TV. I could hear him talking. About how he'd hid in the trunk until Morgan moved her car. How Jense had paid him a hundred dollars and promised a doctor that never came. But what struck me most was our mere presence in the room – that Keoni was gone and we existed. I could see all the small reactions. The little smiles. The painful tics. The glances down in common shame. I saw us as we were. And Kepa was one of us, lying in his hospital bed, hooked up to the antibiotics, clinging to his scrap of half-truth, pathetically eager to share the blame.

"Sharing with Jense and Morgan was easy. My complicity was taking Kepa's eye, then showing him my back. Same thing with Morgan's heart and Jense's cowered manhood. Fidel ignored a premonition. The warehouse was Rizzo's beat. Why wasn't Kepa spotted breaking in? Cory, Jock, Stan, the others, even Easy, we were all in the mix. In retrospect, the risk of violence was obvious. To that extent, we all participated in his death."

"Now that's sharing."

"It's common ground. A reason to forgive."

"I still don't get it. Why do you persist with Morgan? Guilt alone is not enough."

"I sometimes think of her as my child."

"But you said it yourself. You're Morgan's baby doll."

"That's her thing."

"Apparently it goes both ways."

"How's that?"

"You see her as she sees you. Think of your imprint on your two year old. You formed her smile with your own. Trimmed her self-perception with a frown. She saw you as her image."

"Morgan and I are just playing."

"Just playing dolls?"

"A harmless game."

"As long as Morgan's in the doll house."